Dear Mystery Reader:

Imagine your name  ndscape as a character in o_____ Now, DEAD LETTER ma_____lly that it's barely legal. You_____ one of our author's next bo_____ut the coupon in the back _____ DEAD LETTER headquarters in Manhattan, and if your name is drawn, we'll kill you! What's that, you say? Not quite ready to die? Then we'll kill one of your loved ones instead! How's that for reader appreciation? This is every mystery fan's dream, and I hope that we can make it come true for you. The DEAD LETTER staff is eagerly standing by, waiting to kill you!

Three of our deadliest authors round out the exciting DEAD LETTER lineup this month. Mother, widow and tough-as-nails cop Marti MacAlister is back in Eleanor Taylor Bland's KEEP STILL, posh Main Line, Philadelphia, sets the stage for murder in Donna Huston Murray's latest Ginger Barnes mystery and, of course, Jamie Harrison's quirky Blue Deer, Montana, bunch returns in GOING LOCAL. On their own, they're three of the leading ladies on the mystery scene, but when they meet, it's murder!

In GOING LOCAL, Sheriff Jules Clement and the other rich, genuine characters who populate Blue Deer will keep you entertained page after page and hungry for another visit. It's "Northern Exposure" meets Sue Grafton in Jamie's offbeat mysteries. Read on and see why critics and fans won't stop raving!

Enjoy!

Yours in crime,

Joe Veltre
St. Martin's DEAD LETTER Paperback Mysteries

Other titles from St. Martin's **Dead Letter Mysteries**

Mandarin Plaid by S. J. Rozan

Missing Bonds by Bruce W. Most

The King's Bishop by Candace Robb

Agatha Raisin and the Murderous Marriage
by M. C. Beaton

Bleeding Maize and Blue by Susan Holtzer

The Death of Frank Sinatra by Michael Ventura

A Stiff Risotto by Lou Jane Temple

Death in Little Tokyo by Dale Furutani

Louisiana Fever by D. J. Donaldson

Falconer and the Face of God by Ian Morson

Mystery's Most Wanted
ed. by the staff of *Mystery Scene*

Death of an Angel by Sister Carol Anne O'Marie

Hide and Seek by Ian Rankin

Cracker: The Mad Woman in the Attic by Jim Mortimore

The Cold Heart of Capricorn by Martha C. Lawrence

Quaker Testimony by Irene Allen

Keep Still by Eleanor Taylor Bland

No Bones About it by Donna Huston Murray

Dead Letter is also proud to present these mystery
classics by Ngaio Marsh

A Man Lay Dead
Artists in Crime
Death in Ecstasy
Death in a White Tie

ALSO BY JAMIE HARRISON

The Edge of the Crazies

GOING LOCAL

JAMIE HARRISON

St. Martin's Paperbacks

The passage on page 135 is from "The Simple Art of Murder" © 1944 by Raymond Chandler, as first published in the December 1944 issue of *The Atlantic Monthly*.

GOING LOCAL

ISBN: 0-312-96484-6

Printed in the United States of America

Hyperion hardcover edition published in 1996
St. Martin's Paperbacks edition/February 1998

St. Martin's Paperbacks are published by St. Martin's Press, 175 Fifth Avenue, New York, NY 10010

10 9 8 7 6 5 4 3 2 1

FOR ANNA AND MATT

The author would like to thank
the *Big Timber Pioneer*,
from which many of the
"Sheriff's Bulletins" have been
drawn, for its continued inspiration.

SCOTT, MARY LEE HESSE AND STEVE

PROVIDED INVALUABLE ADVICE.

MUCH GRATITUDE TO SUE REENS

FOR THE ORIGINAL, INSPIRED

USE OF THE TITLE PHRASE.

It is annoying to be honest to no purpose.
—Ovid

Looked up the elevator shaft
to see if the car
was on the way down.
It was.
—Tombstone of
Harry Edsel Smith, New York

A LITTLE NIGHT MUSIC

THE WIND WASN'T USUALLY WORTH MENTIONING IN JUNE, but that evening a bluster rose from the south and whipped away the dulcet, green-smelling afternoon. From their lonely side of the water they could see forty miles to the north, and the grass seemed to shimmer and groan, as if waiting for the looming Crazy Mountains to sweep down and crush the plain. Bonnie lost a baseball cap and he clung to his notes and maps and newspaper; it was impossible to cast a fly or keep the flame on the cookstove lit. They hunkered down to eat cheddar and hard salami and fruit, but by nine o'clock they were relieved to get in their tent, if only to keep it from blowing into the reservoir like a high-tech tumbleweed. To her credit, Bonnie never complained or even asked why it was so important that they camp on the bleak plain.

But it was the kind of wind that blew freight cars off the tracks every other year or so, and when Otto woke up a few hours later, having dreamt that someone was smothering him with a pillow, he discovered the wall of his expensive tent collapsing to within an inch of his face, ballooning out again as the gust eased. He thought this was funny and smiled in the dark, humming a song and then going stiff when he realized he heard music over the wind and salvos of rain, that he was humming the song because he was hearing a song, tinny and mournful, a man wailing about his mind having a mind of its own. The line was funny and he began to relax again before another surge of wind ebbed, and he heard the truck engine.

He rolled over, unzipped the tent flap, and peered out toward the invisible mountains. A wet gust blasted through the tent and Bonnie stirred. He hurriedly closed the tent again, fighting dread, hoping that the sound of the truck had been carried from the other side of the lake, crowded with campers and children and barking dogs.

He knelt, still in the sleeping bag, and held his breath. But in the next lull the engine was closer, and he could even hear a voice singing along.

"Up, up," he yelled, staggering free of his sleeping bag, tripping over the startled dog, rummaging desperately in the dark through the too large, too crowded duffel.

"What's going on? Why are you up?"

"Ah, fuck," he said, shaking in fear and frustration. His fingers finally touched metal as he heard the truck engine rev. He ripped the gun free and reached for her arm.

And that was that.

THE LONGEST DAY
OF THE YEAR

BLUE DEER BULLETIN

SHERIFF'S REPORT, WEEK OF JUNE 14–20

June 14—A report was received of a trumpeter swan on the interstate. An individual reported sighting a man who appeared to be ill near a truck. The concerned individual stopped and was told by the man's wife that he had stomach flu. An officer responded with negative contact.

June 15—A gentleman wanted to talk to an officer about a drug deal. The individual had little new information.

June 16—Bees were reported in front of Blue Deer Memorial Hospital. An officer was notified.

A report was received of paint dumped at a river access.

June 17—A complaint was received of a neighbor weed-whacking his lawn at 10:20 P.M. An officer responded and found no one was home.

June 18—An individual requested a welfare check on a family member. An officer checked and everything was okay.

June 19—A report was received of an injured deer west of Blue Deer. An officer responded and disposed of the deer.

A complaint was received of a gun being discharged at a campground. An officer advised the owner of the gun to desist.

June 20—A report was received of a suspicious van with a person sleeping underneath. An officer located the van and asked the driver to wake up and move it.

Some people looked right at you, turned on the charm; others looked all around without meeting your eyes, like dogs scared of giving offense or issuing a challenge; the third group stared resolutely at the steering wheel or the dashboard. Only a squirrelly minority bothered to argue, against all wisdom.

The mayor surprised Jules Clement by being in the second group, but Jules surprised himself by letting the fat man off the hook, bowing to good nature and small-town politics without a threat or a bribe being uttered. Eighty-five miles an hour on the interstate was kid stuff, after all, a five-dollar fine, and it was a relief to pull over a local for a change. The mayor was flushed, beaded with sweat, playing hooky in his wife's car rather than toiling over the problems of Blue Deer, Montana, and once he'd stopped dribbling excuses and relaxed, Jules had been amused to hear just a touch of wonder in his voice. "Glad to see you on the job, Jules. Hope you're healed up fine."

Nothing specific, nothing impolite, just another reminder of how most people lacked imagination. A little gunfire and they assumed he'd grown up. It was June 21, the solstice, Jules's first day back at work in almost a month. The day had a double meaning, the glass half full or half empty, the first day of summer or the longest day of the year. The weather was golden and lovely; on the other hand, he was stuck in a patrol car. Summer meant people wouldn't—theoretically—skid off icy roads, or freeze to death, or shoot each other in hunting accidents, but it also meant that the loonies would be out and about, no longer confined by bad hitchhiking weather or school, no longer lured away by steaming tropical beaches or sterile cities.

Just a week earlier, Jules, seeking a last-minute escape, had flipped to the travel section of the Sunday *New York Times* to see a color photo of the Absaroka Mountains and a headline that read MONTANA: GO BEFORE IT'S GONE. A chunk of Absaroka County was identified as "Hollywood on the Yellowstone," and Jules, heart sinking, realized that his jig might be up. The vacationing nation as a whole already seemed to have descended, or ascended, to southwestern Montana in a kind of berserk westward ho, and Blue Deer, which usually had a population of about four thousand, could now count another thousand hotel guests on a slow day. Maybe more; Jules never paid attention during Chamber of Commerce meetings.

He watched the mayor scoot east toward Blue Deer and made a U-turn away from town on the high interstate, a black backbone against green foothills. He didn't like to bother with tickets, but he loved to drive, and always turned the police radio to its lowest murmur so that it became a white noise of harmless numbers instead of the whine of potential emergencies. He passed a town namesake, a literal blue deer swelling by the side of the road, shimmering in the heat from the pavement. Jules should have moved it out of sight, but with his luck it would have blown when he touched it, and the whole point in his first day back was to try to enjoy the job again.

He shoved the seat back and stretched his legs and worked on thinking about nothing. He drove until he hit the Bozeman Pass and the western boundary of the county, then headed east again toward the Crazy Mountains and the opposite border forty miles away. This was really the county's only paved east-west road; in the ninety miles from north to south there were actually two, but this was due to the Yellowstone River, which poured out of the northern border of the park and split the lower county in half.

By lunchtime, despite an attempt to keep life pleasant by stopping as few people as possible, his equanimity was gone. After three more speeders, a 1965 school bus filled with Deadheads felled by a broken axle, and a dozen loose sheep, the damage award had been won by some ditch-diving Poughkeepsians so riveted by a common antelope that they'd headed straight for it overland. Jules was glad that the antelope had survived the experience and chalked up another defunct minivan to the insurance companies. The people from Poughkeepsie, dappled with Band-Aids, blamed Absaroka County's pretty views and wanted a free hotel room. Jules told them every hotel room in town was booked, but cots were kept in the basement of the Lutheran church for such emergencies. Maybe they'd opt to rent a car and head for Butte, a town that hadn't been crowded since 1920, with the exception of the annual St. Patrick's Day drunk. Jules liked Butte, but then he knew what to look for. The Poughkeepsians scowled and headed east, toward Billings.

At two in the afternoon Jules marched down the bland, modern courthouse hall, slammed through the Sheriff's Department door, tossed his hat and sunglasses on his mounded desk, and slumped against the dispatcher's counter, waiting for Grace Marble to stop typing and look at him. She took a phone call without glancing up, letting Jules stare down into her curly gray hair and cool his heels in heavyweight, uncomfortable leather shoes. After high-tops and T-shirts and worn jeans, his brown uniform felt as uncomfortable as a child's church suit, hot and stiff; his shirt was looser than it had been, but the tie still constricted him and the belt of deadly gadgets jingled and weighed him down.

Grace punched hold. "Someone wants to talk to the sheriff."

Jules gave her a stony look.

"Sweeten up," said Grace. "It isn't a tourist. It's Clarence Bost, up in Martinsdale. He says there's a tent floating in the reservoir."

"It probably blew in. The wind was blowing seventy miles an

hour last week. Tell him if he pulls it out he can keep it."

Grace was sixty or so but her eyes were young, still an unfaded blue and not necessarily kindly, now oozing with reproach. "Some fishermen found it, and say it's heavy."

"No," said Jules. "I'm a month behind. Maybe two."

"You won't catch up before September anyway," said Ed Winton, who'd come up behind them. He opened his paw and a half-dozen speeding receipts floated lazily down onto Grace's keyboard. She drummed her fingers on the handset and Ed smiled. "Nice day for a drive. We want him happy, right, Gracie?"

Grace punched the hold button and used her sweet voice. "One more second, Clarence. We're seeing who's available." She listened for a minute and said, "Of course." Down went the button. "He says it's our responsibility. The reservoir's in Absaroka. And if you stick around you'll have to talk to Scotti about catching up with the court schedule. I told him you'd be back by two."

"I know where the goddamn reservoir is, Grace." Jules retrieved Ed's tickets and shuffled through, signing when appropriate. "Sheriff Clement," over and over, on and on. Five hours back and he was already sick of it. A meeting with the county attorney might push him over the edge.

"The Meagher County guys already told him they wouldn't handle it."

Of course the deputies from Meagher County (pronounced *mar* by local nonbicoastals) would tell Clarence to buzz off; the town of Martinsdale, a mile from the reservoir, might be in their county, thirty miles from the seat in White Sulphur Springs, but the reservoir marked the northern border of Absaroka County, forty miles away from Blue Deer but definitely Jules's headache. Jules could almost hear them cackling in White Sulphur Springs, where they needed speed traps to generate excitement.

"Harvey's on in an hour," said Ed. "Let's go."

Grace was watching Jules, prepared to make Clarence Bost a satisfied man, and Jules nodded. One very small deputy, Harvey Meyers, left to deal with the rest of a five-thousand-square-mile county, if you didn't consider the Gardiner town cop near the entrance of Yellowstone Park, fifty miles south of town. As Jules followed Ed to the parking lot he tried to imagine two Harveys for all of Maryland, a quarter of a Harvey for Rhode Island, eight for Virginia. It probably worked out to something like a gram of Harvey per acre; ten thousand New York citizens an ounce. He searched for his conscience and simply felt giddy at the idea of escape.

They drove north for mile after mile, up the western front of the Crazy Mountains, which came by their name because they sprouted illogically from barren plains like a 100,000-acre stone and evergreen Mad King Ludwig palace. On the way up the mountains looked close, clean and green and white in the sun after night rains, but you'd drive due east on a dirt road for more than half an hour before you felt you'd really reached the foothills. That was the thing about mountains—you only recognized them from a distance, or from an edge or an incline. If you were actually *on* them, especially in a vehicle, they tended to look like hills, even if you were used to very large hills.

Ed's musical imagination had frozen in 1975 when he reached two hundred pounds and the age of thirty. Jules asked him to pick a cassette anyway, and smiled while Ed searched through the box of cassettes, rightfully leery of what he might find. Ed said he wanted to go fast and plugged in *Sticky Fingers,* then hummed along, bobbing his graying flat-topped head, the beefy old-athlete folds of his neck rolling in time to the music. Jules giggled when "Sister Morphine" came on—after his recent stint in the hospital, the song had a new ring. But he didn't bother speeding. There were too many deer in the area, and how could anyone hurry to pull a tent out of the water on a fine summer day even after the decision had been made to enjoy the freedom of the chore? Someone had mown alfalfa, sending a sweet, lush smell for miles, and they drove with their windows down.

The upper third of the county, with only a couple thousand people and two small towns, was Ed's beat, and he brought Jules up to date on the new owners of the Clyde City Tavern, on whether the Wilsall Rodeo would be the usual whacked-out mess, and on how bad the dissension had been at a recent zoning hearing. Jules asked Ed if he'd had a good Father's Day— Ed had four children, dotted around the country. Ed said no, but didn't return the question, and looked uncomfortable. Ansel Clement had been the sheriff who hired Ed, and the real reason Jules wasn't fond of citing speeders wasn't as much a reluctance to ruin their day as the echo of his father's unseen last moments with a trucker on black beauties, a man who hadn't liked the idea of being ticketed. Jules had seen the hole in his father's chest at twelve, and had recently spent quite a bit of down time thinking about it.

Ed rolled his window all the way down and lit a cigarette. "You gotta promise me we'll stop for some food."

"No problem," said Jules. "I'm living for it."

"Get the chicken-fried steak. Or the hot beef sandwich."

They passed a rendering plant and an old Swedish church and Jules made a right onto patchy blacktop. "I'll have the fried fried," said Jules. "You stick to the patty melt."

Ed laughed. He had the kind of big belly that looked healthy, and he was proud of it, regarded it as a sign of a wealthy soul à la Santa Claus. Ed condescended to keep himself under the weight limit for his job.

"Has Bost gotten any easier to take?" asked Jules.

"Nope."

Jules slowed for a pothole and a battered, shotgunned cattle crossing sign, then turned down Martinsdale's main drag. Martinsdale had one grocery, where vegetables were limited to frozen peas and iceberg lettuce, and two bars, one in the Crazy Mountain Inn and one attached to Clarence Bost's hardware store. Recent touches, like the gas pump in front of the post office–liquor store–garage, predated the Korean War. The few hardy tourists who made it this far tended to think the town had been left over from a Peckinpah or Sergio Leone movie, though even the most media-minded couldn't remember something so memorable as the jail. It sat on a slight rise near a boarded-up dimestore, a six-by-six cage with two metal screens for benches and red-painted bars on the door, open to the sky on five planes and to the grass and ants below. The cell was the real thing, still in use when the occasion demanded, on average about a half-dozen times a year.

Jules pulled up in front of the tidy boardwalk on Bost's side of the street; local merchants, faced with crumbled streets and no money, had taken the mud season into their own hands and built up. "Clarence Bost, Proprietor" was stenciled politely on the bright yellow screen door of the Mint Bar. This was Clarence's way of announcing a readiness to argue before his customers even ordered a drink. Ed and Jules walked another four feet and entered Martinsdale Hardware, marked by a blaze orange door that exactly matched most of the hammer and ax handles inside. Clarence, using up old paint, had read *Reader's Digest* on the psychological implications of colors.

The owner wasn't in sight, and Jules, fascinated, peered through the door that joined the hardware and the apricot-colored bar. Clarence wasn't there either. They found him toward the back of his hardware store, behind some dusty toy tractors and warped baseball bats. He didn't acknowledge their presence.

"What's up, Clarence?" Jules followed the owner's gaze into the shelves, wondering if he'd spied a dead mouse.

Clarence Bost still didn't look in their direction. "Problem at the reservoir. Something blue in the water."

It was possible that Clarence, who was at least eighty but used a full bottle of Grecian Formula once a week, might have entered a decline. "Blue?"

"Tent, probably."

"That's what we heard."

Jules and Ed waited. Clarence finally straightened, or attempted to—his back had grown scoliotic with age—and gave them a bleak look. "Little jackoffs from Great Falls rented one of my boats. They ran over this thing and then they tried to pull it out and tipped and I had to pull the first boat out with another one."

"Are they still out there?" Jules didn't care so much about talking to the "little jackoffs," but they might need protection from Clarence.

"They went to the bar." Clarence sighed when Jules and Ed eyed the open doorway to the dark Mint. "The *other* bar. Not mine. They said the smell drove them to drink. They were on something."

Jules thought over the hint of drugs and the word "smell" and decided not to be led off on tangents. "You think they're up to helping us get the tent out of the water?"

"Drove off in the direction of Two Dot. Didn't pay for the motor, but I have their deposit."

Clarence stuck most of his finger into his ear.

Ed sighed. "Can we borrow some rope?"

"Borrow?" said Clarence, curling a thin lip. "What good would rope be to me after you cut a length?"

Ed and Jules stared at him.

"I have to mind my property," said Clarence, picking up a can of paint. "I have to work for a living. The tent's by the dam, and you can borrow my rowboat. Now, do you want some goddamn rope or not?"

The Martinsdale reservoir floated on the high, rolling prairie like a gray-blue hallucination. The Crazies, edged by badlands buttes, domed up to the south, and when clouds swept north with the prevailing wind the sky looked like speeded-up movie footage. Trees were rare on the plains east of the Continental Divide in Montana, and only one stand of battered bonsai cottonwood had survived at the water's edge to illustrate the strength of the winds.

After a flooding May, the reservoir, often reduced to a hundred-acre mud pie by July, was still almost full. Jules counted fourteen campers and tents on the way to the dam, most of them from Billings—Montana's biggest (pop. 80,000) and possibly ugliest city, which was saying a lot, given the competition. Bost had left a rowboat drying on the bank fifty yards past the last trailer, near the dam, and Jules insisted on taking the oars. He regretted this bravado immediately, but Ed, virtually crippled by a hard life and a fair amount of bad behavior, had ruined knees and a horrible back. Jules was the boss, young and theoretically strong but for an almost healed bullet hole in his shoulder. In hindsight, neither of them had been a good candidate to pull a heavy tent from the middle of a deep lake, but they'd been too busy running away from Grace to think anything through.

The promise of the afternoon had faded somewhat in the wash of Clarence Bost's bad breath. The sapphire and fuschia tent bloomed and furled just below the surface, bumping gently against the steep dam embankment. The boys who'd run it over and jammed the outboard motor must have been seeing how close they could come without crashing. Jules gritted his teeth, rowed, and comforted himself with the thought that there wouldn't be much gear inside if it floated so near the surface, and if it had been light enough to blow in to begin with. The tent looked like a huge, lapis-colored sea anemone or urchin, though that stretch of imagination relied on one knowing what an anemone or urchin looked like, and the ocean was a long way away. Jules lowered his arm into the water for a tentative tug, took stock, and looked at Ed.

"It's heavy. This was supposed to be fun," said Jules.

Ed looked apologetic. "It still beats ticketing. Think of dinner."

"We won't want to if this really stinks."

"Bad hamburger won't make me forget dinner."

"Remember when we flipped that rowboat, the one that was burping methane, and found all the fried chicken strapped under the seat?"

"That won't make me forget dinner either."

Jules rolled up his sleeve again and leaned over the edge of the rowboat, but the tent was a foot below the surface and he got wet anyway. He ran his fingertips and his palm along the highest point—a mounded, buoyant object—intent on finding a seam and spare fabric or the tear the motor must have caused so that he could tie on the rope. He paused and ran his fingers back over the shape again, doubting that what he felt could be so horribly familiar.

Jules sat up so abruptly that the boat rocked. He let his wet arm fall limp onto his leg and tried not to black out. His ears rang and the cold started in his neck and ran up to his hairline, and down his torso.

"What the hell," said Ed. "Did your shoulder just kick in?"

Oh God, thought Jules. He couldn't speak, and tried to shake his head while his mind reeled with the statistical implausibility of it all. A happy camper had started a jet ski at the other end of the lake, and it added to the pounding feeling in his skull.

Ed tried humor. "Acid flashback? Piranhas?"

"There's someone in there."

Ed squinted at Jules. "What?"

"There's a body in there. I felt her."

Ed blanched. "Her?"

Jules cleared his throat and wiped his arm dry on his pant leg. He tried a crooked smile. This wasn't surprising, as his face was crooked, but it wasn't usually green. He didn't want to explain that he'd recognized the unmistakable contours of a female posterior, but that the texture had been all wrong.

"Her."

Jules Clement, due to turn thirty-four on July 1, was relatively young for a sheriff. He was tall, almost six-three, and a little too concave after his recent hospital stay. His hair was dark, chocolatey brown, and messy, and his eyes were the same color. His face was somber but quite pleasant, high-cheekboned and handsome but for the fact that a horse kick during a childhood rodeo phase had thrown his right chin askew, so that one side of his mouth twisted up and the other down. Jules only smiled with half of his face, just as he spent most of his working days only smiling with half of his mind.

Jules had a dry, particularly Western take on life that didn't always aid him in his latest reincarnation as the law of Absaroka County. That spring, over whiskeys at the Blue Bat Lounge, an old friend had pointed out to him that no one who really wanted to be sheriff *should* be sheriff, that there was something innately wrong with *liking* life as a cop, even if one were carrying on a family tradition. The old friend, Peter Johansen, a reporter and former assistant prosecutor who had decided opinions about crime and punishment, had been trying to reassure, but Jules had run for office of his own free will the previous fall, and couldn't afterward see his way to simply walking away, despite despair, violent death, and self-loathing. And that had been before things went downhill in the month of May.

The state of Montana, population 800,000 or so, averaged twenty murders a year, with a "modern times" record of forty in 1981. On this endless Monday of the summer solstice, Jules calculated that his county (population not quite twelve thousand) would probably be responsible for a quarter of the state's criminal fatalities before half the year was out. Three that spring, not counting the discovery of a murder from 1972, a shooting and another death that made the books as self-defense (the last two had been a single incident, the one that had given Jules his morphine vacation, and all were the fault of two brothers named Blackwater). All this without counting suicides or accidents or bar-fight manslaughters or vehicular homicides, and so far without a fatal domestic abuse or other standard-issue ugliness. In comparison, two years earlier, when he'd become a deputy, the county was in its third year without a homicide; the next year, when he ran for sheriff, there'd been one domestic. During the three decades plus since Jules had been born at Blue Deer Memorial Hospital, the son of a cop and a Forest Service secretary, only eight other people in Absaroka County had had their lives taken willfully by fellow humans, and one of them had been Jules's father.

So Jules had seen a remarkable number of bodies for a small-town cop who'd been sheriff for less than a year. He'd been an archaeologist before that, so, in a sense, much of his adult life had been spent inquiring into death, yet familiarity hadn't bred ease. In taking the job, he'd never thought the murder rate would go up an order of magnitude, and in returning to it that morning he'd never dreamed the trend would continue.

By the time they had the tent on the grass Jules had resolved, not very quietly, to find a new livelihood, run away and join the circus, become an accountant, a surveyor, a dermatologist, anything but a man who dealt with the dead. The rowboat had worked as a tug for ten yards or so, slowly rolling the tent in the water so that it released a gentle chorus of bubbles. Then Jules had resorted to brute wading strength, up to his chest in the water, moaning from the pain in his shoulder. When the rope reached the squad car bumper Ed punched the accelerator and left ruts in the mud to drag the tent to drier ground.

Now Jules was dripping wet and panting, sharing a momentary paralysis with Ed, both of them standing upwind as if the sapphire mound were a bonfire and they were avoiding the smoke. The tears from the outboard motor were only a few inches long, too small to reveal anything. There were two adult-sized lumps under the nylon and two child-sized shapes that Ed said twice were probably duffels. Ed also muttered something about the wind again, that an eight-mile-an-hour puff might be enough to blow a tent right on into the water, people and all.

"No," said Jules.

"It's what you said, back at the shop." Ed was pissed off.

Jules rubbed water out of his hair. "The tent poles are gone."

"They floated out."

"Someone took them out. Fiberglass poles don't float out of a five-hundred-dollar tent."

"Goddamnit," said Ed.

Jules sighed and made himself move. "Let's flip."

"Nah," said Ed.

Jules handed him the rubber gloves. He handed them back. "You're the oldest," said Jules.

"You're the boss," said Ed. "We could wait for Harvey and Horace." They'd radioed in as soon as they had the tent on the mud.

"If I'm going to lose it I'd rather not have an audience," said Jules. "Horace was finishing a surgery when I called, and Harvey's waiting for him." He pulled on the rubber gloves, swiveled his neck as if to loosen it, and took a deep breath. The sky was deep blue, dark enough to see the crescent moon. He bent toward the zipper, then took out his pocket knife and began to slit the tent open along its base, cutting in both directions until he hit seams. Then he cut up, still not looking inside, and he and Ed slowly opened the interior to the sky.

"Fuck it," said Ed. "I'm too old for this shit." He walked to the patrol car and rummaged for a cigarette.

Jules stayed where he was, shivering in the breeze. One of the smaller lumps had been a duffel, but the other was a dog, a fat old golden retriever with a distended belly and a badly angled back, one paw across the neck of what had, presumably, been a man. The body's head was a puffy sack of bones, given definition only by a black shock of hair, equally dark eyebrows over milky eyes, and a wide-open, screaming mouth. He'd come free of his sleeping bag, but his companion, the woman Jules had felt, still had both legs in her bag despite the fact that the blow that had killed her had been strong enough to tear one breast almost free. Dark brown hair, solidly built, older than twenty and younger than forty. Her face, though unbroken, was too swollen to bear much of a look. Maybe she'd been pretty, maybe not; the idea that what he saw had once been either was unimaginable.

Jules pulled off his gloves and rummaged for a camera in the patrol car's trunk while Ed radioed in a second time. "Try for the state boys, too."

"Say a prayer," said Ed.

Jules started taking photos.

Horace Bolan, internist and temporary medical examiner, and Harvey Meyers, deputy, arrived in the county van. There was no point in monopolizing Absaroka County's only ambulance. Harvey took one peek at the bodies and volunteered to question the campers, by now innocently lighting their dinner fires on the other side of the reservoir. Jules understood the urge to flee, but suggested he wait until they knew what questions to ask.

"So what the hell happened?" asked Horace, wincing at the smell, his bald spot already beaded with sweat in the late afternoon sun. He hated dead patients.

Jules had a theory but assumed the question had been rhetorical.

Horace rattled on. "No obvious bullet holes or knife wounds. Did you find anything they could have been bludgeoned with?"

"In a way." Jules flipped a portion of the nylon and showed the doctor a black pattern on the outer surface.

Horace squinted, uncomprehending. When he bent forward

his paunch got in the way. In terms of health and exercise, he was a do-as-I-say-not-as-I-do sort of doctor.

"It's a tread mark," said Jules. "Does that match up with what you see?"

"Oh, echhh," said Horace.

The woman wore a blue T-shirt, and after Horace peered at her chest Jules tugged it down gently and stared at the lettering.

" 'Blue Deer Wrangle 1990,' " intoned Harvey.

"Great," said Jules. "Goddamnit. You sure you don't recognize her?"

Harvey shook his head. "Hard to tell, but she would have been better off barrel riding."

When they unzipped the sleeping bags, gagging a little at the seep of pink water and fresh smell, Jules focused on the woman's stubby, waterlogged, brightly painted toes, wrinkled as if she was a five-year-old who'd stayed in the bath too long after using her mother's nail polish. She'd lost most of her blood from the blow to her chest, but the man's seemed to have congealed inside, and his lower body looked like a blue balloon. His T-shirt, red and very old, said "Le Grand Aioli, le 14 juillet 1983." Jules checked the label gingerly, and read Hanes.

"What's it mean?" asked Ed.

Jules rubbed the back of his head. "The Big Garlic on Bastille Day."

"What?"

"A festival. California, probably," said Jules.

"You know," said Horace, "we should tell someone in Martinsdale to stop drinking this water."

"They use it for irrigation," said Jules. "Grazing and hay and some wheat."

"Cows get sick, too."

The wind lulled, and in its absence the heat and smell were almost unbearable. They began cataloging all of the tent's sad mementoes while Horace worked on the bodies, with Jules calling out and bagging each item, Ed taking notes, Harvey numbering and labeling the bags. A pair of eyeglasses, probably masculine; a swollen pink roll of paper towel; high-quality sleeping pads, water bottles and flashlights and Carmex; some pens, a paperback mystery, and a red-leather journal Jules didn't attempt to open yet, stuffed in the leg of a pair of men's Levi's; hats and towels and fancy Patagonia long underwear, and more T-shirts, including a medium showing a stick figure on a surfboard and the words "Ride the Big One" and an extra-large advertising an Italian restaurant in Key West. Another extra-large had a front that said "Big Sky Grips" and a back illustrated with Yellowstone's warning against petting bison, a tourist with a camera flying through the air atop horns. The word "grips" replaced "bison" in the standard disclaimer:

WARNING

MANY VISITORS WERE GORED BY GRIPS LAST SUMMER
Grips can weigh 2000 pounds and can sprint at 30 mph,
three times faster than you can run

These animals may appear tame but are wild,
unpredictable, and dangerous
Do not approach grips

"What the hell's a grip?" asked Harvey.

"The equipment guy on a movie," said Jules. "Dollies and stuff."

"I love his air of assurance," said Horace, to no one in particular.

"He's been a bullshitter since he could talk," said Ed.

Jules wasn't in the mood to argue. No wallet, no purse, no names unless they were scribbled in the gluey notebook. Anywhere else it would have been an average yuppie cache of belongings, but in this part of Montana, every item, even the Big Deer Wrangle shirt, pointed to a fairly affluent outsider.

The wind had begun to bluster and swoop. Jules, almost dry, toed a *Blue Deer Bulletin* from Friday, June 11, and wondered if the blob man had been the sort to buy a paper every day, even in the outback, and if this really had been his last purchase. The right-column headline, quite demure, announced CORONER'S JURY CLEARS SHERIFF, but Jules knew that story.

"Echh," said Horace for a second time.

Jules looked and veered away. Horace had opened one of the dead woman's filmy eyes. A tinted contact lens had stayed in place, sky blue on a milky background.

Harvey gagged, and Jules took pity.

"Why don't you go check out the campers now. Go easy on this, so they don't all try to leave at once."

"You might want to wait until we pack up this mess," said Ed. "Once they know about it, they might want to take a look."

He was right, of course, though wanting to see any of it boggled the mind. But now, when Jules looked wearily to the other shore, he saw that quite a peanut gallery was glued to the commotion: half of Martinsdale, and all of the campers, seemed to have found binoculars. Jules reached into the squad car for his own glasses and lifted them. He didn't see any telephoto lenses across the water, which might save them—temporarily—from the front page of the *Bulletin*, but this hope dissolved when he made out the shape of an ancient yellow Mazda pickup heading toward them on the two-track, zipping around the reservoir with aplomb.

Jules sent Harvey and Ed to the far shore, radioed in to Grace, and waited on the car hood. Peter Johansen joined him there, feigning disinterest in the colorful blot on the grass a few yards away.

"So."

"So," said Jules.

"Welcome back to work."

Jules cackled.

"It's true then. You found someone."

"Two ex-someones, just now. I would have called, but . . ." Jules gestured to the grass and bodies and buttes. After fifteen years Peter knew when he was lying, but the rules of their current relationship—cop and reporter—were as elaborate as the protocol between a prime minister and ruler.

"I can't make today's paper anyway," said Peter.

"Good," said Jules.

"When did you get here? I headed straight up when I heard the scanner."

"A couple of hours ago. You weren't going to make deadline no matter what." He started walking, with Peter following reluctantly. "Did you bring your Rolaids? Have a big lunch?"

"Ah, shut up," said Peter. But he resorted to the trick he used when watching horror movies—spreading his fingers over his eyes and peering through the cracks. This was a mildly odd pose to see in a man over six feet and two hundred pounds. Horace, bent over the dead, waved.

"What happened?" asked Peter.

Jules sized him up, judging how much information he might gain in a later trade. "Off the record, I think a truck hit them. Someone ran them over."

"They were camped?"

"It would appear so."

"Seems like I remember something like this happening in Jackson."

"Huh," said Jules. "Seems like a stretch to me." His memory was patchy, but he knew that no one had been killed in the recent tent-ramming in Jackson, Wyoming, at the southern end of Yellowstone Park; in that he saw a world of difference. "You ready to pack them up, Horace?"

"Sure," said the doctor. "I don't know what the hell to do with them anyway. Are we getting any on-site help from the state lab?"

"No," said Jules. "They told Grace they were short-staffed today. You're doing fine."

Horace looked like he wanted to cry. Peter was taking notes, and Jules flicked the pencil from his fingers. "Give us a hand."

"I need to take a photo of them. Soren was off getting the Queen of the Wrangle contestants to pose, so I'm on double duty."

Jules twitched at the mention of live rodeo queens. "No. You wouldn't be able to run it anyway."

"Right," said Peter. "So throw a cloth over them and I'll take a photo and help you lift."

"Blackmail," said Jules.

"Whatever," said Peter.

"What about the dog?" asked Horace.

Harvey and Ed reappeared and said that not a single camper admitted to having been around for longer than three days, and Jules didn't need Horace to tell him that their own campers had been mere mortal shells for a good week. After Harvey and Horace left with the bodies, Jules and Peter and Ed began to quarter the area, first looking for the dead couple's camping site on the isolated far shore of the reservoir. No toilet there, no bothersome kids and dogs and jet skiers and wienie roasters. It was the likely side for an affluent, childless couple to choose, especially a couple who cherished their privacy, who'd been dead for a week without having been reported missing, and apparently without witnesses. Not that anyone would have seen or heard a thing on the far side of the water, a half mile from the nearest ranch road, had the night been cloudy or windy.

The shoreline of much of the reservoir was gradual. It had been hard enough to haul the tent out of the water with two men (especially two half-men), a boat, and a car; hauling it gradually *into* deep water would have been virtually impossible, as well as nonsensical. Murderers were rumored to travel solo, and a high-profile, noisy powerboat was unlikely. The dam end of the reservoir was a possibility, especially given the proximity of the tent when found, but the gravel would have scraped even the most expensive tent, and Jules had noted no signs of such abuse.

So they walked toward the one rocky ledge and drop-off on the reservoir. A little higher than most of the spots, a better view, flatter surface, and shielded from a view of the unsightly campers on the other side by the reservoir's only ratty stand of cottonwoods. Nothing showed on the rock itself, at least nothing Jules could recognize—he was a good tracker but not good enough. He and Ed and Peter moved toward the mountains, looking from side to side as if they were reaping. Ed yelled first, and Jules literally crawled alongside the patchy marks before he found where the vehicle—a truck, probably a three-quarter-tonner from the wide wheel base and large tires—had left the road and crushed a gopher hole. He reversed, found the ruts again, and followed them forward at a crouch, chilled to see that the truck had kept up a skidding speed for ten yards before the tracks disappeared again. Jules found himself surrounded by a half-dozen gouges, made when tent pegs had ripped free, violently and reluctantly.

"The ground was wet," said Peter. "But it didn't rain much afterward."

Jules nodded. The last afternoon shower had hit Blue Deer at least a week ago, but a rain in town didn't translate to water in Martinsdale. The deepest ruts were perfectly preserved, as if the rain had stopped for their benefit; maybe if it hadn't rained at all the couple would have sat around their campfire later and survived. On the other hand, the truck had circled and gone forward at least three times. Whoever had driven it had made up his or her mind with a vengeance.

Absaroka County probably had more pickup trucks than people. Jules did a rough sketch of the tread anyway, and covered the tracks and ruts with tarps for good measure. He walked slowly back toward the car, head down not because he was still searching the grass but because the enormity of the crime had finally sunk in. And there was an apple, a big green granny smith, brown-fleshed and easily a week old but still with distinct, now dried teeth marks. He regarded it, ignoring the incessant static of his car radio, then dropped it in a bag, and shrugged when Ed gave him a funny look.

It was nearly dusk, and Peter left for home, but Jules couldn't bear the idea of stopping when they still had good light. He paced the dam, using his Polaroids for all they were worth on the still surface of the water, his eyes burning a hole in his skull. When he saw the car he guessed the depth at only eight feet or so. After what already seemed like an eternity of wondering who was dead and why, the depth seemed disgustingly minor, chickenshit.

He started to strip, annoying and embarrassing his deputy. "Putting on a show for the tourists? What you gonna do? Find the dog's collar?"

"They're not watching. I'm going to get the numbers off the plate."

"I didn't know you read braille."

Jules dropped his pants, remembered his watch as an afterthought, ballooned his lungs and jumped in above the colorless sedan. The water seemed immeasurably colder than it had that afternoon. The first time down he discovered that in the murk he couldn't clearly make out the plate after all, tried the driver's door and found it locked. The second time he distinguished an L from a 1 with his fingers, and a Z turned into a seven; on the third try he made doubly sure that the first two of seven symbols were in fact 49, the number Montana assigned Absaroka County. This last, taken with the Wrangle T-shirt, was deeply depressing, and on his way to the surface Jules had time to wonder why it would have been so much easier to think that Alabamans or Dakotans had been left to rot in the tent.

He burst onto the dam. "49-BH8L7."

"What?" said Ed.

"Screw you," said Jules, watching the pen move in Ed's hand. He sliced his knee on the rock dam and squinted toward the campers. They waved.

Nutrition, as Ed pointed out, was essential. He'd never lost sight of his chicken-fried steak.

"Chew fast," said Jules. "I'll give you half an hour."

"It's been a long day," said Ed. "Eat, for chrissakes. Have a drink."

"How the fuck can you just say 'long day'?" hissed Jules. "Two murders. Try long week, long month, long year."

"It'll be simple," said Ed. "Not like the last time."

"How's that?" said Jules.

Ed, for once at a loss, looked out the passenger window while Jules drove toward the Martinsdale Inn like an automaton. He ordered a double and, not quite able to face meat, a bowl of chicken noodle soup. Even after the whiskey he couldn't envy Ed his gravy, which was exactly the color of the dead man's face.

While Ed chewed and gossiped with the owner, Mary Peach, Jules stared blearily into the bright swirl of a fish tank. Mary Peach recalled a couple who'd had dinner a fortnight earlier; the guy was dark-haired, and so was the woman, both about medium height. She remembered the man's shirt, which showed a buffalo like the one on the flyers in Yellowstone, and she didn't so much remember the woman as the impression that she rode, and that she was local. Jules kept his eye on the fish, again damning the Wrangle T-shirt. Mary Peach added politely that the woman had been younger, with a great ass, but also seemed to have "lived quite a bit."

Booze, toot, and late nights, thought Jules. They were back

to a rodeo queen with a rich boyfriend, and the truth was probably locked in a purse in the drowned car. As soon as Ed dabbed gravy from his big, dimpled chin, Jules packed him into the passenger seat and sped toward Blue Deer past invisible mountains, squad car lights revolving like the aurora borealis.

Blue Deer, tucked in a hook of the Yellowstone River at the base of the Absarokas, looked larger than it really was when all the lights were on, especially as it had gradually spread out of the river benchland and up the surrounding foothills and buttes. Jules turned the display off when they reached the outskirts. There was no point in trying to advertise trouble, or in competing with the neon. The town's main drag sported six small motels and at least ten of the town's dozen bars, and none of these establishments saw a point to subtlety. Blue Deer was only beginning to try to look old-fashioned, and those who attempted to make it tasteful failed to realize that much of its appeal came from intermittent pawn shops, drugstores, hardware stores. The town had never boasted great wealth—no real mining, like Butte; stick trees compared to Missoula; too many mountains to be a cattle paradise. The big houses were puny by Midwestern and Eastern standards. Too much wind, too much cold, too little wood for heat—houses tended to be stucco and one story or slope-roofed with small upstairs, strictly functional. Blue Deer had been put up cheaply, laid out in one month in 1889 to meet the railroad, anticipating the possibility it might come down just as quickly. Attempting to make it look expensive one hundred years after the fact was futile.

Jules passed the hospital and shook off the image of the van unloading its sodden bodies into the basement ramp, the gurneys moving past cafeteria supplies, old mimeograph machines, and copy paper. He'd told Harvey to plan on shuttling them to Helena by dawn.

When Jules pulled up in front of his house, Ed finally acknowledged the bagged apple core on the dash.

"Where'd you find that?"

"In the field."

"Last meal, huh?"

"Looks like it. Almost makes you want to go to church, doesn't it?" said Jules.

"I do go to church," said Ed, smiling. "Not that it helps me much after a tent like that."

At the station, Richard, the new night dispatcher, handed him a pile of pink slips. Jules threw the lot on his desk and logged into the computer queue for the Department of Motor Vehicles. The license number 49-BH8L7 gave him a ninety-three-year-old named Venus Meriwether, the proud owner of a 1979 Subaru station wagon. Jules knew Venus. Though she was an avid bird-watcher, he doubted that she'd gone camping since LBJ's administration.

He rubbed his aching shoulder and muttered choice phrases from his youth. He tried 49-8H8L7, but it got him nowhere; ditto 49-8HBL7. "Fucking goddamn piece of cocksucking shit," said Jules. He felt the dispatcher watching him and turned around slowly, staring back until the kid looked down.

Jules sighed and shut his eyes and tried to think of how the plate had felt under his fingers. All he could remember was a freezing groin and bursting lungs. He thwacked at the keyboard again—49-BA8L7—and squinted at the screen. A 1992 gray Saab Turbo had been registered to an Otto Karl Scobey, whose residence was listed as 218 South Cottonwood, Blue Deer. Scobey was 48, 5 feet 11, 180 pounds, with dark brown hair and nearsighted hazel eyes requiring corrective lenses. He'd volunteered his organs for transplant and/or his body for research.

Organ transplants were definitely out of the question, though research was inevitable. Otto K. Scobey, Esquire, had been reduced to something that looked like a leaky sack of dirty Styrofoam pellets. Otto alive had had dark, bristly hair and a Slavic face, and Jules could remember him bursting with energy, laughing at his own jokes, and calling a proposed resort in the Crazy Mountains, Dragonfly Refuge, "the world's greatest politically correct nature sanitarium." Jules would have known him in an instant at a cocktail party or at the supermarket, but Otto, in his last incarnation, might have been beyond his mother's recognition.

Jules began to swear to himself again as the ramifications rolled through his mind. The bison-grip T-shirt was explained now: Dragonfly's owner and Otto's boss, a man named Hugh Lesy, was a movie director. Jules tried to imagine a higher profile victim than an environmental lawyer-saint with Hollywood connections, and hoped it wouldn't be the woman next to Otto Scobey in the tent.

He called the state lab in Helena, the capital, and told the night clerk to plan on receiving two bodies by seven A.M. He called Axel Scotti, the county attorney, at home and was told by a sitter that Axel was in Bozeman at an action-adventure movie. Axel probably thought he could count on violent crime staying safely on screen that summer, after a record-breaking spring; Jules didn't bother leaving a message, planning on breaking Scotti's heart at dawn. He tried Ed Winton, and was told by Ed's wife that the deputy was already sleeping peacefully. He reached for the phone book and flipped it open to Blue Deer's ten pages, running his finger down the second until he found Coburg, Sylvia. He let the phone ring at her ranch eight times, then eyed the clock. It was only eleven; he could try to track her down elsewhere, tell her that her ex-husband seemed to be dead, but he'd prefer to wait until Helena removed any possibility of doubt.

Now it was time to find Peter Johansen, for the same reason Peter Johansen had found him by the reservoir that afternoon. Jules threw his tie and hat on the pile in the deep drawer and headed off to swap information.

. . .

Jules hated going out in uniform, but the Blue Bat Lounge was the bar in town most likely to be free of pillars of society, people who might frown upon a fishbowl martini. At the newly remodeled Baird Hotel he could count on half the drinkers around the U-shaped bar giving a little shudder of fear when they saw his gun belt—he might as well have been a serial rapist out on parole. The ones who smiled at him were almost never the ones he enjoyed. This was one of Jules's misfortunes: He didn't like people who supported overly zealous neighborhood watches or tuned in crime shows or belonged to the NRA. He'd managed to convince his deputies that the organization was bad for their health, but challenging the county on an individual basis was another matter. Possibly the only good thing about having shot and killed Ray Blackwater a month earlier (besides the fact that killing Ray had meant that Ray couldn't kill him) was that Jules's college-educated-commie-wimp reputation had vanished in a publicity fireball. Now Jules was a sheriff with righteous blood on his hands, and he kept his nightmares private and let those in the county who wanted to believe so think he was a bad hombre. He was big enough, skinny enough, beaten-looking enough to fit the bill, and when tipsy and loose or especially annoyed could do a good spaghetti-western Eastwood impression.

But when he was tired and demoralized and awkward on his bar stool, Jules probably looked more like a character from *The Grapes of Wrath*. A sunburn from the Martinsdale reservoir didn't hide dark circles under his eyes or a general expression of doom. Word probably hadn't gotten out yet, despite Peter's presence in the bar, but the people Jules knew—an engineer from the train rebuild center, a third cousin four times removed, the plumber who doubled as the high school soccer coach, and an ex-girlfriend's ex-husband, who looked to be rotting into his stool—all seemed to sense something and said hello without meeting his eyes as he passed.

Peter smiled when he saw Jules's face; in the correct perverse mood he could find almost anything funny. He was large and blond and was perched on a bar stool next to a short brunette named Alice Wahlgren, his girlfriend of the last decade, who was currently slumped over a newspaper, squinting at the small print.

"Twenty-three percent of Americans would steal ten million dollars if they thought they could get away with it." Alice looked up from her newspaper and at Jules, leaving the question unsaid.

"After a day like today of course I would," he said. "But there isn't that much money in the county coffers."

"Were you ever tempted to keep a few items in Europe, skip the museums?"

"I was too young to think clearly."

"How about civil seizure? Could be a way through the budget problems."

Jules scowled. "We don't do that."

"I'm just trying to take your mind off your day by saying stupid things," said Alice, patting his back. "I'm trying to remind you that you're a good human. Peter said those people looked like the Pillsbury dough couple."

Jules, who hadn't simply come to ask questions, looked for Delly Bane, the owner. He'd been there two minutes without being served. He picked out Delly at the end of the bar, discussing life with a man Jules had, sadly, once hauled in for driving under the influence. This wasn't grounds for no service; Delly was merely being polite to his friend by not rushing toward his friend's adversary.

"I can't believe it," said Alice. "Your first day back. You were just talking about actually going fishing this summer."

Jules narrowed his eyes at her. It seemed a little early in the game to condemn his whole summer. He hated it when Alice tried to be realistic. Peter and Jules had met at college, in Ann Arbor, Michigan, when they'd spent a day looking at seedy, rundown rentals with two mutual friends. Peter and one of the others looked oddly nervous when a potential landlord stressed the fact that there was an upstairs bath. They'd muttered "In the attic? In the attic?" in a demented echo and finally fled to the cold sidewalk outside, while Jules and his friend went on the full tour. Afterward, Jules discovered they'd been tripping, and somehow took "baths" for "bats"; he still found the memory pleasant, despite or because of subsequent joint misadventures. It was Peter who'd picked up Jules at the hospital when Jules had taken an outdoor flight of stairs on his ten-speed after nine Barbancourt rums; Jules who'd borrowed a girlfriend's car and driven to Indianapolis to retrieve Peter after his race-viewing intake of virtually every known mind-altering substance culminated in the temporary paralysis of half of his face, a small stroke known as Bell's Palsy.

Jules had known Alice almost as long, and introduced her to Peter in New York after college when they'd worked together at Dean & DeLuca. She had never had to witness food dribbling out of the corner of her lover's mouth, or shut his right eye manually, but she still didn't find the story funny. She was dubious about either of them having graced an honors program, and saw some reason for dread when they all ended up in the same town again. But both Peter and Jules had moderated their behavior, Jules a little more dramatically after several intervening years on isolated archaeological digs and the ramifications of his latest career. When they erred now Jules simply fell silent and moved toward home like an automaton, whereas Peter occasionally grew cranky. He'd blame it later on terminal career indecision—he'd ditched the law for reporting after a year of Montana practice. Jules, having built houses, sliced prosciutto, sold books and records, counseled sociopaths, dug for bones, and arrested drunks, went easier on himself in this area—he thought of career indecision as a way of life.

Now Alice looked away while she fiddled with her braid. "Did you identify the bodies yet?"

Peter had been biding his time, letting Alice start things

rolling. Now they both watched him. Jules looked down at his hands.

"You know Otto Scobey, right?"

"Scobey? Of course I do." Peter had had a couple of drinks and started to grin before he put the obvious together. "Oh yuck."

Delly still refused to make eye contact, much less move down for an order. Jules snagged Peter's whiskey and drank half of it while Peter was still rummaging through his jacket for his notebook.

"Oh, hell," said Alice, her pale face, almost as askew as Jules's, a little paler than usual. "Was the woman Sylvia?"

The woman in the tent might be virtually unrecognizable, but she'd never been a five-foot honey blonde. "No," said Jules. "She isn't Sylvia."

"Were they really run over?"

"They really were."

"She'll never go camping again," said Peter, searching for a pen.

Alice had grown up on a farm but prized physical comfort. She hadn't made it through Brownies, and she and Peter usually only camped two or three times a year. Though she claimed to enjoy it her feet were always cold, and she complained constantly about what might be happening to the tomato plants in her absence. Alice liked ordering nature around, and her relationship with the chaotic local climate was uneasy at best.

"Is it about Dragonfly?" she asked. "Someone angry about that?"

"I doubt it," said Jules, craning his neck. "Son of a bitch. *Delly!*"

Delly was there, suddenly, wiping his hands on a towel. "Don't have a hissy."

"Bad day," said Jules.

"Come up with a new line," said Delly, already pouring. "The bar can't buy you a drink every time you need one."

Alice turned back to her newspaper. Jules thought—hoped—she was being polite about the business end of things rather than indifferent. It was still hard to tell.

Peter had a slight edge to him. "Did you know who it was when I was up there?"

"Nah, I dove and checked out the plates." Jules drained his whiskey in three long gulps.

"The car's dumped in the reservoir?"

Jules nodded.

Alice looked up. Jules wondered how she could see the print; the Blue Bat's lighting was as inky as its name. Two high, narrow windows near the front door showed a trace glow of red neon, but in the daytime Delly always left the curtains drawn to protect the fragile eyes of his early customers. Most of the overhead lights were burned out, and by this point in the night the air was opaque with smoke. The Blue Bat carpeting—ceiling to ceiling rather than wall to wall—perfumed the air with the funk of decades. Peter said that Alice could tell which bar he'd been to after the briefest welcome home kiss.

"Are all your stitches out?"

"Most of them."

"Sure hope your shoulder's waterproof. Just think about what was in that water."

"Thanks, Alice." He finished Peter's drink. "How long have Sylvia and Otto been divorced?"

"At least a year, but obviously they still get along. Got along."

Jules didn't see anything obvious. He was notoriously bad at remembering names and details about law-abiding citizens, and thankful that Montana cops didn't spend much time at conventions. But even if he wasn't good at gossip, a few weeks of enforced newspaper reading in a hospital bed had almost brought him up to speed. Dragonfly was big news, potentially the biggest resort in an increasingly popular state: Sylvia Coburg, who'd inherited thousands of acres dotted across Absaroka County from her rancher father, had consolidated her holdings in the foothills of the Crazy Mountains through a series of purchases, sales, and Nature Conservancy and Forest Service swaps. The Crazies had been divvied up in a checkerboard of public and private land when the railroad came through, and Sylvia had simply traded her widely strewn acres for the desired missing squares. Some pristine bottomland here for a new public reserve, a tad of grazing land there; some wooded slopes for the timber lobby in return for another soft valley. In the end, she and Hugh Lesy and their investors had accumulated a series of six alpine meadows: eight thousand privately owned acres surrounded by a buffer zone of inaccessible Forest Service sections. The paperwork had taken years, with construction scheduled for months; the last hearings were only just finishing up.

Jules had learned all this from articles Peter had written, and it was time to make him work. "You're saying Otto didn't mind that she'd taken up with their partner Hugh?"

Peter shrugged. "Otto was still helping out. I heard he wanted to taper off, but anyone would, and they'd brought someone in to help. He had to have written a few miles of briefs by now. I just meant Sylvia and Otto *and* Hugh Lesy still seemed to be on good terms, when you'd see them all out."

"Did Otto have any financial stake in Dragonfly?"

"Only if he was trading work for interest. Otto did too much pro bono to be rich. It's all Sylvia and Hugh and their backers."

"Could one of the backers have had a problem with him?"

"I believe they all live in Los Angeles, and none of them has much of a say. Hugh and Sylvia are definitely in charge." Peter seemed confused by the level of whiskey in his glass.

"Anything funky about the land swap?"

"Have you heard anyone complain? The ranchers love them

for repairing the road and freeing up the lower acreage, the beer-gut mill owners love them for trading them easy-to-log sections, the tree huggers love them for setting up the river conservancy and swearing Dragonfly will be perfect PC. They used horses to log out the new road and the construction sites. They're planning to recycle farts up there. You've got to read their prospectus to believe it."

Jules sighed. He'd prefer to stick to escapist literature. "Some conflict with the new guy they brought in?"

"He's not actually new," said Peter. "They're just transplanting him for the heavy stuff, the last public hearings before they really kick into construction. Otto's still the mastermind."

Jules rubbed his head and wondered if he'd get any sleep that night. "Did Sylvia leave Otto for Hugh?"

"I think there was some lag time in there," said Peter.

"There was," said Alice with authority. She and Sylvia occasionally fell in together, and had once, in fact, sung karaoke together, on an exceptionally cold, drunken February night. Jules dimly remembered a selection of Patsy Cline's most maudlin hits. Alice had been so mortified on waking she'd stayed out of the grocery store for a week.

"Maybe they were too close," said Jules. "That little English prick might have had a problem."

"Hugh is not a prick," said Alice. "He's not like that at all."

Jules stared. Alice sweetened up every summer—more sunlight, lots of pretty flowers—but she tended to be uncharitable in her character estimates.

"How about the Eton accent?"

"Scholarship. He grew up poor in some little town in Wales or Cornwall, one of those peninsulas."

Peter looked vaguely embarrassed. "Hugh hired Alice to do some research for him. Some historical stuff for a new script."

Jules was amused. "Research? Whatever happened to your career as the catering queen of Absaroka County?"

Alice lifted an eyebrow. "You know quite well I have no aptitude for pigs in blankets and cheese dip and hundred-dollar budgets. Besides, I had a history minor. Why be snotty about coming back to your education?"

Jules grinned and reached for his drink.

"You did, after all," said Alice. "Anyway, half of my clients died."

He sucked on an ice cube. "Isn't it a conflict of interest, taking money from a guy while your boyfriend reams him out in the paper every day?" Peter had averaged two stories a week on Dragonfly over the last six months.

"Pffuh," said Alice, disgusted. "I'm not writing advertising copy. I'm not even cooking for him. And if it's payola it isn't working, so far."

Jules thought of leaving and opted for another drink. "Murder kind of ups the ante on ethics. Peter will have to watch his ass when he writes about Otto."

"Sacred Tree Scobey," said Peter, waving to Delly. "The fucker walks on water. Walked."

"Bad analogy, Peter." Alice went back to her newspaper, then looked up again. "So who was the woman?"

☆ 3 ☆

YOU CAN'T WALK ON WATER AT THE BOTTOM OF A LAKE

THAT NIGHT JULES EXPECTED TO DREAM ABOUT PATCHY PINK nail polish, or perhaps missing tent poles, but at four—expecting to be up at six, and halfway through his night's sleep—he instead dreamed of the Martinsdale jail, and in the dream its red door slowly changed into a cobalt blue Moroccan door, one he'd seen years earlier on an archaeological dig, and the prairie turned to sand and the air smelled of spice, and the simple bars metamorphosed into filigreed wrought iron. The snake that crawled across the dirt inside, however, was pure Montana, a fat diamondback, and dreaming it didn't scare him. The snake simply curled up and fell asleep, and Jules opened his eyes for a minute in the dark, then rolled over and postponed the second day of summer.

It was a fine thing, hitting day two with eyes like sandbags, ripped stitches in his shoulder, and a completely justified sense of dread. By nine o'clock on Tuesday morning, when Otto

Scobey's Saab was hauled out of the Martinsdale reservoir and Ed Winton opened a fateful purse and wallet and stared down at a Montana driver's license showing a cheery brunette, Jules knew the crushed woman's name would be Bonnie Siskowitz. By the end of the second round the night before, Alice, Peter, and Delly were ready to swear that Otto Scobey, attorney for the Dragonfly Refuge development, had been seeing a younger woman by that name, and they remembered her as easygoing, thirty or so. Alice called her ample, with the remnants of big hair; Peter, more generous, said "shapely." Delly Bane, with a *c'est la vie ordinaire* gesture, said that Bonnie "had screwed around a little too much to make the grade, but she was still a tomato." He couldn't imagine anyone being mean to her, and more to the point, he couldn't remember having heard of anyone who wanted her dead.

By seven A.M., Blue Deer's two dentists, rousted from bed at six, had each faxed records to the state police lab in Helena, where Harvey had just arrived with the bodies, and the lab sent confirmations an hour later. Bonnie Siskowitz was, in fact, exactly whom Jules had dreaded she'd be: a well-liked bookkeeper at a local supply store with no more than a speeding ticket on her record, a twenty-eight-year-old Blue Deer High graduate, the 1988 Wrangle Rodeo Queen. A sacred cow, as Axel Scotti remarked, rather unkindly, with his head buried in his hands. Jules mused over the peculiarly western irony of a sacred cow dying with a hugger of sacred trees as he trudged back down the courthouse hall to the sheriff's office, passing glass cases of six-guns and hangman's nooses and spurs and brands and, lastly, a logger's awl that had been used to murder a mill owner with a pretty wife in the twenties.

Sexual trespass was possibly the oldest cause of angst on the planet, after food theft and being prey. There was nothing like jealousy; in one form or another it took up the majority of his every working day, and he'd already learned that nine times out of ten the obvious solution to a crime was the solution. Which meant that if Otto Scobey and his friend hadn't been killed by a random crazy, they'd probably been killed by the people who encompassed every motive. Otto had been divorced, and his wife had taken up with a mutual friend. He had no real cash or property of his own—at least to Jules's knowledge—but had spent most of his last three years adding to the cash and property of his wife and that mutual friend. Land *was* money in Montana, virtually the only form of money, and land and money were right after love as motives for putting another human to death.

Land, money, love. Sylvia Coburg and Hugh Lesy. Jules was suspicious of people who were still on good terms despite wrinkles in their affections; his own experience had never borne out such peace of mind. Otto Scobey, environmental lawyer, had angered many of the businesses in town, most of the public servants, and all of the loggers, but there was no need to search for a new sin when so many old ones would do. Really, Jules had gone to the bar the night before to dig something out of Peter that pointed him away from this early conclusion, because he'd always loved Sylvia Coburg. He barely knew and couldn't care less about Hugh Lesy, an Englishman who directed well-reviewed polite melodramas. But he'd known Sylvia since he was a baby, and he found the idea that she might be involved in murder, even as an innocent object of desire, unbearable and unthinkable.

At eight that morning Sylvia answered the phone at Hugh Lesy's apartment at the Baird Hotel, where Peter and Alice had said the couple stayed when they didn't bother with the drive to the ranch. Jules, who'd been struggling with the gentlest wording possible, departed from his script as soon as he heard her voice. He told her that Otto was dead, asked her some simple questions, and told her he needed to ask harder ones, later.

Sylvia was on her way to join Lesy and an architect at Dragonfly; she didn't cry, but Jules didn't expect she'd have a happy drive north, and made plans to meet her on his way back from Helena and the autopsies.

Now he knew why no one had called in saying the couple was missing: They'd been due back the day the tent had been pulled out of the water, which meant they'd probably been killed at the beginning of a planned ten-day vacation. He also knew that Otto Scobey had been married twice but had no survivors beyond an uncle in Phoenix with advanced Alzheimer's. This was a blessing, and Jules trudged down the hall for another cup of coffee, wishing he could bury his head under the pretty pieces of paper on his desk rather than telling the Siskowitzes their daughter was dead. Ed called from Martinsdale, and Jules asked him to return to the Inn (fine by Ed) and Clarence Bost's properties (not fine by him) for more questioning. In the midst of the ensuing wrangle the mayor suddenly loomed next to Jules, materializing with remarkable silence for such a large and graceless and traumatized object. His face was mottled and he started talking without regard for the fact that Jules had the phone receiver in his hand, babbling about the effect of more murders on tourism.

Jules gripped the phone and stared, wondering if the man thought he could simply inject the corpses with adrenaline and make the nightmare go away; on the other end of the line, Ed giggled. The department's youngest, least functional deputy, Jonathan Auber, was in the far corner telling bad jokes about dead people to a salesman from a soda pop supply company, showing no sign of conscience. Ed signed off and the phone blared again immediately; Jules waved, panic-stricken, in Grace's direction. She pointed to four lights on the switchboard and turned away. When Jules finally ripped at the receiver on the tenth ring, the mayor, interrupted mid-monologue, tottered off, pulling out his last few hairs.

It was Helena again, saying they'd moved the autopsy up to noon. Maybe they expected him to take a helicopter; the phone came down so hard that Jonathan finally looked in his direction. Jules stood with his hat in hand, staring at the clock as if it might explain why he'd returned to the job, then headed toward his car, on his way to bring grief to Bonnie Siskowitz's mother and father.

Jules had seen no point in rousting them from bed at dawn. Hiram Siskowitz and his wife ran a popular bar in the valley twenty miles south of Blue Deer, and they always opened bottles and closed at two A.M., whether or not they had paying clients. Doreen Siskowitz, still in her nightgown, became hysterical at the news and beat out the glass bar backboard with her arthritic fists. Jules spent the next hour at the hospital with Hiram, who was subdued and sweet, like a sad, deflated birthday balloon.

They'd loved Bonnie ("christened Boneen; kinda French") but couldn't say that she'd ever been a well-behaved girl. They took solace in her sense of humor and put up with her endless career changes and a long string of boyfriends. They'd only met Otto once, but he'd definitely been a cut above, and Bonnie, impressed, had been very careful around him. Hiram looked at Jules strangely when the age difference came up. Why would he care how old the man was? Age only made it likelier that Otto wasn't into drugs, or wouldn't beat her or live off her. Jules tried to follow this sizable hint with an inquiry into Bonnie's unhappy past, but Hiram insisted that none of his daughter's former lovers had cared enough to carry a grudge; Hiram himself couldn't remember many names. Some were nice, some were mean, almost all of them were stupid, and Bonnie had known this and been bored and annoyed by them, too. But, as Hiram put it, she liked "creature comforts," and people around. "She liked to party." Hiram had loved his daughter, but even grief didn't dent his pragmatism.

An hour and a half later in Helena, as the sheets were pulled back from Otto's and Bonnie's bodies, Jules wondered, as always, why he'd bothered coming. He rarely thought of anything intelligent to ask, and he could never handle certain rituals, most particularly the opening of the skull. Other than being crushed to death and a half-finished root canal on Otto's part, he and Bonnie had both been in sterling health. Even after the tests came back, there would still probably be a forty-eight-hour window for time of death, a wide-open slot should Jules ever be lucky enough to find a suspect. It wasn't as if they'd recover a bullet this time around, and he didn't drive away with any magic details or a clue to the killer's identity, beyond the fact that he or she could drive a truck. No good news either: Though Otto had been deader than a doornail by the time he sank, Bonnie had been alive enough, despite a crushed rib cage, to inhale water in a sinking, dark tent. This was not the sort of comforting detail Jules intended to share with her parents or the local media; his mind was filled with nasty details he had to keep to himself.

Jules drove faster than usual, the better to get to know Hugh Lesy sooner. Twenty miles past the Martinsdale turnoff he cut east, directly toward the mountains, for another half hour, wondering distractedly how many future Dragonfly employees would fall asleep on the road during their roundtrip from Blue Deer. Construction wasn't supposed to have started, but he passed stacks of lumber and steel I-beams and bricks before he even reached the new road to the gateway of the main site, a narrow, yellow-walled canyon entrance to all eight thousand acres of meadows and treed slopes, spawning streams and uninhabitable rocks.

Jules got out of his car at a fork in the road at the foot of the first meadow and tried to imagine a main lodge and forty condominiums, the hot spring pools and saunas and ski ropes and horse barns, equipment shops, holistic groceries, whatever else Peter had mentioned. All the reasons for murder were multiplied by the nature of the business of Dragonfly. There could literally be a motive for every prospective condo. Something in the prospectus, in the deed, in the funding, in the land itself. Dragonfly was sheer real estate, a nature reserve, a potential ski resort, mining museum, spa, outward-bound camp, or four-star restaurant. Husbands, wives, lovers, simple employees: no potential suspect clicked into any one slot, and the emotional unknowns multiplied the practical possibilities.

He stood in the middle of the meadow that would be a resort and thought of how beautiful it all was compared to what he'd seen in Helena. Maybe the buildings would be dotted across the property, a few of them in each clearing, some clinging to the gentler inclines, all of them too well built to really be western. He hoped construction wouldn't go all the way back, five miles or so, to the translucent glacier itself, a narrow thirty-acre valley floored with the coldest blue gray imaginable. There were dozens of glaciers in the Crazies alone, but only one other in the state, down in the Beartooths, that boasted frozen swamp bugs. A warm day, a hatch, a thaw, and a wash of slush, and it had been all over for a family of blue-wing dragonflies ten thousand years ago.

Jules had been about ten, camping with his mother and father and another family, when his first true archaeological question had occurred to him: Where the hell were the rodents? Until then he'd peered down, looking for saber-tooth mountain lions, prehistoric lizards, maybe a very old Crow in the swirl of ancient ants, spring leaves, and pine cones, so close to the ice that the tip of his nose would begin to freeze. It had taken just one Yellowstone River flood to start the change in thinking, to make him realize that the animals caught in such disasters tended to be stupid and common, and that in fact if you were a stupid animal you had to be common, because you tended to die. Hence questioning the absence of mice, rabbits, woodchucks. His father's answer, doled out during a game of euchre, had been half real and half blather: If Jules were able to drill through the ice, he'd undoubtedly find his rodents with their heads in their burrows and their little asses frozen in midair with the dragonflies.

That hadn't been the first time Jules had listened to an explanation and thought "Bullshit." Perhaps he'd so liked the experience he'd deliberately sought out a profession in which people would lie to him as a matter of course. The lies people told their doctors, psychiatrists, spouses paled in comparison. Even people he liked lied to him when he wore his uniform, as if they literally couldn't help themselves. Sylvia probably would, and he prepared himself to be depressed.

He looked down and watched live grasshoppers flit across the road, winging off into soft grass and vetch and broken shale. No grazing for a full year now, and it made an astounding difference, the difference he supposed Sylvia prized, along with the fortune she stood to make, in giving up privacy on the family land. The only tire marks led right, toward the original, ruined homestead, and he sighed as he climbed back in the car and followed a small feeder creek to a burned frame house nestled halfway up a hill.

Sylvia was sitting on what was left of the porch, dressed in shorts and a T-shirt, and they watched each other for a moment before Jules opened his car door and came to sit beside her. They faced a half-timbered new house marooned in daisies a few hundred yards away, surrounded by two trucks and a half-dozen ill-at-ease men. Jules recognized the red blond head of Hugh Lesy, director, producer, developer extraordinaire. They'd met once in a bar, the previous summer, on a night neither of them was likely to recall clearly. Otto Scobey had been out that night, too, and Jules tried to remember whom Sylvia had stuck closest to. He failed; she always had been democratic with her affections, at least socially.

It was a joke now, but Sylvia Coburg—five-one, all honey and cream with the looks of a minute Vanessa Redgrave—had been Jules's baby-sitter and later taught him to ride and rope. By the time he was eleven, when she'd come to parties at his parents' house with her first husband, the idea that she'd once changed his diaper almost killed him. Twenty-some years later, Jules was able to talk to her without breaking into a cold sweat, but he was still prone to an occasional fantasy. By now, she knew it; they joked about it sometimes, and Jules thought it likely they'd still be joking about it when he was seventy and Sylvia eighty-three, unless he got lucky in the meantime. She was still beautiful, and she undoubtedly worked hard to look that way, though without letting it get in the way of her life. She won cutting horse competitions, gardened for blue ribbons at the fair, danced and smoked and enjoyed wine. She'd had two boys with her first husband, both now working in banking on the East Coast as had their father, a Bostonian Sylvia called "the ruler" (the reference had nothing to do with royalty). Otto Scobey, a Berkeley-educated hippie lawyer, had been husband number two. She was a quality pistol, a self-possessed firework. Most of the men in town, of any age, would have surrendered body parts to buy her a drink.

Not that anyone needed to buy her anything. She had the land, and according to Peter, Hugh had the backers and his own money. Otto, apparently, had been the poor, faithful wise boy who helped out.

Jules waited one more polite minute before he looked at Sylvia directly. She gave him a smile, but she looked—relatively—horrible, small and silky as ever but with red-rimmed hazel eyes. Her hair hung down below her shoulders, far messier than usual, and now at least half gray.

"Will that be one of the condos?"

"That will be our house," said Sylvia. "Hugh's and mine. Away from the rest. And we'll call the condos cabins."

Jules felt a hint of bona fide humor, a crease deep in his cheek, the first smile in twenty-four hours. "What about your old ranch?"

"That's conservancy land now. They'll keep a ranger there, rent out rooms."

"Big of you to give up your house," said Jules.

"I'll be reimbursed." She smiled.

Jules loosened his tie and looked at the landscape. She slapped the back of his head, and her voice oozed sarcasm. "You're wondering how I could give up my little private paradise. Try about ten mil over the next five years in home and land sales, between the two of us, not even counting what we might make from the resort itself. I've already made a fortune on the smaller parcels we sold outright."

She hadn't been hurting before, and barely stopped for a breath now. Jules got the sense she'd spent the last few months anticipating criticism and fighting back. "You're too idealistic to face that it'll all go downhill around here anyway. This way people get to see the glacier, and they get to watch birds on the river bottom. More buildings aren't a bad trade, especially if they're cabins that fit into the landscape."

He bet they'd be big, polished cabins, for big, polished people. Your average second-grader in Clyde City wasn't going to get more than a field trip out of the deal, but she was right—that was all they'd ever have gotten. "I'm not very idealistic," he said quietly.

"Besides, I grew up here." She thumped the steps. "This is home."

So much for small talk. Jules plucked a gray sliver of wood from the steps and started gouging a hole in a charred area.

"Did you find out anything more in Helena?"

"No."

"Did he feel much?"

Not "anything," but "much." Jules looked at her, curious.

"He couldn't have, physically. But if he was expecting it, he had time to worry."

"Well, thanks," said Sylvia, bitterly.

"Would you prefer I give you the complete kid-glove treatment? You've got a healthy imagination. You've probably already thought about it, and I need to know if he'd been worried about anything."

She crinkled her face up as if she were trying to make out something in the distance, an expression she'd always used to avoid emotion. Her next words were very dry but spoke volumes of confusion. "It's funny. Otto and I had really started enjoying each other again in the last year. I just don't get it."

No one would call it a direct answer, or a new one. Jules watched Sylvia, and she watched her house, her workmen, and her director. It occurred to him that she and Hugh Lesy could have been twins, all soft, Venetian coloring, both of them usually filled with boundless energy. They were about the same age, too, late forties, and Jules had to cede a point to Hugh for loving Sylvia instead of his scriptgirl or his nanny or a swimsuit calendar model, or behaving like the usual tycoon.

"If you're a lawyer there's always someone on the other side to get pissed off, or someone who thinks you could have done better."

Sylvia leaned over, stretching to reach a cooler. "I've been thinking about it, and I can't remember a single case, a single weirdo who would have been capable of this in the last however many years."

She handed him a root beer and he inched up a step to reach the shade.

"Nothing with Dragonfly?"

"What's to be pissed about?" She took a long, unladylike pull on her root beer, and Jules had the sudden, sharp urge to lick the foam right off her full upper lip. "The mill's happy because we gave them the North Fork sections. The Nature Conservancy and the Absaroka County Environmental Corps are happy because we gave them the Shields drainage, and because we'll leave all the Forest Service trails open. Hell, we're *opening* some. The backers are happy, because they'll make their fortune in the first five years. The county should be happy, because we're paying taxes without asking them for services. We even built our own road." She pulled an elastic from her jeans pocket and had her hair piled in a neat knot in two deft seconds. "Otto got along with people. He was honest, and he was patient, and he was smart. It must have been someone crazy, or someone who wanted to hurt Bonnie. Some asshole cowboy she knew back when she used to ride."

"You ride, and it doesn't mean you hang out with asshole cowboys."

Sylvia gave him an exasperated look. "I didn't know her. I met her twice. She seemed nice, but she was scared of me."

Jules smiled to himself.

She scrunched her face up again, admitting to a secret worry. "I don't have to identify him, do I?"

"Oh, God no," said Jules. "The dental records are enough."

"Did you recognize him when you first pulled him out?"

"Christ, Sylvia, why ask me something like that?"

"Why not?"

"I didn't know Otto well," said Jules stiffly. "Had they planned the trip for awhile?"

Sylvia sighed again. "He'd meant to take a break for months."

"So a ten-day trip just around Martinsdale?"

"Of course not. I don't know why they went there at all. They were planning on the Beartooths, maybe even up to Glacier. They left—I don't know—Thursday or Friday the week before last. It was the morning after the last hearing on Dragonfly, but I can't remember the day."

Jules had done his homework. "Thursday night."

"Oh," she said, not particularly impressed. "Well, anyway, he was sick of Dragonfly, had us bringing in someone who's helped out from the beginning, so he could take some time off and do a little more casework for friends, pro bono stuff for the grassroots people. I think it bothered him, this thing."

She gestured at the pristine real estate and sighed. Jules thought of the stacks of I-beams.

"Anyway, he wasn't doing much for us anymore. So if someone was pissed off at Dragonfly, going for Otto would have gotten them nowhere. It'd be me, or Hugh."

He bludgeoned her with some more questions. Otto had started visiting this part of Montana twenty years earlier, and his L.A. practice had gradually moved away from film work and toward environmental cases. His first marriage had ended in divorce in 1980; she didn't know where that ex-wife lived now. He'd given up California for good around that time, before she'd even met him, and taken a job in Bozeman with an old college friend, where he specialized in land and its queerer rules. Otto had been something of a pro at the arcane, byzantine world of water rights, and when he'd saved enough money he kicked into pro bono environmental fights, using his knowledge against his former clients.

Otto was the reason Hugh Lesy had first seen Montana, and he was the person who'd first suggested his old client and his wife should pool their resources on Dragonfly. And if the outcome had caused him heartache, it seemed unlikely anyone would admit this to Jules. He thought of the half-dissolved red leather journal and wondered if the pages would ever come apart again. He watched Sylvia as she talked, and wondered if he'd be able to separate knowing her from the need to ask indelicate questions. If he were a judge, he would have recused himself from this case.

Jules put down his empty root beer bottle and stood creakily.

Sylvia nodded across the field toward her lover. "Hugh's realizing that buildings take even longer than movies to make, and he's not happy with the local pace."

"It looks like the house is coming right along."

"He's not worried about the house," said Sylvia. "He wants a log barn built up the hill, yesterday. It's another thing we can get out of the way before Dragonfly's cleared for construction. It'll be our barn eventually, but the push is to have it built as soon as possible so it has a chance to weather for the movie. Fade a little, have the green fill in."

Jules turned slowly and looked at her.

"Next summer," said Sylvia reassuringly. "Don't worry."

"Will most of the movie be set out here?"

She smiled softly. "Only about half of it'll need to be filmed in town."

Jules sighed and started across the field. There was no point in wasting dread on something that was still months away when there was so much to drive him witless in the here and now. If things kept going downhill he'd doubtless have quit by then anyway, while Hugh Lesy's movie, whatever it would come to be called, was still in the innocent stage of things, the win-an-Oscar-help-the-local-economy-without-hurting-a-brick phase. A movie crew could temporarily close down a small town, cause whiplash and dreams of grandeur and divorces. This truth had come home to Jules in his first year as a cop, during the filming of a motion picture Blue Deer referred to as *A River Ran Over Me.*

But it was interesting that Hugh Lesy could keep his eye focused on the future, on the day he learned his oldest local friend and partner was rotten. Lesy was rattling off commands in a voice that sounded calm and polite until you picked out the words, perhaps because of the accent. The barn was to be built in three days so the crew would be ready to move on to Dragonfly when they had the legal go-ahead; if cabins had been built that fast a hundred years ago they could be put together that fast now, by idiots with power tools. Then they'd map out the footpaths, a pen for some livestock and another fence to hold next summer's garden. And it better be looking weathered within the year, so if any asshole thought he could get away with using treated wood he should know Hugh would fingerprint the shingles and find him. The barn should, in fact, have been completed during the time all of them were standing in the field together, and why the bloody fuck hadn't it bloody fucking been finished before then? Had everyone been pulling on their bloody puds, picking their frigging noses?

The questions weren't the type people were really meant to answer, and Jules averted his eyes and feigned interest in the half-finished siding, like one dog politely ignoring another's beating. By the end of it Hugh Lesy was bright pink, and the cultured accent Jules had remembered had given way to the kind of fast growl that might have made the grainiest English football fan proud.

The soft voice returned when he apologized for keeping Jules waiting. They agreed that they'd met, in some semblance of the word, both exhibiting the correct amount of humor about that nonevent in the Blue Bat. This was a bad time to talk, a very bad time; in the first place, Hugh couldn't think straight. He'd known Otto for twenty years and relied on his advice that long, and he was literally unsure he could tie his shoes without the man. And it was a bad time because he needed to find a phone and have a story conference, probably from the car, because that was where he and Syl lived these days. He had no choice but to make this call by five o'clock California time, which was almost now where they stood, and then he'd promised an associate he'd meet him about how to handle Otto's death, with the Refuge and all, and the associate was just arriving in town, so there was no way to reach him.

Jules felt winded just listening. Lesy sucked in a breath and stared hopelessly at him with watery, blood-shot blue eyes. "Morning would be better."

"I can see that," said Jules. "Early."

"Syl and I are at the Baird tonight; we could have breakfast there. Would seven do?"

"Fine," said Jules. "Anything obvious to tell me?"

Lesy was sweating profusely just as Jules felt the first bearable breeze of evening. "I haven't a clue. It's unimaginable."

They left it at that. On his way out, Jules took a leak on a pile of expensive shingles, and hoped the coyotes would follow his lead.

Alice fanned her face with a leaflet and made harrumphing noises, but no one noticed. Her eyes grated in their sockets, and her stomach burbled, and her sense of balance was so damaged that she listed slightly to the left. She'd been standing in front of the Forest Service's information desk for a full five minutes without any of the half-dozen people milling in the back of the office showing compassion. It was almost as hot inside as out, and the old Mazda truck had black seats and lacked air-conditioning, and Peter should have made this trip for her anyway, because he knew how to ask questions. They'd stayed up until four, talking about death and drinking Calvados. Unfortunately, she hadn't asked him to ask nicely enough, and he'd left for work in the good car, after slamming the door.

It was not an auspicious day to dig into the nitty-gritty of mining law for Hugh's screenplay, but she'd put it off all the previous week, and there was the small matter of the July mortgage payment.

A man walked around a wall of cabinets toward the front, but bent to open a drawer without meeting her eyes.

"Ahem," said Alice.

The man scratched the back of his neck and opened a second drawer. He slammed the first and Alice flinched.

"I'm doing some research and I need any circulars you might have on mining."

The man straightened, eyed her with weary disbelief, and gestured silently toward a floor-to-ceiling bookshelf stuffed with ring binders.

"Oh come on," moaned Alice. "Don't you have some sort of leaflet on the claim process?"

The man shut his eyes for a moment and rocked on his feet, then opened and shut a few more drawers before slapping some stapled sheets on the counter in front of her. He looked like he'd rubbed his face with charcoal, and one hand was bandaged. Alice was proud of herself for noticing the suffering of another in the midst of her own self-imposed illness.

They stared at each other. Alice glanced down and read "Staking a Mining Claim on Federal Lands."

"This is it?" she said.

He was staring over the counter at her legs and looked away politely. Alice's legs weren't bad, but they were covered with bruises; Alice ran into things on an hourly basis, even when she'd been teetotaling. "It's a start," he said.

Alice scanned subheads. "To Patent or Not to Patent?" "What Types of Minerals May Be Claimed?" "Where May I Prospect?"

"Thank you," she said, looking back up, but the man was already gone.

She stalled the Mazda twice on the way home, and by the time she'd slumped into the chair in front of her computer she was near tears from the desire to crawl back into bed. She settled for an old milkshake she'd found in the back of the freezer and a bag of chips and tried not to get Peter's keyboard too greasy as she typed.

When Peter returned for lunch an hour later Alice had sharpened up considerably; she ran down the stairs to barrage him with questions.

"Did you know that for less than one hundred dollars you can have control over acres and acres of land?"

Peter was staring morosely into the refrigerator. "Generally each claim is limited to twenty acres. Though you can have more than one."

"Whatever. If you patent, it's five dollars an acre, plus five hundred dollars a claim in improvements. And then it's all yours."

He reached for a bowl of leftover stew. "I'm a little distressed that you can act as if you've had a revelation when I've written article after article on the bullshit people get away with under the 1872 law. Do you read what I write? Have you lived here for four years?"

"Peter."

"Alice, sweetheart." He slammed the bowl into the microwave. A fork was inside and the machine arched and fizzled, making them both twitch.

"Can't anyone get a chunk of land this way?"

He held the dripping fork and stared at her, finally wising up and wondering how to tell her she wasn't being fiendishly clever. "You can't build on it."

"You can once you've patented it."

"That takes years, and there's the little matter of actually discovering something to mine."

"It can't be that hard."

He took the Interior Department circular from her hand, scanned it, and began to read aloud.

. . . there must be an actual physical discovery of a valuable mineral deposit on each and every mining claim. Traces, minor indications, geological inference, or hope of a future discovery are not sufficient to satisfy the *prudent man and marketability* rule. Making mining improvements, posting a notice, or performing annual assessment work will not create or perpetuate a "right" or interest in the land if there are no valuable mineral deposits within the claim.

"You can find *anything*, though," said Alice. "Mica, lead, sulphur—"

"Which just means you have to extract more for marketability," said Peter. "And sulphur is a lease. Different scam. Besides, you have to record your claim, show you've spent money to maintain it, and if you want to patent, really own it, the process takes forever. And all you need to know for your research is that a hundred years ago any idiot could prospect anywhere."

The microwave beeped. Peter opened the door and smiled benevolently at a bubbling pound of beef and baby turnip daube.

"Well," said Alice, "if you knew everything already, why did I have to haul my sorry butt to the Forest Service office?"

"Exercise," said Peter. "Let's take a nap after lunch."

Jules could have snuck home while it was still light had he lacked a conscience, but he stopped at the station on the off chance someone had confessed. It wasn't as if the day had ended with a revelation, a talkative psychopath, murdering half-sister, errant big wheels driver from Kansas, crazed logger from Manitoba, or ecoterrorist from Boca Raton. Jules knew exactly zilch about his campers' final moments, and possibly less about his own place in the grand scheme of things. Knowing who they were was no longer reassuring, especially as he'd become increasingly sure that there was something familiar about Bonnie Siskowitz's name beyond her father's renown as a bartender. But Jules had been in New York when she'd been in high school, Europe when she was the Wrangle queen. She had no older brothers and sisters to remember, no connection with his own life.

On the drive south he'd become convinced he knew why, and shoveled through the piles on his desk, finally grasping the wire report received from Jackson, Wyoming, on June 5, the one Peter had brought up the day before at the reservoir.

It had nothing to do with Bonnie, after all, but it was memorable. Jules kept an informal list of hated words, most of which he'd first heard in driver training class. It included terms like "incident," "beverage," "vehicle," "perpetrator," "intoxicated," "individual," "luncheon," and "folks." As in the Jackson police report, which he dimly remembered reading in the hospital: A "male individual" in a "large vehicle" had rammed some campsites outside of Jackson, and another outside of Moose, Wyoming, but both times the "possibly intoxicated perpetrator" honked, as if inviting "folks" to vacate. Both "incidents" occurred in the middle of the day while folks were having "luncheon" at nearby picnic tables, and resulted in five ruined tents but only one injury (a "female individual" sprained her ankle, possibly while running in terror), if you didn't count a shar-pei. A physical description of the perpetrator didn't seem reliable— one camper cited brown hair and a medium-to-slight build, but the woman who'd sprained her ankle claimed he was blond and immense and snapped his teeth at her—but the vehicle, understandably, had made more of an impression. Three witnesses stated the vehicle was a large light green Ford pickup, and the park cops had assumed this meant a Forest Service truck, though none had been reported stolen. All agreed that the individual had hurled a "beverage container" (Budweiser? Molson? Bad ice tea? Jules wanted to know) through his window at the wounded sharpei, but everyone involved had touched the can, then thrown it in the trash with dozens of other such cans before the police thought to check for prints.

Jules had trouble believing that the same man or short-haired woman who'd honked a warning on a sunny day would repeatedly crush an inhabited tent on a dark night. On the other hand, his desk also provided a note from Harvey, tentatively linking the Martinsdale tire tread to a Goodyear lot purchased by the

Forest Service the year before. Perhaps the campers near Jackson had been practice, the tentative beginnings to a dangerous binge. Maybe the guy behind the wheel liked biting apples as well as tourists.

He called the exhausted, understaffed Grand Teton rangers, but they had nothing much to add, even after he'd goaded them with a graphic description of Otto Scobey and Bonnie Siskowitz's mortal remains. The possible truck link was vague at best though there had been two fire camps monitoring small lightning blazes within a twenty-mile radius of Jackson at the time of the first incident. Many of the same trucks and fighters had been transferred to Blue Deer's end of Yellowstone Park by the time Otto and Bonnie had died, digging preventive trenches in a drainage thirty miles south of town. He'd send Harvey to the local camps with the tread in the morning.

Jules sighed and walked toward Grace, who was working overtime like everyone else, eyeing him and tapping her pencil on a mountain of petty complaints. Jonathan, on a split shift, was on the other side of the room, busy cleaning his desk drawer while the criminal justice system of Absaroka County, Montana, burned down around his extra-large, selectively deaf ears. Jonathan had once confided in Jules that a clean desk connoted a clean mind, and had been offended when Jules became hysterical with laughter. Now Jonathan rushed toward Jules when Grace was midway through a litany of small trials, his face red and eager. "Did you tell him about the Daneloffs?"

"No, Jonathan. I haven't gotten to them yet." Grace made it clear that this line was a warning. Jonathan skidded on.

"Jack Daneloff tried to run over Bella with his truck."

Jules signed forms. "I know, Jonathan."

"I mean that he did it again today," said Jonathan. "And I checked and he was in town when that couple must have been killed."

Grace acted busy. Jules lowered his pen and stared at the

deputy. "Jack Daneloff and his wife have been trying to run each other over for the last twenty years. It's their specialty. Are you suggesting that one of them finally decided to branch out?"

"Same M.O.," said Jonathan. "Even if it wasn't Daneloff I think we have a copycat on our hands."

Jules looked him over. Sometimes, when Jonathan was most eager, he also looked oddly blank, as if he was parroting and receiving information the same way he'd watch TV, completely bypassing his brain. Twenty-three, dirty blond and crew-cut, still preferring milk to all other fluids, a fifties youth in a mean, complicated world. He'd been on the force for two months and it was time for the weekly lecture on deliberate thought process. Jules didn't have the heart for the full talk that day.

"You remember what you learned about patterns and coincidence?"

"Sure." But Jonathan looked doubtful suddenly.

"Get out those notes." Jules patted him on the shoulder. "Keep thinking while you're patrolling. Go fill our tank."

"Yessir."

Jules gritted his teeth and looked at Grace, who avoided his eyes and shuffled through her notes. "Let's see. The scene photos came back from the lab, and I've attached Ed's memo on potential witnesses in Martinsdale—"

"Did he find any?" Jules reached for the pile and looked at the first two photos. After the horror of the Helena lab they looked like fashion shoots.

"Just Mary Peach at the Inn, but I guess you talked to her last night. Ed found the Great Falls kids, but they were too hungover and freaked out to be any help. Someone thought they remembered the dog mooching potato chips at a campsite, but that was it."

Jules read the memo. Ed had dug into her background all afternoon, but Bonnie Siskowitz didn't have any noteworthy jilted lovers, annoyed ex-coworkers, funny numbers in her company's ledgers. In the last two weeks of her life she'd slept at Otto's house a half dozen times and spent the other nights either watching videos with her roommate or reading paperbacks or scrubbing her kitchen floor. Otherwise, she'd gone riding twice, attended a baby shower in Bozeman, and shown up early for work most mornings. Her partying days, once involving a healthy amount of cocaine and sweet cocktails, had ended a couple of years earlier when she'd returned from a stint in Boise, Idaho, but no one tied this character renovation to a specific event. The roommate thought Bonnie had been in a minor car accident, but if so, she'd been a passenger, because neither her insurance company nor the Idaho police had a record of such an incident.

Ed knew a hell of a lot more about Bonnie Siskowitz than Jules knew about Otto Scobey. "And no one remembers anyone else hanging out in Martinsdale?" he asked.

"Sorry, honey. But otherwise it's been the usual today. Unidentified individuals shot a stop sign and a cattle crossing sign in Pray. An elderly individual put his car into drive rather than reverse at Vaughn's Drugstore. A couple from Missouri flipped their raft just below the island bridge, but no injuries. And there's a rock fall on the river road. Jonathan cleaned up one bunch this afternoon, but we just got a second call."

"Where the hell is the county crew?"

"Handling some washed-out pavement near Springdale. An irrigation ditch busted through."

"Why didn't you send Jonathan out again?"

Grace made a face. "He wanted to wait for you. One large rock is blocking a lane, so someone has to get there by dark." She handed over another wad of paper. "And I'm leaving in an hour whether Richard shows up or not."

Jules had heard that Richard, the new night dispatcher, had trouble with the alphabet and froze, deer in headlights, when more than one line rang. He had a fuzzy memory of scaring him the night before. "You have a hospital meeting?"

"No, I'm going to go have a gin and tonic, all by myself, and if anyone talks to me I'm going to have two."

Not wanting to push Grace over the line into alcoholism or, worse yet, have her quit, Jules headed south toward the fallen rocks and mused about Jonathan and the Daneloffs and cars, lately the next best weapon of choice in the New West after the eternal, sainted firearm. Whenever Jules asked Bella and Jack Daneloff why they were always standing in the driveway when the car started up, the question seemed to confuse them. Where else would a person stand? Not that staying away from pavement had helped the soupy remains in Helena.

Ten minutes later he stood in front of a virtual boulder in the middle of the river road, wondering how a sole human was supposed to solve this particular problem. He found a branch in the ditch and, using it as a lever, managed to move the thousand-pound chunk of granite in the wrong direction, smack onto the yellow line, before the stick gave way and he nearly lost his toes. Jules hurled the branch onto the cliff face above the road and started for his car, doing a double take when he recognized a dry buzz and made out a sandy brown, pissed-off coil in the rocks fifteen feet above.

Jules strode to the car and punched the radio. "Get the goddamn road crew, Grace. This thing weighs a ton."

"Ha, ha, ha," said Grace.

"Literally," said Jules.

He pulled a caution sign from his trunk, straddled it over the rock, and decided to work on his attitude by continuing to loop away from Blue Deer. Maybe it was time to become an archaeologist again, really delve into the local serpent population. He plugged in a gospel tape and yodeled along as he let the valley unroll. It might be more crowded than it had been in his youth, but it was still beautiful, green and gray and white under a dark blue sky, with the Yellowstone higher than most years, a fat brown ribbon dividing the valley.

Within ten minutes the landscape looked beautiful again, he felt young again, and life was all so lovely again that it took him several seconds to realize that the car approaching him at ninety-five miles an hour on his radar was really heading right *at* him, passing two RVs and showing no signs of vacating the south-bound lane. Jules had spent the whole last month feeling glad to be alive, and spending two days with spongy bodies hadn't dented this resolve. He veered to the gravel on the right, praying for a hard shoulder, at the same time that the oncoming forest green BMW finished its pass and glided into the northbound lane. Jules had a glimpse of a smiling man in sunglasses, and with this vision his blood pressure seemed to shoot out the ends of his chaotic hair. He kicked into a string of bad cowboy language, punched on his lights and his siren, made a U-turn, and floored the accelerator violently enough to have the sensation of G force.

There was still something strange about speeding down a highway, talking and listening to air, usually air with the voice of a sixty-year-old bird-watcher named Grace Marble. After working too many shifts in a row he'd find himself in his own ancient Chevy truck, talking back to the music or hurling abuse at the traffic, as if he were still in beautiful New York.

"Stop it," said his radio. "Who taught you those words? We're taping this."

"Har dee har har," said Jules. "I show him at ninety-three."

"Still," said Grace, "I thought you said no more car chases."

"He'll pull over," said Jules. He turned the volume down and passed the traumatized Winnebagos. The BMW, a mile away, had slowed to eighty or so, and grew larger every second. Jules was going ninety-eight by the time he braked to ride its bumper, and the driver finally slowed and signaled.

It was a relief to turn off the sirens, and his footsteps on the gravel seemed to echo. The well-tended asshole behind the leather-covered wheel—pale, tall-looking, with brown hair—had rolled down his window but had failed to turn down his radio, and Jules recognized an old ska band with mild amusement. No wonder the car had been going so fast. The driver was rummaging through his wallet, head down, sunglasses on, and Jules fought the impulse to jerk him through the open window by his white, well-scrubbed neck.

"I've charged so much gas lately," said the man, "that my license is probably wrapped in one of these receipts."

"Or in one of those tickets," said Jules. "Turn the goddamn radio down."

"Yes sir," said the man, punching a button on the dash, the search through the mess of cards on his lap growing frantic. "Actually, it's a CD."

"Actually, I don't give a flying fuck," said Jules. "Your license is face down on your right knee. Hand it to me, remove your glasses, and keep both hands on the wheel."

No cub scout could have been more obedient. Their eyes finally met and Jules gave a little shake of his head before checking the license for a stereo identity, the pale gray eyes and long nose and unmistakably serene, smug expression in color and in life, the name, the height, and birth date in black and white.

Everett Parsons gaped. "You're the fucking *sheriff*?"

Everett sounded panic stricken. "Jesus," said Jules. "I'd think this would be good news. What the hell are you doing?"

Everett ogled Jules's badge. "I quit my job."

"What job?"

"I've been a lobbyist for the last four years."

"I thought you worked for a logging company."

"Mining, logging. Call them a consortium of useniks." He radiated assurance, just as he had in high school, when no reasonably intelligent, sane person feels assured. This talent had annoyed Jules almost twenty years ago, and he felt the annoyance again, now. No allegiances, no problems—Everett had always claimed it made life easier.

"Shithead," said Jules. "At least you quit." He warmed like any good liberal at the prospect of the world losing a right-winger.

"Let's call it a vacation," said Everett. "You're not looking much like a Bolshie yourself these days. When the hell did you turn into a cop?"

"A couple of years ago."

"Why?"

Obvious questions annoyed Jules. The conversation was beginning to retrieve its edge. "I wanted to move back and there wasn't much to do around here. It seemed like a good idea at the time. And since when have you been in a hurry to get to Blue Deer?"

"I'm heading back for a funeral. And it's a new car. I was seeing how well it works."

"Of course it works, Everett. It's a BM fucking W. It's probably been working since you left Boulder or Salt Lake or Jackson or wherever, right?"

"Just fine." He was still grinning like a maniac, his face so pale it glowed in the dusk lighting. Perhaps quasi-environmental lobbyists never actually took walks in the sunshine. Jules imagined Everett on a dank subfloor of the Capitol, working from the bedrock up, a mole hero for whoever was paying his way.

Everett shook his head in wonder. "Are you really going to give me a ticket?"

"I really am. Welcome back."

"The least you could do is buy me a drink."

Jules cackled as he scribbled out the cite. "I'll try to forget the reckless part of it. Maybe you forgot tickets outside of town are five dollars."

"Is that still two drinks around here?"

"At least," said Jules, signing off and handing Everett his copy. "But I can't buy you one now, and anyway you said you had to go to a funeral. You don't seem heartbroken."

Everett shrugged, peering at the fine print. "Business associate. I've got plenty of time to drink."

"Well," said Jules, "I don't. But by tomorrow night I'll probably be ready to kill for a beer. The place has been hopping."

The proverbial lightbulb went on behind Everett's pale gray eyes and he grabbed Jules's sleeve. "Jesus, you're the one who's dealing with Otto, then. You're the one who hauled him out of the lake. Reservoir. Whatever."

Jules stared.

"Otto Scobey," said Everett.

"I know the name," said Jules. "Believe me."

Everett squinted at his face. "I've been doing some work for a little resort up here. Didn't anyone you talked to mention me? No one gives me any goddamn credit."

Jules regretted his lecture to Jonathan about patterns and co-incidences, and hoped he wasn't becoming a conspiracy paranoid. "Maybe we should have that drink."

"Okay," said Everett. "I'll follow you so I don't get overenthused again."

"Good idea," said Jules.

I FOUGHT THE LAW
(AND THE LAW WON)

JULES SHOWED UP AT DAWN ON WEDNESDAY MORNING FOR HIS getting-to-know-Hugh-Lesy breakfast, still off-kilter from lurking, work-related panic and several getting-reacquainted-with-Everett Parsons drinks the night before. He was not happy to be at the Baird again: A woman named Edie Linders, a divorced mother of three who was no longer fond of Jules, had taken a job working the front desk. Jules knew he'd misbehaved, badly, during the time they'd been biblical together, and didn't blame her for her lack of warmth. Had he chosen to forget, Alice, who was Edie's best friend and a real pro concerning Jules's lesser moments, would have reminded him. He'd prefer to try to make up for it, but Edie's husband had recently reappeared. Jules didn't have much use for the man, and the feeling was mutual; according to Alice, Jules's time spent in Edie's bed was the only reason Andy Linders was back. Jealousy, the universal motive, was hard to avoid lately.

Edie, a small, curly-haired brunette, had been working the night before, when Everett had checked in before they headed for the bar. Jules had tried a feeble joke about needing a jail cell, saying that one of the Baird's air-shaft specials might do in this pinch. You can't help being an asshole, said her eyes. Poor idiot. She gave Jules a dark look, pointed out that much of the hotel had been renovated, and graced Everett with a pearly, megawatt smile. Everett gave as good as he got, and they worked over the kind of room he'd prefer as if they fully intended to share it. Jules put two quarters down for a *Blue Deer Bulletin* (DEAD CAMPERS FOUND DROWNED—they had been extra dead, in a way, but it always maddened Peter that he was rarely allowed to write his own headlines) and rubbed his eyes while he waited for Everett to sign his credit card and rezip his metaphorical fly.

He hadn't been expecting Edie to have a back-to-back shift; she probably hadn't been counting on seeing his smiling face that morning either. When he walked in for breakfast, she hadn't even bothered to say hello, and Jules brooded on his overactive sexual past and nonexistent sexual present in the dining room while he waited for Hugh, who looked a little ruddier than usual when he limped into the room with Everett in tow. Hugh was wearing shorts today, and Jules's eyes were riveted by the map of white scar tissue on his knees.

"I was in stunts before I moved to cameras," said Hugh, apparently used to men staring at his legs. "I'm happy to still have any joints. A bit like your line of work."

Everett slumped into his chair and looked out the window. Hugh picked up the menu. "You certainly got Ev started last night."

Everett's features were so even, his movements so graceful, and his hair so thick and dark and healthy-looking that his deep pallor had seemed vaguely normal at dusk and in the bar. Now he looked near death. "I stayed," he said, draining a glass of ice water. "Had another drink with Hugh, bought the receptionist one at the end of her shift, called some people. Closed the bar."

Jules felt smug even though he'd started the day with a handful of aspirin. He got some preliminaries out of the way, givens: Where were you when Otto and Bonnie's lights went out? Why do you think they went out? What did you think of the light itself? Everett had been in his apartment in Boulder, Hugh in Great Falls with Sylvia. Bonnie had been an innocuous, pleasant woman they hadn't known well; Otto a benevolent friend, a mentor and genius, a man with no downside. Jules played with the sugar packets and tried to remember the days when he'd been less pessimistic about human nature.

The third time the waitress came by they were ready to order. Jules, almost beside himself with hunger, had eggs over easy, grits, sausage, and grapefruit juice. Everett had pancakes with a V-8 juice on the side, an evil-sounding combination. Hugh ordered the menu and Jules wished he'd brought along Axel Scotti, Blue Deer's token Italian, for a speed and quantity-eating contest. Biscuits, gravy, sausage, eggs, hashbrowns, half a melon, and an extra-large glass of milk.

Everett took two bites of pancake and ordered a fruit salad and a side of toast. "They're not what I remember from being a kid."

"You probably don't like bubble gum these days either," said Jules. "You haven't eaten any in the last twenty years?"

"No."

It was a sad detail. While Jules quizzed Hugh, who chewed through the dictionary on the topic of his former partner, spitting food as he wrapped his tongue around his bacon and explanations at the same time, Everett was silent, apparently fascinated by his bowl of rubbery grapes and strawberries. Maybe this was his reaction to a hangover; though they'd gone to high school together, Jules hadn't known him well enough in their school days to remember how Everett typically handled such mishaps. Hugh was actually funny, not a common happening in interviews about murder, earnest without being too obnoxious, and when he was obnoxious he seemed to sense it immediately, and would turn to relentless self-deprecation with a Monty Pythonesque edge. As in: "I'm simply so pleased the people who know this state have accepted me. I want to live here the rest of my life. I've never before felt so at home in a place." He was compact and dense, in constant movement, and utterly awake. But he became still when he listened and it was a little shocking, as shocking as when Everett, so impassive that morning as to resemble a statue, suddenly woke up in the midst of a piece of toast and told a joke about his grandfather's death, drunk, in a car. The punch line was something like, "I want to die like my grandfather died, in his sleep, instead of screaming like the people in the other car."

Jules ordered another cup of coffee. Hugh looked mildly embarrassed and took a second peek at the menu. Everett went back to his fruit and a daydream; he'd said his piece to Jules the night before, mostly seconding what Jules had already heard. He'd known Otto for five years and had last seen him on June 6 in Boulder, as Everett packed to move; Otto had been coaching him on his mouthpiece role, bringing him up to snuff before feeding him to the Absaroka County factions. Last night Everett had explained to Jules that he'd been chosen as a replacement because he was (a) available; (b) local; (c) familiar with Dragonfly, as he'd helped from the beginning, almost three years earlier; and (d) Republican, a decoy for liberal Otto, whom Everett called, somewhat unfortunately, a bleeding heart. Over drinks, Everett had also called Otto "the West's most boring lawyer"; over juice he praised his "deliberation and granite intelligence," while Hugh sniffled and ate his fourth egg.

There was also the small fact that Everett's father, Donald, was one of the county commissioners, the most reactionary asshole of the bunch. Jules had no doubt Everett would handle the public relations aspect of Dragonfly as well as he'd handled his last cyanide leaching gold mine in South Dakota, or "selective" logging in Washington state, during the years he'd spent as a sort of secret weapon to trot in front of subcommittees once or twice a year. Dragonfly was relatively kind by any ecological measurement, and Jules was sure Everett, with scads of stock-owning politicians in his pocket, would have no problem greasing the permit process. Having him on the job was a little like opting for a hydrogen bomb when a single cannon would do, but as Peter had pointed out, the object was not to even let protest begin, to mollify and balance questions out of existence. A bird sanctuary here, ten square miles of logs there, profit for everyone. Jules wondered how much Hugh and Sylvia were paying him.

Hugh had last seen Otto at the hearing ten days earlier and he'd only met Bonnie once. He'd thought she was a bit of a piece of work, a titch hard. Hugh thought a psychopath must be at play. Jules pointed out that this was obvious. What Hugh meant was a stranger, maybe someone who'd watched too many episodes of "Mr. Bill" on "Saturday Night Live" as a tot, had a thing for squishing. Maybe a deranged vet who'd seen Bonnie bathing. Maybe someone who didn't like tourists or fancy tents.

Everett snorted and ordered a soda water. Jules drained his coffee and tried to be patient. "Why was Otto cutting back on his work, anyway? Why take time off just when the process was almost complete?"

Hugh had just slid an entire egg into his mouth, and took a moment to chew before answering. "He always was quite an outdoorsman, and he'd just had it, needed time off, impulsive young girl and all, and Everett had said he could fill in early if necessary, even though he was going daft himself and really needed a break before—"

"Daft?" Everett rolled his bloodshot eyes at the ceiling.

Hugh smiled, flashing white teeth that were virtually perfect but for the center two, which square-danced together. "Well, wobbly. Right? Quitting your life of crime as a pig's politician and all. Anyway, the point was that even if the rest of us were nuts, it was fine if Otto took a break."

Jules worked on a piece of recalcitrant bacon, mesmerized by Hugh's teeth. Bless the British for allowing imperfections, he thought. However healthy, they were easy to spot, unlike Everett, who could have been a dentist's poster boy. "Had anything been worrying him?"

"Just the usual. Driven to exhaustion by friggin' paperwork. A little pissy because he was getting some dental work done, on a mush diet, and let me tell you, Otto enjoyed his food. After that last meeting he just bolted with the lady." Hugh grinned. "You might call it a midlife crisis."

"She was younger than me," said Everett with a slight edge of resentment. "And I'd heard she was wild. Did we go to school with her? Did she have any angry, pimply boyfriends?"

"She was in grade school when we graduated, and no, we haven't found any angry, pimply boyfriends." Jules met the waitress's eye and stared pointedly at his empty coffee cup.

"So strange that you know each other so well," said Hugh. "Anyway, it was just a case of the little shit getting a good man down. His teeth, and his car failed on the way back from Boulder. Maybe his pecker had failed him."

"He was a mess even before the car, when he got to my house," said Everett. "Wanted to quit everything. I expected him to start screaming 'life's too short' everytime he had to wait for anything."

"He seemed fine to me," said Hugh.

The back and forth, the potential divisiveness of the two of them, began to grate on Jules, and he wondered how easy they'd find it to work together in Otto's absence. "No nonwork problem past the car and the teeth?"

"Not likely that Otto would mention it to *me*. Sylvia and all. Not that there was any problem between us, but it wouldn't do to push the question."

"No problems lately with Dragonfly?"

"Just delays, and we can't afford any more. We're already a year late. Last fall we had a little landslide, and between the rocks and the creek we had to put in a new half mile of road. This year it's just been those nasty county commissioners. We were scheduled to start construction May 1, then June 7, and then it slid to June 21, and on and on. Now we'll probably wait till after the Wrangle and the wake and all, even though we should have the go-ahead this week. We have to have the buildings framed by the time the weather moves in, and everything rolling by spring. Keep the backers happy, start making our money back, and I'll have to make a movie then, help pay for my share of this disaster."

Everett stood abruptly. "I believe I should go to my room." He managed to make it sound as if he'd misbehaved just then, rather than by incurring the hangover the night before. Hugh expressed concern and they waved him off. Jules tilted his chair back and noted that Everett had enough energy left to make small talk with Edie.

Jules turned back to the table and life as he knew it. "What's the movie about?"

Hugh plucked one of Everett's grapes out of the bowl. "Well, we're still dicking with the script. I wanted to remake a movie like *How Green Was My Valley* without all the cutesy Welsh stuff, bring it west and throw in some John Wayne and Dashiell Hammett. Mining as *noir*. I hired a lady named Alice Wahlgren to do a little research for me, pick some stories for background."

"I know," said Jules.

"Of course you would," said Hugh, touching a finger to his forehead. "Everyone knows everything here. At any rate, I want to get into the difference between the feeling the world might cave in on you if you were a miner underground in this landscape, to the feeling you might just float off the plains above at the end of a shift. There's very little in between here."

A point. Most people didn't notice.

"So if I can get that down, I'll have a good movie, no matter the actors. Fucking actors," Hugh said with feeling, stabbing his last bit of egg white. "The great thing about Dragonfly, the really wonderful thing, is that I'll be able to skip the cocktail-party crap, live here with Sylvia, and be human again. Of course, that's what everyone wants, and I know I'm part of the crowd problem. Plus all you people who just want to move back. I mean, Everett's people had a cabin five miles away from Dragonfly. He *loves* it up there, and part of the deal is that he'll have his own cabin when we finish up, take a couple of acres for his own. Everyone needs a place to run away to."

Jules couldn't recall Everett's family owning anything more tactile than a bad business, but he couldn't remember everything. The only place he had to hide in, these days, was the men's bathroom at the station. He sighed, and waved for the check.

Jules sent Harvey, armed with tread maps and a list of further questions, to the closest fire camp, and tried to organize his knowledge of Otto Scobey and the Dragonfly Refuge deal and partners. He discounted the background investors, who seemed as uninterested in who and why and what as was possible with a huge outlay of cash. Though Jules was no financial whiz, he'd taken his share of economics classes; even without the final polish, any fool could see Dragonfly would make a bundle, barring a fire or major embezzlement scheme.

He pooled scraps of notes and logged onto the computer. Hugh Lesy, forty-nine, born Cardiff, Wales, in the Director's Guild since 1976; generally well-respected, usually well-reviewed. One prior marriage, to a Newport princess type (two boys in their late teens), divorced in 1986. He had moved to Blue Deer when he'd taken up with Sylvia the year before, but he'd kept an apartment at the Baird for the last eight years, and he seemed genuinely to love the town. In the beginning he'd avoided the other Hollywoodites who littered the prettier chunks of the county, realizing that if you want to really live in a place it's better to know your electrician's kids' names and like your neighbor than to bother with details you could just as easily pick up in *People.*

According to Axel Scotti, Jules's best source after Peter and Alice, in the last few years Hugh had relaxed a little too much in this regard, dropped out of the weekly poker game at the Bucket, and many of the locals now regarded him as a snob. It was a fine, difficult line, and with the advent of Dragonfly Hugh had probably concentrated on those friendships that were politically and economically helpful.

It was obvious to Jules that Otto had been instrumental in finessing the project through all the usual tortuous government channels, and that exhaustion might truly have been the reason he wanted to pull out. Everett Parsons had worked with them on and off since the inception of the project, and his full-time hiring had been Otto's idea, according to Everett and Hugh. They'd been on opposite sides a number of times, and Otto had taught Everett tricks and appreciated the knowledge of a devil's advocate. The real question was why Everett would want to bother, why he'd give up thousands of dollars and the pleasure of having his ass kissed to work on a relatively tiny project in his hometown. His excuse was fatigue, and no one admitted to bad feeling between the older man and his pupil.

Then there was Sylvia. Jules entered her name and current address, and decided to leave it at that until he checked out everyone's alibis. Doing more was a waste of time, not because he couldn't believe she'd kill, but because her biography was common knowledge.

He reached into his one neat drawer, pulled out the soggy red-leather journal from the tent, and tried to open it. Grace was talking to a sister about another relative's phlebitis, and Jules wandered over to her, looking the picture of patience. He sorted through Jonathan's tickets from the night before while Grace chatted about ballooned veins. Jonathan had nailed the high school principal for going six miles over the speed limit on Blue Deer's least traveled street, and cited several out-of-state people for expired plates. As always, he recorded every address where he'd seen a basement light on, taking this as evidence of dope farming.

Grace had hung up and was watching the expression on his face. "He's trying all the time."

"Shit," said Jules. "Any more applications?"

"A couple."

He nodded, feeling happier. "Do you happen to have a hair dryer?"

"What?"

"For some wet stuff. From the tent."

The first ten pages of the journal took half an hour, during which he ate some of the molasses cookies he'd snagged on the way out of Grace's house with the hair dryer. It wasn't so much a diary as an ongoing task list, and the fact that Otto had filled every minute of the day and felt the need to remind himself of every detail was a mixed blessing. A lot of the simple calendar entries were enigmatic without being compelling: do this, file that, petition for summary judgment now, doctors, clients, hearings—a traveling lawyer's desk. The man needed a laptop, and Jules wouldn't know what it was worth until they had gone through the office files. Mixed throughout were earnest bits of thought, most of them sad. Otto had evidently lacked self-esteem, though. from the almost clinical entries having to do with women over the last several years (Jules should have skimmed the parts about Sylvia but didn't) he hadn't lacked for sexual self-confidence, and Hugh's supposition of "pecker trouble" seemed to be wishful thinking. Jonathan would have turned purple, but Jules simply went into a funk. Life was flitting by, and he was too busy to remember what he missed.

The clippings tucked into the end of the journal were too lightweight for the hair dryer. He brought them down to the station kitchen, peeled them apart carefully, and laid them out to dry. Three pieces on different subdivisions, a story from the *Denver Post* about Everett leaving his job, and two stories on campsites in the Beartooths and Glacier Park. He scanned them briefly and turned to the refrigerator, hoping in vain for leftovers.

Jules was edging for the back door and food when Harvey returned and announced that their sketch of the tread marks had matched the tires on five of the nine trucks at the fire camp. Small differences, of course, but all unidentifiable from the details they had.

Jules rubbed his head. "I suppose they've all been in constant use over the last ten days."

"Yep. No point in dusting. I checked with the Gallatin and Lewis & Clark stations, and they all got tires from the same order."

"So most of the Forest Service trucks in the West could match up."

"Yep."

"Do they keep the fire camp ones locked up in the main yard?"

"Nope. They're all out there on the flats. The guy in charge, someone named Ankeny, has the keys hanging behind his desk, and he's never inside."

Harvey took out a toothpick and worked his mouth over nonchalantly. Jules would have put money on the fact he'd stopped for breakfast. They'd both grown up in Blue Deer, and they made a particularly cranky Mutt and Jeff pair when they worked together. But Harvey was good at his job, though he pretended to be stupid when he found ignorance convenient. He looked like a human feather, with a thin pink-gold face under straight, thin, white-blond hair. He was tiny, at the bottom of the law enforcement size chart, only one hundred thirty or so and five-five, but his fragility was deceptive. Harvey, an ex-bantamweight wrestler, had once flipped a 300-pound cowboy over a table at a bar. He would say "I don't know how," or "why me," or "I think I'm coming down with bronchitis," and then, when he knew he was stuck, could find a miscreant or lost hiker or stolen car in record time. Jules had tried praise, derision, bribery, and threats before finally realizing that Harvey was simply lazy, and would always need a cattle prod to get out the door.

This time around he'd theoretically done the job, and started to walk away. "Hang on," said Jules. "Did you check out the names at the fire camp, see any weirdos on the rolls?"

Harvey patted his pocket and pulled out two grimy pages. "Is any coffee made?"

"I'd love some," said Jules. "Thanks for your devotion."

He started to read. Payskill, Leroy Dean; Poest, Brantley Lee; Buggley, Dawn Celeste. God, but names could be awful. He skidded through the next twenty, recognizing two shoplifters, last year's salutatorian, and a second cousin. Contway, Ricky B.; Nilsson, Brady K.; Jordan, Eugene F.

Jules stopped and blinked. Bonnie, Bonnie, Bonnie, he thought. Bonnie Siskowitz, a name on a blotter, a beating victim of Eugene Franklin Jordan, a.k.a. Genie, thirty-one, five-foot-ten and one-half, 160, ash blond hair, blue eyes, meaner than most KKK prison foremen in Alabama; an ex-heroin addict and a native of Blue Deer, but most recently a resident of the state penitentiary in Deer Lodge on a crystal meth dealing charge.

Jules was halfway down the hall. "Harvey!"

"Give me a break. I'm cleaning the pot."

"Clean it later. Were any of the workers hanging around camp?"

"Just the guy in charge." Harvey was drying his hands on a dish towel, looking suspicious.

"We're going back down there. Now. Bring your vest."

The fire camp on Eight Mile was a small one, with only a dozen ragtag tents. Not quite the field of the cloth of gold but an endless, bleak, boulder-strewn succession of unphotogenic canyons. Eight Mile had been mined at the turn of the century and never fully recovered, with shale from the old dredge piled along one side of the rock walls and a tangle of sagebrush and old railroad ties on the other. Hence its Forest Service martyrdom as a test site for trenches, water drops, experimental fire retardants.

The office was empty, keys dangling unprotected, just as Harvey had prophesied, and the camp seemed deserted until Jules spied somebody napping in the shade of a large boulder. The man, about Jules's age, stocky and dark and smudged on most surfaces, opened one bloodshot eye when Jules was still ten feet away.

"Now what?"

Jules smiled. "Are you Patrick Ankeny?"

"Not if you've grabbed a crew member for anything."

"Not yet, but I'd like to. Is Genie Jordan around?"

The man covered his face and moaned. "What'd the prick do?"

Harvey fidgeted and Jules stonewalled. "Is he here?"

"I sent him into town with the cook. Let me look at the schedule, see when they're due back." The man climbed to his feet with an audible groan, shook Jules's hand, and limped toward the tent. "I'm so sick of smoke I could puke. I can't believe I asked to get out of the office."

"Wanted some fresh air, huh?"

"Har, har, har." Ankeny rummaged around on his foldout desk, seized a tattered list and examined it. "They should be back by noon tomorrow. Like I explained to Deputy Meyers, we're not talking the elite corps here, not your ideal experimental staff. They save those people for the areas with expensive real estate. We get people like Genie, who may or may not show his smiling face again."

"They have a truck?"

"Yeah."

"He's got no license and two DUIs."

Ankeny shook his head vehemently. "No keys to Genie. I know enough to draw the line on him. He just caught a ride for his days off, said he was going to see a girl in town. The cook's to keep the truck."

"Got a plate number?"

Ankeny's face was incredulous. "Do I look like I keep track of anything here? In my former life, when I had a place to keep my pens, when sane people sat at the next desk . . ." he gestured around the tent.

What Jules saw made his own professional life seem like a marvel of order. "You have records on these people?"

"Locked in a file drawer in a basement somewhere, sure. Personally, I don't have a clue, and I don't want to have a clue. I didn't hire these douche bags, and I'm not accountable. The big boys will find a way to shred the records when one turns into a mass murderer."

Jules possibly had a funny look on his face, and Pat Ankeny stared at him, suddenly at a loss for words.

"How long's Genie been here?"

"A couple weeks. Since the camp was set up anyway."

"Do you know where he was before this?"

"No, I don't know. Probably the Jackson fires. What the hell did he do?"

"Like you said, you don't want to know." Jules headed to his car; Harvey had already retreated.

Ankeny yelled after him. "What do I do if he shows up here?"

"Act normal and let us know immediately." He paused by the open door. "What's your usual job?"

"Claims and permits and campers who eat the wrong mushrooms. I transferred to the Blue Deer station from Great Falls a couple months ago."

Jules started the car and Ankeny cupped his hands for a last word.

"FYI, most of our trucks wouldn't make it as far as the Martinsdale reservoir."

Less than fifty streets in town, but Jules's own ancient Chevy looked as much like the missing truck as anything else they found that evening. No one at either of the town supermarkets had so much as seen a cook from a fire camp or a mean, stringy potential shoplifter who doubled as a fire-fighting hero, and the questioning only made everyone ask, in tones of horror, where the fires were. When they finally tracked the camp cook to earth at the bowling alley, he said he'd given the truck to Genie for a "date." Ankeny's words notwithstanding, Genie had taken off in the trucks plenty of times in the last two weeks, said the cook; if the cook hadn't handed him the keys, Genie would have hot-wired the thing.

Back at the station at dusk, Jules printed out Genie's rap sheet. A dizzying series of pages spooled out but he waited to touch them until Bonnie's name flicked by. In January of 1990, in Boise, Idaho, she'd accused Genie of assault. In February she'd dropped the charges. And that was all there was to read. No more mentions of Bonnie; Genie had drifted for a while, hitting up a sister in northern California for hospitality before wearing out his welcome with a DUI and an alleged assault in an Arcata rest room (the arresting officer commented that "the accused felt the complainant was staring at his privates. This doesn't seem likely") and heading back to beautiful southwestern Montana for the first of his run-ins with Deputy Jules

Clement et al. According to the sheet, Genie was still on probation for a second DUI and for selling methamphetamine in Helena the previous fall, and one of the conditions of his probation was that he not drive a motor vehicle unless heading to or from a place of work.

Jules started over at the top of the sheet and began a salvo of phone calls. Genie's mother and brother claimed not to have talked to him in three years, despite Jules's own memory of having arrested Genie at the trailer that passed as the family homestead only eighteen months earlier. High school friends, old girlfriends, fellow felons, bar owners—no one remembered having seen the asshole in several months. Jules called the Siskowitzes, who said Bonnie had lived in Idaho with a girlfriend for about six months, but couldn't recall Bonnie mentioning anyone named Genie, Eugene, or Jordan. Then again, said Hiram softly, he doubted he could remember everyone in between. Was this man related to Arnie Jordan, the cemetery caretaker? They'd just been talking with him about where to put poor Bonnie, and now that Hiram had Jules on the line, when *could* they have their daughter? They wanted to bury her. Jules promised Bonnie would be back from Helena by Monday, admitted to the hideous coincidence that Arnie Jordan was Genie's uncle, and hung up kicking himself: Why *would* Bonnie have mentioned the man? Genie was unmentionable.

It had been another day of not making any new friends and not paying attention to the ones he had. Peter and Alice had left a few messages, all ostensibly to do with having him over that weekend or planning his birthday the next Thursday, July 1, but in Jules's mood it was easier to pretend he had no friends than to accept sympathy. It was also easier to not recognize a question than to lie. Peter was still digging into the story, and past Genie, Jules had nothing to give him, and no intention of discussing the hopped-up firefighter.

At dark he headed home via Otto Scobey's house. He didn't

hope to find much; Ed and Harvey, both of them thorough, had already gone over and under and through everything right after they'd finished up at Bonnie Siskowitz's house. Otto's office had proved to be just a room he'd rented from another attorney named Biddle, and used at most twice a week. The secretary they shared could remember nothing interesting; Otto hadn't done anything meaty, like divorce work. The files that Jules had scanned were run-of-the-mill, a few that seemed to be favors for friends—wills and letters—and the rest taken up with property disputes, pro bono stuff for local environmental groups, the nuts and bolts of Dragonfly. He'd hauled them all to the station for a closer look, but tonight he needed to get to the soul of the matter, and that meant actually trying to know the unknowable—Otto Scobey's mind—through the place where he had lived.

South Cottonwood was Blue Deer's fanciest residential main drag. Otto's place was especially nice, a single-story Craftsman from the twenties with a big, open front porch. Bugs didn't fare too well on the plains of southwestern Montana, and few people bothered with screens. The back was completely obscured by a handsome wood fence, tall shrubs and fruit trees, and a collapsed trellis, all very private and envy inspiring. Jules hadn't bothered with details like keys, and found one on the dark door ledge, the second place he'd looked after lifting the floor mat. Otto had been in Blue Deer long enough to understand the town.

The house was pleasantly lived in, distracted and messy like the yard and the owner Jules remembered. A dark anteroom, an old-fashioned parlor with stacked files, some books, and odd items like broken cross-country ski poles and a wooden barbershop statue of an Indian propped up in a corner. He peered through a door to the left and made out more books, some snapshots, including at least two of Sylvia, and a clean desk, then walked straight ahead, through a swinging door into the sudden light of an equally old-fashioned kitchen.

Sylvia sat at the kitchen table, the warm night breeze from the open back door billowing her blouse, with a feather duster on her lap, and a stack of files on the table in front of her. Her face was stiff and blank and her right arm was twisted behind the wooden chair. It wasn't a comfortable position—nothing about her was relaxed, even though she was now trying desperately to look at ease—and it only took Jules a moment to make out the shotgun behind the chair.

He didn't move.

"I told Otto I'd look after the bird while he was gone," said Sylvia. "I can't see stopping just because he's dead."

One tiny, elegant arm gestured toward a ruby-colored parrot in a huge copper cage. The bird was watching Jules intently.

"What were you going to do? Shoot it?"

"I didn't know who you were," said Sylvia defensively. "And it's a him. Moe. Otto had him for fifteen years. Hugh doesn't want to live with him. Maybe you'd like to take him?"

"Sylvia," said Jules heavily. "I'm not interested in the goddamn parrot. Would you please let go of the gun and tell me who the hell you expected to show up?"

"It's not loaded."

"Fine. Please answer the question."

"Well, whoever killed Otto, of course."

"I guessed that much," said Jules, crossing the floor and picking up the shotgun. It was loaded.

Moe, on cue, jammed his beak between the bars of the cage, looking longingly toward Jules. "Hi, honey, you're home."

Sylvia burst into tears and threw the feather duster at the parrot. Jules emptied the shotgun and searched for rejuvenating liquids. She stopped crying just as quickly as she'd started, which was good because all he found was water, moldy orange juice, and spoiled skim milk, with solids limited to canned tomatoes, rye crisp, birdseed, and brown rice. Sylvia said water was perfect and explained that Otto had been trying to lose weight ("for Bonnie"), and found it easiest to do this if there was nothing he *could* eat. He'd never learned to cook anyway.

The thought of Otto's eternally enforced diet sent her over the edge again, and Jules spent the lull trying to determine the best way to approach her. He wanted to look around the house, but he didn't want to leave her alone for a number of reasons. He told her they had a suspect, and would find him soon; he sketched the man's character and motive.

Sylvia stared at him and laughed. "Why would Otto run from a little idiot like that?"

"Who said he ran?" asked Jules.

She shrugged and got up to retrieve the duster. "Figure of speech."

He got a little testy. "A few days ago you said everything was peachy. Now you act like the man had something to worry about, and you keep a loaded gun with you in his house."

"Well, you tell me," snapped Sylvia. "You've got the damn files. I haven't lived with Otto for a year, and I lost track of client problems longer ago than that."

"I haven't had a chance to look all of them over yet, and you've got your elbows planted on these. What are you looking for?"

She sighed. "Current papers for Everett. These are all old. Bullshit permits we filed years ago."

"Years ago when you were still married? Did anyone have a chance to back out?"

"Of course they did." She was really angry now, her small face scrunched into a mean knot. "Both of them wanted to stay involved."

"For you or for money?"

"Money, you twerp."

Jules smiled. Maybe she'd lost track of his age. "Why'd you get divorced?"

"None of your goddamn business."

"Come on, Sylvia. Cut the shit and just tell me."

She walked to the sink and splashed cold water on her face, then felt around blindly for the paper towel. "Otto had had a few lapses at conventions, and one day I woke up and wasn't interested anymore."

"You filed?"

"He understood."

"You filed before you started up with Hugh?"

"Pretty much," she said, amused. "I'm forty-seven, and a free woman. And we both know how lonely a town this size can be."

Pretty goddamn lonely, thought Jules. "What do you think of Everett?"

She smiled wearily. "I think he's a nice boy. A bit of an I-want kind of boy, but who isn't."

"Boy," snorted Jules. "Everett's my age and he makes a fortune."

Sylvia looked at him evenly. "I think you're a nice boy, too."

He stood up and started to leave, and she reached for his arm. "When can I have Otto back? I need to plan the wake."

"Helena should be done by Monday."

She looked relieved. "I was worried it might run into next weekend. The Wrangle and stuff."

Thirty years into knowing her, he finally realized she was crazy. Hugh was worried about a movie; Sylvia was worried about a horse. Otto had had all sorts of reasons to ease away from them.

"You're riding?"

"Just in the exhibition, if I get my ass in practice. Not my own horse, I don't have time for that this year. Plus I'm on the fair committee, so it's a hectic time." Now she was businesslike, avoiding the present. "When you finish up, give the files to me. I might know what to look for."

"So pass it on."

"Oh Jules." She smiled. "Don't be such a crank. I'll be looking for a psycho bronc rider he might have offended, just like you. But I have a favor to ask. Feel free to say no."

"Sure," said Jules sarcastically. "Ask me anything."

He left with the files, wondering if she'd meant she'd know what to hide. He also wondered how she'd convinced him to adopt a dead man's noisy bird. Moe sang "I Wish I Were an Oscar Mayer Wiener" all the way home in the truck.

Four full-time cops did not make for a forgiving schedule, which was why Jules had Grace soliciting résumés. It meant that after five hours of sleep he was in his car again at six-thirty, checking on some frequently burgled storage bins near the interstate, quartering Blue Deer for a Forest Service truck, and sipping bad coffee. At 7:50, on a second loop around town, a succession of shit began to hit the proverbial fan, all enunciated in an increasingly apologetic voice by Grace. Four missing chain saws in the mill compound, a found briefcase of prescription medicines, and a missing camper (the vehicle rather than the individual) gave way to a vicious squabble between neighbors about a failure to maintain a golf-course-style lawn. Jules was freed from this skirmish by a flipped truck filled with buffalo hides, bound for the tannery near Billings. He'd never before considered the weight of an untreated buffalo hide, nor the way fifty of them might smell on a warm summer morning. The reek followed him back into the patrol car, where he took stock of a uniform saturated with buffalo fat and planned on a shower for lunch.

The next call canceled that plan, though it coincidentally had to do with water: A construction crew, hooking up a sewer line, had dug a little too close to the main. When the county crew showed up, "words" were exchanged and authorities duly called. But when Jules arrived everyone seemed to be getting along fine, a dozen excavators and county employees in a circle around a ten-foot-deep pit, all of whom asked about his gooey uniform and distinct aroma. He peered in at the dented pipe, wished them luck, and then did a double take.

"That coupling looks like it's moving."

"Ha, ha." Someone began to tell another dead skunk joke.

"Getting bigger and moving."

"Jules," said Renny Beasley, the foreman. "You've had a hard day already and it's not even noon—"

"Run!" screamed Jules.

It seemed unfair that the pipe would actually give first in his and Renny's direction. All the men ultimately got wet, but Jules and Renny were lifted ten feet through the air and pinned on the grass for the five seconds it took the pipe to fully explode. In the aftermath, as a good portion of the city water supply collapsed the foundation hole, Jules took solace in the fact that he now looked and felt quite clean, wet and refreshed on a ninety-three-degree day, and just bruised enough to be reminded, for the umpteenth time that week, that he loved life. After all, the water had broken Renny's nose and mangled his glasses.

So Jules was in a good mood, considering, working on his Buddhist's glass-half-full attitude, when he pulled over at Clancy's Fry & Chew Drive-In and let himself dry in the sun on his patrol car hood while he waited for his order. When members of the public stared he smiled sweetly and said "bad day." He swallowed a barbecue sandwich in a matter of seconds, ordered a cone for dessert, and was laughing with a grade school friend about how much of his time had been spent wet lately when a light green Ford pickup with a faded Forest Service insignia barreled right past them down Blue Deer's main drag at what seemed to be the speed of light but was probably a measly fifty miles an hour. Jules dropped the cone into the waiting mouth of his friend's dog, made his patrol car in three long strides, and peeled out, sirens blaring, before another car had passed.

The truck, unbelievably, accelerated, and Jules said a prayer for Blue Deer's baby carriages. When the Ford ran the red light at Cottonwood he radioed in; a second later the truck careened to a stop in front of the Baird and a single figure leapt out of the passenger door as Jules shot past, braking furiously and screaming obscenities. The man slammed through the bar door and Jules followed him into the lobby, jumping chairs and tables, a surprised tourist who'd been knocked flat, and a pile of suitcases, wondering all the while where the agile fuck he was chasing thought he was going. This wasn't New York, and there weren't many places to be lost; then again, if it was Genie, intelligence had never been his strong suit, and high school track had been his last shining moment. Jules had a brief glimpse of Edie's face as they careened through the dining room and smacked through the swinging double doors of the kitchen. A waiter at the far end of the kitchen sized up the situation and spread his body against the back door. Jules anticipated injuries, but the man he was chasing actually stopped, then turned to Jules.

Eugene Franklin, giving him a fuck-you grin in a hotel kitchen. Jules felt like his head would explode, and roared before he started running again. Genie pulled the waiter out of his way, ricocheted through the open back door, and smacked right into the side of a linen delivery truck. He fell to the ground, rolled on his back, and aimed his foot at Jules's approaching groin. Jules zigged to the side and caught Genie on his exposed posterior with a heavy black police shoe, flipped him onto his stomach with the force of the kick, jumped onto his back, and pinioned his arms.

They both observed a moment of silence, punctuated by heavy breathing. Genie squirmed and Jules tightened his grip, remembering the time Genie had shot at a friend who beat him in a footrace. More clean, athletic fun.

"Suck my cock," muttered Genie, speaking with an effort.

"Nah," said Jules, clicking on the cuffs. "I'd rather have a meaningful conversation."

"You do this every time someone speeds?"

"All for you." Jules climbed off Genie and wiped dirt from his knees. He was happy to see that Genie's cheek lay on some stray gravel. A car tried to pull into the alley and Jules waved it away. "You weren't even supposed to drive on parole let alone go fifty-five downtown. You've also evaded and assaulted an officer."

Genie sighed. "So help me up."

"I'm comfortable where I am. When's the last time you saw Bonnie Siskowitz?"

"What?" Genie had spent his lifetime trying to look smarter than he was, but Jules had to admit that now he looked confused. Maybe it was his position, or the dirt on his lower lip.

"Your old girlfriend."

"I haven't seen that cunt since she whined about me."

"Well, I have," said Jules. "And something about the way she looked makes me think you're lying."

NATIVE SONS

PROGRESS REPORTED IN MURDERS OF LOCAL WOMAN AND LAWYER

As if lawyer was a third gender. Peter, who'd wept over every child abuse case he'd ever prosecuted and pro bonoed his mortgage unto death before becoming a reporter, had been flattened by another bad headline. Jules, incognito in jeans on Thursday night, sipped his whiskey carefully, alternating with water, trying for pacing.

June 24. The sheriff's department reported several leads today in the killings of Bonnie Siskowitz and Otto Scobey, whose bodies were found in the Martinsdale reservoir on Monday. An unidentified man, apprehended by Sheriff Jules Clement after a dramatic car and foot chase this afternoon, was a former acquaintance of Ms. Siskowitz and may be, according to unnamed sources, a potential suspect for several reasons.

Jules studied the *Bulletin*'s photos of Otto and Bonnie for a long, melancholy minute. A swarthy man in a suit and tie, laughing; a pretty woman in a cowboy hat, trying for Mona Lisa mystery.

Jules dropped the paper on the bar. Peter sat in the stool on his left; on his right, Everett read the previous Sunday's *Los Angeles Times* and chuckled about mud slides and seismic tremors. Jules supposed there were certain acts of God lacking in Absaroka County, omissions to be thankful for. He didn't have to worry about black mambas, ferry accidents, tornados, Ford pulling out of town. Maybe he should start reading the state-by-state news in *USA Today* to fully realize his good fortune.

Jules picked up the *Bulletin* again. It was a good way, or at least a realistic way, to conduct a postmortem on the week and prepare for Friday.

COUNTY OFFICIALS BRACE FOR WRANGLE

The Blue Deer Chamber of Commerce hosted a special lunch planning session yesterday, attended by members of Rotary, the county commissioners, and other officials. According to Art Kapot, chamber president, Blue Deer's hotels are averaging a 70 percent reservation rate for July and August, and local restaurants report that business is booming. Advance sales for Wrangle tickets, to be held July 2, 3, and 4, are also going well, and 42 entrants are listed for the parade thus far. Last year the parade boasted 49 entrants. The theme of this year's parade is "Proud to Be Old and New," with a grand prize of $200 and $50 for the Mayor's Choice Award. The entrance fee is $10, with no fee necessary for the Kiddie Parade. Prizes will also be given in other categories, including Creative & Colorful, Hoofs & Harnesses, and Spark Plugs & Pistons.

Jules considered all the different ways the town might interpret the theme. There were rest home citizens older than the oldest building in Blue Deer, whereas the big new item was a stoplight.

In other business, the chamber of commerce voted to allot more money to the fair Junior Rodeo, set for July 16, and tabled a plan to rename the city/county complex until the next meeting.

Mayor Travis Brushcobb voiced concern about a recent rash of crime and subsequent publicity. He suggested merchants stress Blue Deer's low incidence of theft and minimize . . .

. . . its recent rash of capital crimes, thought Jules. Good luck, fearless leader. He'd told the mayor to use the word "anomaly," but this advice hadn't panned out.

. . . recent "bad luck." "Blue Deer's people are good people," said Mayor Brushcobb. "There's just more of them these days, and a few bad apple weirdos can make a bushel look brown."

Mayor Brushcobb said that in a private meeting with Sheriff Jules Clement, the sheriff had also cited population as a concern, especially with the advent of the summer vacation season, and suggested that he might request additional deputies in his next budget. Recent estimates show Absaroka County gaining approximately 500 permanent residents last year, up from 200 in 1991, for a total of approximately 12,041 souls.

The cow population, however, stood at 55,000. This was a more salient fact, as the rodeo drew near, than Absaroka County's 3,500 walking lambchops or even its 2,000 horses. Through the Baird window Jules and Everett watched the early arrivals prepare for a Friday night, all the feral boys crawling out from under their cars and trailers, arriving in town via Greyhound and pickup and horse trailer, circling, conning, practicing their peculiar mating dance, shimmying down the sidewalks like silverfish, scooting around the heartfelt ropers and earnest ranch hands, the locals who worked too hard to travel much, who truly liked singing the national anthem and still said *ooooooh* during fireworks. The rodeo wasn't until next week, but the closest event this weekend was in Kalispell, not a hard-core rodeo town, and the big deal circuit rodeo was in Provo, too antialcohol to be preferred by what the mayor had been known to call "the undesirable element infiltrating our grand tradition." No one wanted to think of a land settled by killer boys, who'd been given twenty or so years to roam in a grassy, mountainous vacuum before population and its amenities, including fencing and the law, finished them off. Some of them bred; Jules was forever listening to their watered-down descendants brag about their credentials in bars. The others were loggers, realtors, broken rodeo hotshots, bad cops, gas pump clerks, and hunting guides.

As the current crop floated into the Baird, either harassing the bouncer or complaining that the scheduled band was blues instead of country, Everett and Jules and Peter laid bets on who would survive the next fortnight and decamped for the Blue Bat and Delly, who brooked no cowboy shit. Everett, in a fine mood, had bought the first rounds, and given an impressive stand-up routine. He told stories about the fat-ass politicians who loved him (one of whom Peter had recently quoted as saying, "If you don't like gun control, buy a congressman"), complimented Alice to Peter, and lectured Jules about why he should run Edie's husband down with a patrol car, accidentally on purpose. He explained how Hugh managed to get anything done, anywhere, without apparently leaving his car, and told filthy but affectionate stories about his last girlfriend, a rubber products heiress, and about another woman, an old friend who was showing up to take some pictures for Hugh, a woman he described as a walking sexual device.

This led them to Peter's incipient article on the contestants for Wrangle Queen. All of them thought it was quite nice that beauty in Blue Deer was practical, and not as weight-related as elsewhere. There weren't many ribs showing in the current crop, and they all agreed that a padded seat was an advantage in a bouncing saddle. Peter pointed out that this finally wasn't the world's most exciting assignment; Everett pointed out that at least his job had variety.

That day's paper also had a piece on a man who intended to suction gold in the Yellowstone River.

"Just like the old days," said Everett, snickering unpleasantly.

Jules was dubious, even after a lifetime of watching the landscape being pillaged. "He'll screw up spawning, gouge the bank. You can't add a piling without a hearing, so how can he dredge?"

Peter shrugged. "He's got a claim. It's holy right. I was just explaining it to Alice."

"The Forest Service got to be freaked about the example," said Jules. "Thousands of claims to worry about. They don't want to encourage every idiot to actually do something with them."

"They're freaked, all right," said Peter. "I talked to the Bozeman honcho, Larry Nellikov, and he said the big companies want to squash it. They don't need the bad press."

"Poor Larry," said Everett, still grinning. "He'll be besieged by assholes with pie plates."

Peter raised an eyebrow. "I hear, by the way, that you lobbied to keep the 1872 law when it came up last time."

"My favorite law, a landmark in the annals of pork," said Everett. "I was working for a mining company at the time. What would you expect?"

Something else, evidently. They smiled at each other, and Peter stood to pay his tab, probably on his way home to a four-course French meal and some affection. The world was patently unfair, and Jules, marooned with a Republican, bent over a crossword as if he were fascinated. Everett got into an argument with Delly about the recent playoffs while Jules rubbed his eyes and tried to see life from a remove. He needed enlightenment, and it was not to be forthcoming in the Blue Bat. Everett was now raving on about the coincidence of a certain baseball player being traded back to his hometown, and Delly was pointing out that this might be surprising if the hometown wasn't Manhattan; a whole lot of people had that in common. This led to a discussion of how coincidences weren't so impressive in Montana, population 800,000, for the opposite and obvious reason. Everett said he still wondered at the idea that Jules had happened to ticket him on his way into town. Jules, his attention fading in and out, had been thinking of the true coincidence of eating a cone and seeing Genie drive by, and pointed out that if Everett continued to spend all his time in bars, he was bound to run into everyone he knew within a week.

Everett persisted. "We went to high school together. And we've been gone for years and we're both back here at the same time, messed up in the same problem."

"Whatever makes you happy," said Jules. "We better buy a drink for Delly. He went to school here, too. We all peed in the same urinal."

A flicker of annoyance passed behind Everett's pale gray eyes and then it became a smile. He started in on politics with the man on the next stool, a realtor, talking loudly as he discussed weepy liberals, Democratic graft, welfare cons.

Jules knew he was being baited, and ordered a beer with an aspirin chaser. To the naked eye, always deluded by a love of mankind's imagined commonality, he and Everett were peas in a WASP pod. They were Saxon mothers' sons, less than a year apart in age, from the same mongrel stock, both families on the land for the same amount of time, and with roughly the same lack of money. Both had gone east to school on scholarship, and both had received honors and gone on to graduate degrees—not exactly standard maneuvers in a town as small as Blue Deer. They were even physically similar—dark-haired, pale-skinned, tall, lean, and moderately athletic—though Everett was by far better-looking.

But Jules came from a family of union members, Swedish Lutherans, FDR Democrats; a do-unto-others family without the wealth or condescension or middle-class pretensions or guilt that characterized many other virtuous clans. Clements liked to drink and play cards. They argued vehemently, went to church spottily, always wrote thank-you and condolence and congratulation notes, and saw most of the movies that floated through town. They canned produce from their gardens, used the library, voted for their fellowman, and didn't take taxation personally. Jules's mother, Olive, whose family had been a mix of Cornish and poor-white miners, fit in easily: She had never been a good housekeeper, lacked patience, went bird hunting, liked good and bad novels, and sometimes swore. Once, when Jules was about eight, Olive and his father, Ansel, went to a fancy Christmas party, Olive feeling lively in a real dress, a strapless number. They danced for hours, but in between songs Olive managed to drink an entire bottle of brandy—"by mistake," she said later—and she stayed in bed the whole next day while Ansel and Jules and his sister, Louise, told jokes at her expense and ate all the Christmas cookies. Otherwise, she'd been fully operational at all times. Jules still wished she had more down time; in hindsight, she'd been exactly his current age on the night of her greatest aberration.

Jules had kept his family's general philosophy through the University of Michigan and Columbia, and Everett kept and strengthened his through Dartmouth and law school at Georgetown, and these facts encapsulated their near total philosophical differences. Both families had been big on guns, but Jules belonged to a long line of Swedish socialists who happened to be police, while Everett belonged to a long line of John Bircher vigilantes. His considerable charm hadn't been inherited from his father, Donald Parsons, who was a raving conservative, the kind of prick who wrote letters to the editor suggesting members of a local cult, "worshipers of a false idol," be denied county services, or accusing the school board of pederasty, or labeling the sheriff a "communist, atheist dope-smoker." Jules took great and secret pride in this last arrow, a fond reminder of his youth, and every time he was forced to attend a county meeting, he and Donald did their best to eat each other's throats out. Donald loved to boast about his son's success, tell the lunchtime restaurant crowd about how Everett was "cleaning the slop out of Washington and Jew York"; Donald himself had dabbled in a variety of professions, and had always managed to accumulate money despite small glitches like losing his realtor's license or being sued for libel or embezzlement. These days he was selling insurance and making life miserable for his fellowman as a county commissioner.

Jules had mixed feelings about Everett, always had. The young Everett had gotten away with acts that the pint-sized Jules had been nailed to the wall for, and Jules had always been a good liar.

Now, in the bar, Everett headed for the bathroom and Delly interrupted a silent wave of ancient resentment. "I heard Everett was working on that Dragonfly project."

"That's right," said Jules. "Do you know the other people who are involved?

Delly was amused. "You must mean Hugh, now that Otto's left the planet."

Jules made a face.

Delly wiped glasses and made him wait. "I like Hugh. He's funny. He doesn't mean to be a prick, he just is one." He put the glasses away very carefully and headed down the bar to serve a couple. Jules eyed the bathroom door and drummed his fingers.

Delly wandered back. "Hugh can drink everyone else under the table and stay as happy as Bozo the clown, whereas our old pal, Mr. 'I'm home, kiss my ass . . .' " he jerked his thumb quickly toward Everett, now talking to the woman Delly had just served, still out of earshot.

"How about Otto," asked Jules. "Did you see much of him?"

"Off and on. Came in a couple of weeks ago."

"Remember the date?"

Delly gave him an are-you-crazy look. "Two or three weeks ago, afternoon, midweek, probably, because it was quiet."

"You'd have been watching the playoffs then. I can't rely on your testimony."

"Well, fuck you," said Delly, marching off. The mere mention of the end of the season had caused fresh distress.

Jules tried to appear patient until Delly returned. Everett was winding up his conversation.

"Was Otto alone? What did you talk about?"

Delly watched Everett. "Yes, he was alone. I didn't get the impression he hung out with his asshole buddies for fun."

"Not too cozy?"

"They all came in last time Everett slimed up, a couple of months ago. Three A-types just waiting to eat each other."

Jules was leery of Delly's tendency to exaggerate. He usually stuck to sports, but you never knew. "They were fighting?"

"Nah. Watch three men sitting at a bar for half an hour and you just know."

Delly started humming and Jules bit off his next question, one he'd already asked: What had Otto talked about, alone in the bar in the last week of his life. Everett was at his elbow again. "Remember her?" he asked, looking back toward the woman he'd been talking with.

"Sure," said Jules.

"When'd she get so mean-looking?"

Around the time her husband starting beating her, thought Jules. It was none of Everett's business, and he pulled out his wallet to settle up.

"I hear the guy you nailed was with a fire crew." Delly was in front of him with a full glass of whiskey. "Mr. Parsons just bought it."

Jules put his wallet away slowly, aware of the fact that Everett's attention was locked on him.

Delly held the full glass away.

Jules cleared his throat. "Someone on the experimental crew down by Eight Mile."

"I heard a rumor that it was a Forest Service truck that nailed that tent. And that the guy was someone I've tossed out of here a few times."

"Who's your little canary? My pal Peter?"

Delly smiled.

Everett leaned forward. "So they keep track of those trucks, and you traced one?"

"Not exactly."

"Who's in charge of the camp?"

Jules gave Delly a dirty look. He knew better. But Everett knew enough people in the Forest Service to dig this up himself. "His name's Ankeny."

"Ankeny. I think I've met him. Is he part Indian?" asked Everett.

"I don't know," said Jules. "He's dark but he could be anything."

"What do you mean?"

Jules stared at him. "Hungarian, Turkish, Chilean. Why?"

"Just curious about the name." Everett smiled. "Of course, if I went by names, I'd think you were a French Jew."

Jules fixed his gaze on the back bar and hoped Everett's political tendencies didn't take him that far.

"How'd your parents come up with it anyway?"

"An uncle. And July." Everett looked confused, and Jules noticed he also looked very, very tired. Maybe this was why he was acting like an idiot. "I have an uncle named Augustus and an Aunt Mae, if you get my drift. Are you okay? You look like shit."

"I'm not sleeping well. I have nightmares. It might have something to do with the fact that I've been drinking like a fish."

"It might," said Jules. He had sympathy for people who arrived home at a complete loss; he'd returned in horrible shape himself, three years earlier, and he hadn't had to immediately attend to a murdered partner.

"I took you off track," said Everett. "You were saying you'd arrested someone today."

"There's this guy named Genie," Jules said wearily.

Delly smiled, satisfied, and put the whiskey glass on the bar.

Since Jules happened to be a raving liberal, he, as a matter of habit and philosophy, veered from patronizing suspects or resorting to violence, assumed innocence as often as possible, and often ascribed bad behavior to a bad environment. On the other hand, once somebody did "go" bad, he wasn't particularly forgiving; too many people with an equally long list of excuses stayed good.

Like most cops, he had his own fairness code. No busts for joints; as little hearsay and use of informants as possible; an avoidance of entrapment, be it in bar alleys, hotel rooms, or real estate offices. The code fell apart when it came to Eugene Franklin Jordan. To say that Jules didn't like him was to miss the point: Genie was one of the few people, maybe the only person, Jules had considered killing. He hadn't seen him for a year, but before that he'd answered five calls about him, all domestic abuse incidents involving the two women stupid enough to sleep with him. Both women had had young children and speed problems. Genie had christened Jules to that kind of ugliness.

So when, on the fifth call, Jules had run through a house, he left the screaming woman on the bed to Harvey and followed a skinny blur out the window, knowing full well whose ass he'd glimpsed, also knowing that Genie owned a gun, and hoping he was holding that gun. Genie, always rabbity, ran naked through the spring dusk and Jules ran with his pistol in his hand. They'd gone two blocks before Jules had a clear enough view to howl a warning and strike a stance. And at the time the disappointment he'd felt when Genie actually stopped and turned around, with his obviously empty hands up, was very real. As Jules walked up to him, unclasping handcuffs, Genie had smiled, and Jules had smashed him across the face with the butt of his Beretta. It was still his greatest act of police brutality, but the only complaint around Blue Deer had been that Jules hadn't bothered to cover Genie's gray-white body on the walk back to the squad car and the waiting crowd.

Jules still wanted to shoot Genie, but he also knew it was the kind of ugliness he would have to watch for in Jonathan, who'd come by a fascination with police supply catalogs after Jules's injury. As a sort of trial by fire, Jules delegated him to quiz Genie's numerous acquaintances and relatives on Bonnie and other females, and hoped the experience would teach him care. Jonathan hadn't grown up in Blue Deer, but he hadn't learned sense in Rapid City, couldn't tell you a thing about the town past how great the Red Lobster was, couldn't explain how the badlands came to be or why the reservations existed or where the townspeople worked or why they might have settled there and stayed. He didn't seem to come from anywhere other than an abstracted shopping mall, a television sitcom, a Beaver-Cleaver-meets-Oprah suburban sprawl. After a season in Blue Deer, he had yet to exhibit curiosity about anything most people found interesting in the area. He said he liked to camp, but hadn't bothered checking out Yellowstone yet; he claimed to love fishing but after the spring floods felt strongly (the most passionate emotion Jules had noticed so far) that the river should be dammed. He didn't read newspapers or books, or watch the news; he read *Sports Illustrated* and enjoyed target shooting and mowing lawns and dirt bike riding. He hadn't learned silence yet, and drove the other deputies and Jules nuts on joint patrol, but on the other hand, it was hard to pull anything memorable out of an hour's conversation. Jules had taken a stab at music once, but Jonathan looked appalled when Jules listed the stuff he liked, told him he was weird, and blushed for having criticized.

Jonathan, it seemed, liked country and western, and not very interesting country—Billy Ray Cyrus and Vince Gill and Reba McIntyre. He confessed to branching out as far as Mariah Carey and Michael Bolton. Jules blanched and played the Clash's *London Calling* while he cooked dinner that night. He didn't intend to tell Jonathan that he'd gone to the Palladium concert on the front of the album, playing hooky in New York with Peter, both of them coked out of their twenty-year-old socially responsible punk brains. Until he'd met Jonathan, he'd never felt old *because* he'd misbehaved in his youth.

Jonathan was dogged, though, and if nothing else he'd bore Genie's friends to death. He was like Genie's white shadow, both of them lifeless and sterile. Genie was local, entirely of the town, but in another sense he shared Jonathan's strip, a landscape found throughout the west; as Jules grilled him about his movements over the last few weeks, Genie's litany, half left up to Jules's imagination, was predictably grim. Get up at noon, have a Coke, eat a Big Mac, hang out, get a little fucked up, drive around, get a little more fucked up, head home with whoever was putting up with him, pass out, get up late and eat a Poptart with a Mountain Dew, bully the bitch into a blow job, slap her when it didn't work, take some of her money and wander over to Kentucky Fried Chicken. Meth to wind up, beer and schnapps and whatever downer he could get his hands on to wind down. He'd hated working on the fire crew, gotten roped into it because of parole; Ankeny was "a little red shithead." Genie hoped he'd get fried when the real fires started.

Jules and Genie had logged a lot of hours together over the last two years, but this was the first time Jules had bothered considering how wide the gulf was between what Genie was and what Genie thought he was. Genie thought he was an outlaw, a latter-day Billy the Kid or cracker confederate, a noble, put-upon, genetically superior white hero, Montanoid Allman brother, high plains Hell's Angel, the sort of whining Romeo who thought rape was romantic and the world was crap for finding him repellent. Jules, after testifying against Genie at his parole hearing the year before, had been thrilled when one of the wardens told him Genie had been cornholed by Gabriel One Bear, Deer Lodge's largest Blackfoot, who probably didn't think rape was romantic at all. Jules had cackled happily in the car all the way home, hoping Genie enjoyed his last three months.

But this time around, during questioning, Jules was tempted to believe him. When Genie got the point, figured out Bonnie was dead and he was the likely man, you could almost hear the panic switch kick on. Then he leveled out, got fast and nasty with his answers. Jules and Harvey traded off in the interview room: No, Genie hadn't taken a truck before, hadn't been to Martinsdale for years, didn't give a shit about that cheap slut Bonnie; couldn't even tell you what color pubic hair she'd had or who she might have been sitting on lately. He hadn't known she was dead, and he didn't care. He didn't know Otto Scobey. He didn't know Hugh Lesy. He knew who Sylvia was, and he'd love to show her what he could do. They didn't have any right to hold him without bail; they didn't have anything to charge him with except for maybe running and driving without a license, and he could prove Jules intended him bodily harm, and that he was running for fear of his life. He hated Jules and Harvey. They were stupid, homo pricks, and someday he'd make them pay.

In the sense that both he and Harvey remained impassive throughout, Jules could call it a good interview, but he had to admit that something—guilt—was lacking in his favorite felon's expression. Maybe it wasn't guilt in the sense of conscience; more that Genie seemed sure he *couldn't* be in trouble, possibly because he hadn't done anything. But in the end, Jules decided to put aside his second thoughts and believe Genie had honed his acting skills in the last year. He asked the judge to deny bail, and kept his doubts to himself.

The state lab in Helena returned Otto and Bonnie on Friday afternoon instead of Monday morning, though not necessarily in one piece. Ed and Jules unloaded the couple's possessions into the garage behind the station and sent the van with two black bags on to Blue Deer's sole mortuary. The dog was nowhere in sight, probably deep within the great landfill in the sky. Jules prayed Sylvia hadn't wanted to bury him with his owner.

Jules hummed in lieu of making small talk with Axel Scotti, who watched bleakly as they sorted the evidence. Axel had already asked twice about when to hold the inquest, and both times Jules had argued to postpone until they had a better handle on Genie Jordan. As Jules pulled another Ziplock from the pile, Axel lit his cigar and started in again. The county needed a ceremony at all costs, especially given that Fourth of July and Wrangle were only days away. A nice double inquest on Tuesday or Wednesday would fit the bill. .

"The papers will still be filled with it when the crowds come on the weekend. No progress. It'll look like shit."

"People will take action *for* progress."

Scotti already had an eye on the following year's election. "Jesus," said Jules. "Do what you want to do. Why do you even ask me?"

"It's the polite thing to do. You give them any mileage, they'll bring back a city force next election. You keep your head down and your dick in your pants"—this was doubtless an allusion to Jules's spring—"and it'll be easy to get money for guns, especially if you steer clear of taking a position on gun control."

"I've already stated my position. And I don't need more guns. We have the Berettas. I need people."

"Well, for Christ's sake, don't restate it publicly and give them so much advance warning."

The city force had been disbanded in the early sixties, when all five of its officers were accused of being part of a burglary ring. The sheriff's department had assumed city duties without becoming strictly beholden to the mayor or city council. This fine point was meaningless because the mayor and the council loved the county commissioners, who controlled the department's money, and had the power to stick Jules's head in a blender and punch the "on" button. It made Jules violent, thinking of the pudgy fuckheads like Everett's father who wished they could cut AFDC or high school information programs (Jules had once said "AIDS" during a speech in the middle school gym, and several Holy Roller parents went after his badge), while suggesting a rural force needed one man and ten bazookas, the war's generals buying toys for its foot soldiers and looking hastily away.

He stared moodily at Otto Scobey's soggy car, on the other side of the garage. He opened the driver's door while Scotti continued talking about the rules of public office, then the back door and the glove compartment. Everything of obvious interest had been sorted, examined, fingerprinted, and bagged at the station—Bonnie's purse, Otto's wallet, a mileage book. Jules pulled the trunk latch before he remembered Otto and Bonnie had stored their food and trash inside, and that he and Harvey had elected to leave it there.

"Aargh," said Scotti. "Are you trying to get rid of me?"

"Yes," said Jules, giggling. He peered in, then lifted items out one by one. The food was still mostly recognizable by its wrapping—crackers, soup, cheese—with the exception of a table grape stem and two pits, plum or apricot.

"Don't look in there," said Scotti, squirming.

Jules was thinking of a frozen apple core, and Otto Scobey's dental work, and the care taken by the campers to remove even the organic trash. He threw the lot back inside and slammed the trunk shut.

"How many people did we arrest last year, during the Wrangle?"

"About twenty. It was rainy, pretty quiet."

"Do you know Hugh Lesy?"

"Sure. Nice guy. Gave me a cameo in his last movie, greased me over lunch a couple of times about Dragonfly."

"Know Everett?"

"Only by word of mouth."

"Was Otto a good lawyer?"

"Absolutely."

Scotti and Peter didn't usually agree, which was one of the reasons they no longer worked together. Jules sighed and Scotti sensed a weakened opponent.

"You're digging in the wrong place, and it doesn't do to piss the wrong people off."

"You mean the right people."

Scotti smoothed his velvety black hair, which seemed to have elevated when he smelled the garbage. "I should also counsel you to do something about Genie by the end of the day."

Jules kept his silence and started opening the moldering bags from the tent. The lab hadn't found a thing out of the ordinary, and no one had made an attempt to dry out any of it. The combined scents of mildew and bad meat and Scotti's cigar made the already hot morning seem steamier. They might as well have been standing in a bayou, digging up murdered blacks, or so thought Jules, who had a fuzzy, Northern, bigoted opinion of hot locales specializing in cotton, tobacco, or barbecue, even after a few perfectly pleasant stays in the Deep South.

"Jules, what are you going to hold him on?"

"Parole violation, driving without a license, no proof of insurance, speeding, attempted assault, resisting arrest. Some combination."

"What about bail?"

"What about it? This is murder." The tent still had standing water inside, with dirty red rings where some had managed to evaporate.

"You've talked to twenty people, and none of them have remembered Genie having a grudge against Bonnie, or any contact between the two of them since whatever happened in Idaho. His whole history is limited to drugs and domestic abuse, no violence like this—"

"The doctor in Idaho said she was hospitalized for two days. He jumped up and down on top of her."

"And then she hit him with a cast-iron frying pan and had him arrested. And she dropped the charges a couple of weeks later, so where does that leave the revenge theory? He doesn't even seem like he's on anything right now, does he?"

"No," said Jules. "He was faster than usual. But whatever you say about his record, he was driving a truck that matched these marks"—he held up a corner of the tent—"and Bonnie was the first and only person to press charges for more than a day, out of six domestic arrests."

Scotti began to chew on his cigar. "I think it was a crazy. I think it was the guy in Jackson, and I don't think the guy in Jackson and Genie are the same person."

Jules, examining the boat-motor rend in the fabric, looked amused. "You think Genie's sane?"

"You know what I mean. Someone out of a textbook."

"A heavy equipment operator who was beaten as a baby and diddled by his stepdad while mom watched. Someone who chops up poodles in the privacy of his apartment and puts food coloring in his bathwater."

Scotti was only momentarily nonplussed. "Right. That lady in Jackson swore the man wanted to bite a chunk out of her butt. I mean, Otto was a smart guy. He would have known if there was somebody to watch out for, and the people you've talked to say he was just another middle-aged happy camper with a younger woman, getting away from his workload in the great outdoors. I can relate, and I'm going camping with Jetta and the kids in two weeks, and I don't want to worry about a lunatic crushing us in our new sleeping bags. You must understand that."

Jules nodded automatically, but he wasn't really paying attention. One side of the tear on the roof of the tent was marked by a ragged half circle. When he lined up the other half he had a full circle, just about the size of a bullet hole. And when he ran outside into the bright light, dragging the tent behind him and ignoring Scotti's inquiries, he could just make out a dark blush around the hole, on the inner surface of the tent, that smelled faintly of gunpowder despite a long soak in the Martinsdale reservoir.

Scotti understood when Jules called the funeral home, where the owner, and coincidentally the county coroner, Ed Babaski, was just about to give Otto and Bonnie their final bath. Jules tested their hands for gunpowder himself, and by dark knew that Otto hadn't been such a happy camper after all.

☆ 6 ☆

PRAYER
CHANGES THINGS

BLUE DEER BULLETIN

SHERIFF'S REPORT, WEEK OF JUNE 21-27

June 21—An individual reported sighting a car with a skull on the dashboard.

June 22—A report was received of a rock fall on the River Road. The caller was concerned about snakes. An officer responded.

A request was received for assistance with a domestic situation. An officer reasoned with the individuals.

June 23—An individual reported a stolen vehicle. An officer responded and discovered the vehicle had been repossessed.

June 24—A report was received of juveniles hot-rodding on the train track. An officer warned the juveniles.

June 25—An individual reported that a family of raccoons had invaded his garage, made a mess, and played with his puppy. An officer was assigned.

A report was received of four llamas loose in the cemetery. Their owner was advised.

June 26—A report was received of a man sitting on top of a slide at the park without moving. An officer responded and reported the man needed rest.

June 27—A rattlesnake was reported in a cattle trailer. An officer was notified.

An individual complained of someone putting a garden hose inside her window and soaking her bedroom.

"You know," said the woman behind the wheel, "you're a real prick."

Jules looked up from the ticket, startled by the urban accent. He stared at her opaque sunglasses, then let his eyes stray to her dark roots. He didn't trust people who chose to be blond. She'd backed out of a parking spot near the Baird so suddenly that he'd nearly rear-ended her, then accelerated over the town speed limit as if the revolving lights and shrieking siren behind her had been meant for someone else, perhaps the librarian she'd been tail-gating.

He lifted his own glasses and grinned, genuinely amused. "Do you know me?"

The big red mouth pursed a bit and the sunglasses tilted toward his badge.

Jules fell into a hick number, biting his lip while he laboriously printed her name, a prize-winner: Opal D. Meek. If a driver expected country boy politesse, he beat down the side that dearly wanted to behave like a pissed-off New York narcotics cop. He signed off on the ticket without asking why she'd come by her opinion and handed it over, wondering what would happen if he called her Opie. "You can pay your fine by mail, or drop it off at the courthouse. I've supplied you with a court date if you'd like to contest."

"You actually allow for differences of opinion here? I'm so impressed." She scanned the ticket. "Of course, if I thought there was no one behind me, and you say you were there, I'm just shit out of luck, aren't I?"

"Yes," said Jules with another big smile. "I'm afraid you are. But if you feel like arguing over twenty-five bucks I'd be happy to suggest a local attorney."

"I'd rather just argue now," she said.

They stared at each other, or rather Jules looked into her opaque lenses and imagined she was a large bug, which was odd because what he could see of her looked a little like a model.

"Sorry, you'll have to make an appointment."

He tipped his hat before he walked away. He'd worked all weekend and now, putting in his requisite Monday morning patrol hours before he could return to small-fry like double murders, he'd blown the week's supply of patience. He was the only one on duty until eight that night, because Ed had the next ten days off. The timing was hideous, but Ed's daughter, who'd always hated cowboys, had elected to be married in Seattle, and she'd made her plans the winter before, when the force had been almost twice as large. One officer, a sluglike psychopath named Bunny McElwaine, had been offered an early retirement. Another had experienced a midlife religious revelation after finding a half-eaten farmer in a pigsty, and moved to Utah. Jules had suspected the third had a bone to pick with minorities, a hobby with few outlets in blindingly white Montana; after being reprimanded for an off-duty incident at the Crow reservation, he'd wangled a Border Patrol job and headed for El Paso.

Jules hadn't missed any of them until he'd tried to hire new officers, and been told that the county was temporarily out of cash, had, in fact, borrowed money from the department payroll fund and wouldn't repay it until fall. Enough money was left for Jules to hire a rookie, and Jonathan had arrived for an interview in April a banana skin sent from Heaven or possibly South Dakota.

He spent the rest of the morning writing tickets with less reluctance than usual, making all sorts of people miserable: nitwits, gerries, his favorite checker from the supermarket, high schoolers, a banker named Eldridge Anderson, the guy who owned the title company, a man his mother had dated briefly when Jules was heading off to college, the local masseuse, two out-of-towners besides the charming blond woman. At noon all the tickets cascaded down on Grace's typewriter, including one for her daughter Betty, who'd driven at fifty through a fifteen-mile zone, trying to get a sick baby to the medical clinic. Jules cited her in the waiting room. He hated doing it, but he'd only been called in after she slugged Jonathan—off duty, but still Mr. Letter of the Law—and speeding was better than an assault charge. Grace lost her powdery I'll-bake-cookies-for-you-anytime-honey smile and loomed like a Hitchcock mother. Jules promised to take Betty, divorced since her seventh month of pregnancy, to lunch, and wondered what hideous revenge awaited Jonathan.

Two divers from Helena entered the station in full frog regalia in the midafternoon, and Jules drove them north. It took five hours to find one of the missing tent poles (Jules saw no point in spending more taxpayer money on a search for the others) and a Colt registered to Otto Scobey in the reservoir. The pistol, safety off and lacking one bullet, lay in the silt about thirty yards out from where the couple had camped, a throw that Jules figured was about right for an average, reasonably athletic murderer.

No, said Sylvia and Hugh and Everett that evening, in complete and annoying agreement, their partner was emphatically not in the habit of hauling handguns along on camping trips; to the best of their knowledge he didn't even own one. This didn't rate as a revelation: By then, Jules already knew that Otto had bought the Colt at a gun store in Bozeman only two days before he set off on the trip, although he hadn't bothered scribbling that appointment into his journal.

He'd spent most of the weekend after work reading Otto's files without finding anything obviously suspicious in the corporate papers or permits or labyrinthine land trade arrangements. On Monday night he finished up, and on Tuesday he dropped the lot off at the Baird for Sylvia, leaving them in the relatively civil hands of Edie, who seemed to always be on shift. He would have liked to have shown them to Peter, asked him what might be missing, but he could imagine Scotti's reaction to showing a reporter a murder victim's files.

On Tuesday morning, Jules and Scotti spent an hour hashing over the evidence or lack thereof. The lab results had finally come in, rife with the usual autopsy gibberish of staph, E.coli, strep, and gram negative rods. Otto and Bonnie had been dead about as long as Jules had guessed they'd been dead, since June 13 or so. They'd been killed six to nine hours after a meal of wine, cheese, ground meat, and fruit.

Beyond the owner of the inn, only one group of witnesses claimed to have seen them, a couple from Missoula who'd camped Saturday and Sunday nights, and said the sapphire tent on the far side of the reservoir was gone when they'd woken at eight Monday the fourteenth. They'd noticed because the golden retriever had circled the reservoir the day before and kept their little girl, a tireless stick thrower, occupied, and she'd been bored and peevish Monday morning without such entertainment. The woman had run into Otto Sunday evening at the inn and said hello, but he hadn't been talkative.

Jules didn't suppose you would feel talkative if you were packing a handgun for the first time in your life, and why else would a man and a woman with no children, no boat, and a limited time off camp on an open, windy plain? Otto had wanted to see someone coming, and it didn't sound like much of a vacation. It had been the craziest weekend anyone remembered in Martinsdale because of a parade Saturday to celebrate the town's hundredth anniversary, and the town had been (relatively) packed. The locals had spent all of Sunday picking up the streets and talking to each other about the doings. But it had been windy after all, because Clarence and the others remembered the parade streamers filling the trees, and napkins and paper plates and newspapers tucked against all the fences. Jules tried to imagine what the wind had been like on the isolated side of the reservoir. Maybe this was why Otto hadn't had time to get out of the tent or aim his gun. On a quiet night, even if he'd been sound asleep, he would have heard the engine of a large truck, especially if he'd been listening for a pin to drop. People usually ate early when they camped, by eight or so, and Otto and Bonnie had to have been dead well before the predawn glow at four-thirty or five, because whoever had killed them needed time to pull the poles out and dump the tent and car. And the gun.

Jules, trying a by-the-book approach, had boiled the mess down to one question: Why had Otto been worried? Everything else followed that, little ifs like "Why was Sylvia in her ex-husband's kitchen with a loaded shotgun?" He'd checked into Hugh's, Sylvia's, and Everett's movements quietly, without bothering to tell Scotti. Everett's landlord placed him in Boulder, packing for the moving van that had loaded up Monday afternoon. Hugh and Sylvia's architect put them in Great Falls, and recalled they'd planned a stop in Missoula to check chefs. They'd been closer to the scene, with few set appointments and vague memories; nothing was airtight, but nothing, so far, showed a lie.

The detail that most confused Jules was the gun's absence from the tent. It had been found far from where the boys in the boat had torn the hole; it hadn't fallen out. Removing the tent poles had been a practical matter, insurance that the tent wouldn't pop out of the water like a sea capsule carrying an icky version of James Bond and Pussy Galore. But why bother going inside? Nothing else seemed to have been removed from the tent or the car—money and I.D. had been left where they might have been expected to be left, locked in the glove compartment of the Saab. The only point that mitigated against the idea of a random, raving maniac was the removal of the gun, the gun that pointed to Otto—nonhunting peacenik—having dreaded the random, raving maniac's arrival. He'd been worried, no matter what his friends claimed.

This was how Jules put it to Scotti, and Scotti didn't want to hear it. There was no good news for Scotti's random psycho theory, and no good news for Jules's halfhearted Genie dream. Try as he might, Jules couldn't imagine a man like Otto Scobey being afraid of a man like Genie Jordan. The timing seemed wrong, too; everyone put Genie in Idaho Falls during the days before Otto left to go camping, when Hugh and Everett had dithered over whether he'd been troubled by something. Most of Bonnie's acquaintances in Boise, where she'd apparently only dated Genie for a total of two months, had failed to even recognize his name, and the two who did said something like "Oh, him" and were sure Bonnie hadn't seen Genie after she filed charges. Friends in Blue Deer said she'd been happy and relaxed and smug about vacation time, with not a hint of the tension Otto had suffered, while she packed for the camping trip. Genie had reported for work on Friday, June 11, and Patrick Ankeny, after some real sleep, was virtually positive no one had left his camp during the first week at Eight Mile. Jules pointed out that Ankeny had thought that Genie would never use a truck either, but Ankeny pointed out that Genie was too much trouble not to miss for a long period of time, very enthusiastic about setting fires and worthless at putting them out. He might not have noticed a short absence or one truck less, but if Genie had been gone for most of the night he would have noticed the peace and quiet.

Genie had been in Jackson around the time of the first crushing incident, but the Forest Service office there showed no record of him working on local crews, despite the fact that Genie had claimed this work on his application with Ankeny and in his interview with Jules. (He'd reversed himself when he realized Jules wanted him to be there.) A girlfriend of Genie's said he was staying with her in Gardiner by the time the shar-pei was injured in Jackson. When Jules tried to warn the girlfriend about her lover's nasty habits, she called him a pig and spit in his face.

And that Saturday, while Genie was sucking his thumb in a Blue Deer cell a woman camping in the Pryor Mountains had woken to find a man crouched over her in a dark tent. He'd bitten her twice on the leg before the woman found an extra-large Maglite and tried to brain him. He'd run from the tent and jumped into what looked like a Volkswagen Rabbit, and though he hadn't run over the tent some witnesses testified he'd tried, while others claimed he just seemed panicked.

Scotti agreed to postpone the inquest until after the Wrangle, possibly until July 9 or 12. Jules agreed to talk to the judge, and bail was set. The new girlfriend talked to the bondsman, using her double-wide for collateral. At noon, Jules opened the cell door himself, and managed a smile when Genie scooted free and flipped him the bird, a moment immortalized by Soren Rue, the *Bulletin*'s official photographer, who had a talent for shooting unprintable moments. At least Genie had managed to keep his face out of the paper until then.

In a town as small as Blue Deer, you usually recognized obituary names. Today, Alice, a relative newcomer, knew all three entries, as the first two were Otto and Bonnie, and the last was a ninety-two-year-old man from down the block. She hadn't known Bonnie had been a National Merit Finalist, or the second runner-up for Miss Montana in 1988, or that her middle name had been Amanda. She hadn't known that Otto had first come to Montana for a summer job in Yellowstone in 1963. And she hadn't known that the man down the block had lost his mother and two siblings in the influenza epidemic of 1918.

It was all a little overwhelming, and made her want to run into her garden or cook or jump Peter's substantial bones or even do something that might make her really sweat, like tennis.

But now she was faced with the tawdry, not particularly life-affirming business of making money. She'd given up any organized attempt at catering when most of her clients had died in May, and knew she was luckier than most English majors to have Hugh Lesy's research to fall back on. She would rather have weeded around her twenty-six tomato plants, but as Peter had pointed out, they wouldn't be there to pet in November, when she'd be gnashing her teeth over the checkbook and once again giving up dreams of a vacation in Mexico. The problem with Peter was that he had a long memory, and always remembered what a jerk she'd been through the winter, and didn't necessarily sweeten up on cue. He was German year-round: even, affectionate, and clinically depressed; overintelligent and overfond of wine.

Alice finally attempted a succinct description of the claim process and the General Mining Law of 1872 for Hugh. He'd told her he liked to elaborate himself, and resented too much truth. Alice could take three paragraphs, no more and hopefully less, to describe a century's worth of legal pillage.

She started with the theory: In 1872, the government rewarded anyone willing to move west. Land grants to the railroad, still the biggest landowner in Absaroka County after the government; cheap land to farmers who promised to stay; cheaper land to miners who promised to dig. The mining rules and prices had hardly changed since. If you could prove you had found a valuable mineral, and could extract it for profit, you could "locate" a twenty-acre claim for a $5 filing fee, and maintain it for $100 a year. That claim gave you virtual control over the land and the right to cross over public land to reach the claim. If you wanted full title, actual ownership, and fulfilled all requirements (discovery of a mineral, some development and improvement of a site, a Bureau of Land Management survey, a posted note of intent, and a $25 filing fee), a patent was yours for $5 an acre on a load claim, $2.50 an acre for a placer. You could will it or sell it, and you could pretty much ruin it as you saw fit. There were 4,500 claims and patents in Absaroka County and its two neighbors.

Alice reviewed her paragraphs and printed. Her own handiwork distressed her, and she hauled a pile of library books out to the hammock. Two hours later she was wallowing in the unheroic west, a brittle place whose romance had more to do with bravado than ethics. She skipped the lengthy blather about vigilantes—she believed they'd jumped to conclusions—but took notes on the raving assholes they'd chased, the men like Henry Plummer who led posses valiantly, never catching anyone, naturally, as he'd been the leader of the gang of thieves they sought. It all reminded her of stories about the old Blue Deer city police, who'd robbed the town blind for several months and simply stored their booty and change into uniform to revisit the scene officially. She read about staged suicides and actual murders, solved by frozen ink; about Evil Roy Slade and whores who sifted the ashes of charred miners for gold; about claims and claimants buried under avalanches, and pack camels scaring horses, and being mistaken for deer. She skipped anything having to do with dead children and politics, each being unbearable in different ways, and veered into a chapter on the hideous, cattle-killing winter of 1886 before she remembered that the movie was supposed to be about mining, not about something edible.

She looked at her watch and decided to pick some peas. She could read when it was dark outside and she didn't have a feeling life was ignoring her. Hugh wouldn't be in such a hurry anymore, what with his partner dying.

Two hours after Jules lost his only true suspect he arrived late at Bonnie's funeral. The back pews were packed—no one wanted to be watched for this one—and he took a seat next to Bertha Nickelskin, who patted his thigh and blew her nose into a flowered hankie, having begun her mourning early. Bertha had played bridge with Jules's mother, Olive, for at least thirty years and was the president of Absaroka County's Lutheran Women's League, which meant she was a pro at funerals. This latest occupation had begun in 1980, when Bertha retired from a prosperous career as Blue Deer's last madam; the writer who'd claimed American lives lacked second acts had probably never traveled this far west. Jules would have liked to have asked his father what sort of arrangement his force had struck with Mrs. Nickelskin and her employees, but by the time the question had occurred to him, Ansel was buried in the same cemetery where Bonnie Siskowitz would end this day.

Jules was flipping through the *Book of Common Prayer* when someone tapped his shoulder. He turned to see Sylvia directly behind him.

"How's it going?" she whispered.

"Fine," he answered automatically. "Would you like to trade seats, so you can see?"

"There's nothing to see," she hissed. "Will you be there for Otto tomorrow? I just remembered that it's your birthday Thursday."

"Sure," said Jules. "I hadn't planned anything."

"That's a shame," said Sylvia.

The music began, an organist hammering the keys ten feet from the nondancing black casket. "Umm." Sylvia leaned closer to his shoulder and lowered her voice even more. "I need to get the rest of Otto's files back from you, if they're still decipherable."

"I already dropped them off for you," said Jules. "Yesterday morning."

"Not the stuff from his office. The stuff he kept at home or had with him." She scrunched her face. "The stuff that probably got wet. The Forest Service files, his map, stuff like that."

Jules shook his head. Sylvia gave him a blank look, at a loss for once in her life, and her voice went up an octave.

"Nothing in the car or the tent?"

"No files," said Jules. "A journal, some clippings. Maybe he gave them to Everett or Hugh."

Sylvia stared at him, and Bertha Nickelskin buried her razor-sharp nails in Jules's knee. "Turn around," she hissed. "You're being rude."

Jules gave Sylvia a last confused look and obeyed. The minister appeared to be hyperventilating; Jules had heard a rumor he took a beta blocker every time he faced a full church.

> *I will lift up mine eyes unto the hills, from whence cometh my help.*
> *My help cometh from the Lord, which made heaven and earth.*
> *He will not suffer thy foot to be moved: he that keepeth thee will not slumber.*
> *Behold, he that keepeth Israel shall neither slumber nor sleep.*
> *The Lord is thy keeper: the Lord is thy shade upon thy right hand.*
> *The sun shall not smite thee by day, nor the moon by night.*
> *The Lord shall preserve thee from all evil: he shall preserve thy soul.*
> *The Lord shall preserve thy going out and thy coming in from this time forth, and even for evermore.*

This song of degrees had been read for his father, too, and was one of the roots of Jules's distrust of organized religion. His father had indeed been kept from the sun and the moon, and Jules couldn't believe, at twelve, that this was a favor, that his father didn't ache for fresh air. Twenty years later the word "preserve" still made him think of a soul pickled in brine, the smell surrounding him in the funeral home basement as he looked for gunpowder on hands.

When he turned after the service, Sylvia was gone, and though he left a message on her answering machine, she didn't call back that night.

Jules slept until seven on Wednesday morning, and it felt like a luxury despite his history as a marathon sleeper. He gave himself a full hour, and was humming by the kitchen window as he spooned coffee into the machine when he saw a figure in his garden patch.

Alice before noon. The world grew stranger on a daily basis. He pulled on pants and a T-shirt and padded across the dewy grass toward her.

Alice screamed, perhaps unnerved to begin with by the experience of seeing the morning so early. She was absolutely undone, but this didn't take much at the best of times. She'd dug and planted the patch for him ("Just annuals and vegetables. You don't get perennials until you get a life"), while Jules was in the hospital, and though he'd had great plans of contemplating the greenery with a book and a drink and a lawn chair, he'd only made it out twice to water so far.

"Hungry?" asked Jules. "Planning my birthday dinner?"

Alice snorted. "Sorry, sweetheart. This salad is for poor dead Otto's friends. Get in line."

"Okay," said Jules, wishing he'd waited until his first cup of coffee to be social.

"You haven't even weeded."

"Jesus, Alice. It's been a little crazy lately."

"And just think, it's not even prime fireworks time."

He drank his coffee before he tracked Hugh and Everett down to earth in the Baird dining room. Sylvia was there, too, smiling and a little too bright-eyed.

"I was confused," she said. "Otto did leave the files. Hugh has the originals for safekeeping, and Otto also gave Everett a set of copies."

"Oh," said Jules.

Hugh and Everett smiled.

"He gave them to you before he left?"

"No," said Everett. "He left them at the front desk, here."

"But you were in Boulder," said Jules.

"I'd planned to make a run up the next week," said Everett.

"I'll be right back," said Sylvia, popping to her feet. "Just a bathroom run."

Jules stood there, trying to define the tension. They all wanted to look as if they fit together, and the strain was showing.

"Your package was at the desk, too?" he asked Hugh.

Hugh was in mid-bite, and took a minute, nodding. "The package for Ev was marked hold for arrival, so mine probably got lumped with it, or the girl simply misplaced it. At any rate, it's been too busy for me to have thought to mention it to Syl."

The girl. Jules looked toward the door, and there she was, ushering in some hungry-looking people dressed in stripes and polka dots. He caught her eye and waved to her to come over, but Edie stood her ground and continued to seat the bright people.

Jules looked back down at Everett. "And you decided not to?" he asked. "You decided not to come up here?"

Everett looked alarmed. It only lasted a second, but it was satisfying. "I was on call," he said. Jules watched Hugh fiddle with utensils. "But nothing came up, and there was no point in making the trip until Otto got back. Besides, I had a cold, and I wanted to camp myself, and I needed to finish packing."

They stared at each other for a moment. Jules turned away and met Edie's equally unfriendly eyes. He crooked one finger, pointed to his badge with the other, and gave her a shit-eating, not very pleasant, grin.

This wasn't a good beginning. "Can I help you?" she asked icily.

Jules rubbed the back of his head and gestured to the table. "Hugh and Everett said Otto Scobey dropped off some files before he went camping, and I wondered if he dropped them off with you."

"He didn't leave any files here. He left a note for Sylvia and that was it."

Jules looked at Hugh and Everett, who looked blankly at Edie. "He would have left them on a Thursday night or Friday morning, June 10 or 11. They may have been misplaced over the weekend."

Edie pointed in the direction of the lobby office, five by six at most. "I had a back-to-back, worked both shifts. You're suggesting I'd miss files for several days in a place like that?"

"*I'm* not suggesting," said Jules, gesturing toward the table. "These gentlemen are."

"A note," said Edie. "For Sylvia. That's it. I remember because it was my first week on the job. I worked from three to eleven that night and seven to three the next day. And even if he came back in the middle of the night or after I left Friday, I worked on Saturday and Sunday, too, and I never saw anything larger than a phone memo for any of them."

Finally, a succinct human. Jules felt a wave of complicated affection. "Is that it?" asked Edie, giving all of them an unreadable smile.

"Thanks," said Jules. She was already halfway through the door, just as Sylvia returned from the other direction.

Hugh stared into space, away from his lover. "So," said Everett evenly, "you're prepared to believe a waitress you've been to bed with rather than a local businessman."

"I am prepared to believe anything that makes sense," said Jules, with only a trace of humor.

"Dear God, I thought you two liked each other," said Hugh heavily. "Perhaps the truth is somewhere in between."

"Perhaps," said Jules.

Hugh straightened in his chair. "I keep wondering what he thought while it was happening."

"Why wonder that?" snapped Sylvia. "What would be the point?" They all stared at her.

"I'll need to see the original files," said Jules softly.

Otto Scobey's wake began with a train of thirty cars snaking along the bumpy dirt two-track to Dragonfly for the dusting of his ashes. Peter and Alice and Jules parked in the meadow and walked to the canyon at the farthest end, where Sylvia's great-grandfather had sunk the first of a series of unsuccessful prospect holes in 1871, near the dawn of Absaroka County's white era, back when the land was still a free zone, a buffer Crow and Sioux hunting ground north of the closed Bozeman trail, before the railroad or Custer's arrival or statehood or Yellowstone as a park, before anyone realized there was no gold whatsoever in the Crazy Mountains. One shaft was still more or less visible, framed and blocked by old logs near the creek. It was quiet and windless, and when Sylvia poured Otto's ashes into the creek the larger chunks of bone made an audible plop. No minister; Hugh, visibly nervous, said that Otto had felt God from the ground up, and anyone who stood on it could speak for him. He ad-libbed for some time, to the effect that Otto could usually convince everyone with him that work was fun, and that now he, Hugh, couldn't imagine enjoying much of anything, let alone work, and that Otto had been an example to them all. Hugh read some Rilke, and two men standing in front of Jules, one of Hugh's producers and a former law partner from L.A., sighed and flecked pieces of grass from their soft, expensive jackets.

Sylvia stepped in front of the crowd, and read a psalm without any asides at all. He'd forgotten she'd taught Sunday school in a former life.

> *The earth is the Lord's, and the fulness therof; the world, and*
> *they that dwell therein.*
> *For he hath founded it upon the seas, and established it upon*
> *the floods.*
> *Who shall ascend into the hill of the Lord? or who shall stand*
> *in his holy place?*
> *He that hath clean hands, and a pure heart; who hath not*
> *lifted up his soul unto vanity, nor sworn deceitfully.*
> *He shall receive the blessing from the Lord, and righteousness*
> *from the God of his salvation.*

An ecolawyer couldn't have dreamed a nicer verse, especially from a book that held few comforting passages. But if you were Otto, would you want your ashes dropped on your rival's land, especially if your rival had also been your boss?

The whole afternoon was enjoyable, as funerals went. Only eighty or so in the late afternoon sun, the proverbial million-dollar view, the smell of grass and trees, no one crying, everyone past the shock of the death itself. Jules sighed and rocked on his heels and counted the trees clinging to the canyon wall. It was almost his birthday, and he wasn't dead.

It was half a mile back to the car, another decent touch, though one that caused problems for those women wearing black stiletto heels. Jules held the door open for Alice and climbed into the backseat. Alice had wanted to loiter and see the mine shaft, and now she bargained for a glance at the next meadow, the large one where Dragonfly was finally under construction, or maybe the farthest meadow, with the private houses and the barn. Seeing the barn would help with research. She lost again, and Peter roared out, trying to beat everyone who might actually slow down for a rut in the dirt road. He wanted to skip the wake and work; Alice said he couldn't, if only because she was catering it and she wanted him to be polite to her employers. Peter said that the last reason would be short-lived, because Alice, historically, fought with everyone who employed her. Alice didn't bother arguing the point. She'd lost the urge to fight to the joy of summer and her garden, but Peter had some justifiable bones to pick after a spring of niggling complaints and sourness. They settled: He agreed to attend the wake, and she stopped insisting on a tour, possibly because she had remembered that she was supposed to get to the Baird before the guests.

It seemed as if the tension between the two had been constant in the last months, and Jules lolled in the backseat and watched the earth unfurl, clouds spooling out in a high wind that barely touched the car's patch of surface. The grass was already browning after two solid weeks of clear heat. He hoped Alice and Peter would snap out of it for any number of reasons, many of them selfish, like the possibility that his once-a-week edible meal might atomize. If things went badly, it could be a horror show in a town the size of Blue Deer. He'd known couples, including Alice and Peter a decade earlier, who'd found Manhattan too small after breaking up. There might be a dozen bars in Blue Deer, but only two or three were worth going to, and the whole notion of being out with Peter when Alice walked in with a date—or, worse yet, out with Alice when Peter walked in with or without one—was chilling.

Alice grabbed Tuesday's paper on the dash, made fun of a couple of headlines, and settled into the AP stories. A tubby conservative claimed a readership or viewership of eighteen million (the *Bulletin*'s editing left this unclear). "Eighteen million like him," said Alice. "The world is a scary place."

"It's bullshit," said Peter. "He's just trying for safety in numbers."

"You're telling me there aren't eighteen million conservative white overweight males in the United States?" said Alice.

"Who can read. White overweight conservative males who can read."

"Oh," said Alice. "Well, if they can read the sports page they can read that shit."

Jules had been about to ask her for the sports page—literally a page in the *Bulletin*—but now turned back to the landscape. Alice wanted to know who the woman had been with Everett. Peter said she was the old friend Everett had mentioned in the bar, the "walking sexual device." "Did you look at her legs?" he asked, looking at Jules in the rearview mirror.

"No," said Jules, surprised at himself. Then again, it had been a funeral.

Silence from the front seat. Jules was slow to realize he was supposed to keep the trip painless.

"Have you heard from Rita?" asked Alice.

Jules came away from the landscape with a jerk. Alice was watching him, craned in her seat. "Me?"

She gave him a sidelong look. Peter cackled and passed a sports car.

"A card, yesterday," said Jules.

"A birthday card? That's sweet of her."

"No. She didn't know about that. Just a card." He was tracking some irrigation pipe, wondering who on earth owned so much land, and when he turned away from the window Alice was still watching him.

"You don't really care, do you?"

"Nope," said Jules.

"End of subject," said Peter.

Jules smiled at Alice and she gave him a slow, evil grin in return.

"What's the deal with Edie, anyway?" asked Peter. "Are she and Andy still trying to get along?"

"Yup," said Alice.

"That's great."

"It's great if he's really given up on the rest of it."

"What the hell's the rest of it?" Being left out of the loop on anything made Peter angry.

"The girl Edie saw him with last week. A little hardbody, tight ass and strong hands. I can't believe it."

Ecofiends unite, thought Jules. He could believe it, and he was thrilled. Edie, whose only shortcoming was a tendency to dance obsessively when drunk, was wasted on a man who aspired to sell all the stereos in Montana, and still kept his bad seventies albums in a tidy row. Edie was Italian and Jewish and lived up to most of the stereotypes: She was, to put it politely and fondly, appetite-oriented, which was one of the reasons she and Alice got along so well, but she was saddled with a Norwegian prick who kept his shoes in freezer bags. Jules, though Swedish, did not know where most of his shoes were.

Peter was stern, troubled by the description of Andy Linders's athletic friend, and Alice laughed and extracted a cigarette from his pocket. They'd both started smoking again while Jules was in the hospital, and he supposed he might as well feel flattered. It was hard to imagine a less fashionable time to start, unless it was next year, but regulations came late to Montana, if at all.

"What the hell are you supposed to be researching anyway?" he asked Alice.

"Other than your nonexistent social life?"

"I actually saw her working," said Peter. "She was lying in the hammock, but she was taking notes."

"I already turned a batch in a few weeks ago," said Alice without annoyance. "I read a really wonderful story yesterday. A hunting party in 1865 was sighted by some Crow at Mission Creek, I think before we pared away a few more million acres, and two guys were killed and the third wounded. The Crow didn't know his gun was empty and he hid from them in a thicket all night long, while they circled around and laughed and drank and kept yelling things like, 'Good evening, Charlie,' and 'Hey, Charlie, watcha doing in there,' and 'Hey Charlie, let's play cards.' "

"Was his name Charlie?" asked Peter.

"No," said Alice. "That's the point. And then all the Henry Plummer stories, stealing Bannack silly with a gang, throwing parties for the vigilantes who couldn't figure it out. Though Hugh already knew about that one."

"Yeah? So who was in the gang?"

Alice gave him a sidelong look. "You know, Peter, you don't have to be a cranky because I'm asking you to go to a party. And this isn't a dissertation. But if you want proof, their names were Ives, Shears, Stinson, Helm, Pizanthia, and six or seven others, most only known as 'Whiskey Bill' or 'Mexican Frank' or maybe 'Pissant Peter.' It happened in 1863, and they hung all of them right around Christmas. And the man who hid from the Crows was named Hughes, so maybe his first name was Charlie, but I doubt they were all on that basis."

Jules, staring due south at the Mission Creek drainage where Charlie and his buddies had swapped names, was smiling broadly.

"Ah, darling," said Peter. "I was just teasing. Keep telling stories."

Alice swatted the hand that snaked toward her leg. "My favorite is about two men named Crandall and Daugherty, who came out of Yellowstone near the Clark's Fork in 1869 and told another group they'd found gold. They were all going to meet at the headwaters the next summer, but Crandall and Daugherty never showed, and it wasn't until the following year that another prospector found their heads on their picks on the bank of the creek. Their tin cups were placed in front of them, to show they'd been surprised during dinner."

"Thank you, Alice," said Peter. "You always especially like it when food's involved, don't you?"

"That would be Crandall Creek, right?" said Jules. "Near Soda Butte."

"Why don't you just give me the stories, and I'll take the money," said Alice. "Fortunately, Hugh doesn't really care if they check out or not, as long as they make 'emotional sense,' and involve lots of color."

"Local color or pretty rocks?" asked Jules.

"Both," said Alice.

They passed a tow truck and a car in the ditch at the White Sulphur exchange, and saw Harvey gesticulating at three very pale people, probably the owners of the folded car with Oregon plates, the ones responsible for the spray of deer on the pavement. The animal was a shell, and Harvey did not look happy. Jules waved and the deputy gave him the finger with his right hand while his left shielded it from the accident victims.

Harvey, in his own way, could be wonderful. Jules wished for a vacation for everyone, and decided he'd throttle the commissioners if they denied another budget proposal at the meeting next week. He was locked on such sweet thoughts when he fell asleep.

Fifteen minutes later, Alice and Peter shook him gently and hauled him onto the curb in front of the Baird Hotel, where the wake itself was to be held. The manual, turn-of-the-century elevator was broken, as usual, and they all grumbled as they climbed the four flights to the top floor and Hugh's apartment. It was large, with two bedrooms, a long living room, dining room, kitchen and wet bar, four former singles that a director of violent westerns had opened up for himself back when the Baird was peeling apart, slowly and inexorably. Hugh had heard about the apartment at the director's funeral, and followed up on it through his friend Otto. The dead man had been an unlikely idol for someone who specialized in pretty English social comedies, but Jules could now imagine an eight-year-old Hugh watching westerns in his tiny Welsh town, six-guns strapped on a small white waist. He almost envied him: a western kid watching a western became dubious early on, especially if he'd already been kicked in the face by a horse and been raised by left-wing parents who indoctrinated him to the bottomless downside of the story.

Hugh essentially owned the apartment the way octogenarian Hungarian princesses owned apartments in hotels like the Carlyle, combing pugs that peed on the Aubusson and subsisted on cucumbers and bisque. According to Edie, via Alice, he had a standing morning coffee order but was otherwise a sweetheart. Sylvia joked that she'd taken up with Hugh for the sake of his place, and the forty-five-minute drive to her ranch probably helped the attraction. Since she'd moved in she'd made the roof into a slightly seedy Fifth Avenue penthouse, French doors leading to a garden with pots of perennials, framed vegetable beds, and even pots of vines working along the trellised edges.

Alice headed toward the kitchen and began to fret about the food with Edie. Meanwhile Sylvia darted back and forth with drinks, looking almost feverish. She made huge martinis for them, and Jules and Peter tried to ooze as directly as possible toward the lawn chairs on the porch. A half dozen of Hugh's friends loitering near the bar were discussing their first vacations in Montana, all of them falling into the habit of the wealthy, who tended to go on vacation as they would go on safari, finding fault with the native bearers, making much of roughing it. Peter and Jules listened without comment; this was the reason Peter hadn't tried to become a fishing guide, and part of the reason Alice constantly disagreed with catering customers. One actress named Sally, someone he'd met during the mess in May, eyed Jules and whispered into the ear of a blond friend, the woman Everett had brought to the funeral. The woman turned and stared at him frankly, and though he thought he knew her he couldn't place the memory. Tall, with short blond hair and long, skinny, bone-white legs.

Out on the roof he gave Peter grief for even remarking upon those legs, saying it was a return to New York, emaciation as beauty. They spent the next few minutes being deliberate assholes with each other, but as they were both essentially private they could rarely sustain such stupidity. They looked over the town of Blue Deer, framed to the south by the Absarokas.

"You are the king of all you survey," said Peter. "Happy almost birthday and good luck."

Jules didn't know whether to laugh or cry, and settled for a sip. Sylvia trotted by with a handful of flowers. "I wish she'd go take a nap."

"I think she did. She looked worse at lunch."

"You go along for the catering confab?"

"Nah."

"Interview? She have anything new to say?"

"No interview." Peter looked uncomfortable. Jules stared and tried to make him more so. A flock of Californians passed by and looked curious but settled into the chairs at the far end of the roof.

"Legal business," said Peter.

"What kind of legal business?" asked Jules.

"I couldn't tell you before, and I can't tell you now, so lay off," said Peter.

"But you're not a lawyer anymore," said Jules.

"Oh, yes I am," said Peter. "I'm a dues-paying member of the bar association. I'm playing hooky, and I might play it for forty years, but I can still file papers and dispense advice."

"If you're not going to tell me anything, why'd you bring it up?"

"I *didn't* tell you anything. If you're not going to tell me anything, why are you asking me questions?"

They settled into a surly silence as Axel Scotti and his wife and Alice came up behind them. Jetta Ganter Scotti was a second cousin of Jules. After she wandered off with Alice to inspect Sylvia's flowers, Scotti lit his cigar. .

"Genie behaving?"

"I hate to say so, but yes," said Jules. "I have absolutely nothing to tell you. Do you have anything to tell me?"

"Only that the mayor wants us to have a meeting next week, and he's going to tell you he doesn't want any more crime, but unfortunately they've still misplaced the money you'd budgeted for new officers. Permanently misplaced it."

Jules turned to stare at him. Scotti sucked the end of his cigar and pointed to Peter. "Not a word from you, sonny."

"Misplaced?" Jules could feel his pulse thudding.

"They're trying to figure out whether it went toward the new Christmas lights or road repair overtime."

"I can't believe they wouldn't know," said Peter.

Jules could.

"I probably shouldn't have told you before this weekend," said Scotti.

"Why did you?" asked Jules, smelling a rat.

"Because you need to give it your all and then ream them out at the meeting when they don't treat you like God. Because some of them want you to quit, think you're too much trouble, and I don't think you'd really want to, if you have time to think about it," said Scotti.

Four stories down, they watched the *Bulletin*'s new editor, Theodore van der Vent III, climb out of his Range Rover and trip. He was the heir and brother of the previous owner, Ada Santoz, and he'd taken advantage of his sister's death to abandon Toledo for the mountains.

Scotti was watching, too, and looking smug. "Teddie must be a joy to deal with on a daily basis."

"You're fishing for a deputy prosecutor, aren't you?" said Jules.

Scotti smiled. "Peter could work for an asshole like me, rather than assholes like that. I can offer him money, challenge, civic pride, and I can usually get out of my car without falling down."

"Look where civic pride's taking me," said Jules. "He'll have twice the hours for the same amount of money. He'll always be the heavy, play God, prosecute petty thieves and breaking up miserable families." He could have gone on for another ten minutes, just for the sake of annoying Scotti, but it was too disheartening.

"I need help," said Scotti. "You're talking about yourself."

Jules looked at Peter. "It's not half the money," he said. "It's twice it, and Alice wants a better kitchen."

Jules became aware of a rhythmic squeak. The blond woman sat on the swing ten feet away and stared into space as if daydreaming, her eyes blank and her mouth open. He looked away, down onto the sidewalks again, and saw Ankeny heading toward the hotel. "You know him?" he asked Peter.

"Patrick? Sure. He's great, especially compared to the asshole he replaced."

"Otto knew him?"

"I'm sure Otto knew everyone in the Forest Service. Otto lived in their files."

"Otto, by the way, did leave a will," said Scotti.

Peter and Jules both took a sip.

Scotti smiled. "Most lawyers don't get around to it, but he left about twenty grand in savings to the Audubon Society, and his house and other belongings to Sylvia."

They all thought it over in silence. The creaking swing was beginning to annoy Jules, who was trying very hard to not ruin his night by thinking about his morning, or personnel budgets.

"What you gonna do for your birthday?" asked Scotti.

"Work. Get ready for the bull riders to get their ya-yas out."

Scotti snorted. "I remember how you used to spend it."

Jules smiled. "I used to spend it being an asshole, but that was a long time ago."

"He got extra mileage for being a college boy," said Scotti to Peter. "A girl in every alley. I tried to tell him bull riding was definitely the hard way to get laid."

Peter, who'd always thought Jules was fibbing, was amused. "Why do you remember all of this?"

"Because I married his cousin around that time, and I'd just started as deputy county attorney. When Jules got trotted in after one July 4, the extended family suggested I have the charges dropped."

Jules was pink. "Charges?" asked Peter.

"In flagrant delicto with someone. A little nudity in the wrong backyard."

Jules sighed. The swing creaked again and he turned. Everett and Sylvia were talking to the woman now. The lens of the camera on her lap glinted as she rocked, with one long white leg tucked beneath her. Scotti, who wasn't the world's finest husband, tapped him on the shoulder.

"Do you know her? I think it's someone Hugh's hired to take photos of the rodeo."

Jules looked again at the woman on the swing, who was watching him while Everett and Sylvia talked next to her. For one awful second he wondered if they'd gone to bed together in some former life, and he'd forgotten; this was unlikely. He searched her face for clues and she smiled slowly, red lips pulling back from white teeth. It came to him and he grinned back.

"I gave her a ticket a few days ago."

"She's quite a piece of work."

"You should hear her talk."

Sylvia turned away from Everett and started talking to the

woman. They made a strange picture together, one at least five-eleven and as smooth and cold-looking as a mannequin, the other almost a foot shorter and pleasantly the worse for wear, having lived every minute of the aging process as fully as possible. The woman nodded toward Jules, and Sylvia waved while Everett watched.

Jules put his glass down and walked over.

Half an hour later he'd finished his second martini and was trapped, alone, in the sitting room, his escape route blocked by Everett and Opal D. Meek, a.k.a. Diane, who seemed to be discussing the fate of the earth while leaning against the doorway to the stairs. Alice and Peter were on the other side of the hall, squabbling about when and how to leave. Alice started to notice things after three drinks, and Jules usually tried to make himself scarce when such heightened sensibilities and vocabulary kicked in, especially because the things she noticed almost always had to do with Peter's drinking.

He decided to give them another five minutes to make peace before he made for the fire escape, and flipped open one of a stack of bound magazines. There, in a 1948 *Atlantic,* was an essay by Raymond Chandler on detective fiction. Splat on the table like an omen, a dab of advice from gumshoe purgatory:

The hero's tie may be a little out of mode and the good gray inspector may arrive in a dogcart instead of a streamlined sedan with siren screaming, but what he does when he gets there is the same old futzing around with timetables and bits of charred paper and who trampled the jolly old flowering arbutus under the library window.

There'd been some changes, thought Jules, unwilling to accept the obvious truth of the quote. What woman fainted, and who knew what a bitter almond smelled like these days, and what modern word for a car could equal roadster? He was still staring at the page when someone turned off the light. Sylvia stood holding a flaming chocolate cake, and everyone sang.

There wasn't a flowering arbutus for a thousand miles, but Jules still drove to Otto's an hour later for a second look at the collapsed trellis at the side of the house. The heavy flame honeysuckle vine was still attached, its gnarled trunk split but already curing gray in the air and light, and the wood of the trellis base was rotten. *Obviously,* the thing had fallen of its own weight, but the troubling fact remained that one of the horizontal rails, about two feet up, had also broken. Jules eyed the window, six feet from the ground, considered the rail again, and bent over the deep, perfectly heel-sized indentation in the soft soil, just where someone might have landed had he lost his footing. Half of a columbine plant had been pushed into the soil, and it was well shriveled. He could have hauled Alice, the gardening expert, out of the Baird bar to date its death, but doubted her word would stand up in court.

Jules couldn't remember which of Otto's rooms lay inside the window, and stepped gingerly into the flower bed to peer through the glass on tiptoe. His two large martinis kicked in and he started giggling.

It was the library.

☆ 7 ☆

THE ETIQUETTE OF DRINKING (HAPPY BIRTHDAY TO YOU)

IN MONTANA, THE QUESTION "CAN I GET YOU A DRINK?" WAS still the number one panacea for all that ailed, as opposed to that of the East and West Coasts', "Do you want my therapist's number?" The shrink in the bottle, the bar as church social; most summers turned into a long, collective lost weekend. Drinking for the sake of drinking was still socially acceptable, but you were never supposed to discuss it until after the fact, and you had to hold your liquor like Gary Cooper and other famous Montanans of the past, transplanting the cowboy's no whining mentality to the martini. Some silliness was enjoyed and forgiven, especially if there was no one relying on you, no compelling need to think anyway. It proved you were pleasantly human and gave everyone else something to talk about.

Jules, of course, had to be more careful than anyone in town short of the judge, who hadn't wanted to misbehave in thirty years. In a sense, drinking was a wise public policy decision—

bar and restaurant owners trusted him and called when trouble started, instead of waiting until it was out of hand. Jules visited the bars stubbornly but carefully, off duty, off call, usually walking home if he had more than two drinks. And he was well versed in the obvious drawbacks, both personally and professionally. His days and nights were filled with people who'd blown the rules, who'd chosen to forget they had a responsibility to others, usually children. He'd been old enough, before his father died, to remember hissing arguments between his parents on the subject, and even in his teens and early twenties, when most of his friends guzzled mindlessly, he'd had an eye on the hereditary mixed blessing of being a Swede with a cast-iron liver. He in fact so loved to drink that he drank carefully to not lose the right, and was horrified whenever he crossed over the very fine line between happy and drunk.

But birthdays were apparently exempt, and the jokes the night before had turned into a self-fulfilling prophecy. Alice, his very own Greek chorus, had put beans in his ears and made sure his glass was full.

BIGGEST WRANGLE YET

Doom, thought Jules. The paper had turned into a fortune cookie. Maybe Alice was secretly writing headlines.

Blue Deer can anticipate a stuffed-to-overflowing Glorious Fourth, as a bumper crop of county guests began arriving in earnest today for the three-day Wrangle.

Why don't they just say "tourists," thought Jules. Or come clean with "aliens." This wasn't Peter's story in yesterday's paper, but Jules looked forward to shaming him with it. It was the only thing he looked forward to.

Most city merchants have said it's the busiest year ever, with county hotels and campgrounds virtually filled as of Wednesday afternoon, and many rodeo entrants forced to stay with their animals at the fairgrounds.

That'll make for a good mood in the cowboys, thought Jules, watching the orange juice twitch in his hand. Come see my love shack, *cherie*. Love my horse, love me. He'd be suctioning them out of the playground equipment, prying them from alfalfa fields. Maybe they'd try doing it underwater. Maybe they'd drive to Yellowstone for the night, find final communion with the grizzlies, try a Jacuzzi in some extra thermal water.

The final contest for the year's Wrangle Queen will start at the main arena at five o'clock Thursday with riding and motivational speech competitions, with the crown awarded by Mayor Brushcobb that evening. A street dance will follow immediately, featuring the live music of the Whoopee Riders, and the blocks between B and Cottonwood will be closed to automobile traffic.

The Wrangle parade, with 65 floats planned, will begin at three o'clock Saturday, barring inclement weather. The rodeo competition will begin at eight P.M. on Friday, Saturday, and Sunday nights, with fireworks following all shows and a grand finale on Sunday.

Jules gave up trying to sit upright at his kitchen table and slumped on the couch, paper in hand, while the coffeemaker burped out a second pot. This weekend was potentially the worst of the summer, but it was also only the first of nine potential award winners, and he was not starting the tourist hell season or his thirty-fourth year on solid ground. One good brush with death, two dead bodies, the humiliation of a freed suspect, a funeral, a wake, the deadfall of a birthday with nothing pleasant to anticipate, four hours of sleep, his worst hangover in more than a month, maybe even a year, and now every moving segment of his body astounded him and seemed unbearably fragile. He peered down at his feet and wondered how they'd survived three and a half decades without being crushed, how they knew automatically how to move. The idea that people twice his age still had working parts shocked him. The notion of repeatedly enforcing all the laws he used to break, of dealing with loud explosions and whistling rockets, querulous tourists and vomiting drunks and maimed riders and loose stock animals, all day long for the next four days, was appalling.

At six A.M. on the day before the Wrangle, Jules was *rooont* by all of it, to use the local parlance. His skin crawled and the back of his head pulsed where it touched the couch. The coffeepot finished its struggle but he couldn't bring himself to move. Several old girlfriends would have told him he wanted to be fired, and they all would have been right. Thankfully—or not—they were not around to tell him so.

He confronted the hideous, pathetic, embarrassing memory of his night. He'd headed from Otto's yard to the Baird bar and started talking with Everett, thinking he'd pry out an admission about footprints in the flower bed, perhaps a full confession to murder and the abc's behind it. Sadly, Everett didn't care to discuss whether or not he'd crushed a coworker, and preferred to wax mordant about his favorite current topics: the nature of the birthplace, their families, their past. His mother was a glassy-eyed drunk, his sisters manipulative Barbies, his father a psychotic prick. The men in Everett's family specialized in self-pitying, indirect suicide—his grandfather had driven a car into the Yellowstone, and his father was a diabetic alcoholic—and Jules's male relatives specialized in being murdered during run-ins with self-pitying, indirect suicides, men like the trucker who'd offed Ansel Clement during a fit of pique with his life and wife, or the drunken rancher who'd aimed at an enemy and shot one of Jules's great-uncles by mistake, back in the twenties.

At the time, Everett claimed the point was that Jules could at least *like* his family, even if half of them were dead. In hindsight, hungover on a couch, the point seemed to be that the two of them were in danger of carrying on the tradition.

Everett had moaned on, singing one old song after another. Rich people didn't appreciate what they had, they took everything for granted. Everett hated them, even though he spent most of his time around them and voted for them and wanted to be one. Why were he and Jules slaving away for peanuts for lesser mortals? Didn't they, for God's sake, deserve to be happy and rich, attended and worshiped?

"Not really," offered Jules, in one of his last sane responses. His companion, after all, had a brand new BMW and had definitely lost touch with the little people. "I've really been quite an asshole for much of my life, and so have you."

"But think of the competition!" howled Everett, suddenly snorkling with laughter. "Everything's relative!"

That was the disarming thing about Everett: he knew he was a jerk, though he occasionally forgot. He danced from subject to subject, mixing flashes of brilliance with banalities worthy of Jesse Helms. Jules had remembered him as a kind of Teflon jokester who'd spent high school tricking everyone out of seeing him as human. Now Everett was definitely out of his shell, and even when he drank little, not the case that night, he was so wound that almost everyone in his presence guzzled.

So when Everett cried about his dead brother, Jules bought him a drink, and when Jules didn't cry about or want to discuss his dead father, Everett bought him one. When Everett cried about Otto—not "It should have been me" but the more selfish, less clichéd, "What if it had been me?"—Jules bought him two (it was a long conversation), and knew he was losing objectivity with his suspect. When Everett fell down on the sidewalk and refused to get up, wheezing with laughter about a passing cowgirl in silky purple jeans, Jules hauled him back inside, and suggested they move on to beer. They did, then switched to a fine Sonoran tequila the owner wanted Jules to try, a reward for not breaking anything when he'd collared Genie.

This was the big regret period of the night, the time when Jules would normally have had a glass of ice water and faded off down a sidewalk, with or without company. Instead, he'd watched Edie dance with her estranged husband and had another tequila with Diane Meek while their mutual friend slept in a nearby booth. It seemed she was a photographer, an old friend and lover of Everett's (she somehow stressed *old*) who'd arrived to record the rodeo for a documentary Hugh was considering, as well as the scenery for next summer's movie and the building of Dragonfly for posterity. Though she looked amused for most of the night, not much humility was in evidence, nor was she particularly charming, even by a drunk's lenient standards; she said mean things in a short space of time about everyone from Otto ("a bore," though she'd only met him once), to Hugh ("an idiot"), to Everett himself ("a hopeless, sad case"), to everyone out of earshot in the bar and the town itself. In a way, she was fascinating, especially as Jules, bombed, didn't really listen to much of it. She had, after all, already levied a similar opinion in his direction. He'd thought at first she'd said she was from New York, but this turned into Newark, where her auto mechanic father had been abandoned by her mother, whom Diane swore had been a Lithuanian leg model, a mannequin prototype. The father had hauled her to relatives in eastern North Dakota, where she'd gone to high school. This side of her history was oddly touching, and made sense, even though she looked as if she'd walked out of a Helmut Newton photograph—they didn't grow them that tall in Eastern cities. She was probably in her early thirties, with small, very pointy features, blue eyes and virtually no breasts. All and all it was a scary combination. If Jules had a favorite look, this wasn't it, but her mouth was so wide and generous as to be obscene even without lipstick, and it transformed her face, warmed it right up to the boiling point.

The mouth was really all Jules paid attention to as they talked, and he'd have to live with the hideous but vague memory of what he'd said in return toward the end of their public conversation. He doubted anyone else had heard or even noticed, though he dimly recalled a look of amusement on Sylvia's face early on. Alice and Peter had spent most of their time debating at the bar. A blues guitarist from Chicago was playing, and Alice wanted to dance, and Peter wanted to go to bed. Alice thought that was a fine idea, but first she *had* to dance; at some point Jules was sure he'd seen her lock her legs around Peter on the bar stool and refuse to let go until he obeyed. Summer and tequila were a potentially deadly combination with her; she always perked up a little too much after the long, sordid, navel-gazing winter, leaned out, drank wine with a better attitude, and laughed at bad jokes. By August she was capable of pure trouble—it had been during such a late summer heat wave a decade earlier, during a breakup with Peter, that she and Jules had looked at each other cross-eyed.

Not that they'd erred again. When Peter left and Alice launched herself at Jules—wanting, honestly, only to dance—he had other fish to fry. Everett woke up and proved game, to put it politely; when Alice and he began bouncing off the walls, Jules and Diane exchanged a look and went up the stairs.

He reached for his coffee cup again, thought of a specific Diane moment, and felt his skin crawl. This was not his normal reaction to a night naked with someone else, but then he'd never had such an antiseptically filthy night in his whole life. He hadn't been a good boy, strictly speaking, since he was fifteen or so, but he'd never been one to spend time with a woman he didn't enjoy in a variety of ways. No beauties as necklaces, no idiot fascination with nasty ladies. But here he was, celebrating the most innocent of days with a woman who reminded him of another Chandler phrase, "gimlet-eyed," words redolent of a forties sense of machination, the naked gesture performed as carefully, as coldly, as the mixing of a cocktail. Even during his days in cowgirl Eden he'd had better sense, despite no grand instinct toward kindness, but when he asked himself why, the answer—why not?—was distressingly familiar.

A little errant youth in Blue Deer's armed public servant number one. No one would call her cuddly, and Jules had left the hotel at five, unable to sleep for a variety of reasons, overjoyed that Edie wasn't lurking behind the desk.

He stuck to the couch for another ten minutes, then suddenly vaulted to his feet, shook himself like a dog, drank the pot of fresh coffee mixed with a quart of milk, and filled the bathroom sink with cold water and ice. He took a deep breath and submerged his head, raised it and took another deep breath, and kept this up for five minutes. It was reportedly the Paul Newman hangover cure, a drastic measure; as usual, when Jules looked into the mirror, dripping and frozen, he didn't look a thing like Paul Newman. Nor did he look like an officer of the law. He resorted to another shower, this one cold, drained the rest of his orange juice, and squirted forth, near hypothermia, onto the sidewalks of the sober, fun-loving, daylit planet.

At the still quiet station, beset by an immediate relapse and Richard's silent curiosity, he swallowed three ibuprofens, checked his fly, and finally pulled out the set of missing files he'd snatched from Hugh the morning before, the originals.

Dragonfly seemed determined to educate as well as profit: During the longest hearing, one held while Jules was in the hospital, Otto had spoken of corporate retreats and symposiums, linked shows with the museum in town to teach tourists how to enjoy the area without destroying it. Enough variety existed in one eight-thousand-acre chunk to teach everything from paleontology to botany to wildlife management. There was even mention of shoring up one of the old, unsuccessful mines in the back of the property and turning it into a kind of living mine, but Everett and Otto doubted insurance would be workable. Mines were by definition unsafe, and Absaroka County abutted the Yellowstone caldera, right up there with the San Andreas fault in terms of seismic instability. A flattened corporate sponsor would be bad for everyone.

It was all deeply uninspiring. Jules read through the transcripts of the commission meetings, Otto saying absolutely nothing of moment and gliding the thing through. Some tension about delays and the permits necessary to rebuild the road after the landslide: time was money. Everett had added memos from the beginning of the project, and most had to do with hot-wiring government permits, but nothing objectionable seemed planned for the area. Up-to-the-second systems for fuel storage, water filtration and recycling, heat and waste; setbacks on all the structures and stream reclamation on the former Forest Service acres; the least intrusive possible methods of road building and strict protection of vegetation and the namesake glacier.

Grace had arrived, and Jules took three doughnuts from the bag she offered without apologizing for his selfishness. She might not remember his birthday, but he did, and someone needed to help him survive it. He pulled Otto's journal out of his desk drawer, then located Otto's secretary's log and compared it to the journal appointments and files and the station's own notes, a maddeningly slow process. Otto had scooted around the country—L.A., Houston, Washington—during May, then made the quick drive down to Boulder on the first weekend in June, before camping. He'd been due back Sunday night, but a cryptic scribbled note moved his Monday appointments to Tuesday and Wednesday, and the same pen noted a drop-off Tuesday morning at River Automotive, presumably for the car trouble Hugh and Everett had mentioned. Tuesday was all clients, especially after the delay, simple property purchases and disputes. On Wednesday, after Otto had driven to Bozeman to buy a gun—no entry for that—he'd raced back to Blue Deer to get his hair cut, then had a root canal session and a doctor's appointment with Horace Bolan, who hadn't recognized his patient ten days later. They were all things Jules supposed you might do before a vacation, also things you might try to get out of the way in a single day, any day. Otto had fit another four clients into the afternoon, according to the secretary's notes, but the journal listed two additional appointments, written on a bias over the neatly penned others: *Stop at FS, PA, forms* and *BB 4:30, H.*

The second was obvious: *Blue Bat, 4:30, Hugh,* but when Jules had tried to decipher the first one, he'd thought it impenetrable. Now, in a weakened condition, it seemed too obvious, too easy. *Forest Service, Patrick Ankeny, forms.*

It was a little too early to call Ankeny, whom Jules thought he'd seen dancing the night before. He sighed deeply and cracked his first soda of the day, knowing he'd crash and burn by noon.

The map Sylvia had mentioned at Bonnie's funeral was there, marked everywhere in a Sharpie code that looked confusing at first but translated well. This section had been traded to the state, this one from them; the final property was outlined in red, surrounding Forest Service sections in blue, roads in black, prospective trails in green. A car couldn't get closer than three miles to the glacier, which would make building three planned cabins near there a logistical nightmare and a wonderful idea. He'd have to rent one when he had a life.

Otto had marked building sites, septic fields, water pipes and gas tanks, and shaded the steeper areas, according to the Forest Service's squiggly altitude lines, a light gray. A dozen yellow rectangles and squares and trapezoids were dotted throughout, and Jules drew a blank for several minutes, until he wanted to growl from sheer frustration. Most stretched up the rock faces, though some extended a few hundred yards into the valleys; all of them were on the public land but most abutted the private holdings; one lay near the old mine area, and another lay across from the canyon entry road, on what was still state land.

Jules stared at the map for another few seconds, then rummaged through Otto's newspaper clippings in the back of his drawer, the ones he'd dismissed earlier. He flipped a roughly torn article on a subdivision and scanned the small announcements again. Lost and found, four miscellaneous wanteds, an uninteresting home sale by owner and five legals, one by a Pam E. Nitz, petitioning for emancipation from her parents, and two other notices, both postings of intent to patent a mining claim. Jules muttered the coordinates aloud to himself and turned back to Otto's Forest Service map. The first, assigned to a T. Boyd in Billings, lay on the far western edge of the county, by Trail Creek and the Bozeman Pass. The other, posted by B. Stinson, lay squarely on Dragonfly Canyon, and Otto had marked it with a yellow blob.

None of the other clippings included legals, and Jules returned to the first. One other had dealt with a subdivision near Missoula, but this one was on Horse Creek in the foothills of the Crazies, about ten miles downstream from Dragonfly, and Jules scanned the article once more but still found nothing that linked one project to the other. On the flip side, in the wanteds, one announcement stood out: "Patented mining claims, all or part interest. Call 555-1739." Jules punched in the number and got a busy signal just as Jonathan slumped in, half an hour late and flushed.

Jules crooked his finger and explained the questions at hand without bothering to chide Jonathan on tardiness. But the second time Jonathan said "I don't understand," Jules snapped.

"Call the number, see if it's Boyd or Stinson buying claims. We don't have time today to go digging around in Forest Service files. I'll check into the subdivision."

Jonathan seemed to be listening, but his breathing was heavy and his face was pink. He looked like Jules felt. "Call Boyd in Billings?"

Jules's temple began to pound. "Call the number in the classified ad, a Billings number, and if it's Boyd or Stinson, then tell me. Right?"

"Right-o," said Jonathan.

"What the hell happened to you? Are you sick?"

Jonathan shook his head miserably and made a woofing sound. Stale bar breath smote Jules full in the face, and nearly pushed him over his own thin line.

"Sit down," said Jules. "I thought you stuck to milk. Any particular reason you decided to start drinking on our worst week of the year, in the midst of a rodeo and a double homicide and everything else we don't even know about yet?"

He was yelling. Grace watched from her station, fascinated.

"I don't know why," said Jonathan. His flush had been replaced by a green tint. "I got carried away, and I met this lady."

"Meaning you didn't get any goddamn sleep either."

"Meaning she was kinda weird."

Jules felt another wave of weariness flood his body. The parallels were unbearable, and he felt old. "How weird?"

Jonathan was in agony. "I saw her take a pill, and she kinda bit me."

"Bit you?"

"*Bit* me."

Jules stared at him and tried to control an incipient case of giggles. On the up side, he hadn't run into the fun couple. "Any city council members or commissioners see you guys together?"

"Oh geez," said Jonathan, completely serious. "Shoot. I don't know."

"Why don't you go into the bathroom and try to get it out of your system. Grace has some topical antibiotic. If you see much swelling, go to the clinic. Can you work?"

"I don't know." He stood and crumpled the newspaper clip in his hammy young hand. "Could you do me a favor?"

I am, thought Jules. "What?"

He whispered. "Could you ask Grace for the cream?"

Jules hissed back. "Jonathan, she doesn't have to know where the woman bit you. She doesn't have to know that a woman bit you at all. Right?"

"Right," said Jonathan. He lurched away, then stalled. "I almost forgot. Happy Birthday."

Jules almost blushed for shame. "Thanks, Jonathan," he said. "I hope you feel better."

Grace charged toward him across the room, appalled, and locked his aching head in a bear hug. "How that goof would remember and I'd forget. What could be wrong with me?"

She gave him another doughnut.

After Jules redeemed himself as a human by wiping Jonathan's miserable face with a very cold, very wet towel, he dialed the Baird.

"Happy Birthday," said Sylvia.

Someday, maybe, someone will say that to me without sarcasm, thought Jules. "I need to talk to you."

"Can't today. I've got ten thousand things to do up at Dragonfly, and then I have to ride."

"I could say I have to take a nap," said Jules. "But I'm not saying it."

She laughed at his pain. "It's your job. Mine is to get the horse I'm riding this weekend into shape, and right now she's skittish."

"Sylvia," said Jules, losing patience, "it is my job to talk to you, and I'm afraid my job is more important than your hobby."

"Well, screw you."

He'd heard the edge in her voice all along, and now it had cracked. He rubbed his forehead. "Did you notice anything missing from Otto's house?"

"You got the files yesterday. Did you leave them in the bar last night?"

"You mean the files you said he'd have with him, wherever he went? I just read through them. I mean missing from his house. Somebody broke in a couple of weeks ago."

"Nothing's missing. And what do you mean, a couple weeks ago?"

He didn't want to get into trellises, pry marks on windows, faint mud smears, and other potential figments of his fevered imagination. "You really looked around, made sure? Were you thinking someone else would look, too? You were very attached to that shotgun."

"I just wanted the work papers," said Sylvia.

"Which work papers?"

"The ones you've just read. I've got to go."

"I'm coming over later."

"Suit yourself."

He slammed the phone down.

Jules spent the rest of his birthday afternoon chasing banalities and mishaps like a dog chasing his tail, wondering why on earth details didn't make way for larger questions, like murder. A middle-aged diver misjudging water depth under a Yellowstone bridge; skunks on the rampage through the town garbage; a double-wide, hauled down Blue Deer's main drag on one of the busiest days of the year, taking out a line of rearview mirrors.

Ankeny was in the midst of a meeting, and sounded harassed and ill when he finally came on the phone. Sure, he knew Otto, had dealt with him several times out of the main office. He remembered seeing him a month or so earlier, but how could Jules expect him to remember anything beyond that, on short notice? He thought Otto had made Xeroxes, and he'd been at one of the older cabinets, and it might have been one of the claims or patent cabinets, but Ankeny couldn't remember, and Otto knew his way around and didn't have to ask any goddamn questions, like other people. Jules decided to try another day.

Jonathan, still green, delivered the daily update on Genie,

who'd been remarkably, disappointingly obedient about the terms of his bail. He'd stuck to Gardiner, or at least was in the bonded double-wide every time the Gardiner deputy checked on him, and Jules's spies told him that the girlfriend was intent on cleaning him up. The news was the same today, which meant that Genie had gone a solid week without getting high, a new world's record, even if he hadn't had a choice in jail. He'd even boasted to the deputy about a job that weekend, working the chutes at the rodeo.

The mayor stood in the doorway, and he didn't have any balloons in his hand. Jonathan started to run for it. "Wait," said Jules. "Did you figure out the patent?"

"Same guy," said Jonathan, oozing out of sight past the mayor.

A fine answer, if Jules hadn't asked about two names. He stood for the mayor and let it go. He let almost everything go that day, including a message to call Diane. He didn't want to work, and he didn't want anyone to touch him, and he didn't want to celebrate a thing; he mostly wanted to lie face down on his couch, but he would never have made it back to his feet, and by the end of the day it was time to carry through on his threat to Sylvia.

No one was at the desk in the lobby of the Baird, and he peered into both the dining room and the bar without seeing a preternaturally cheery and secretly pissed off brunette or any other employee. He was back in the lobby, wondering if four flights of stairs were worth a direct assault on Sylvia and Hugh's apartment, when he heard the old elevator grind into life and made out Edie's shoes, ankles, knees, and dearly remembered torso. He came to his senses and affected a disinterested stare out the window as she slid open the grate.

"Can I help you, Jules?"

"I wondered if you could ring Sylvia for me," he said.

She smiled, fresh as a daisy and holding a remote phone. She was wearing a very short skirt, and he was annoyed to see that married life agreed with her.

"She's still off with Diane and Hugh and Everett. They were all going up to Dragonfly. Would you like the car phone number?"

"No," said Jules, too quickly.

Silence. He knew she was trying to be patient. "Would you like to have dinner?" he asked, a question from Mars that confounded him as soon as he'd uttered it.

She snorted. "Lord, your timing. And I'm working anyway. No thanks."

Her first response didn't bear too much thought. "Well," said Jules, retrenching, "I'd like to double-check on that note you said Otto left for her."

"What about it?"

"Did you read it?"

She looked shocked. "Jesus, no. This is a *hotel,* and anyway, he had it in an envelope. I was going to dial up to the room, because I knew Hugh was in, but he said his car was running, that he was leaving for a few days, and asked me to give it to Sylvia directly."

Jules rocked on his feet ever so slightly.

"You look horrible," said Edie.

"Gee, thanks," he snapped. "That's just the sort of thing I've been hoping you'd say to me again."

"Sit down," said Edie. "Wait right there."

He flopped on the couch. Edie reappeared with a huge iced tea and Jules chugged half of it, almost weeping for small kindnesses. The moment was too good to last.

"Can I ask you a question without you taking it the wrong way?" asked Edie.

"Sure," said Jules, synapses screaming danger.

"Why . . ." Edie was tapping the phone antenna against her thigh. "Why on earth . . . oh, never mind."

Jules gritted his teeth and put the iced tea down. "What?"

She pulled the antenna up and down on the phone, then reached for the afternoon's *Bulletin*. The headline was NO PROGRESS ON MURDERS, which was better than SHERIFF GETS BLIND DRUNK.

"Never mind. It's none of my business. And I wasn't going to ask because of what you and I did, but because I just don't understand. I mean, you're smart, and this woman is just about the nastiest person I've ever met. I understood Rita, but . . . "

Jules reached a personal limit. "What are you getting at?"

Edie watched some guests descend the stairs. "She's a bitch, and Everett's unstable."

"What is this, cause and effect?"

"I guess he was singing opera off the fire escape at dawn. He was still singing when I got here."

"Why didn't you call the station?"

"I didn't want to make trouble for him."

Mr. Charm struck again. Jules's already foul mood grew fouler, but Edie either didn't notice or didn't care.

"And maybe you don't know, but they used to go out together, and I think they still sleep together."

"I know entirely too much," snapped Jules.

She looked at him in disbelief. "How could you be so stupid?"

"Whatever—" he hissed out "ever," "whatever would lead you to believe that I'm smart in that particular way? Whatever led you to believe that I actually thought first, or liked this woman? Why would you expect more from me than your husband? Why am I the unforgivable jerk?"

She turned vermillion, tossed the paper at him, and marched toward her cubicle.

"Jesus," said Jules, seizing the paper and following her. "I'm just here to do my fucking job, and I get this."

"If you were doing your job you would have asked me questions a long time ago. I see these shitheads every day. I know when they sleep and what they eat, and who they eat and sleep with. You've grilled every other idiot in the county but you'd rather not even have to *talk* to me."

Jules slammed the paper down on the desk. "You're seeing your husband again. I spent two weeks in the hospital and you didn't feel talkative then."

"I'm divorced, and I'm not talking about *seeing* you. We didn't have a goddamn thing left to talk about, and anyway, Alice said you were having fun with the nurses. This is different. This is business. You're not any better at seeing the difference now than you were before you were shot, are you?"

"You actually think there's a difference in a town like this?"

They glowered at each other until Edie let her glance stray into the lobby and sat in the office chair with a sigh. Jules looked around. At least a half-dozen of her customers and his constituents were frankly fascinated. He shut his eyes and let it all go, and when he opened them again and looked at Edie, he only thought of how much he still liked her, and how little she liked him, and how he deserved everything she had the energy to dish out.

"So," he said. "Who do they eat with and who do they sleep with, and why?"

Hugh and Sylvia had been given to very vocal arguments, and so had Hugh and Otto, before Otto left for Boulder. When Otto took off, Sylvia had said something to the effect of finally being back to work, though a week later, when Edie had given Sylvia the note from Otto, Sylvia had been quite surprised and upset to learn he'd left town again.

Which was odd, thought Jules, shutting his own screen door behind him two hours later and overjoyed to be alone, as Otto had supposedly planned the vacation for some time. Moe the parrot immediately began to scream "Hi, fuckface," and as Jules dropped a bag of groceries and more of Otto's files on his kitchen table he wondered at the man's sense of humor.

Edie had only worked three night shifts in the last month—she had children and hated the sound of the elevator slowly lowering after midnight—but on the night Diane had shown up, after they'd had a screaming argument that floated all the way down the stairwell, Everett had apparently left by the fire escape, because she saw him go upstairs twice during her shift but never down. And yes, of course she could have been in the bathroom, but everything echoed in the Baird at night, and the next day the ladder had been dangling into the alley.

Which was odd, thought Jules, loading groceries into the refrigerator, because in school Everett had been so deliberate, so careful to not seem the fool, that his sole sport had been tennis. No climbing, no diving, no high jump. He wouldn't ski because he wouldn't go on the lift. Neither would Alice; maybe that was why they liked to dance together. Everett hadn't danced much in school either, but he and Alice had acted like they were in a depression era marathon, and kept it up until the bar closed, long after Jules had made his clever departure, according to Edie. Jules thought about his leave-taking and cringed, but they were past that now, and Edie was only mentioning Alice because the incident worried her. Jules said something about alcohol as Dutch Courage, turning everyone into Mr. or Ms. Happy, but this was not a reassuring thought, and they both knew it.

He played his answering machine reluctantly. Axel Scotti, wanting to talk about Genie; Ed, checking in from Seattle; three friends with bubbly birthday greetings; and his mother, Olive, ostensibly calling for the same reason but more likely worried about the fat cat he was watching for her. Olive had been so disgusted with Jules for having been shot she'd gone to San Francisco to visit her daughter, Louise, and her two grandsons. Jules had pointed out that, unlike his father, he was alive; Olive had pointed out four inches wasn't enough of a difference for her, and shouldn't be for him. She planned to stick with the fog for the summer, despite her dislike for Louise's second husband, and the chaos of her household.

The fat cat in question, Fred, was currently flicking his tail under Moe's cage, being serenaded by a song that sounded like "Squish Goes the Weasel." Fred weighed nineteen pounds and hailed from Brooklyn, where Jules had found him ten years earlier. When he'd left for Europe and a series of archaeological digs, and dropped Fred in his mother's lap, Olive had called him a sweet little orange thing. Now in obese middle age, Fred was still terrified of most moving objects, a paranoia possibly due to the big bull's-eyes he wore on each side. Moe had figured this out, and made little lunging hops at the cat for the pleasure of watching him jump.

Two gifts from his mother and sister had arrived the day before, and he opened them like a kid, savaging the paper and tossing it at the animals to break up their argument. Good binoculars and an expensive photo book about the excavation of an Iron Age village in Turkey. They were obviously grooming him for bachelor old age. He called San Francisco to say thanks, and tried for sympathy from his sister, but she was incapable of giving it without referring back to herself. Jules was let to know that his sleeplessness was nothing compared to the deprivation suffered by a woman with a new infant. Never mind that Louise's youngest, Arthur, hadn't been an infant for three years and had always slept like a rock, or that Jules had helped out with her oldest, now fourteen, for a month after husband number one had taken off for a cooking job on St. Martin and hadn't been seen again. Jules tried again when his mother came on, and she merely told him to get a different job. Both of them accused him of being humorless and surly, and he decided to live up to the accusation by telling them, metaphorically, to screw themselves as he hung up. Five minutes later he realized he hadn't thanked them for the presents they'd sent or talked to either nephew. He spent a long time on the front porch, looking at pictures of Turkish mountains while he sipped a curative beer, before he dragged his sorry ass to Peter and Alice's for dinner.

Alice hadn't left her bed until three that afternoon, but it didn't matter, because she and Peter had splurged on shellfish from Seattle. They'd done it to make him feel like he was somewhere else, she said, and it had seemed like a wonderful idea until the stuff arrived while she was throwing up that morning. Now Alice dropped the mussels and clams in a sinkful of cold water, and Peter opened a bottle of white burgundy, which they all drank ardently on the back stoop. When it was gone, the shellfish and bread and salad sounded much better, along with two more bottles, and following an apricot tart with candles, they faced a little brandy. After that Jules faced his pillow and vowed to be a better man at some point in the future.

BULL RIDERS
DO IT BEST

SOMEONE, PROBABLY MOLLY IVINS, HAD CALLED TEXAS "THE land where the lunatic is normal." Maybe she didn't know about Montana, or maybe the two states didn't have to be in competition. Perhaps lunatics in Montana were less glaringly obvious than their Southern counterparts. Fewer clock towers, fewer people, smaller hats, and more snow; in winter, Northern maniacs tilted toward quiet, pickled melancholy and solitary suicide rather than indulging in the almost joyous Texas habit of taking the whole town along to hell. But in summer, the distinctions blurred, without the pleasure of border food or musical accents. The same cowboys, on the same endless loop of injury and hangover and quick love, spread across the west and into Canada. Non-Westerners who stumbled into the horse opera either wilted and retreated, appalled, or leapt in with the behavioral equivalent of a cannonball: Harvard doctorates—male or female—convinced after four whiskey ditches or sloe gin fizzes that they could kick a jukebox into submission without breaking a toe; Alabama junior leaguers—again, male or female—vomiting margaritas out of deflating rafts, not noticing the bridge abutment ahead.

Jules didn't fully subscribe to the heroic notion of the west, wasn't the sort of homeboy who bought into the mystique. History conspired against it: He'd checked the fine print on the station calendar as he finished out the month, trying to prepare himself for the holiday by seeing when the full moon might hit. June 23 had been the anniversary of the first spark in the 1988 Yellowstone fires; June 25 the day Custer had made his final idiotic decision in 1876. Almost everything in between—drought, reservation starvations, dead wolves, dead immigrant babies, and overgrazing—fit the pattern.

Jules had always wanted to play Indian during cowboys and Indians, always wanted to be the one to kill Custer, an affinity for the underdog that made his most recent career choice perverse. Even when he'd been in the rodeo himself, during the great testosterone surge of his late teens and early twenties, he'd been not quite of his background and recognized the glorious idiocy of it all, been amused by the ironies even as he flew through the air. Maybe he'd been defensive about heading east for college and wanted to be tougher than the assholes he'd left behind, maybe he'd only taken life seriously when in motion, always loved the edge without admitting it. Bull and bronc riding was a marvelous excuse for bad behavior, especially if your father had been a martyred sheriff, and you were the valedictorian who left every September when the weather went downhill.

Scotti's memories were peanuts compared to Jules's: No matter how hungover and depraved from the festivities or bruised from the rodeo itself, he'd gone to bed or alley or field with someone he'd never met before and didn't intend to meet again. It was just the way things were, an annual late birthday present, a ritual Diane had managed to revive.

He'd stopped finding such self-abuse even remotely interesting after he graduated from college, the last summer he came home. He was working on a construction crew with a friend (David Eaton, now, amazingly, the fire chief), on a big, fancy project in the valley. He and David had done some mushrooms, and when they headed down to the river to clean off their mortar and compare space cowboy notes they were confronted by three large angus bulls in an ugly mood. The bulls snorted great loops of spittle, inhaled, and charged. How stupid, thought Jules as he chugged at full speed through a wavering green landscape, barely able to remember where the house was, or why it was where he belonged.

Now he had cowboy boots but he preferred sneakers, and usually remembered that things, sexual and otherwise, just happened. This was really the only attitude he could take on the eve of chaos.

The first Montana rodeo had supposedly been held in the late nineteenth century by an enterprising Frenchman named Pierre Wibaux, to amuse visiting nobility, and every July, Blue Deer headed full circle. By the time the Wrangle actually began Friday evening, tourist hell had fruited like an overripe, oozing melon. At nine that morning, temperature eighty-five Fahrenheit, the local Best Western discovered a dead, naked, and very rich Nevadan in one of its showers, the probable victim of a heart attack. At nine-thirty, a waitress at Morton's accidentally poured a pot of coffee into an Ohio State senior's lap, and the senior broke her nose. At ten forty-five, a family reunion in a city park gazebo turned ugly when one cousin threw horseshoes at another. Fifteen minutes later and a hundred yards away, a confused couple from Maine drove into the lagoon, nearly killing some fishing eight-year-olds.

At noon, the locals kicked in with a seemingly infinite variety of explosions and accidents. Blue Deer lost its first digit to fireworks when a fourteen-year-old, packing gunpowder into a cardboard cylinder, taped one end and decided to tamp the other down with a ball peen hammer. At one-thirty, temperature ninety-six, some prematurely baled hay burst into flames in a valley barn, and shortly thereafter (thankful for no dead animals; no spreading grass fire), Jules and Harvey argued about who'd get to cool down by swimming halfway across the Yellowstone with a rope to pluck some wet rafters from a shoal. Jules won, but Harvey elected to help push the boat, and both of them enjoyed goofing on the trapped fun-seekers. "Didja check out that paw print, Harv?" "A big one, Jules. I haven't seen one like that since I was a kid. Remember that time we only found the arm?" "He's probably come down for water. Might be watching us right now. You sure all your kids are accounted for, ma'am?"

This cooled-down, chuckly stage of things only lasted twenty seconds, because it seemed one ten-year-old girl wasn't accounted for, having drifted off in the missing boat when she decided her family didn't appreciate her. It took a couple of hours to track her down at Dairy Queen, where a kind group of bombed fishermen had headed after plucking her from a bank. Jules thanked everyone, apologized to the mother for literally the hundredth time, and took his angst out on the next call, an impatient truck driver who'd rammed a Winnebago away from a diesel pump, and clubbed the driver with a nozzle when he'd dared to complain. Jules tracked the man to earth in a diner bathroom and threw him in jail.

By then it was four o'clock, and on a sidewalk downtown, lecturing a would-be shoplifter, the heat radiated up from the pavement and bounced down from the brim of his hat to settle on his cheekbones. It wasn't like New York, with the great moist blast of urine hovering over subway grates, but the kind of dry sear that made you think of deserts and circling buzzards. The heat was peaking now, and would last through the first half of the rodeo, when he could add in flies and dust and the smells of manure, hot sugar and fried fat, tobacco and whiskey, cheap strawberry lipstick and nervous sweat.

Jules used his hour off to take another cold shower.

That night Jules took in the Wrangle from the inside out, listening to the national anthem and the cheers and the dull thuds from behind the chutes and concession stands, booting teenage miscreants off the grounds and confiscating their beers without bothering to write them up. The schedule was the same every night: bareback, saddle broncs, the clown's act, more saddle broncs, team roping, and the ladies' exhibition; steer wrestling, calf roping, and more clown; barrel racing and two sessions of bull riding. The bulls and bucking horses had names like Angel Dust and Twist and Shout, Goose Step and Close Encounter.

Genie was working a chute. Jules had never seen him surlier, and was amused by the fact that Genie couldn't slack off in this job without losing his macho. He didn't want to push him over the line, and walked to the edge of the grandstand to watch the ladies' exhibition. He looked up in the grandstand and a white arm flashed at him. Diane, grinning like a fiend. Everett, who'd always had a horror of all things animal, was next to her, acting like he knew what he was talking about, and Jules wondered what he made of it all, whether what had gone on two nights earlier made any difference to him.

Sylvia and her fellow maniacs called themselves the Lucas Loonies, after a female bronc and trick rider named Tad Barnes Lucas, who'd made a fortune in the thirties. Two of Sylvia's aunts had won prizes throughout the Western circuits during World War II, but women had been barred from most rodeo events besides barrel-racing since the fifties. Most of the women in the group spent the rest of the year at more polite cutting horse events, and the ones who were Sylvia's age, who'd given up bronc riding for safer breakaway roping, rode at the rodeo for reasons that had less to do with feminism than boredom. Half of them were overeducated readers of South American fiction, like Sylvia, with too much money and too much time, part of the last generation of women who wouldn't automatically work. They could have run corporations, but this wasn't part of the marital plan, and so they opted for a little self-imposed pain. The Lucas Loonies were a practical measure, too: Blue Deer didn't have the money for a traveling trick show, trained buffalo and the like, and the once popular wild horse stampede (won by the first person who saddled up and rode, no matter how long the moment lasted) had been ruled out for insurance reasons. Greased pigs and barrels were a treat saved for the fair rodeo. Sylvia, eternal board member, had taken a typically hands-on approach a decade earlier, and only in the last two had she given up saddle broncs for breakaway roping, which only required a high speed chase, an accurate toss, and a braking horse.

She did a tidy job the first night out, only six seconds to the flag, and he gave her a few minutes before he wandered over to where she perched, smug and dusty and pretty next to Hugh, who looked absurdly proud and happy and wandered off after a few minutes to buy lemonade. Sylvia teased him good-naturedly about the night at the Baird, digging a bit for confirmation; but Jules was having none of it.

"Any idea why Otto'd be concerned by mining claims on Dragonfly?"

She looked at him in disbelief.

"He'd marked them on his map."

"Just cleaning up details, probably. There's nothing worth mining up there."

"So why so many claims on the property?"

She looked exasperated. "I don't know. There are claims on every square mile of this county, and whoever the old crazies are who own them, they'd never get it past a planning commission. Otto checked *everything*. That's why he was Otto."

They both looked straight ahead, at the arena. The bull riding had begun, and Jules shuddered for his teenage spine. "Any more ideas on that break-in, what might have been missing?"

"Otto probably locked himself out," said Sylvia, pissy now.

Jules thought of the key on the porch. "Know why he and Hugh had a meeting the day he left to go camping?"

She looked at him so coldly that he doubted for the first time that they'd ever make it back to their former easy friendship. "There was a meeting that night. They usually got together before meetings."

Jules held his tongue through two more riders, letting her relax her guard, shoot the shit with some other riders. Then he touched her arm. "Sylvia?"

She smiled, finally really looking at him. "What, sweetie?"

"What did Otto say in the note he left with Edie, in the last note?"

Sylvia stiffened and jerked away. "None of your business."

"You sure?"

"Nobody's but ours, ever." She climbed down and walked away.

It was an easy night, with only one injury, a bull rider who separated all the muscles from his rib cage on his left side. Jules helped Al and Bean, the paramedics, haul him into the ambulance and watched them drive away, knowing they stood to have a worse weekend than he did. After the clown lit the first night's fireworks, he helped the fair committee clean up stragglers and headed home, but half an hour later, at eleven-thirty, he and Harvey and Bean and Al mopped up the first mangled drunks of the summer on an especially bad curve in the valley. Two dead and one critical passenger, an elderly tourist from Utah, in the car that had been heading north, innocently and peacefully sticking to its own lane. The southbound cowboy, actually an apprentice electrician, had swallowed approximately eight rum and cokes before he decided to pass on a double yellow line. Jules especially minded when drivers missed the lesson by dying, and when they died horribly enough to make him throw up.

Three dead people in one day was a record, even by that spring's exacting standards. Jules rejoiced in small things, like the fact the *Bulletin* didn't have a weekend edition. But when Saturday actually arrived, nothing much happened beyond the requisite misadventures with fireworks, stray animals, alcohol, vehicles, and a wash of complaints about noise. The relative calm was almost eerie. One man claimed his small terrier had died from fear during some rocket blasts down the block the night before, and Jules was at a loss; what did people expect on a holiday dedicated to gunpowder?

At four that afternoon he stood in the blazing sun, dark brown uniform scorching into his shoulder blades, sweat trickling down his nose, his spine, the backs of his knees; children's screams and smoke and sirens and the smells of horse shit, popcorn, and beer in the air. The parade was only half over, and despite the quiet morning the day seemed endless and awful again, filled with happy, moronic faces; the horns of antique cars; Future Homemakers and Farmers of America, all of them tossing candy. A bagpipe band brought him to the edge of nervous collapse and violence. When an eight-year-old, really too old to be chasing tossed Tootsie Pops, stepped on his foot, Jules's fingers tightened on his baton before he bestowed an unpleasant smile on the tot. This reaction appalled him, and he spent the next few minutes wondering what sort of sadist or good samaritan might actually be suited for riot duty in larger cities. Jules usually prided himself on having at least some sense of humor, but it had given way to a wave of self-pity and fatigue.

Jules gave up the pretense of being a Beefeater and wiped a wealth of liquid salt from his high forehead. He rocked on his feet, trying for some sort of Buddhist quiet, then focused on a small herd of llamas, followed by the barrel riders and the Queen of the Wrangle and her runners-up, who had the shiny, desperate looks he normally associated with bad television pageants. The new queen, a certain Tawnee Arlee, bounced into view and waved to him, and Jules waved back, looking so alarmingly wolflike that her hand fluttered momentarily to a stop. According to Friday's paper, she wanted to join the Peace Corps, but today she looked as if her lifelong ambition was to inspire a namesake plastic doll. His mind flashed over the black and white photo of Bonnie Siskowitz, big hair, big smile, happy moon face, then veered away.

Jules decided to sweeten up, and waved to the manager of a sporting goods store, who was chucking armloads of popsicles from a Corvette, and to another old friend who ran the local preschool. Old cars, dwarf horses, Shriners, and a Wyoming cavalry unit. Floats for softball teams, the lumber mill, the credit union, and a dude ranch; floats for hardware stores, truck stops, and furniture stores. The queen of the parade, a ninety-five-year-old named Ruby Montcrief, blew him a kiss and slapped her eighty-year-old consort on the back as they putted by in the bed of a Model T. Off and on he saw Diane and her camera zig into view down the street, crouched at an extreme angle in very long jeans. The fire truck chugged past, manned by David Eaton, Jules's old cohort in hallucination. A half-dozen men with shovels marked the end of the parade.

Jules started moving toward downtown through the swarm, feeling like a sheepdog on strike, and stopped in his tracks when he saw a very small back facing an angry, flushed Hugh Lesy in an office doorway. Everett stood nearby, facing politely away, and met Jules's eyes just as Sylvia slapped Hugh's face and marched off down the sidewalk.

Saturday afternoon at four the wind whipped up and a short, thorough thunderstorm turned the rodeo grounds to mud. Jules, heading home to change into Clark Kent, watched the feral boys take shelter under tavern awnings, saw their cowboy hats swirl off, and wondered again why anyone bothered with them in the second windiest town in America.

It was his night off, but he had to go to the rodeo anyway, because he'd promised Alice. Her younger cousin Lucy, a museum restorer from Seattle who was due to marry a doctor that fall, had arrived the day before and wanted to go, and Jules was the best person to explain "what it all meant." Just about nothing, thought Jules, but he was a sucker for Lucy, who had silky black hair and silkier black eyes.

So that evening Jules helped Peter dig fence-post holes for Alice's garden and watched his hostess and her cousin drink wine and weed the flower bed. Alice epitomized the saw that the lasting legacy of a liberal education was expensive taste but no money with which to indulge it. Somewhere in the back of her come-the-revolution soul she was to the manor born, and switched at birth; selling truffles at an absurdly luxurious food store in Manhattan had probably cemented both sides of her nature. Now she was lecturing Lucy on the kind of sheets she should register for. At least two hundred count, all cotton, and don't forget the goosedown comforter, the Pillyvuyt plates and hand-blown goblets, the hundred-dollar Italian saucepans and three-hundred-dollar French copper roasting pans and the Monet-pattern gravy pitcher from Tiffany's. Lucy already seemed to be reconsidering her relaxing stay in the country and the choice of Blue Deer as the site of her wedding, and chugged wine from the stress of it all.

They moved on to invitations, fine points like the difference between "the pleasure of your company" and "the honor of your presence." Peter refused to join in and wrestled with the box fencing. Jules filled Lucy's wineglass and voted for "invite you." Alice caught him and gave him a look that said "Just try it, mofo." She'd already told him, on Lucy's last visit, in plain English, that the mildest flirtation would result in his death, or at the very least in a cancellation of meal privileges.

The fact that Alice might be living vicariously was not lost on either Jules, who tried to sip his wine, or Peter, who'd lived happily (he thought) with Alice for nine years without whispering the "M" word in a weak moment. Jules had always found this avoidance self-defeating, and now he snagged two more shrimp and told them he had to head to the fairgrounds early to take Jonathan through his paces.

"Thank God it's summer," said Peter, waving him off.

It seemed like an easy night. Jules hauled Jonathan around, introducing him to the concessionaires and pointing out the obvious holes in the fairground fence. He saw Diane photographing the stock pens and the fireworks setup and led Jonathan in the other direction before circling around to show him all the barns and exhibit buildings where people shouldn't be.

Which was where they saw Diane again, snapping away at them. She said she wanted to ask him some questions, do a little groundwork for Hugh on the documentary; she hadn't been to one of "these things" since she was ten, and other knowledge had supplanted such memories. Huh, thought Jules, still warm from the afternoon's wine and fully recovered from his birthday wallow in shame. It was almost eight, and people were streaming through the main gate; he sent Jonathan off into the dust cloud.

"So," said Diane, holding up her arms in puzzlement, "where will they keep the fair animals? Do you have time for a tour?"

"Certainly," said Jules, taking her arm.

Diane nixed the empty, dusty cattle, horse, swine, and poultry barns—all of them clearly labeled—and settled on sheep. Jules wandered back to the arena a half hour later, hoping that he wasn't covered with cobwebs or hay, and that the send button on the radio he'd stuffed in his jeans hadn't been inadvertently pushed during their melee. The fact that he felt wonderful was a sad testament to his moral depravity, but he wasn't in the mood for introspection, and perhaps this last was the best birth-week gift of all.

Alice and Peter and Lucy were in the grandstand, a couple of rows above Hugh and Everett, who looked awful and admitted to having gone out the night before. He climbed down the bleachers twice to use the bathroom, and Hugh headed down three times to check on Sylvia, whose borrowed mare had been acting up. Both of them were as jumpy as rabbits, which amused Jules, who was feeling heavy-limbed in a pleasant, postcoital way. He'd have liked to ask Sylvia why she'd slapped her suitor that afternoon but hated to ruin his mood, and was quite sure, anyway, that it had to do with Otto's last private note to his ex-wife. Jules only had to leave his seat once (Jonathan was busy with a vomiting teenager, and Jules left him to the task), when a tourist with an expensive video camera punched a horse in the head for slobbering on him, and was immediately and brutally attacked by the horse's loving owner, a large calf roper from Laramie. The victim wanted to sue, and probably would, despite Jules's patient explanation: never, ever punch a quarter horse during a rodeo. What kind of fucking fool was he anyway?

Back on the bench between Alice and Lucy, he discussed the finer points of bareback riding without admitting that he enjoyed watching the riders fly. On to saddle broncs, and the announcer cackled about "losing a pedal," and noses spurted blood; the crowd, mostly from out of state, was having a wonderful, Roman time. Jules was happy that they were mostly watching violence instead of taking a hands-on approach; even Genie was being constructive for the second night in a row. He watched Diane slide around in the crowd with her camera, a cold parting of waters. Once, when she caught him, he winked, still trying to hold the upper hand, be the law, knowing he was already on an incline. The next time he saw her she was the only one whose head pointed toward him in the short west stands, everyone else watching a fallen bronc rider to see if he could move, and she pursed her lips in a moue before widening them to a perfect *o*. Then she laughed, a silent sound in the roar of clapping as the rider gimped out of the arena. Jules felt the wave of the blush rise to his temples, deaf as Alice asked for a second time how they made the horse calm down so fast and slapped his thigh with her program. They'd picked up cocktails at the bar stand, and Lucy was giddy, indecently happy for someone who spent her life removing specks of dirt from lesser paintings.

Sylvia's turn came five minutes later. He'd watched her ride Friday, and dozens of times before that; he'd watched many of these women ride many times, even if he wasn't always watching their horse or their hands. He'd never, ever, seen a horse move out of the chute at top speed with its head back, ignoring the calf, spasming and twisting, and it was likely no one else in the arena had either. So there was a prolonged silence, a kind of refusal to take it all in, as the lanky bay quarter horse loosened Sylvia in the saddle, flailed again so that her tense face was down about its shoulder, rammed into an arena pole with that shoulder, and collapsed there, stopping utterly.

By then Jules was moving, looping over Hugh and Everett and everyone else in front of him. He vaulted the grandstand fence and hit the dirt at the same time as the clown and Harvey and Al and Bean.

The horse was dead, pink foam at its mouth and runny shit streaking down its back legs. Sylvia was face up underneath, both eyes closed and one oozing blood, buried under the body from her chest down. Her fingers were wrapped in the mare's mane, and as Jules and Harvey hauled the horse's head and neck up she started to come up along with it, loose as a piece of fabric. They couldn't hold it, and tried again at the count of three. This time Bean got her halfway out, and with the third massive pull he lifted her free of the mud and the horse.

As if it mattered, thought Jules. People weren't supposed to bleed from the eyes, and hundred-pound women weren't supposed to lie under sixteen-hundred-pound horses. He stayed on his knees by the horse's head and stared into its open mouth. The mare had swallowed her tongue.

Bean strapped on an oxygen mask and Al ran toward them with a stretcher. The clown was crying and making funny little hops, and other than these sounds and the announcer telling the very calm crowd to calm down, all Jules could hear was the sound of Hugh Lesy screaming from somewhere behind the chutes.

Jules walked back to the hospital at six on Sunday morning, four hours after he'd left. There wasn't much point: Sylvia had fractured three vertebrae, snapped six ribs, bruised her heart, and shattered her pelvis. All of this was moot, even the likely paralysis, because of the damage to her fractured skull, the fact that her brain had enlarged, and she'd spent several minutes without breathing. Now she was shunted and tubed and wrapped temporarily together, but if by some miracle she opened her eyes when Hugh said her name, no one expected to see recognition.

Hugh was alone in the cafeteria, asleep with his head in his arms. Jules woke him and told him nothing was different, and nothing would be different after he'd gone to the hotel and slept and come back. Hugh wanted more coffee; Jules bought him a cup to go, loaded him into his car and then the Baird elevator with Edie's help, and got him through the door of his apartment. It wasn't a good time to ask him why he'd been arguing with his dead partner, or his nearly dead lover.

Jules walked on to the station. Downstairs, in the jail, he found Archie baby-sitting two morose drunks, an unbelievably quiet tally for a holiday Saturday. He worked through the bullshit on his desk, throwing most of it away, and shocked Richard the dispatcher by bringing him a fresh cup of coffee. He called the Wrangle committee to encourage them to start early that evening, make the goddamn bull riders happy—they'd been canceled the night before, in the postaccident pall. If the horse had walked out the show would have gone on, even if Sylvia had been deader than a doornail, but a dead horse was a formidable obstacle. Jules double-checked; yes, the committee had finally gotten the mare out of the arena. The owner, Sylvia's old friend Nelson Henckle, had been screaming that he wanted the mare autopsied as Jules followed the ambulance to the hospital. At the time it had been beyond bad taste, and now Jules simply shied away from what it might mean.

On Sunday night the rodeo opened with the mayor saying a little piece about Sylvia, how everyone should say a prayer for her and continue to support the sport she loved. Jules stayed by the chute and tried to ignore the pablum. He actually smiled at Genie, probably the single most unnerving thing he could have done, and when Genie, who looked shaky anyway, began to screw up with the pull, he wandered through the grounds, looking dull-eyed at the steers, the hot dog buyers, the vaguely off-center weekend partyers, a little wobbly in the homestretch. The temperature was falling, and it looked as if it might rain; there was some comfort in sharing a mood with the weather.

Edie was there with her children and husband, and he saw Diane wander about with her camera, but he'd looked over the grandstand a few times before he saw Everett seated in the second row with his parents. It was a bit of a flashback—Everett wore the same trapped look he might have worn at high school games, when his parents insisted on sitting with him. He'd always hated them; no wonder he had mixed feelings about coming back.

The night began with the postponed bull riding, then segued into the regular schedule. When the exhibition women appeared wearing yellow ribbons, he buried his annoyance to concentrate on the breakaway, standing in the aisle of the grandstand near where he'd been when Sylvia had hit the fence the night before. He didn't see a thing to help him understand the horse's death.

At nine-thirty it was time for the big event. In Australia, kids could learn to rope with kangaroos; in Blue Deer, they could learn to ride on sheep. Jules usually loved such slapstick, but tonight he thought sourly that they were all up past their bedtime. The sheep had names like Steel Wool, Sweater, Coyote Killer, Woolite, Lanoliner, Shear Energy, Mint Jelly, and, improbably, Couscous, and planted child after child facedown in the dust within seconds. A few hung on to the rudimentary saddles until they were parallel to the dirt, and a couple had to be pried off by the exhausted clown; the winner, a four-year-old girl, lost her seat in the first few seconds but hung on to the tail for a full circle, a little like an extra in *Ben-Hur*.

The clown came out again, this time pulled by four sheep in a Radio Flyer made up to look like a motorized chariot, carrying some fireworks and dragging others. After four falls he settled down and arranged his shipment, then began a long gag about looking for the wicks, lighting the threads on his overalls by mistake, the wires on his vehicle, his hair. The winning mutton rider trotted back out, to be presented with a ribbon, some sparklers, and a Barbie Doll. The four-year-old stared at the doll as if it were a Martian, deeply offended, and the clown reacted to the moment of tension by asking her in mime if she knew how to light the sparkler.

She did, of course, but after that she wanted to show him how to light the rest, and the clown started to jump around in alarm. He pushed her away, and turned his back; as anticipated, the girl made a run for the fireworks again.

It was meant to be a joke, but it was a bad one, and Jules started to twitch at the vision of the small pudgy body approaching the rockets with a lighted sparkler. Maybe the clown was drunk; all the kid had to do was zig and dart forward. He looked up in the stands, wondering where the parents were, and found them, on their feet and screaming, right behind Everett's mother and father, whose son had his hands over his eyes.

The clown shooed the little girl, more forcefully this time, and having tired of his own joke, lit his fire stick. She'd already proven her tenacity, and lunged at him again, so excited that she didn't notice her sparkler was long gone. Jules started up the rail corral. The clown lurched and pushed the child backward again, yelling this time and dropping the firestick, and she finally broke into a scoot back toward the announcer's box. Jules started to reach back down with one foot, relieved, as the man leaned forward again, flicked his lighter on a wick, and held it there for perhaps a second, obviously nervous, looking over his shoulder for the girl's possible return. Jules looked up at the stands again, hoping the parents had headed to the announcer's box, and instead saw Everett leaning forward, biting his lip. Not to worry, thought Jules, turning back toward the clown and mystified by what looked like a pink cloud, confounded by the massive report that followed. The clown seemed to disappear and all hell broke loose as the fireworks blew into the dirt and toward the stands and the stock pens like a horribly patriotic and apparently endless missile attack. Jules vaulted the fence for the second night in a row, and hauled the howling clown away from the buzzing crater.

The rodeo crowd gave a large growl when the Wrangle committee president, an unpopular banker, announced that the bronc and bull riding finals might possibly be postponed. When he suggested, ten minutes later, that these events would definitely be postponed for another day, and likely never held, the growl steadied into a muted roar, and the grand finale fireworks, set to an amplified, very patriotic country song, didn't seem to dent their unhappiness. Jules, who had been searching the muddy crater in the center of the arena for remnants of the clown's fingers with Harvey, turned off their spotlight and sized up the situation. He radioed Jonathan, on his way back after delivering the two almost complete digits they'd found to the hospital, left Harvey at the arena, and headed for downtown.

The streets were quiet. Jules tried to think clearly, but all he came up with was a wild, tired mix of images, everything from *High Noon* to *The Blob*. He warned Delly, and the bartenders at the Baird, the Bank, the Bucket (formally the Bucket of Blood), Sister Suzie's, the Nugget, the Player, the Pour House, and Ernie's Moonlight Lounge, zigging between various establishments as the traffic grew louder and more raucous and the inexorable human swarm filled the streets.

Three men and a riot. Suddenly the idea that every bartender in town kept a baseball bat made Jules feel warm all over. Maybe they wouldn't pull out their shotguns. Blue Deer hadn't had a riot since the rodeo glory days of the mid-seventies. Jules couldn't remember the reasons behind the last one, but he thought it had been more good-natured than what he faced tonight, mostly because he'd been one of the people charging down streets, screaming, hurling objects, and feeling untold joy. In the early eighties, in New York, he'd been part of another riot, this one over the eviction of squatters from Tompkins Square Park, and he'd felt the same righteous giddiness right up until the moment a baton caught him on his thigh.

These memories were not helpful, and Jules was horribly aware of the ironies. For the next hour, during which time Harvey and Jonathan arrested three men at the rodeo grounds for assault and malicious destruction (of a rival's pickup), everyone downtown, or at least a troublesome core of twenty or so, seemed intent on drinking away the ugly mood, but the situation imploded at about ten. In a suddenly cool east wind two men from Idaho walked out of the Bucket and started whaling away at each other in the middle of Yellowstone Street. Friends brought out bar stools to watch more comfortably, and one of them—trying, ostensibly, to slow down the fighters—threw one of the stools through the plate-glass window of a menswear store. Someone else climbed through the window into the store, grabbed some clothes, and retrieved the stool, which they then used to shatter the windshield of a mint-condition Mustang.

Jules called in David Eaton and the water trucks. At about that time Peter asked him for a quote.

"Not now," said Jules.

Half an hour later he saw Peter take down an ugly specimen with a pool cue, apparently in reaction to someone spilling his drink. At about the same time Genie turned back into the Tasmanian devil, and Delly, with fiendishly clever and fitting placement, sprayed him with Coca Cola, right up his nose. A few minutes later he saw Alice and Edie and Lucy and the owner of the Baird slinging vegetables from one of the balconies. He saw Diane once, angling her camera with every hair in place. No one seemed to notice that it was forty degrees and raining. He saw Patrick Ankeny drive away, wiser than all of them.

It wasn't easy to slow down someone without doing damage to that person, or to yourself. Jules resorted to the sheer trickery of a soccer player, tripping, feinting, sliding, as the sleet gave way to snow; trying, given Absaroka County's finite handcuff stock, to talk people into going home once he had them pinned. At the outset, he'd told Harvey and Jonathan (the message was really meant for Jonathan) that he didn't want to see anyone so much as touch a gun. As a result, Jonathan took two people to the station, Harvey eight, and Jules passed on the other dozen who refused to hear reason. They didn't bother with stray window breakers, and concentrated on the true psychopaths, the people who showed signs of looking for tires to burn.

Jonathan ended up needing stitches on his forehead, which might have made Jules feel guilty about his gunfire ban if he wasn't sure somebody would have used the gun on its owner. Harvey was full of lumps but energized, as if he'd finally woken up, and wanted Jules to go to the truck stop for breakfast. Jules got him to take Jonathan, instead. He was coated in a mixture of soda pop, mud, and blood from his own minor scratches, and had lost his appetite.

At four A.M., having rousted the street crew to start on broken glass, and talked Mark Roseau, the Gardiner deputy, into baby-sitting what remained of the night, he drove home through the falling snow. It was almost dawn, and he saw a figure crouched on a curb at the Depot. Jules wanted to slide past but his conscience gave a last spasm, and he climbed wearily from the car.

He tapped the man on the shoulder, and the man slowly lifted his face, tears shining in a streetlamp. It was Everett, and even though Jules had thought he'd seen every possible expression on his placid, ivory face in the last few days, the sheer suffering he saw now took him back a step.

"What's wrong?" asked Jules finally.

"What's wrong?" said Everett. "Sylvia's wrong."

"Oh, Everett—"

"You don't understand. I *saw* it happen. Why would anyone live in a place like this?"

"For Christ's sake, we *all* saw it happen. And you and I've seen something like it happen a dozen times before."

He was silent for a long time, and Jules shifted impatiently in the cold. "Maybe you don't understand how I felt," said Everett. He stood up slowly and unsteadily.

"How you felt about what?"

"Sylvia."

He'd used past tense. Jules watched him rock on his heels.

"Maybe I don't," he said. "Why don't you explain."

Everett shook his head and crossed the street, headed for the Baird.

☆ 9 ☆

WELCOME TO THE WORKING WEEK

BLUE DEER BULLETIN

SHERIFF'S REPORT, WEEK OF JUNE 28—JULY 4

June 28—A report was received of two spooked horses heading through town toward the river. An officer responded but could not locate the horses.

An individual reported dead chickens in a parked pickup truck.

June 29—An individual reported seeing a woman park in front of a local business and letting three children out of her trunk. An officer responded but was unable to locate the woman.

June 30—Two individuals reported encountering a possible drunken woman. An officer responded and advised the woman was recovering from a stroke.

An individual complained about objects being flung from a downtown hotel roof. The caller was informed that a funeral was in progress.

July 1—A complaint was received of fireworks being shot off. An officer responded and discovered they had been shot off.

July 2—An individual requested a welfare check on a family member. An officer checked and discovered the relative was ill.

An individual reported a calf on a frontage road. The owner was contacted and said it happened about a hundred times, and that he no longer wanted the calf. An officer advised him that he was responsible for the calf's location anyway.

July 3—A report was received of boys lying in a puddle in an alley, blocking traffic. The boys were taken to the hospital for observation.

An individual reported that a man was pounding on her door and threatening to break her window. An officer responded and reported an intoxicated male, who was confused about addresses.

July 4—An individual complained about a possible violent situation. An officer responded and discovered a barbecue in progress.

An individual reported a group of magpies harassing a cat. An officer suggested she scare away the magpies or let the cat inside.

Complaints were received of havoc downtown. The county took on several unexpected guests.

On July 5, the day after a ninety-degree Independence Day that many people celebrated by being locked up, Jules woke to four inches of snow. This was impressive not so much because of the season—Montanans didn't store their sweaters in the summer—but because he'd only been asleep for three hours. By ten A.M. on that Monday two more inches fell, but by noon it had all been dissolved by sleet and the day's high of forty-two.

There was a thousand-page book about and by Montanans, called *The Last Best Place*. Jules had enjoyed reading most of it, but on bleak days he enjoyed the irony of the title even more. This was, after all, a state where the thermometer could drop seventy degrees in the space of a work shift, where the weather was the last true element of the wild west and frozen pepper plants brought grown gardeners to tears summer after summer. The more you tried to control the land, expected it to be reasonable, like Alice, the more skies whacked back at you. Jules had been born in Montana, and he loved the place, had picked it anew by returning after more than a decade of absence, but that didn't mean it was an easy place to live.

The land around Blue Deer was achingly beautiful, the landscape as a map of the soul, with long cold sadnesses and sudden, verdant, short-lived frenzies of happiness and new life. Some winters addled Jules; sometimes he thought he'd read too much Steinbeck as a kid, been inoculated with a purely fictional vision of pastures of heaven. He took perverse pride in the weather, adored boasting—albeit with no choice—about the highs and lows. It was a Blue Deer habit—in most other states acts of God were minimized, but here the pride taken was messianic, a wallow in the glory of extremes, all partaken in the whitest of white counties. If the East ever had a bad winter, Jules's sympathy goose was cooked with old New York girlfriends, who could sometimes be lured into visiting just to see the thermometer read minus forty from the safety of his bed.

Not that the weather was necessarily worse than that of other, more populous states. People in Montana made the sign of the cross when faced with humidity, and told stories about the dread bugs and reptiles and mass murderers of Florida and Alabama and California. When buildings blew over, they usually landed on grass. When midsummer hail shattered windows, the air that blew in was clean and free of killer bees. When the steering wheel froze in place and trees shattered in the winter, at least the sun was often out when it happened, as opposed to Minnesota and Michigan, which had bad restaurants, too, and much worse suicide rates.

It was only at certain times of the year, or when enduring certain people, that Jules's affection for the landscape turned bitter and made him want to lash out at all the idiotic, self-justifying romanticism aimed at packaging the state for investors and tourists. Jules, who'd grown up with family stories about hard winters, dead babies, and depression-era haying disasters, accepted some pioneer heroism, though his father had always been careful to puncture great-aunts' stories by comparing the suffering on the Crow, Blackfeet, and Flathead reservations. Jules had inherited his father's sarcasm (once, when he was ten and whined about being stuck with his older sister's bike, Ansel Clement had said, "Tell it to Anne Frank") and recognized the murky flip side of the last best place: Montana had gotten some of the last people to have the balls to move.

The state had received its share of bold lawmen and pretty English ladies and political and religious refugees and starving, canny northern Europeans with large families, but it had also been settled by the failures and outcasts of other areas and the immigrants too slow and tentative to have reached the richer lands of the eastern plains in time. The phrase "the last best place," currently twisted to evoke larger-than-life purple sunsets and the Marlboro Man, might as well have read "the last habitable place," then and now. Didn't anyone find it suspicious that Montana, indisputably beautiful, *had* been picked last? Who in their right mind wouldn't have preferred the climate of Napa Valley before the crowds arrived? As for warring natives, the army had been a lot faster to massacre for the cornbelt farmland of Iowa and Kansas and the gold of Colorado.

So there was nothing out of the ordinary with the lovely camping weather of July 5. The weekend's spasm of firework repair would give way to hypothermia treatments at the clinic, and even the town's seediest hotels would fill with soggy, traumatized vacationers. Most tourists would want to sue, brandishing mileage books and frostbitten fingers as if they were signed contracts for a Mediterranean cruise, but even New York apartment leases cited acts of God, and at five thousand feet in the Montana Rockies, July snow was as humdrum a disaster as a flood in Mississippi or a child losing an eye to a firework.

Not that the latter had happened, at least to his knowledge. Jules walked to the hospital early that morning for the sake of making footprints and having the cold flakes settle on his aching head, and was relieved to learn his colony there hadn't grown since he'd taken Jonathan and one of the rioters in for stitches a few hours earlier. The nurse on duty said that Sylvia's respiration and blood pressure had stabilized, great news he supposed, but a little like learning a terminal cancer patient had low cholesterol. They were lessening the morphine dose, because it depressed her breathing; Sylvia, as the nurse pointed out quietly, was past hurting. Jules peered through the open doorway but couldn't make himself sit next to her.

Richard Berko, a fifty-six-year-old ex-taxidermist from West Virginia, a taxi owner moonlighting as a clown, was lightly sedated and sleeping, his left hand a bear paw of gauze. His face was abraded, eyebrows and lashes and chest hair and fingers gone. He had some old bruises on his forehead, and in the aftermath of the riot, Jules could only imagine someone had tried to warm up on Richie, the likeliest candidate imaginable.

An eyelid flickered as Jules slid the chair toward the bed. Even without his makeup Berko looked like a clown. He could have been a ringlet-headed Marx brother but for the slack parchment face and yellowish brown eyes of tertiary alcoholism. That morning, Jules had described him to Peter as "kinda dun colored," trying to turn everything into a joke with some rodeo horse talk. Palomino and chestnut women, roan boys, and here he was again, with the candidate for the glue factory.

It wasn't Berko's fault he'd been blown up, though had the tiny sheep rider gone with him Jules would have found plenty of room for blame. Renee, Jules's favorite nurse during his own hospital vacation, had told him he was the clown's first visitor, and Jules soon understood why. Not that some whining wasn't called for. It was the way Richie Berko whined, the high keen, every sentence a nasal plaint. He claimed that no one cared enough, one way or the other, to want to do him harm, but the fact that he admitted this didn't make it any easier to listen to him. He'd never been married, never jilted anyone, owed no money, denied ever having been in a fight in his life. He was after all alive and theoretically sensate, at least compared to the woman down the hall. He had insurance, and he hadn't had to drive any of the July 4 drunks home. He could still be a clown; he could still drive a cab. He could eat, drink, make love if the man or woman existed who could bear him.

Jules didn't bring up any of this, but patiently took a list of Berko's neighbors, roommates, former business partners and clown compadres. When he backed out of the room he had eleven names, and not one of them was promising. Berko's loneliness was so thorough and so well deserved that Jules ached to charge from the hospital and marry the first woman he met, buy a round at the bar, procreate like a rabbit, and take up team sports again.

Two hours later, Jules and Harvey stood in front of the third fireworks stand, slush slowly settling on their shoulders. The owner was grumpy and hungover, with a visible welt showing through his thinning hair; most of the unsold fireworks were piled in boxes behind him. Harvey was holding up a one-inch flutter of colored paper, what was left of the suspicious-looking tube that hadn't matched those it was surrounded by.

"Recognize this pattern?"

"Are you joking?"

"What's your sturdiest tube?"

"Are you joking?"

Harvey gritted his tiny, pearly teeth. Jules had already given up and was searching the boxes. The owner sat on a bench and rubbed his head.

"Don't bother with those," said Harvey to Jules. "We're looking for something with at least nine tubes, each at least an inch across and eight inches long."

The owner giggled. Harvey and Jules both glared.

Fifteen minutes later they found a "Bozo Blaster" at the bottom of the box, a direct match to the scrap of paper. The uninterrupted pattern sported marching clowns, and Jules and Harvey both thought this over in a long, depressed moment of silence. "Any idea of how many of these you sold?" asked Harvey.

"Are you joking?"

Harvey laid the Bozo Blaster directly onto the man's sore scalp. The fireworks salesman blinked and Jules tried to keep a poker face while visions of lawsuits danced through his tired brain. "They're one of your most expensive, twenty-five bucks easy. You're the last stand on the way out of town, and you were closed most of last week. *I* brought my kids twice and you were closed both times. So I don't think you sold much, and I think you can try to remember."

"Maybe half a dozen, and no, I don't remember. Kids all look the same, parents all look the same."

"You think *we* look the same?" Harvey's voice dripped irony.

The man looked nervously at Jules, six-three, brown-haired and pale-skinned, and at Harvey, five-five, white blond and soft pink. "I'll think about it," he said. "I'll try really hard, but for now I need to rest."

Harvey had a burr up his butt and wanted to haul the guy in. No room, pleaded Jules: The jail had five cells, two of them hastily constructed in a concrete evidence locker the month before, when the need for additional human storage became apparent. On Sunday night and early Monday morning, sixteen men and three women had been stuffed into these spaces, and when Jules got in all but three were still sleeping soundly. The happy sleepers included a saddle bronc rider from Arkansas, a roper from California, a meth salesman from Toronto, two concession workers from Yellowstone Park, the owner of the local lube shop, a surly veterinarian, and other sundry citizens. The early risers included a self-important chamber of commerce employee, and though Jules could claim his early release was for the good of the town, it truly came down to not wanting to listen to the little bastard. Number two was Monica Monsanto, who'd been there several times that year, and who always became alert with fear for her children (whom she loved) several hours after arrival. Harvey had called her mother to stay with the grandchildren the night before, and since Jules had no lessons left to impart to her, probably never had had any, he let her go at six without a fine.

Number three was Genie, propped bleakly against a wall in the green-painted center cell. Jules dealt with the other two first, then opened the door before anyone else had woken. They walked silently to the coffee room. Genie was visibly shaking, and used two sugars and two creamers, but this was his only sign of self-pity. No whines all night long, according to Archie. Jules was impressed.

"What the hell happened?"

"Delly shot me up the nose with the pop hose."

"That came after you tried to take out the back bar. What got you rolling? You were working, everything was great, and all of a sudden you're breaking mirrors."

"Fucking rodeo job started everything." Genie fidgeted in his seat, looking like he wanted to cry. "Fucking horses."

"Why was this the start of anything?" asked Jules.

"Well, the lady got pancaked, for chrissakes. It was just the start of everything being whacked out," said Genie. "I saw them go through that chute, I saw her eyes figure she was fucked. It's a fine line, man. You're going great for a week and then *sppllaaaat.*"

The sound Genie made was a close approximation to the sound Sylvia had made hitting the corral fence. Jules poured more coffee in both their cups.

"I had to take something to even out after that," said Genie.

"Unhuh," said Jules.

"It's a prescription, man. You can check."

Jules kept his silence.

"Then the clown. Christ. Red shit blowing through the air. Fuck that."

"So I guess you decided to have a few drinks."

"Who wouldn't?" asked Genie. "Can't we go outside so I can have a smoke?"

"Nope. How'd it come down to Delly and the hose?"

"Weirdo in the bathroom." Genie smiled, bits of creamer gooing in his yellow-stained mustache. "I was going, and saw this guy was looking at me."

"That's it?" Jules remembered an incident on Genie's rap sheet and felt a migraine coming on.

"Well, yeah. I was all shook up anyway. Couldn't get zipped fast enough to catch him. You know, I saw the white light." Genie drained his coffee.

Boys will be boys, thought Jules. Homophobia rules. "So you thought it over and took out the back bar when you couldn't find him."

"Like I said, the guy *looked* at me," said Genie.

"Oh God," said Jules. "Take it as a compliment."

He let Genie go, and by the time he'd waved him out the door the complaints had begun to roll in. Four of the cells had been full before the riot, a backlog due to the fact that Deer Lodge, the state penitentiary, was packed and not accepting. That spring every jail in the state had banned smoking, and every waking rioter now seemed to need a hangover Marlboro. Harvey led them to the courthouse one by one, alphabetically, and the process seemed endless. By the time Peter arrived to cover the grand event for the *Bulletin* a second insurrection loomed, but things quieted down with such a sympathetic audience; when Peter finished, he and Jules toyed with the idea of what might happen if they slid a few dozen Twinkies between the bars. The kitchen was crowded with cops and lawyers watching arrest videotapes on the one machine, all of them giggling, and at noon, someone had the sense to order four pizzas.

At three in the afternoon the last bondable county guest, a Roto-Rooter specialist named Zellman, headed off to see the judge. Jules bypassed his own littered desk in favor of Harvey's, and gingerly fingered the bundle of pyrotechnic fun that had separated Richie Berko from his fingers. Harvey had taken it to pieces and labeled all the parts. It was easy to identify the remnants of the one aluminum tube that had held something special, probably an extra load of common gunpowder added at any time over the last week, since the stands opened. Richie Berko was a lucky guy, in a sense, but it was doubtful he'd look at it that way. Jules poked a shard of metal on the desktop and headed for his car.

The rodeo grounds were a wasteland of cold mud and manure and trampled bits of trash, abandoned but for a surly cleanup crew, a few steers, and a committee member or two. The sleet started again as Jules stripped off the crime scene tape. Harvey, who'd already scoured the site, had left behind a couple of beribboned stakes in the small crater, and assured Jules there was no point in looking for more fragments, and now he wondered why he had bothered coming. He looked around, hoping for an original idea, and saw a pair of barely pubescent identical twin boys, whose combined weight couldn't have been over 150, still lurking outside the chutes with two bedraggled horses and a sawhorse. Would Jules please let them ride? They were waiting to head back to Nevada until their dad "recouped some losses." They actually used that phrase; what could Jules say, especially since they helped him haul the clown's drum and firetruck from the arena?

The sleet let up again, and Jules sat on the arena fence with the chute rope and watched the boys bumble through an approximation of roping and cutting in the cold mud. The horses seemed especially huge and snorty with tiny riders. The boys didn't know what they were doing but the horses did, veering slightly to the right on the first charge past the sawhorse, neck down and pissed off; screeching to a stop when the rope hit dirt instead of wood. It took Jules another run before he began to pinpoint the sequence of what had gone wrong two days earlier, the way Sylvia's mare had veered left even before it had thrown its head back and collapsed. Something had been wrong from the beginning. It couldn't have been a stroke, and if it had been a heart attack the attack had already been in progress. He wasn't sure what difference it would finally make, but he wanted to know what had happened, and he was sick of waiting for other people to give him half-shit answers. Jules yelled at the boys, and said he wanted to show them how it was done.

He'd only ridden once in the last decade, and knew immediately he'd made a huge mistake. He cut some circles, trying to get used to the feeling of all those errant pounds moving beneath him. Then he decided to skip preliminaries and asked one of the boys to run the chute.

The horse's surge was a terrible, invigorating shock, and Jules had to ask for a second try. This time he not only focused on the angle of the wall but threw the loop at the right time, and when the gelding punched on the brakes Jules was out of the saddle and hitting the ground running, having momentarily forgotten the point of the exercise. He was so proud of himself, the kids and the half-dozen idle watchers so stunned, that he would have howled in happiness if he wasn't more confused than he'd been when he got on. How slowly could a heart attack kill? He'd figured out, at least, where Sylvia's horse had hit the fence, and was staring at a brown stain on the corral wood when he realized one person was still clapping, and looked up to see Peter.

"Hoka."

"Smartass," said Jules.

"I'm just checking out the scene of the crimes, too."

Jules kicked some mud off his black shoes. His uniform was covered with horse hair.

"Figure of speech," said Peter. "Right?" He looked tired and unhappy, a little past the humor of jailhouse interviews.

"Right." Jules climbed the fence and perched next to him.

"At least for Sylvia. This whole summer is turning into one long accident. I feel like a sports writer, trying to come up with new words for disaster. Her bad luck."

"Right."

"And the clown was more bad luck, an accident or a prank."

Jules sighed. "It would appear that one of the fireworks may have been modified. We'll have a little lab work done."

"What on earth was left to test?"

"Some cardboard and metal, and two detached joints."

Peter shuddered. "Doesn't it just come down to gunpowder?"

"Your basic Chinese, packed a little too tight or in aluminum. Or a dab of TNT or plastic."

"Some went missing from the Forest Service a couple of weeks ago, right?"

"Right."

"You know," said Peter, "your vocabulary was once considerable."

"Right." Jules smiled. "The tests will take a couple of days. Then you really should talk to Harvey, because he's a whiz at this. He was a pyromaniac as a child and his experience is coming in handy now."

"Hah," said Peter. "Harvey might have jaywalked once, but I bet that's the limit of his law-breaking."

"Hah," said Jules. "He burned down a barn and blew up a garage with a bunch of other kids. A year later there was the incident of the tractor gas pump, which blew a crater in his uncle's yard and started a thirty-acre grass fire. They sent him away to Pine Hills for six months."

"No shit?"

"No shit. We used to call him firefly because he was so little and white. And there wasn't anything random about it. He did a lot of research, probably got his only A in physics our sophomore year."

Peter lit a cigarette. Jules almost wanted one, anything for a change. "Of course he got to start over, like everyone else, so this isn't an area of excellence you can mention in the paper. And it's not like he's the only kid we're acquainted with now who blew up a mailbox."

Peter did not appreciate being teased and cocked an eyebrow. "Who?"

"Guess."

"Genie."

Jules snorted.

"You."

"Jesus," said Jules. "How late did you stay out last night? Everett Parsons."

Peter frowned. "Why would Everett want to blow up a clown?"

Jules sighed. "He probably wouldn't."

"Why think of Everett at all?"

"I don't know."

"You've got a problem with him. You've got an edge on."

Jules kept his mouth shut and rubbed his cold hands together. Peter smiled. "Take it out on the rioters. I've got to wrap up the story somehow, and I don't want to get into personal accounts of how my honey and her cousin threw water balloons."

"That's not why you're here," said Jules. "And I don't think you need anything more on the clown either."

Peter flicked his butt into the mud. "Is Sylvia going to die?"

"She's not going to wake up."

Peter looked toward the boys, who were still wrestling with their horses. "Just tell me," said Jules.

Peter pulled out another cigarette. "When she came to me on the day of Otto's wake she wanted advice on a new will. He was in her old one."

"Who got his share?"

"I think she was upping Hugh's chunk, but she didn't really say. She wanted to know how she might phrase a proviso."

"Keep going."

Peter sighed and reached for another cigarette. "She wanted to shift the proportionate shares among the people in her will, depending on how she died."

Jules stared.

"I don't know what she ultimately had in mind," said Peter hurriedly, "but I gathered that depending on her death, say if she'd died violently, someone would have lost out."

"Did you write the will or not?"

"No, or I'd have more details for you. She always used Biddle, but he was on vacation, and she had some questions, so she asked me. End of story."

"Do you know if she met with him?"

"She couldn't have," said Peter. "He was in Seattle for Ed's daughter's wedding."

Jules wished he'd gone to Ed's daughter's wedding.

"You can't plan a horse landing on someone," said Peter.

"I wouldn't have thought so," said Jules. "But maybe someone got lucky."

Jonathan, stitched up and looking awful, was trying to clean his desk instead of going home and getting some sleep. It was sweet, also pathetic, and Jules watched for a while before he interrupted.

"Remember that patent I asked you to call about?"

Jonathan shook his head.

"A snippet in the paper, some classifieds. One offering to buy or sell patented claims, and the others announcing the intent to patent."

Jonathan rubbed his neck, in obvious pain. "I remember calling. I know the one guy said it was his."

"The claim in the Crazies or the one in the valley?"

Memory dawned. "The valley. He didn't know about the other."

"Why didn't you tell me?"

"You didn't ask."

Fair enough. Jules slumped toward his own desk, but Grace dropped a note in his lap as soon as he sat down, before he could dial the phone. "They've called a meeting for tomorrow night. Scotti says be there or be dead. Also, the fairgrounds just called, wondering if they can rake the arena and clean up."

"I just left there and I took the tape with me," snapped Jules. "And I already knew about their goddamn meeting. Did Harvey send the fireworks to the lab yet?"

"I don't know when he would have had a chance," said Grace, piously, as if it were all his fault. The world was a snarl of loose ends, and anyway a confirmation that the fireworks had been extra explosive would only state the obvious. But another officer or two to make the calls and ask the questions would have come in handy, and he wondered if the mayor and his cohorts realized what kind of mood they'd have him in.

"Do you know if Nelson Henckle lives in Clyde City or Wilsall?"

"His kids went to Clyde."

Jules flipped through the white pages of the phone book, exactly twelve of them for the whole of Absaroka County. He found Henckle on Rock Creek Road. Jules remembered the place now: Kentucky-style paddocks, aspen-lined gravel avenues and a roofed arena. Subdivision profits at work.

He worked his way through two of Henckle's patronizing employees before he got the man himself.

"I *told* you I was getting an autopsy," he said, surly and patronizing. "I just bought that mare this March, and she was expensive, and if something was wrong with her when I bought her, I want my goddamn thirty grand back, plus the charge for having the vet school look at her poor stupid carcass."

Horseflesh had gone up in price since Jules had last wanted to be the Lone Ranger. These days he felt more like Tonto. "How soon will you hear back?"

"A week or so. Why the hell do you care? Is Hugh gonna sue me? Sylvia's little bankers?"

"I'm curious," said Jules, wondering why people were so relentlessly mean-spirited lately. Maybe guilt. "Did that mare have any funny habits? Veer one way or another?"

"For thirty grand?" Disgust oozed over the phone line.

"Did you notice anything right before the run?"

"That horse was fine until she dropped. We're talking a goddamn heart attack and I want to know if it was congenital. She was more than ready to go. I've never seen her start so hard."

"Was she scratched up at all? Bleeding?"

"What?"

"Never mind," said Jules. He hung up and called the vets at Montana State, and sweet-talked them into adding a couple of toxicological tests to Henckle's bill and sending him a copy of the report first.

The weather was shit, and maimed people littered his fair town. Jules's reaction was to want a real dinner. He'd bought groceries a few hours earlier while checking on a shoplifting at the supermarket, and now he dropped the bag on the counter and discovered that Fat Fred had thrown up over much of the kitchen floor. Moe hurled abuse on Jules as he crawled along, cleaning it up, and continued to jabber as he cooked and started washing two weeks' worth of dirty coffee mugs. A year or two earlier, cat vomit would have revolted him past appetite, but he'd seen too many truly horrible messes since then to be fazed.

Moe talked on, most of it gibberish, but this night Jules imagined, while he did the dishes, that the phrases were Portuguese or Swahili or Finnish. He couldn't pretend that they were your basic romance language. *Don tawori odo. Watta battamine. Askan kenni.* Some lines sounded Slavic, others distinctly African, via Berlin or Stockholm. Maybe Moe hadn't been born in a pet store in San Diego, as was most likely, but on a smooth, slow tributary of the Amazon, where life wasn't quite pristine but still pleasant. Perhaps he'd scammed scraps between fat blood-laden tropical bugs, old avocado salads and mango and the occasional rock shrimp, from what passed as the local fancy restaurant. Perhaps he'd shat on the heads of tourists, just as Jules would love to train him to shit on the city council and county commissioners now. At least the tourists spent money and actually enjoyed what they woke up to, as opposed to the mayor and Donald Parsons, who were too proprietary about their concrete to glance out the window.

Jules opened his freezer and reached past the apple core for an ice cube, then smelled burn and hurriedly flipped both chicken thighs. Moe continued his monologue, and Jules kept trying to ascribe meaning to the squawks. It reminded him of trying to decipher song lyrics. He should call Alice and hold up the phone; she was the queen of this, having once been convinced that the lyric "solar sex panel" was actually "soul-sick sparrow." Afterward she'd argued convincingly that both were equally unlikely.

Jules plated his meal and sat. *Don tawori odo.* Moe wasn't a dog, but he had his points; he tended to get excited when people ate, which was pleasantly weird and hadn't happened much lately. Now he'd started the cycle over again, beginning with the Hawaiian-Italian phrase. He sounded just like Sylvia, suddenly, instead of like a man, and Jules wondered what Otto's voice had been like. He couldn't remember, but then Moe kicked into his West African song again, as if to remind him.

Jules forgot about dinner and fed Moe a strawberry. Moe cackled and said *mine.* He said it five more times with each bit of strawberry before he burst into *watta battamine* again. Jules scratched his crooked jaw, feeling like a movie character, hot on a shallow clue. Parrots didn't speak toddler, or chimp. They weren't supposed to reorder or maim grammar to their own devices, they were supposed to *parrot,* perfectly, what had been said. And no one had said *watta battamine* to Moe. *What's mine* maybe; *what about mine,* possibly. *Don tawori odo* and *askan kenni* where still completely inexplicable. Jules rooted through his scary refrigerator and surfaced with a half-fermented grape. Moe spouted again, the same phrase but with *sweetie* at the end of it, and now Jules understood the extra word.

What about a mine, sweetie? said Jules.

Don't worry, Otto, said Moe, singsong and soft. *Ask Ankeny.*

The bird and the sheriff stared at each other. "I think I've gone over the edge," said Jules, finally. "Your brain is the size of this grape. Or smaller."

"Don't worry, Otto," said Moe, again.

Jules ate his dinner.

An hour later, after a long conversation with an old friend in New York, the phone rang again just as he climbed into bed, and he found it under a pile of muddy clothes in the corner of his bedroom, left over from the night Sylvia was hurt.

It was Renee, from the hospital. "We have a problem," she said. "Jonathan's already here, but I can't reach Horace, and we could use you."

Jules retraced his path of the morning at a faster pace, and reached the parking lot in time to see Jonathan's taillights speeding away. Three people were crying in the waiting room around a pile of religious-looking pamphlets, and the harried receptionist pointed down the hall. "Renee's putting out fires," she said. "We had a little faith healing incident."

Out in the hall Renee nearly knocked him down as she ran past him toward Sylvia's room, where someone was wailing. Jules accelerated, feeling an odd relief, but when he came through the door everything was the same except that Hugh and Everett and Diane were there, and Hugh was pulling out his hair, and tugging on Sylvia, whose machines beeped just as relentlessly as before. Renee shoved Hugh into a chair and adjusted some tubing, and when Hugh popped forward again like a windup toy Jules collared him.

"I saw her move," said Hugh. "The man ripped out a wire and her hand moved. You're asking me to decide whether to give her food or not, and she moved."

Jules gave Hugh a gentle push and he settled back into the chair, exhausted. Everett, pale and agitated, paced, and Diane left the room. It seemed a man from Nevada, an "Apostle of the Holy Triumvirate," had given the patients and visitors a megaphone lecture on miraculous recovery, the laying on of hands, and the evils of science. Every last patient in the building was being murdered by machinery, and he was there to do something about it. Then he started ripping out I.V.s and hauling people from their beds, until Jonathan arrived and used his recent riot experience to bring an end to the experiment.

Now Renee concentrated on Hugh, and spoke patiently of muscle spasms, tightening ligaments, the CAT scans and other tests, the deep falling dream still moving through the cerebellum, so that the body jerked in fear without knowing what falling or pain meant anymore. She didn't put it that way, but that was how Jules imagined it as he tried not to look directly at Hugh. When she finished he followed her into the hall, and behind them he heard Everett comfort Hugh, and repeat everything Renee had said.

"It's hard enough to die without this sort of shit. He screamed at the visitors, told them they were killers, said they just had to have faith."

"I can't imagine Hugh really believing she'd wake up," said Jules. But even as he spoke he realized that Hugh was the kind of intelligent man who never quite caught up with real life, who might spin his wheels indefinitely in some sort of confused middle ground of hope. It was the kind of mindless optimism that made making movies and resorts possible.

"You'll let us know the minute that jerk gets out, right?"

"I won't let him out," said Jules, wondering where the current cell population stood. It would be so much easier to kneecap the asshole and put him on a bus for California. "Did Jonathan do well?"

"Jonathan was great," said Renee. "When you *have* to let that shit out of jail, he can watch the door." Renee patted him on his hip, hitting the Beretta he'd stuffed in his jeans pocket instead of anything more meaningful, and spun off toward the nurse's station.

"You know her, I guess," said Diane.

She was sitting on a bench against the wall on the other side of Sylvia's doorway, wearing a sky blue miniskirt and no stockings. "I do," said Jules.

"Personally or professionally?"

None of your business, he thought, but she was smiling at him. "Both. She was my nurse last month."

"Ah," said Diane. "Men and nurses."

Ah, thought Jules. Men and amoral blondes.

"When I was a little girl I intended to be a nurse," said Diane. "But eventually I recognized I lacked compassion."

Jules snorted. At least she'd realized it in time, before a child with cancer or an eighty-year-old with a broken pelvis had to endure her indifference. When he saw Renee now, he understood that few things were more intimate than the bare skin of a woman's arm as she propped you up to pee in a dish or rolled you over to change a dressing. He'd seen more than Diane's arm.

Diane lounged against the wall. Inside the room, Everett murmured on.

"I've been wondering why I'm here."

"I believe you're supposed to be photographing the local color."

"I can get work anywhere," said Diane, stretching her legs. "It was time to check on the sweet idiot."

"Is he really such a mess?" Everett was telling Hugh that he was lucky to have been loved, and lucky to love a woman who'd die doing exactly what she liked doing.

"Everett's already insane. This isn't helping."

A brain-dead woman. What an inconvenience. "He's doing pretty well tonight, better than the last few. I thought he was going to faint when the clown was shooing the little girl away."

"He wet his pants in grade school, too. He's never been able to handle anticipation."

"You've known each other how long? A decade?"

She smiled sadly at him and he noticed how cold and pale her eyes were, no matter the expression she willed them to show. "At least. It's the first time he's asked me to keep an eye on him, though. I've never seen him so bad. Quitting his job, being around his parents. It was a bad idea."

They fell silent and watched Renee lead a very pregnant woman in a winter parka toward maternity. A hand fell on Jules's shoulder. "I'd like to buy you a drink," said Hugh.

"Sure," said Jules.

They ended up at the Baird. Two hours later Hugh was still talking, now explaining why he'd moved from Los Angeles. Jules hadn't asked for explanation; the thing spoke for itself, and it didn't seem like a good time to introduce the topics of talking parrots and mining. "I wanted to get out of there. I wanted to be with her, because she made me feel wonderful. Just wonderful. I know it sounds trite, but it's true. I told her once, as an excuse, that I had a bad feeling about California, and she loved to tease me about that. Look at me now, what do I really have? No children, a job that bores me profoundly, no real home, a lover being held together by machines who can't tell me how to live anymore. What on earth . . ."

Hugh stopped and stared out a small window, his body sagging on the stool. There was a fine line between the kind of young Englishman who was gold and peach and handsome and the middle-aged man who looked like a boozy bulldog. Hugh had just crossed over, like Winston Churchill before him. Jules stacked quarters on the counter.

"Do you understand?" asked Hugh, after a minute. "A month ago I loved my life, and now I don't want it anymore. I don't want to build a fucking resort. I don't want to make a goddamn movie. I want to go to sleep and have it all disappear."

Jules understood. He looked down the bar. Everett, the human yo-yo, and Diane, the woman without a smidgeon of normal human guilt, were talking. Everett was staring at a waitress, and Diane was telling him that something, presumably the waitress, was his civic duty. "It'll do you a world of good." Everett had downed two double vodka and tonics in quick succession on arrival and listened to her with a daydreamy, bright-eyed look on his face that was familiar and dread-inspiring. There didn't seem to be a rule of thumb for how many drinks it took him to reach that point, and Jules couldn't tie it in to suspicious tablets, trips to the bathroom, the presence of anyone in particular. Perhaps he was having a strange reaction to hay fever medication. Diane's blank look when Everett moved off doubled his unease. If Diane was worried about Everett, everyone should be.

Peter and Alice were at the Baird, too, and though Jules could tell they'd rather not have company, they could hardly ignore Hugh, the man with a true reason to be unhappy, even if he'd begun to rant.

Now the topic was bad luck, listing everything that had gone wrong in real estate and life.

"Don't forget the first two wells you dug and the septic bid," said Everett morosely.

Hugh shook his head sadly. "The landslide taking out the road."

"And then the mixer nearly killed Sylvia."

"Yeah, I threw the gizmo away," said Hugh. "It was a juicer. Shoddy Japanese piece of shit. Healthy my ass."

"What'd it do, attack her?" Alice was leery of appliances.

"Shorted," said Hugh. "Burned her pretty little arm." He drained another glass. "If we'd made it to the wedding, there'd have been an earthquake."

"No," said Jules without thinking. "Weddings always go well."

Everett was amused. "How would you know? Everyone but you has tried it once."

Jules looked at him in astonishment. "When'd you fit that in?"

"Somewhere between his first two breakdowns," said Diane quietly.

"Now, sweetness," said Everett, "don't be getting hard on me." He turned to Jules. "Wasn't that a line from a play we had to read? 'Diana is hard, but sometimes her bosom goes cloudy'?"

"I can't recall," said Jules. He nodded toward the door Peter and Alice had just disappeared through. "Peter and Alice aren't married."

"They live it. They just don't like to admit it."

Jules heard a small sound and turned back toward Hugh, who'd covered his face with his hands.

"Tears in his beer," said Everett, looking out of his element in a T-shirt. "Let's pick up the tempo here. You clean out your jail yet, Jules?"

He patted Hugh on the back. "Just about."

"Rodeo boys," said Everett, snapping his fingers at the bartender. "They just keep bouncing up, but the smart ones die. You used to do it, too, didn't you, Jules? What'd you ride, Jules, anything?"

Jules turned to him. Everett might as well have been wearing a neon light for a hat, flashing *mood change, danger*. He was too tired for such shit. "Pretty much, Everett."

"Horses, bulls, a little bit of everything?"

Jules barely nodded. At least Hugh had stopped crying, and was peering down the bar.

"Just last night Diane was humming a song about bull riders. You know that song, Jules?"

Jules met Diane's eyes. She looked away first. "Yes, I know it."

Diane picked up her bag. "Everett, if you're going to be an asshole, I'm going to leave."

"Diane," said Everett softly, "I'm going to be an asshole. Go away."

They watched her go. Everett slapped the bar. "God, I feel like a local, again, a native."

Hugh snorted. Jules ran through escape options. He felt badly for Hugh, but could only take so much.

"Loco?" said Hugh. "Enunciate."

"Local," said Jules. "But it means the same thing if you say it in a bar."

"I'd love to be a local," said Hugh, smiling.

"It doesn't have to be a near-death experience, no matter what Everett says."

Everett stared. Jules smiled back.

"I should never have left," said Everett.

"You know as well as I do you have to leave to know what you like." Jules sorted his dozen crumpled dollar bills. "You wouldn't have a clue otherwise. You'd be tribal, like your dad, and you'd hate it."

"I've only been back a week and I already hate it," said

Everett. "You're so goddamn earnest, you believe everything everyone says. How're you gonna bop Little Miss Strange again if you sound like that?"

Carefully, thought Jules, beginning to feel annoyed at Diane for fleeing the sinking ship. "Why make a big deal about a visit home? If you enjoy it, admit it. If you hate it, get another job. Shit or get off the pot."

"Enjoy, bullshit," said Everett, struggling toward a milder mood. "You have to own, and people like us don't. To belong to it, it has to belong to you."

"How much land does a man need?" muttered Jules.

"Tolstoy," said Hugh.

"Turgenev," said the bartender, delivering another round. He spent every winter reading thick novels stacked between the bottles.

"Fuck all of you," said Everett, looking weepy. "He needs enough to make him happy."

"He needs enough for his grave," said Hugh, looking away.

"It's the only way I'll own a nice view," said the bartender. He looked up at Hugh. "Nothing personal."

"Not to worry," said Hugh. "I wouldn't have a pissing acre if it weren't for Sylvia."

It seemed to Jules that none of them, as white males making more than twenty grand a year, had much of a reason to bitch. But he kept his mouth shut, because Everett's concept of fairness was quite obviously different from his, and probably had been since birth.

"Here's my theory," said Everett, raising his voice and settling snugly on his stool for a speech. "To be local, to stay here, whether you own any of this shit land or not, you must be stupid, dumber than a box of rocks. Wind, rattlesnakes, trailer homes, ugly shirts, and big white asses." He cocked an eyebrow at Jules. "Tell me why I'm back here. Tell me why you're back here. Small hat sizes, that's why. The lights are on but no one's home. We're night-lights instead of three-way bulbs. We're, we're, we're . . ."

The bar, collectively, sized him up, ranching men and pool-playing women estimating the strength of opinionated bones.

"Shut up, Everett," said Jules.

"Just give me another phrase for stupidity."

"One too many times through the gene splicer," said Jules. "Swinging on a family tree with no branches."

Everett gave him a foul look. His parents had been second cousins. He pointed toward a corner. "Look at that guy. He looks like he's never been in a room with ten lightbulbs before."

"That guy," thankfully, was playing pinball, and the only human in the room who wasn't fascinated by the mess playing out at the bar.

"All this interest in light, Everett," said Hugh mildly. "Maybe you should try a new career."

"We're . . . How do you say *c-o-y-o-t-e*, Hugh?"

"*Kiiyoteeee*," said Hugh, drunk enough, fascinated enough, to be obedient.

Everett leaned forward until his mouth was two inches from Hugh's recoiling ear. "*Ki-yote*, you dumb Brit cocksucker. Think *buy* boat. For me. Now." He giggled. "Where'd you get coyoteeeee? Loony Tunes? Your fantasy life? You think you can *live* in this town and say it that way?"

Hugh's eyebrows were near his scalp. This was probably not how he'd intended to wind down from Sylvia's hospital bed. Everett patted his employer's head and Jules stiffened.

"How do you say *c-r-e-e-k*, Hughie?"

Hugh finally put his beer glass down. "I say *creek*, Everett. Like *meek*. How do you say it?"

Everett howled with laughter again. "I say *crick*, you *prick*!"

Hugh was still on his stool, but Everett, after one small popping sound, was now on the floor. Hugh drained his beer. Blood flooded from Everett's mouth, but he had the happy smile of a blissed-out infant. He actually gurgled with laughter, eyes shut, then fell quiet.

"He has what you'd call a character change problem when he's under the influence." Hugh dabbed at his forehead with a bar napkin and peered at the bartender. "A round for the bar's patience, please."

Jules sighed in the blessed silence. "What's his room number?"

"Let the twit lie," said Hugh. "He's been complaining about his back, anyway. The floor may help."

"Sadly," said Jules, "I'm the sheriff. I may be off duty, but I don't get to sit in a public place drinking with a bleeding man on the floor next to me."

"I can," said Hugh. "My patience has been sorely tried this last week or so. I believe Everett should seek psychiatric help."

"I believe you're right," said Jules, climbing down from the stool and chugging his water.

"Perhaps you could recommend somebody. I'd be happy to pay."

"I'll look into it. The room?"

"Four-o-eight. Sorry to have created more trouble."

"Somebody was going to do it," said Jules. "You've got quite a snap there."

"Thanks," said Hugh. He smiled. "I used to want to kill people all the time. Now I stick to beer. Everett would do well to note my example."

They looked at each other for a beat before Jules bent, pulled one of Everett's arms over his back, and hoisted him up. He was in the lobby before it occurred to him that Everett had had no response at all to movement, and when he flopped him on the couch he checked his pulse.

"That tickles," said Everett, with his eyes still closed. "Stop it."

"Asshole," said Jules.

Edie was watching him, packing up her stuff at the end of her shift. "Everett needs to go to his room," said Jules.

"I can see that," she said icily. "You're back to your old habits."

"I didn't hit him," said Jules.

Her expression was dubious. "I'll call Diane."

"She'll need help."

"No, she won't."

Jules turned, pointing; maybe they were discussing two different people. But Everett was sitting on the edge of the couch with the straight posture of a tea-party attendee, his eyes bright again and smile cheery, though there was the small problem of the drying rivulet of blood running from his mouth into his collar.

Jules turned back to Edie. She almost looked sympathetic, but not quite. "I'll call her," she said.

Jules waited. Diane, true to character, took her time, and it was ten minutes before Jules heard the tap tap of her stilettos on the open marble staircase. By then Everett was snoring.

"Can you help?"

So much sarcasm in three words. "Sure," said Jules.

She turned to Edie. "I'd appreciate the elevator, if it's not too much for you."

Ick, thought Jules. He met Edie's eyes, and then Diane's. It was safe to say that none of them liked each other at that moment, but they crammed the lobbyist into the manual elevator and Edie slammed the glass door and the metal grate. Diane hummed, and Jules stared at the skin on the back of Edie's neck, watched her overshoot the floor and slam the lever back in place. She stood to one side as Diane waltzed past and Jules dragged Everett out, pulled the grate shut behind them, her eyes holding Jules's for a moment before she descended from sight.

Jules dumped Everett onto his single bed and walked out into the hallway. Diane's adjoining door was still open, music playing. She was sitting by the window in a rocking chair, the last person he would have expected in such a pose.

Jules opened the door of his dark house at four, climbed the stairs, stripped, and wrapped himself in a goosedown comforter. He dozed for an hour, then gave up and headed back to the kitchen. The sky was just lightening and he flipped back Moe's blanket.

"Welcome home, fuckface," said the parrot.

"I'm feeling smart," said Jules.

"I'd like a berry, ma'am," said Moe. "Hubba hubba."

BLAME IT ON CAIN

WRANGLE WEEKEND MARRED BY ACCIDENTS
  BAD FIREWORKS MAIM CLOWN
  23 ARRESTED IN SUNDAY NIGHT RIOT

No progress has been reported in determining the cause of the accident visited upon Richard X. Berko, 56, the rodeo clown who was injured in an arena explosion Sunday night. Deputy Harvey Meyers of the Absaroka Sheriff's Department told the *Bulletin* that the possibility exists that the fireworks were tampered with, and an investigation is ongoing. Mr. Berko is a patient at Blue Deer Memorial, where a spokesman announced today that doctors there had been unable to reattach four of the fingers on Mr. Berko's left hand.

Four, thought Jules. Imagine that. How about that opposable thumb. He also liked the inference that such a feat might have been possible. Horace, who'd been in Vietnam, said he'd rarely seen such itsy-bitsy pieces.

Sylvia Coburg, injured in a separate Wrangle accident on Saturday night, is listed in serious but stable condition at the hospital. Doctors there previously described her head injuries as "grave." Ms. Coburg's misadventure resulted from the sudden death of her horse during the team roping. The mare's death has been ascribed to heart failure pending further tests.

Unrest on Sunday night, termed a "minor riot" by Sheriff Jules Clement, resulted in a total of 23 arrests, with 18 individuals being held overnight. By this afternoon, all but two had made a plea or been freed on bond. Sheriff Clement offered no explanation for the unrest beyond "alcohol," but likened the situation to college students pulling down goalposts. "Almost everyone we dealt with last night deserved their own padded room, but unfortunately we only have five cells," he said.

Jules, twitchy with caffeine and light years past common fatigue, was reading Monday afternoon's paper on Tuesday morning because he hadn't gotten around to it the night before. Both Harvey and Jonathan had worked overtime throughout the weekend and had the day off; Jules was all alone, trapped in the station for the day, and the world was an unfriendly place. He stared out on the cold gray landscape, his eyelids grainy, morale at a new low even though the year had accustomed him to feeling like dogshit. He rubbed his eyes, and this brought on a pink blur like that of Berko's disappearing fingers, and pink blurs brought him back to the way he had celebrated the traumatic weekend with Opal Diane Meek.

Here he was, lurching toward midlife and losing sleep with someone he didn't particularly like. Jules didn't mind acknowledging mistakes, but forgetting about them was preferable. This was especially difficult when you repeated the mistake in question. On the other hand, his mood had called for something, and they were both adults with a sense of humor, and this wasn't going to be another case of diminishing expectations.

"Yuck," said Jules aloud.

"Yes?" said Ed.

Jules jumped. "What are you doing here?"

"I came back a day early to make up for my inconvenient vacation."

Jules brought his head down on his desk in sheer relief, then gave Ed a big hug before he filled him in and left to complicate Patrick Ankeny's professional life.

Ankeny was so cheerful and bright-eyed Jules hardly recognized him.

"I told you, I can't remember anything about Otto's last dropby."

"You weren't able to remember that day, but now you look pretty rested up."

"More than I can say for you."

"Thank you," said Jules. "Now think."

"By the way, are you really seeing that blond woman?"

Sometimes I shut my eyes like a good American boy, thought Jules. "Don't ask."

"Didn't she used to be with Everett?"

"Different terms, these days."

"Huh." Ankeny looked dubious. Jules sympathized. "Well, Otto came in midmorning or so—"

"You know Everett?"

Ankeny looked startled. "I knew both of them. Of course, Everett usually skipped me, went for the big guns, friends in high places. Made all of our lives faster."

Jules backed up. "Did Otto Scobey ever ask you any questions about mining?"

"Actual extraction?" asked Ankeny.

In hindsight the comment was dry; at the time, Jules simply thought it over literally. "I don't know, but the questions wouldn't have been philosophical."

"Patents," said Ankeny. "He asked me questions about patents. You want my full, recovered memory? He came a couple of times, once back in May, and then the last time I saw him. You just asked me about the last. The first time he wanted to know about outstanding claims on the property, what its history was."

"What could you tell him?"

"I said he could go digging in a lot of dusty places through a lot of dusty maps, or he could make his life simpler by just asking his wife. I mean, the private sections in the checkerboard have always been in her family." Ankeny was sorting papers efficiently between three trays, and Jules wished he'd consider a career in law enforcement. "See, I thought they were still married, and I felt bad as soon as I gave this advice, because he obviously didn't like it. And anyway, he wanted to know about the old public land, too."

"Why did you think he didn't like it?"

Ankeny shrugged. "Didn't want to take the short cut and ask her."

"Why do you think he wanted to know, to begin with?"

"Probably thought he found something. They all think they've found something, even people like Otto who should know better. Or maybe he just wanted to be safe about the trade land. The state isn't any more reliable than a bad realtor—there could have been chunks of private land in there, buildings, holy land covenants, anything."

Jules was offended. "My mother worked for the service for thirty years, and I can tell you they knew what was private and what was public most of the time, and if they couldn't they sent up a surveyor."

Ankeny looked amused. "You think we have the staff to keep the last hundred years' worth of claims and patents clear? There's something like twenty thousand mining claims in the Gallatin. The best the rock guys can do is try to make sure the new ones are free and clear, that we actually own the land we're giving away. And not counting the cabins we rent out, there's another few dozen standing buildings in there, and a lot of them were built on claims. What if Dragonfly got their condos built and found out after the fact that someone owned twenty feet of a duplex?"

Jules grinned.

"Now, the last time he came in he just wanted to make copies, like I said. He had a map and a list of claim numbers. I didn't pay him much attention because I was packing for the experimental burn."

"No questions?"

"Just on procedure, claims to patents, stuff like that. How long it took. Otto was a pro at water and timber, but he didn't have a clue about rocks."

Jules pulled out the map from the files Otto had left behind, with the yellow-marked claims. "Was this the map he had? Can you help me track down these locations?"

"Aren't Otto's Xeroxes around? He was at the copier all afternoon."

"No," said Jules. "They're not in his files."

Ankeny started to ask a question, then thought better of it. He led Jules through a metal door in the back of the office, into a warehouse and through a warren of dusty cabinets. He jerked open a drawer. "Do you want to read through all of these?"

"I'm a little short on time," said Jules.

Ankeny shrugged. "We'll just Xerox the rough application then. That'll give you locator names, corporations if they're not filing as individuals."

"Thanks," said Jules.

"That's okay," said Ankeny. "By the way, I started in the Blue Deer office. Your mother hired me, and she always said you were a pain in the ass."

Jules came away with all twenty-two patents and claims Otto had marked within the Dragonfly territory. Four dated back to the 1870s and three from the 1930s, the last time prospecting might have seemed like a real economic option; one had belonged to Sylvia's grandfather, and would have come to her with the rest of the estate. The other fifteen all dated two years earlier, and were split between four names, apparently a loose association of locators. Two, Hazel Lyon and Ian Dillingham, listed a Boston address, and the others—Bartholomew Stinson and Nicholas Thalt—gave an apartment on West Fifteenth Street in Manhattan. Information listed none of them, and the whole process had taken another four hours out of his life.

He decided to put a bad mood to his advantage. Everett's car was in the Baird lot, parked next to Edie's. Screw all of them, thought Jules, slamming the door of his squad car. Everyone's worst nightmare, a depressed Swede. But he took the back door into the bar, to save her the pain of seeing his face.

Climbing the Baird stairs helped sharpen his funk. He pounded on Everett's door and heard a dull moan from within. He'd guessed right, and kept pounding.

"Long time no see," said Everett grumpily. "Thank you for the visit." His lip was dark blue, the size of a roll of Lifesavers.

Jules couldn't openly blame Everett for two murders, but he could hold him responsible for a good deal of personal physical discomfort. He took the direct approach of kicking the boy while he was down.

"Why did you tell me you didn't know Patrick Ankeny?"

"The guy at the Forest Service?"

"See what I'm talking about?" said Jules.

"I can't remember every pencil pusher, every day," said Everett. "Maybe I was drinking."

"What the hell would be new about that?"

Everett cinched his robe. "One lush to another, right?"

"Why would Otto check out mining claims to Dragonfly?"

"Do you think I'm psychic?"

"What day did you say the moving van picked up your stuff in Boulder?"

"What?" They stared at each other. "Are you going to keep this up for a while?" asked Everett.

"Maybe," said Jules.

"I'll dress then."

Everett disappeared into the bathroom. Jules walked to the window and saw Hugh crossing the street from the post office to the Blue Bat, probably after another wonderful visit to the hospital. All of them were candidates for a month's supply of grapefruit juice. He turned back to the room and quietly poked around. Neat and tidy, like one fraction of its guest's personality, silver-framed snapshots carefully arrayed on the bureau. Some children, probably nieces and nephews, but nothing of his sisters or parents. One of Everett and friends and a lot of pine trees, probably from Dartmouth, and a photo of Diane, her hair already bleached but looking much younger, posed with another girl on a beach. Maybe it was the mystery wife. Jules bent closer but saw nothing interesting in the bland, button-nosed face.

It made Jules remember a suicide's room, and he felt a jolt of fear. The shower stopped and he found a chair, and sorted quickly through a pile of magazines. He wasn't up to Everett's favorite political rags, and opted for *Playboy*. While Everett whistled and sounded rejuvenated, Jules took in the Playmate's likes (hot chocolate, midnight swims, and poetry) and dislikes (violence, cold weather, and shallow people; Jules started to giggle at this point) and marveled over her incredibly recent birthdate. Talk about not remembering the moon landing.

When Everett came out Jules grilled him for half an hour, pretending to not notice that Everett needed coffee in a desperate way. Everett, typically, pretended not to need any.

Even with Ed around, it wasn't the kind of day that allowed for a nap. At six o'clock Jules wandered down the courthouse stairs, expecting to meet several other battered, overworked public servants in the basement meeting room on the other side of a cinderblock wall from the county jail. During silent chunks of particularly tense meetings in the past, Jules had been able to hear the clank of a cell, Archie removing dinner plates. There were three such rooms, in which Absaroka County's citizens could be tested for a driver's license every other Wednesday, or attend Lamaze and First-Aid and Defensive Driving classes and cow-calf seminars or meet as part of Trout Unlimited, the library board, Big Brothers and Sisters. There were dozens of other socially responsible options in a given month, even in a town the size of Blue Deer: Weight Watchers, Alcoholics Anonymous and Al-Anon, Alateen, Sexaholics Anonymous, Overeaters Anonymous, the Battered and Formerly Battered Women's Support Group, La Leche League, the Bird Club, the Historical Society, the chamber of commerce, the hospital board, People Concerned About Those with Disabilities, the Absaroka County Economic Development Committee, the Absaroka County Environmental Council, the Ministerial Association, the Business and Professional Women's Group, and the Pioneers Club (with half its members still first generation).

Instead the room was empty, and Scotti and the mayor and Donald Parsons blocked the doorway. They didn't seem happy with life in general. Everett's father was dressed in golf clothes, despite the bad weather, and probably regarded a frigid July 6 as yet another public relations disaster, equal to, if not greater than, two murders and the coma of the Historic Society's and fair committee's biggest booster. Donald Parsons gave Jules a dirtier look than usual, and this took Jules aback.

"I thought there was a meeting," said Jules. "Where are the other commissioners?"

"There was supposed to be one," said Scotti grumpily.

"We must have given Grace the wrong impression," said the mayor, his bristly gray hair shining with sweat. "Donald's here to represent them. We just need to have a little chat, at some nice place. Everyone could use a drink, don'tcha think?"

Jules found himself not wanting one for the first time in twenty years. Fifteen minutes later, in a corner of the Elks' bar, he ordered an old-fashioned and scanned the photos of mostly dead club members on the wall. He met his father's amused eyes and turned to face the other men at the table.

"So," said Jules.

The mayor cleared his throat. "Well, it's obvious why I wanted us to meet."

Scotti was mangling a drink straw. "Not really," said Jules.

"Our problems," said Donald Parsons. "You might say the county is getting a bad reputation."

"We have to work on our attitude," said the mayor. "We have to find the hoodlums who ruined the rodeo and harmed an innocent clown, and we have to arrest whoever murdered a couple at one of our loveliest spots."

"We thought of inviting your friend Pete," said Everett's father. "See if he could slow things down a bit, put a better emphasis on the good stuff in our area instead of harping on these temporary dramatic difficulties."

"Peter already has slowed things down," said Jules. Peter hated being called Pete. Jules would make a point of telling him.

The mayor kicked into a prepared speech, and Jules, in a trance, listened to every third word he bleated, and gradually made out a pattern. Murders in a safe place, accidents in a safe sport. If it's so safe here, why did I get shot this spring, thought Jules. Why are we always losing assholes to the mountains and the rivers? As far as the assholes went, obviously because they were told it was safe, and they'd forgotten centuries of contrary, constructive knowledge. What was safe about precipices, subzero temperatures, large carnivores, a high unemployment rate, felling large trees or operating grain threshers? What was safe about getting on an angry fifteen-hundred-pound animal with a brain the size of a hamster? No one who sat on one sober *thought* doing so was safe, so why would this fat fuck, whose idea of physical risk was climbing into a sand trap after a golf ball?

The mayor discussed the need to preserve the "friendly, small-town flavor" of Blue Deer, while lengthening its tourist season and "encouraging appropriate housing," a not so secret push for various subdivisions and projects, Dragonfly included. Donald Parsons's post as commissioner certainly hadn't hurt Hugh and Sylvia, but there would have been plenty of like-minded individuals had he not existed. The whole thing had turned into a warm, cozy cluster fuck, and this proved to be the point the mayor was oozing toward.

"One of our council members has wondered if it might be possible to go after our fireworks supplier." Donald Parsons looked at Jules and Scotti expectantly. But for a thirty-year age difference and a cherry red nose he and Everett were identical. It made Jules think of Dorian Gray.

"It had been tampered with, after the factory," said Jules wearily. "A different tube had been inserted into a nine cluster. It's not their fault."

"I don't suppose there's been any progress in the last couple of days," said the mayor forlornly.

"Nothing I'd go public with," said Jules. "We are, as you know, severely understaffed, and I'd intended to push forward with the hiring of two new officers until I heard, recently, that the money allocated for this is still missing."

"Not really *missing*," said the mayor. "We'd asked, back in November, if we could borrow against your budget for Christmas lights, and you said you could live with the situation."

"I could live with it, temporarily," said Jules. "That was eight months ago. I need more officers, period. We've already got the smallest force per capita in the state, and now we have the highest murder rate. I didn't plan on five murders within three months."

"Now Jules—"

"I thought the point of this meeting was to solve the current problems. You want to say you're too cheap to hunt down a multiple murderer?"

"Oh God, don't say that," said the mayor.

"Two people does not a multiple murderer make," intoned Donald Parsons. "I have trouble understanding why there hasn't been more progress on the case, no matter how many deputies you have."

Pecked to death by dumb fucks, thought Jules. "Don't say what?" asked Jules. "Cheap or murderer?"

They winced at each.

"I'm budgeted for six officers," said Jules. "I want, and need, six officers. I've been collecting résumés since I got back to work," he continued, "and I've come up with five solid candidates in only two weeks, in all my spare time. Three men, two women."

"You advertised?" The mayor was appalled.

"That money really is gone," said Donald Parsons.

Jules looked at him evenly. "If you'd like to have a force at all, I suggest we all think of ways to raise some."

That sank in for a few seconds. "I've noticed a lot of speeders in the last week," said the mayor hopefully.

"No speed traps," said Jules. "It's unconstitutional, and it's labor intensive, and there's an innate risk to an officer every time we pull someone over. Raise the price of a parking ticket. Give me some court money."

Scotti stirred, a sign of life.

"According to the rules on record, the Sheriff's Department is to be reimbursed for extra hours put in on the Wrangle, the fair, and the Oktoberfest. We have not been for several years. I have to assume this money is simply being held, and might be made available."

"Your predecessor didn't need that money," said Donald Parsons. "I have real misgivings about your abilities and judgment."

Jules smiled at him. "Raise the money."

"Now Jules," said the mayor. "Don't go turning mean again."

"Excuse me?" said Jules. "Again?"

"Part of our reason for calling this meeting was to air troubling complaints about your conduct," said Parsons, doing his best imitation of a Roman senator in a bad sixties movie.

"Jules," said the mayor patiently. "We're casting back to a bad time, but then here we are again. And your first day back, *before* you found the bodies, some individuals complained, said you were 'snide.' " He looked down at his notes. "A couple from Poughkeepsie, New York. You told them they were 'looking at nature the hard way,' and suggested they go to Butte, of all places. Now why would you do that?"

Jules opened his mouth and Scotti kicked him in the ankle. He reconsidered. "That's the complaint?"

"You reportedly hit a man in a bar last night," said the mayor, looking almost apologetic. "That man hasn't lodged a complaint, but—"

"Everett?" said Jules in disbelief. "He was drunk, and his partner smacked him. Ask Hugh."

"Are you calling my son a liar?" asked Donald Parsons.

"Not necessarily," said Jules. "There's always the option that he's a drunk."

A hot night in the Elks' Club. The bartender craned her head, and some wizened men playing euchre stared openly. The mayor broke in: "Whether or not you hit someone, we feel we need to question your judgment for having frequented a bar where such a thing could take place."

Jules was astounded. "This whole town is a place like that. Every last one of us has been in that bar."

"Fine," snapped Donald Parsons. "That doesn't answer the question of why you were there, reportedly harassing two of our better businessmen."

"Why?" asked Jules.

"Why."

"Because I happen to think one of them killed two people."

A half hour later Scotti followed him outside and caught his elbow.

"It's a great thing," said Scotti sweetly, letting himself be pulled along. "Sheriff's been drowning sorrows for a few months now, screws a multitude of women, and maybe punches a commissioner's son, who just happens to be involved in the biggest project in the county. Then he says the commissioner's son is one of only two lousy candidates for the state penitentiary. It would be wonderful, romantic, if this were 1900. But it isn't fucking 1900, not even 1930."

The old behavioral fuzzy line. "You're saying I don't always keep correct company."

"Well, you sure as hell haven't this year."

Jules continued past his squad car on a march toward home, remembering all the reasons he'd left town so absolutely fifteen years earlier.

"Have you?" snapped Scotti, parent of a teenager. He tugged Jules's arm.

Jules turned to face Scotti, and snapped his arm away. "Do you happen to feel I do a good job?"

"You didn't tonight." Scotti walked away.

It was the same old problem, a profound difference in sensibility and experience. Nights like Tuesday made him feel that he didn't belong in Blue Deer anymore, that he shouldn't want to, didn't deserve to, never had. He was all over the map, like Everett. Late at night he thought of the loneliness of that hotel room and wondered what made his own bedroom any different.

The weather was warmer the next morning, and Jules had breakfast with his cousin Joseph Ganter, Jetta Scotti's father, who'd called at a typical near-dawn hour. Joseph told stories about the bad old days, something he could do without romanticism because he'd reached his late seventies. Jules asked Joseph about mining in the Crazies—"enough said," said Joseph—and told him about Alice's research. Joseph waxed poetic about the vigilantes, whom he blamed for much of the subsequent bullshit about the west. In Joseph's opinion at least, a couple of the men in Plummer's gang had been better than the men they'd killed or than the men who lynched them, abhorrent pricks like Nathaniel Langford who made a fortune after the fact. He liked the irony that Plummer had been paid a salary to protect while he murdered, practiced a kind of bloody embezzlement.

Joseph had always been good at reading Jules, and knew almost everyone in town, and most of the stories he told that morning were probably his way of telling Jules to stop complaining, live with the job, remember why he'd come home. They all had to do with the randomness of human behavior, the fact that you never could tell when someone would blow before the fact, so why would you think it might be easy to figure it out after? A woman finally chopping her abusive husband to bits, a trucker making a cop pay for his own unhappy life. Neither of them were that different from the good kid blowing up on the playground one day, reacting to a few years' worth of bullshit from a smartass rather than the actual last straw comment. This was a specific memory Joseph had of Jules at twelve or so, something that happened soon after Ansel Clement had been killed, so that Joseph had gone to talk to the principal because his cousin Olive, after all, really had to work. And one of the reasons Joseph was worried this morning was that the boy Jules had beaten to a pulp was Everett Parsons. Jules must remember, said Joseph, dropping the pretense of a casual breakfast and piling butter and brown sugar on his Cream of Wheat, that the people who really felt they were decent, like Donald Parsons, were usually the filthiest shitsuckers of all. Remember your Dante, said Joseph, who'd left for Yale fifty-some years earlier. Pick your holes for them but never lash out; save yourself for the real problems.

Once again, virtue had to be its own goddamn reward. Jules said as much to Joseph as he polished off his hash browns, asking if this was in fact his point. Joseph just laughed and said let me know if you figure out an easier way.

Jules left a note of apology on Scotti's desk and drove to the hospital. Richie Berko was scheduled to be released that morning, and Jules wanted to corner him one last time by chauffeuring him home. Richie, however, was drying out and barely able to talk, and still claimed no one wanted him dead, despite evidence to the contrary. Jules dropped him at his sorry doorstep, near his sorry orange Happy Cab, and hoped he'd keep a few drunks off the summer streets.

As part of his Be a Better Human campaign, Jules had ensured that Harvey and Jonathan each got two days off that week. It wasn't likely he'd have known what to do with one himself. This meant patrolling again. He'd hoped to give the mayor his money's worth by citing the man's extended family, but none of them seemed to be on the road. In the next two hours he gave out eighteen tickets anyway, a personal record that didn't make him feel any better about life.

At noon, his pattern slowed by a single car, no-injury accident, he watched a maroon pickup slide through one of the valley's only stop signs at twenty-five miles an hour, and flicked his lights on. The driver, with a passenger on the seat next to him and three kids in the bed of the truck, didn't respond, though the three kids all waved. Jules had just resorted to the siren when he recognized the children and the profile of the woman on the seat next to the driver, and gave a little howl of regret.

"What?" squawked Grace from the radio. "What's wrong?"

"I'll tell you later," said Jules.

The kids kicked in as soon as he pulled himself out of the car, asking if their dad was in trouble, if Jules would come to their house again, shoot some gophers. Jules smiled and joked about his aim without answering, but they didn't seem to notice this and prattled on until Edie told them to be quiet. Andy Linders's take on things was a little harder to pin down, and Jules avoided patronizing questions like, "Do you know why I pulled you over?"

"I'm afraid you missed that last stop sign."

"I was following someone who missed it, too. I'm taking my wife to work."

Linders had lost most of the blood in his knuckles from gripping the wheel. Jules was happy to see both hands, but excuses still annoyed him, as did the proprietary, out-of-date phrase "my wife." "I didn't see the person you were following. I saw you."

Edie shifted in her seat, and the three boys retreated to their comic books. Her ex-husband had his eyes fixed on Jules's star—in Montana, sheriffs really got to wear them—but Edie didn't look his way even once.

Jules palmed Linders's license and said that he'd be right back. By the book, again; it wasn't good form to let on you might have known the driver in advance of pulling him or her over, might in fact manufacture a reason to pull the driver over. Especially if you'd known a man's former wife in the biblical sense, and she was examining the dash from the passenger seat, hating you very quietly. But he didn't bother calling it in, and he didn't bother with the ticket. He sat in the car, looking at the seat next to him, and thought of good guys and bad guys and Joseph. Ninety seconds later he was back at the pickup's window.

"Watch it, okay? You follow this route enough to know people barrel through here in the summer." He handed the license back.

Linders had spent the interim preparing for a fight, and his disappointment was obvious. "Wait a minute."

"What?" asked Jules, who'd already turned away.

"I know why you pulled me over."

"I pulled you over because you ran a stop sign onto a busy highway in third gear."

"You pulled me over because you knew who I was."

He had a stubborn, dark, bearded face, and Jules thought it looked like a mean face. Honesty was the best policy. "If I'd known who you were, nothing short of an accident would have made me turn my lights on. I didn't know. But now I see you live up to your reputation." He smiled and Linders looked down. "Drive on, or I'll ticket you for the stop and for carting the kids around in the bed."

Linders was motionless, staring at his wheel.

"Drive on," said Jules softly, walking away.

They were still sitting there, obviously arguing, when he pulled away, but the boys waved good-bye. He cut back toward town on a high bench road, skidding around graveled corners, then bought more time and avoided dishing out more tickets by following another dirt road. When a name finally came clear in his memory he hit the access ramp to the freeway and accelerated to ninety, wanting to know if he was right and not caring to ticket the people he'd passed who were doing eighty. As he made out a wavering yellow Volkswagen Rabbit, he said a little prayer for the driver to notice him in his rearview, but the car kept wandering between lanes. Jules slowed to watch, still willing to give him or her the benefit of the doubt. Then the car veered over to the shoulder, straightened, and a beer can sailed out the window.

It was like a cartoon: everything you shouldn't do with a sheriff a hundred yards behind you. As Jules passed the people in between, lights and sirens on full bore, they smiled and waved and he smiled back. Rare public acceptance, but it was still all a pain in his ass.

The Volkswagen driver still didn't seem to notice him, and only stared dully in Jules's direction when he pulled alongside and held up an open palm. The Rabbit weaved again, and Jules dropped back, swearing, and radioed in the plate. Jules tried pulling up again as he waited for a response and this time the driver, a heavyset blond man about his own age, snapped his teeth at him but slowed a bit. Werner, Robert, of Red Lodge, said Grace. Huh, thought Jules, and asked Grace to check if the first three figures of the plate might happen to match up with those taken down after a biting incident in a tent in the Beartooths a week earlier.

Grace checked, fast. "Oh my," she said. "Should I tell Ed to bring a muzzle?"

Jules wished someone else's day had turned into a nightmare of coincidence.

Alice should have kept working, but ten pages into a dry book about the economics of Rocky Mountain mining camps in 1870 it occurred to her that it would be a fine, cool day to put in a second batch of greens and favas and romano beans. It took a full half hour to locate the seeds under some fishing equipment and food catalogs, and another forty-five minutes to make it outside with them, because she'd started sorting all the packets and looking through the cheeses in one of the catalogs. When she hit the garden it was two and at least eighty-five degrees, and she almost gave up when it seemed her neighbors, whom she was actually fond of, were having a full-blown reunion a foot from the fence, and might want to say hello. Alice, having grown up on a farm followed by a decade in Manhattan, had trouble with the in-between. But she persevered, pulled out the gone-to-seed spinach and peas, and started in with the hoe.

By three, when Jules screeched to a stop and headed toward her like a torpedo, Alice was fairly sure she'd lost five pounds in sweat alone, and her suffering was such that it took her a minute to take in the strange expression on his face and panic.

"Peter."

"What about him?" Jules looked alarmed.

"Tell me."

"Tell you *what*?" he howled.

"Is he okay?"

"What do you mean?"

They took stock of each other.

"Why are you here?" asked Alice.

"Do you remember talking about Plummer's gang?"

She squinted at his face, wondering if she should check his pupils. *"What?"*

"What were the names of the men?"

"Why would I remember that?" Alice kicked a hose with her clog.

"Because you did already, on the drive back from Otto's funeral."

My but he was testy. He actually looked like a cop today, lean and mean. "I remembered them then because Peter was giving me a hard time. I rose to the challenge."

Jules was glaring at her. Alice moved into the shade. "Stinson. A guy named Piranha, or something like that."

"Pizanthia," said Jules, gritting his teeth.

"See," said Alice, "you know all of it anyway. Go away."

"Where'd you dig the names up? What book?"

Alice thought, sweating on her hoe. "Blue and yellow cover, topmost on the pile on the computer monitor. It's by some lady who used to run the university library, came out in the fifties. Or maybe in the laundry basket at the top of the stairs."

He found the book on her nightstand and skimmed it sitting on the bed. Ten minutes later he heard Peter's truck and moved to the kitchen, rather than remind anyone of their sole tryst in the distant past. At any rate, he'd found what he'd been looking for: two of the people who'd recently filed mining claims at

Dragonfly—Stinson (Buck, not Bartholomew), and Lyons (Haze, not Hazel)—had been hung in January of 1864, a hundred miles away in Alder Gulch, with Henry Plummer, the sheriff of Bannack. Nicholas Thalt and Ian Dillingham, the other claimants, were two of the men they'd killed.

Peter fiddled in the refrigerator while Jules read, and now asked if he'd like a beer. Jules most certainly did, along with some professional advice. Peter told him that, yes, legal names—real names—would be recorded in the full claims, and why didn't they go see Ankeny right now. He wouldn't write a word about it. Cross his heart.

Ankeny was off watching a wildfire in the Gallatins, but Peter was an old hand at the files. It only took him half an hour to pluck out the papers and determine that Ian Dillingham had been Hugh Lesy, Nicholas Thalt had been Otto Scobey, Buck Stinson had been Everett Parsons, and Hazel Lyons had been Sylvia Coburg. Jules spent a full minute staring at her signature.

He stayed for dinner and told Peter about the meeting the night before.

"Cool down," said Peter. "Why shorten your life over those assholes?"

"I can't do it anymore," said Jules. "The point is that life's too short to begin with."

"What are you gonna do, use your education? Dig arrowheads and daydream?"

"Sounds goddamn wonderful."

At ten he pushed through the glass doors of the hospital, still in uniform, and glanced at the stencils that announced visiting hours had ended an hour earlier. He supposed all-night admission was one of the perks of his job. The main hallway seemed too bright, but the ICU area was dim and soothing, and the nurse's station was empty. Jules moved a box of tissue from the visitors' chair and sat at the foot of Sylvia's bed, the Naugahyde cushion exhaling softly, matching almost exactly the whoosh of the oxygen machine.

All of the nurses avoided looking at Sylvia, who'd volunteered, been on all the hospital boards, raised funds. Back when Jules had been in the hospital, and his roommate had only emitted beeps, Renee had explained that you stopped looking at someone when there was no one left to look at. In the daytime, in the midst of the hospital's efficient, reassuring bustle, this seemed fair and businesslike. In the quiet dark, it was easy to understand why the near dead had never been left alone a hundred years earlier, before people tried to believe those beeps constituted company.

At night, watching Sylvia's face in the glow from the window, he understood that there was no way the figure on the bed would ever move or speak again, but there was something comforting in listening to the movement of blood and air, even in hoping those sounds would stop soon. A terrible ache and weariness flooded through his body and he leaned his head against the back of the chair.

He'd probably only slept for half an hour when Renee patted his head and he jumped. "I thought I just saw someone come in," she said.

"Nah." He smiled. "I've been here for a while. It's the quietest place in town."

It was his second night in a row at home without drinking himself halfway to infinity or having someone blow up or die or having sex with someone who unnerved him. It was a fine thing, despite the boring refrigerator and the fact that the cat had thrown up again, this time in the bathtub.

Now Fred and Moe, out of Jules's sight in the kitchen, were heckling one another, which meant that Fred, "never God's smartest creature," in Olive Clement's words, was meowing steadily and atonally at Moe, who had just screamed, "Mine, all mine," for the twelfth time. Jules threw a magazine through the open doorway and they both shut up. He fell asleep five minutes later.

He awoke, sweating, from a nightmare a few hours later. He flung himself off the couch and washed his face in the bathroom sink, then stood still until his heart slowed down. By the time the phone rang ten minutes later he had the refrigerator door open, trying to decide between a peanut butter sandwich and leftover pasta. It was four A.M.; he rehearsed a speech to Harvey as he picked up the receiver, but as soon as he recognized the nurse's voice he understood. Sylvia was dead.

FLORA

HORACE, WEARING PAJAMA TOPS OVER A PAIR OF KHAKIS, WAS striving to be patient. "You know, Jules, people *do* just die. Especially after a horse crushes their skull."

"I thought she was stable."

"She wasn't going to be the same."

"I *know* that," said Jules.

"It was probably a blood clot we missed, something we couldn't see. There was potentially a lot we couldn't know. It's a blessing."

A woman was giving birth on the next hall, sounds like a dying bear echoing down the linoleum every three minutes or so with miraculous vigor, and it was all especially miraculous if she was the woman Jules had seen waddle in thirty-six hours earlier. He looked down at Sylvia, and up again quickly. He knew Horace was upset, too, and that he was right—Jules had hoped for the same thing. But the idea that there was no finite answer, that he'd been taken by surprise again, enraged him, and counting to ten wasn't panning out with Sylvia's rumpled, unwakeable body still lying in the bed between them. Horace had shut her eyes, but one lid kept rising stubbornly, and now he was fussing with her sheet. She'd grown yellower since they'd started wrangling above her, all the blood finally obeying gravity.

A nurse ahemmed from the doorway, but Jules and Horace stayed rooted until they heard Hugh's voice in the hallway, off a note and guttural, saying "Because I want to." Jules moved to the corner, but Hugh probably didn't even see him. He walked in, kissed Sylvia on the lips, and pulled up a chair, just as he had the day before. This time he didn't bother talking, and though his face was wet it was also impassive.

Jules dragged Horace into the hall. "When will you autopsy her?"

"Why the hell autopsy her?"

"Because," said Jules, letting his face settle into its dourest expression, not difficult considering the hour and the circumstances.

Horace could look stony, too. "Have someone else do it then. I'm not touching her."

"It's your job," said Jules. "She was your patient, and you know her chart. And I want it kept quiet. If I send her up to Helena there'll be a stink."

"Who's going to tell him?" Horace jerked a thumb in Hugh's direction.

"I will."

"Oh, goddamnit," he said, stamping a plump foot. "I'll take some samples now, but I won't look at her until Friday night. I've got two surgeries today, and Amy and I have plans for tonight."

Plans, thought Jules. What a notion. "Can you put off your plans till Friday night?"

"Jules," said Horace, "it's my twentieth anniversary. I am

buying my wife a nice dinner, plying her with wine, telling her my love is eternal, and spending the rest of the night in bed with her. These are things that will already be difficult enough to enjoy given this—" he gestured toward Sylvia. "You think I'm going to be in the mood if I cut her up first?"

"No," said Jules. "You're right."

SYLVIA C. COBURG

Sylvia Charlotte Coburg, 47, of Blue Deer, Montana, died early Thursday morning at Blue Deer Memorial Hospital of injuries suffered on July 3 during a riding accident. Funeral services will be held at noon on Saturday, July 10, at Emmanuel Lutheran Church, with Rev. Fergus Grabow officiating. Interment will follow at Cottonwood Cemetery in Blue Deer.

She was born September 29, 1945, on the Coburg Ranch near Springdale, the daughter of Gustav and Ellen Coburg, and attended grade school and high school in Absaroka County. After attending Smith College and several years spent teaching in Blue Deer, she lived for a number of years in Boston, though she returned to her family's ranch outside of Blue Deer every summer.

She enjoyed riding and gardening, and traveled widely throughout her life. She was active in the Blue Deer Historical Society, the Hospital Fundraising Committee, the Fair Committee, the Wrangle Committee, and Big Brothers and Sisters. She is survived by sons Compton and Christopher Baslington, of Boston, and her grandmother, Carlotta Edmark, of Springdale, and was preceded in death by her parents, an infant daughter, and her second husband, Otto K. Scobey.

Memorials may be directed to Blue Deer Memorial Hospital.

Peter finished Sylvia's obituary at noon on Thursday. He could have written it in ten minutes at the beginning of the week but hadn't felt up to it; he didn't care if the *New York Times* started its in memoriams when the subjects were toddlers. One of the advantages of Blue Deer was that you could live in hope without someone ridiculing your optimism. At least that had once been the case.

He cracked his knuckles and considered the wave of items littering his desk. All of them made the next hour of his job amusing in a well of heartbreak, but he doubted they diverted Jules in such a pleasant fashion. In Absaroka County's last day or two, there had been a flurry of organic problems, most of them based on failures to correctly gauge Mother Nature and mankind's role within her. The downside of the environmental movement flowered every summer, but the material for the day was still impressive even without the stuff he couldn't write up, like Everett in the Baird the night before: Three separate bad mushroom incidents marked the high-altitude chanterelle picking season (locals rarely made such mistakes, but all the adventurous California imports were dropping like flies), a tree-logger incident, two fresh grass fires, a nasty rock slide, a nearly fatal heroin overdose (this particular Floridian had been discovered, oddly enough, lying in a flower bed dotted with Icelandic poppies, but Peter doubted he could fit this idea into a story), a steam burn from an innocent-looking hot pot, and three overturned rafts (taste that sweet, piney, *Giardia*-laden water, and kiss your cameras good-bye). Earlier that week, an Arizonan had located one of Montana's only poison ivy patches and attempted to inoculate himself by eating budding leaves, and a Texan had tried smoking wild geranium with nasty results. Blue Deer Memorial Hospital was overflowing. Even Sylvia was part of the week's pattern: Sooner or later, after thousands of rides on something bigger than you, the odds were on your luck running out.

Peter tried to build up steam, but it was hard. Alice called twice, crying, and he almost managed to talk her into floating down the river with him, but on the third call she told him she'd decided to go for a drive by herself.

He filed the stories and rode his bike home, intending to fish anyway.

. . .

Bad was relative. All the incidents Peter boiled down into a single article hadn't actually made Jules unhappy. A little psychosis was to be expected when fine weather followed a cold snap. No one had died, except for Sylvia, and all of the lesser miseries conspired to distract him from her death. The tent-crushing camper connoisseur had been remanded to Carbon County authorities that morning and had, naturally, a wonderful excuse for the weekend Otto and Bonnie had died: He'd been in a Dillon jail, charged with suddenly biting the shoulder of a woman on a neighboring bar stool. In the midst of it all Jules had gone over Otto's Forest Service map again and found no discernible pattern in the ownership of the claims, but a call to Ankeny was slightly more illuminating.

Genie was perking up a little, sliding downhill since the holiday, but it was little shit, nothing worth pulling him in for. An altercation in a Gardiner bar; a friend picked up in the girlfriend's car for some crystal meth and trace cocaine; a report—denied—that Genie had been driving the car himself; a report—denied—that the woman had ejected Genie in the middle of the night, and that Genie had responded by kicking in the door and dragging the girlfriend out by the hair. The Gardiner deputy, Mark Roseau, found some wood splinters and noted a bruised hairline, but Genie and the woman sat side-by-side on a couch while he talked to them, and claimed they'd been locked out together. It was depressing, in a vague way, but given life's other problems and the pattern of Genie's past, Jules didn't give enough of a shit or know how to stop him from hanging himself.

Everett, though, took the cake. He'd apparently responded to Jules's inquisition by starting the day off with a beer, instead of coffee, and had once again gone on to star in a movie of his own making, tentatively titled *Beyond the Deep End.* This was only Jules's third summer as a cop, but he'd had an eye for unbalanced assholes all his life, even when he'd been one himself, and Everett was beginning to rank high. An early afternoon drive had ended in a French kiss bestowed on a truly unattractive Bozeman waitress, after which he'd burst into tears and apologized. He'd driven on to Ennis, where he'd received a warning from a deputy after throwing beer bottles and one of his shoes into the Madison River. Once again he'd talked himself out of a free meal, saying he'd drive home to Absaroka County and rest up, but the Ennis deputy had been troubled enough to report the incident to Grace, who decided not to pass on the story to Jules so soon after his wrestling match with the Jackson biter. Ed had checked up on him instead, and discovered Everett at his parents' house, pruning a jacaranda hedge back into infancy with a chain saw. Donald Parsons didn't look happy, but wouldn't admit it, and Ed left them to their private war.

Now Jules read that Everett had been involved in a call that came in from the Baird at one A.M. the night before, the matter dropped at three-thirty, with the individual in question under the safekeeping of Peter H. Johansen, Esq. For further amusement, Jules had Jonathan's traumatized incident note, so simple that it was suspicious. The bouncer at the Baird claimed Everett had attacked him. Peter, speaking for Everett after the bouncer retaliated, said that Everett had been greeting the bouncer, and that the bouncer's subsequent attack upon his client had been unjustified, and that the bouncer's subsequent fall had been accidental.

Nowhere in Jonathan's labored paragraph did he spell out exactly what Everett had done to offend the bouncer, who resembled a large gland. Jules guessed he was glad he'd been busy at the hospital, looking down at Sylvia's dead body. At least he hadn't had to handle both nightmares. He thought about the bouncer, and realized, suddenly, that he strongly resembled the Bozeman waitress.

Ed strolled into the station, saw Jules's silently shaking back, and assumed grief or a long-anticipated nervous breakdown. He patted Jules on the wrong shoulder. "Take the rest of the day off," he said. "Go fishing. I'll take care of the little shit."

When Jules pulled up to the curb, Peter was standing in the street in front of his house, looking distraught. The hood was up on his 1973 Mazda pickup.

"Let's play hookey."

"It'll have to wait. I just got a call from a client."

"I heard that you started practicing again last night," said Jules. "Maybe you should take some time off first, think it over."

Peter looked uncomfortable. "That was in the nature of friendly advice. This is emergency advice, and Alice took off in the Subaru, and this is running really hot."

Jules peered at the Mazda's sorry engine block, then heard a pinging sound and crouched down to watch oil drip into a pie plate underneath. "You could take my truck."

"Your truck is older than my truck."

"My truck works."

Jules's radio shrieked static, and he scrambled for the volume. "Hang on."

Peter lit a cigarette and sat on the curb. "Do I look like I'm going anywhere?"

"Jules," screamed Grace.

"Pipe the hell down," said Jules.

"We have a disturbance at the reservoir."

"Oh dear," said Peter, popping to his feet again.

Jules stared at him. "What kind of disturbance, Grace?"

"White male caucasian, mid-thirties, brown hair, tall, shot two boats and started a grass fire." There was a pause in the static while Grace reviewed her notes. "Apparently he also danced a bit, and a fisherman claimed to see a gun. Actually, he shot the boats, ran into town, had a drink, made a call from the inn bar, and then started the fire."

"Son of a bitch," said Peter. "Goddamn it all." He hopped up and down a couple of times in the street.

"Are you sure he was on our side of the county line?"

"Clarence phoned. I'm sure."

"Did you call the fire department?"

"White Sulphur did us a favor and sent their guys. We're down for backup, but they thought they could contain it."

"Where's Ed?"

"He just left for Emigrant, dealing with an accident. Car versus cow."

"Harvey?"

"Brandon had an orthodontist appointment in Bozeman, and Michelle couldn't take him because—"

Jonathan needed his sleep. Jules watched Peter kick the Mazda. He was beginning to get the picture. "Okay, I'm leaving."

He replaced the handset. "I gather your client corresponds to this description."

"I *had* planned to fish today," said Peter. "Even before you showed up. I can't believe I told him I'd come. I can't believe I didn't run away an hour ago."

"I'll give you a ride," said Jules. "We can find Everett together."

No one said anything for at least five miles. The drive was just as pretty as it had been a month earlier, when Jules and Ed had headed north to pull a tent out of the water on another beautiful day, but the grass was much browner, infinitely more flammable.

"So what happened last night?" asked Jules, in between Grace's fascinating updates.

"Everett went local," said Peter, popping a root beer and wishing it was something else, though open intoxicants were a bad idea in a squad car. "A lot of kids were in the bar for a band,

and Everett didn't like them, and he especially didn't like the way the bouncer was treating them at the door. He started talking about how stupid and surly people were, and things accelerated. And Alice wouldn't dance with him again because he let go of her halfway through a swing."

"Is she okay?"

"A funky wrist. Nothing broken, and it didn't hurt until this morning." Peter seemed to lose track; he was fascinated by the radar detector, but the next car headed toward them at a disappointing sixty-one miles per hour, and he sighed. "He tried a waitress. The waitress wouldn't dance. Diane wouldn't dance; she seemed pissed off. He talked about how no one loved him, and then he started talking about how Sylvia couldn't dance anymore, and Hugh left."

"He just gave another monologue?"

"Pretty much," said Peter. "It was a lot like that time Hugh hit him, but I'm leaving out little details, like when he tugged on Alice's blouse and looked down the front."

It seemed that Everett had grown increasingly moody in the welter of noise and hot bodies as the band wailed, and Peter and Alice had stopped paying attention until he rose from his stool, trudged purposefully toward the three-hundred-pound, mushroom-necked bouncer, and gave the man an open-mouthed kiss, holding his ears to anchor the moment. Then Everett pulled back, smiled and said something, and the bouncer, blind with confusion and fear, seized Everett by his rib cage and shirt, careful to keep him at arm's length, and slammed him against the wall ten feet away.

Peter drank some of his soda. Jules watched a red-tail hawk dive for a rodent and miss.

Everett had bounced and landed on his feet, still smiling, and headed back to his drink next to Peter. The bouncer shrieked and charged and Peter stuck his foot out. The man went down and Peter walked away, hauling Everett along with him, directly to his room. Jonathan had knocked on the door a half hour later, because the bouncer wanted to file assault charges.

"He told his friends he felt raped," said Peter, mouth curling in the corner. They both knew the bouncer, who thought of himself as God's gift to female drinkers, had a bad history with the word "no."

But he was easy to appease, because by the time Jonathan arrived Everett was doing his best cherub imitation as he dabbed blood from his cheek and the back of his head. Since the bouncer refused to articulate to Jonathan just how he'd been attacked, and showed no injuries, and since Everett had obvious marks on his perfect skin, and since Jonathan lacked imagination, it was not difficult to get Everett off the hook. Everett claimed that he'd been reading in his room and someone else must have caused a problem. Said he was reading Wodehouse, if you please, but by then Jonathan was so confused that he didn't bother with the inconsistencies or the subtleties.

Everett had explained to Peter and Alice that the bouncer's sour mood had annoyed him, and he'd wanted to sweeten the man up; apparently the whispered comment after the kiss and before the wall had been a warning about steroids shrinking genitalia.

"How long did you say you'd known this guy?" asked Peter.

"Second grade or something," said Jules, trying to decide if he was amused or annoyed. "I would never have thought he'd turned into a fruitcake."

"Try a fruit," said Peter.

"I don't think so," said Jules. "He's been around, he's been married. Though he might be more democratic in his tastes than his politics."

"I guess there really is an old girlfriend who calls all the time," said Peter, watching the radar again. "According to Edie, who's been asked up."

"I'm sure she has," said Jules evenly.

"And Diane's a piece of work."

"Yes, she is," said Jules.

"I guess they used to sleep together."

"I guess they did," said Jules.

Grace interrupted to tell them that the protagonist of the current story had taken off some of his clothes. Jules sighed. Peter leaned back and closed his eyes.

"Alice is so coy about this shit, but I overheard her and Lucy and Edie talking in sign the other night, and I gather Diane's not limiting herself to her old pal."

"Do you," said Jules.

Peter frowned. "I hate being teased with gossip. I hate being curious. It's like throwing water balloons at a slumber party, but the windows are closed. I'm too old for this shit, and so is Alice."

Jules sighed again. "I am, too."

They drove another mile in silence, Jules so lost in his failings that it took some time to register that Peter was staring at him, horrified.

"Biological need," said Jules.

"Omigod," said Peter.

"One more word and I'll smack you."

Two more quiet miles, and Peter broke the rule. "You know," he said, "I honestly think most intelligent males would have the sense to stay away from someone whose first name is Opal."

"Is that so," said Jules.

"Yeah. But it's a tradition with you. Remember that dipshit India?"

Jules made a face.

"How about Eugenie?"

Eugenie had died, laughing, in a car accident, and had nearly taken Jules with her. He had loved her, and one of these days he'd remember to take her out of his meaningless will. "Stuff it," he said. "Names have nothing to do with it."

"Why didn't you tell me?"

"Etiquette." Jules shrugged. "Time constraints."

Peter couldn't hide a shit-eating grin. "Tell me how this came about."

"I'm not sure myself." Jules slowed for a gopher. "You know what she's like?" he said suddenly. "She's beyond etiquette. She's like a mob car—you get in, and all the locks go down. She's like the blond scissor-kicker in *Blade Runner*. She probably tortured flies as a moppet. I'm stunned I've survived her without permanent bodily harm."

Peter looked shocked. "Oh. I didn't know."

"I didn't tell you," yelled Jules, "because I was fucking well observing etiquette."

When they reached Martinsdale, Clarence Bost was waiting for them in the middle of Main Street's dented macadam. Though Clarence had missed the commotion, as he was a block away in his house eating a sandwich, he'd designated himself town spokesperson, and the half-dozen people who stood behind him nodded enough for Jules to be sure the story was substantially correct.

Everett hadn't so much shot the boats as turned them into colanders, reloading a shotgun several times for the task. The fishermen on the scene had plenty of time to get to the bar to fill everyone in, though it seemed no one had thought to call the police at this early point. Everett had joined them in the bar and drained a vodka martini before the bartender had understood why the fishermen were suddenly nervous. Everett then asked to be placed in the jail, but wanted an assurance that someone would make sure no rattlesnakes approached the red cage. When a joker a few stools down pointed out that this had happened once, only forty miles away in Ringling, Montana, Everett changed his mind about imprisonment, headed back to the reservoir, and started the fire.

Having to listen to Clarence made Jules cranky, but it probably saved them time. Jules edged toward his car.

"I'll be writing to the paper if you don't arrest this man," intoned Clarence.

"Don't worry about it," said Jules.

"You guys don't get much done. Can't count on you."

"We got a goddamn tent out of your goddamn reservoir."

"There wouldn't be lawless behavior out there if you came by more often. White Sulphur sent a guy for our parade, but you visit when it suits you."

Clarence certainly knew how to talk himself out of sympathy, but Jules decided not to change the subject. "On Sunday, the day after the parade, were there many people left in town? Do you remember any of them?"

"What are you talking about?

"Just what I said. How's your memory? Do you remember anyone having a drink or eating in town?"

It was easy to goad Clarence, who probably remembered how many ants he'd stepped on that day. "Some campers with a kid, and those dead people."

"You told me you hadn't seen them before."

"A man can change his mind," snapped Clarence.

"Who else?"

There was a long silence. Peter twitched and watched smoke rise from the direction of the reservoir. "Cleanup day, right?"

"Right."

"I didn't feel so good."

"I understand," said Jules.

"Some kids. A couple from Tulsa, in an Airstream."

Jules waited.

"Another guy came in, asking if there was anyplace to eat besides the inn. I said my place."

Jules kept his face still. "What'd he look like?"

"Can't remember. He left."

"Nothing? Color of his hair?"

"Nah. He was polite. That's all."

"How old was he?"

Jules felt Clarence think, an almost alarming phenomenon because Clarence wanted him to feel it.

"Thirties, forties. Not older than sixty."

Jules hated Clarence Bost.

They bumped along the two-track toward the far side of the reservoir, where they'd spent so much time a few weeks earlier. The BMW blocked the trail, but Everett was reading something in a lawn chair at the edge of the shrinking, mud-ringed reservoir, a hundred feet from the fire truck and two lounging men. The ground in between the man in the chair and the men by the truck was patchy black and smoldering.

Jules took his time walking toward Everett, taking in the scene. His face was singed pink, and lumpy from his last three bar outings. His arms looked burned, too, and his white T-shirt was sooty. His legs were poached, undoubtedly because he only wore underpants, navy boxers with white polka dots.

"So, Everett," said Jules quietly. "Fancy meeting you here."

"Well, hello," said Everett. He lowered the torn page he'd been reading. "How are you?"

"Fine, just fine," said Jules. "But what's going on? You a little upset about Sylvia?"

A bleary look passed over Everett's eyes and he shut them for a moment. "I came out here to take a walk, and noticed the fire. Luckily, they've gotten it under control."

Jules rubbed the bridge of his nose. "Keep trying."

Everett smiled, charmed. "I was smoking a cigarette after a little picnic, and thinking about life."

"You never smoked a goddamn cigarette in your life," said Jules.

Everett rolled his eyes, exasperated with Jules's lack of understanding, nonchalant despite his smudged underpants and scorched toes.

"Where's the shotgun?"

"My father's favorite grouse gun is about eighty feet that way." He pointed to the ten-acre mud puddle and went back to his reading.

Jules tried to determine what was different, beyond the obvious, and it came to him that Everett didn't usually wear glasses. Jules was about to speak—could an especially bad new prescription send a fragile psyche right over the edge?—when he realized that there were no lenses in the glasses, and made out the one surviving dark sliver of a very dead pair of Ray Bans.

"That's it," said Jules. "That's fucking it."

"Pardon?" Everett looked startled. Jules closed in on him, jerked him out of the lawn chair, and shepherded him toward the patrol car, stuffing him into the backseat and locking the doors.

"Do you want to speak with your client?" he asked Peter.

"Not particularly." Peter peered toward the car. Everett waved through the glass. "Maybe later."

"I'm not charging him with anything," said Jules. "I'm taking him to the hospital. Drive that thing back to town, will you?" He gestured toward the BMW.

"Sure," said Peter. "Good idea. Don't ticket me, okay?"

Everett gave a dim little giggle from the back of the patrol car.

"He could probably use some more ventilation," said one of the White Sulphur firemen. "Part of the reason he's so pink is that he was dancing until a few minutes ago."

"He's so goddamn ventilated brain cells are pouring out of his ears," said Jules. "I'm leaving anyway. I'll send someone to finish up later. Any idea how he really started it?"

"We found a book, and we found some matches. They were lying on the blanket, right in the center, there."

Jules stared at Everett's oblivious profile in the patrol car, then trudged over and looked down at a smoldering, unreadable cover. He flipped it open and it fell to page forty, with the facing page ninety-five and a lot of ripped out edges in between. The book was *Sand County Almanac,* and Everett had started his blaze with the chapters from July through December, "Great Possessions" through "Home Range."

The hospital confirmed that Everett had first-degree burns on the soles of his feet and a third-degree burn on one elbow. He'd singed his eyebrows and the hair around his face and on his chest. The doctor on call could find no immediate evidence of intoxication or drug-induced dementia. Jules had to bully her into admitting and sedating Everett, by now patiently waiting in a plastic chair, as gentle, innocent, and pink as a newborn lamb.

Jules walked to the pay phone, then realized he lacked a quarter. The receptionist, by now one of his better friends, loaned him one, and Jules dialed the Baird.

"Hugh's line is busy," said Edie.

"Try Diane's room," said Jules. "Please."

She didn't bother with a comment and put him through. After the phone had rung eight times he hung up, hard, and borrowed another quarter.

"I'd like to hold for Hugh, please," said Jules. "No one picked up."

"Of course," said Edie. "Sorry. I think Diane's up there with him." The line went blank, and Jules had time to wonder about a lot of things, including how much time a quarter bought these days, before she picked up again. "How about a message?"

"How about you sweeten up?"

"Huh," said Edie. "How about you get a rabies shot and then we'll see."

Well. He took a mental step backward and actually stared at the receiver. "Please tell Hugh that Everett won't be making the meeting tonight, and please tell Diane that he would probably appreciate a visitor at the hospital. He was involved in a little fire, and has some minor burns, but otherwise it's a job for the little men in the white coats."

That got her. Jules found the silence on the other end of the line quite satisfying. "Oh dear," said Edie.

"Maybe you'd like to stop by, too."

"Oh, shut up, Jules."

Jules lay in bed that night, trying to change the course of his thoughts by enumerating all the words for insanity. Amok had always been his favorite, the most elemental and foreign from Latin roots. Unhinged (he saw little clasps unfurling in Everett's mind). Deranged, raving, frenzied, psychotic. Dementia was a lovely word, like a woman's name from a Greek classic; perhaps it had been used that way, and he'd forgotten his education. Dementia and her mate, Delirium, leapt from a high cliff with their toddler twins, Phobia and Mania. Cretin, imbecile, moron were less interesting because they suggested no grand, deluded exaltation, no flying too close to the sun, no bats in the belfry, loose screws, flipped lid, lost marbles.

Everett was either mad as a hatter or had a drug source Jules could only envy. He was touched, daft, psycho, starkers, cracked, addled, crazy as a bedbug. Jules looked at the clock and read 5:17. He thought of turning on the light and looking for one of the six books he'd started in the last month, but he fell back to sleep trying to decide which.

"They'll find something in his bloodstream," said Scotti at breakfast the next morning. "That'll shut Donald up. Why else would a man dance in his underwear?"

"Let's just say," said Jules, "that the man has a lot on his mind."

"No shit," snickered Scotti.

"Maybe he's just crazy." Jules chugged a glass of water and looked around Morton's, Blue Deer's greasiest diner, wondering what food might possibly get the day off to a good start.

"Swap a couple of letters, and you go from weird to wired," said Scotti. "Maybe he ate too many Twinkies." He tapped his menu on the edge of the table. "You may have a drug bust in your future."

"I think this is organic," said Jules wearily. "Everett's too conservative to want to have fun. Republican drugs like cocaine just don't do this sort of thing to a person."

"Republican?" Scotti didn't look happy.

Jules shrugged, beyond political wisdom.

Scotti was pissed off. "I guess you'd have the best guess, after living in New York."

In New York it had simply been a question of population. Head for head, Blue Deer won the weird war. Maybe having more room to fall apart encouraged people to fall apart.

"Let's get Donald to lock him up for a while."

"As if you'd get that turd of misery to admit anything was wrong," said Jules. "I wouldn't pin my hopes on that."

"We could bargain, say we'll drop the charges if they put him away." Scotti continued to drum the table with the menu. "This place put a big ad in the paper. New food, fancy chef for breakfast, lunch, and dinner. A diner should be a diner, no matter how upscale. Which means someone should have taken our order ten minutes ago."

Jules looked at the menu, alarmed. To his relief he discovered that upscale didn't mean low fat. He pretended not to notice when Scotti brought the menu down on the table with a resounding thwack, but he wished he wasn't wearing his uniform. Everyone stared at cops.

A tiny, dark-haired waitress appeared, and regarded Axel Scotti through narrowed eyes. "You rang?"

"We need to get to work," said Scotti pleasantly. "Do you know how to take an order?"

"Do you know how to say please?"

They smiled at each other, like minds meshing gears. Jules sighed, and foresaw his cousin Jetta cuckolded again. It was another five minutes before they got down to the business of the following Monday's inquest. There wasn't much to be said; afterward, Jules gave Scotti a brief account of the mining claims.

"You're saying they've claimed their own property under fake names? Why?"

"Not their own property. Parcels on the adjoining Forest Service land."

"Why?" said Scotti again.

"I'm not sure yet."

"Are you going to talk to them?" Scotti said this a trifle sarcastically.

"Of course," said Jules, trying to swallow his toast.

"Well, when?"

"When I drive Everett to the station from the hospital."

Scotti gave a gentle burp, patted his stomach, and looked at his watch. "Seems like discharge time is upon us."

Jules was fairly sure that Scotti wanted a second helping and the waitress, with no witnesses. "Sylvia would have inherited Otto's claim, right?"

"Right." The county attorney dabbed at his mouth and scanned the room.

"Who would have inherited hers? Hugh or her sons?"

Scotti lost his well-fed Romeo look and stared at Jules. "According to a rather confidential talk I had with her attorney, Mr. Biddle, yesterday, the claim—"

"Claims," said Jules, marveling at how quickly Scotti had dropped his usual manner of speech.

"The claims would likely have gone to Hugh. Lenny and I just had a casual talk, no true details, but it was my understanding that the children had the entirety of her other property, but the resort average is substantially his."

"Imagine that," said Jules, draining his glass of orange juice, and wishing he'd remembered a vitamin.

Jules wasn't one of those people who felt so normal that they believed themselves untouchable. A little good acid and a hereditary tendency toward depression went a long way, and at the very least inspired humility. Normally he would have felt great empathy for someone in Everett's fragile state, but Jules's heart hadn't been very warm in the last few months to begin with, and he was fairly sure Everett had killed at least two people. Until the day before Jules had felt Everett was feigning grief as part of an elaborate con, a way for a bloodless reactionary to get away with murder, but even the most devious killer would be hard pressed to fake mental illness by stripping and walking through a fire.

Jules trudged down the hospital corridor, sure that Everett was insane from guilt in the best tradition of a Russian novel. He remembered the bar, Everett's paean to land and resentment toward Hugh. But nothing Jules could detect in the Dragonfly setup promised to reward Everett. Killing Otto didn't seem to get him any closer to a few acres and a picket fence, at least without Hugh's help.

Everett was dressed and ready, perched on the hospital bed watching two nurses smoke on the lawn outside the window.

A central symptom of insanity was that it made other people nervous. But Everett seemed relaxed, and rummaged through Jules's pile of cassettes during the ten-block drive to the station.

Jules stopped for Blue Deer's only light. He was almost positive it had never been green for him. "Why'd you get divorced?" he asked.

Everett jumped.

"You told me you were married, once. What went wrong?"

He cleared his throat. "My wife felt I lacked ambition."

There was a woman who wouldn't find a spouse in Blue Deer.

"You've set land speed records in ambition, at least compared to most people," Jules said mildly.

"Back to the idea that everything's relative," said Everett, wearily. "Sometimes that's not good enough. My wife grew up poor and unhappy. My wife grew up with a chip on her shoulder, and I couldn't do enough to make it go away."

"Is this your explanation for coming unglued?" The car ahead of him hadn't noticed the light had changed. Jules honked.

"That would be a cheap shot," said Everett heavily.

"Go ahead and take one," said Jules. "An explanation might help my patience."

Everett shrugged and stared up at the Baird as they passed. "I'm anxious," he said. "Death and taxes, the Dragonfly deal, Hugh's mental state. Sylvia. I told her bad things came in threes." He looked at Jules. "I hate my parents, my parents hate me. I hate me. And then there's Diane."

Jules was sorry he'd asked.

"Wouldn't you?" said Everett.

"Wouldn't I what?"

"Hate me."

"Now that's a cheap shot," said Jules, pulling into the lot behind the jail. "I'll get you a cup of coffee, and we'll see if Hughie's here on time."

He wasn't, of course, and Jules took a certain pleasure in the sight of Everett waiting next to his desk, awkward and out of his element. Everett kept staring at Grace with a confused expression, and Jules, in a leap of intuition, explained that she'd probably been his Driver's Training instructor. This relieved Everett greatly, and he and Jules swapped stories about Grace bellowing "Shift" and "Brake" and "What the hell do you think you're doing?" in their teenage ears. Hugh arrived in the midst of the conversation, and looked as if he'd been plunked down on Mars.

Pleasantries over, Jules outlined a few bones of contention. He wanted Everett to realize that he had not hit him several nights earlier, that in fact he was one of the few people in the county who hadn't in the past week or so, and that he hoped Everett was capable of remembering that Hugh had hit him without this causing ill will.

He aimed to bore them to death, to so confuse them with the length of each question that they lost bearings. They both looked dizzy for a moment, and then Everett turned to Hugh. "You? You hit me? Good lord, how embarrassing."

Hugh stared at him. "Of course I hit you, you crazy shit."

Point two: Hugh and Otto had had an argument on the day Otto left to camp, but Hugh had said they had a completely amicable relationship.

Jules stopped there and waited for Hugh, who stared at him. "Small town," said Jules finally.

Everett, able spokesman, leaned forward. "That's how they *talked.* I'm sure they were—"

"Everett," snapped Jules, "I don't believe you observed the argument, and if you did I want to know about it."

Hugh ahemmed. "We were talking about who was going to handle what in the future."

Jules raised his eyebrows, unsatisfied.

Hugh looked uncomfortable. "Otto had decided to stay in overall charge. He said that Everett was a marvelous salesman, but wouldn't do for a tactician."

Everett stared at Hugh.

"And what did you say?" asked Jules.

"I said it would be hard to explain this to Everett."

"Is it possible this change of heart had something to do with mining claims?"

Hugh stared at Jules. "No. Just general stuff."

"Did you know I used to be an archaeologist?" said Jules.

"Everett told me," said Hugh. "I found it quite an interesting change of career on your part. In North Africa, right?"

"Mostly," said Jules. "A school friend of mine who worked

in the Southwest once put in a mining claim on a site to prevent it from becoming part of a subdivision."

"How clever," said Hugh, smiling. "Did they get away with it?"

"Yes. Another tactic I've heard of was to put in a claim to prevent other researchers from inspecting a doctored site."

"Nasty," said Everett. "That wouldn't work now."

"No," said Jules. "And in Europe and Africa it's much easier to openly bribe or buy the site. The point is that Otto had been looking into mining claims and patents on the public land around Dragonfly. Everett told me he didn't know anything about claims in the area."

"I don't," said Everett.

"Though four claims are specifically in your name, Everett, and another eleven are split between Hugh, Otto and Sylvia."

Silence. Hugh turned cherry red. "We do," said Everett. "Pretend I never said that last. I've been a hired gun too long."

"You sure as hell have," said Jules. "This was your end run around the possibility of logging?"

Hugh nodded. Everett sighed. "We put it together a long time ago. We couldn't afford to buy more Forest Service parcels, and this was our way around potential problems."

"If the Forest Service allowed logging, we'd have the claims," said Hugh. "They were sited to block access to the drainages. And if all else failed we had the easement to the road in. Otto was careful, Otto watched our ass."

Grace dropped a pink slip on Jules's desk. "Richard Berko returned your call. He could barely talk."

Jules threw the slip on a growing pile and met Everett's bloodshot eyes. "Why would Otto look into claims if he already knew about them?"

"I don't know," said Everett. "Especially as it was his idea to file for claims to begin with."

Jules made out a lukewarm soda can on the corner of his desk, and cracked it without offering them anything. "Did he perhaps figure out there was something valuable on the land after all? I ask because if there is something worth mining, I can't discount it as a motive. Hugh"—Jules nodded toward the director—"now holds eleven of the fifteen claims you filed together. Sylvia inherited Otto's, and Hugh inherited Sylvia's."

Everett and Hugh exchanged a look. "I did the literal ground work," said Everett. "There's nothing up there. The claims were meant as insurance, a way of controlling the land without really having to pay for it. A mining claim is an absolute. If someone held claim to the base of a hill, there was a good chance the hill would legally be off limits. Hugh could kiss his profit good-bye if the condos faced a clearcut."

"Or a mine," said Jules.

"No one has ever found worthwhile mineral deposits in the Crazies," said Everett. "And no one ever will."

"But you had to find something to locate the claims."

"Oh," said Everett. "We found enough gold for that near the old shafts. Had a little picnic."

Hugh was smiling at the acoustical tiles, remembering. Jules was annoyed. "What, you just went up and panned?"

"Jules, I have a degree."

"Biology and law, right?"

"Geology," said Everett, grinning. "Not that the methods change much with time."

Jules drained his soda and crunched the can decisively enough to make Hugh jump. "Why'd you use fake names on the claims?"

"Less suspicious," said Everett wearily. "Who'd believe Otto Scobey wanted to mine? And they weren't really fake names, they were corporations as locators, all strictly legal. I did it through a friend to speed things up, and he understood."

"Why lie to me?"

"You never really asked," said Hugh, suddenly taking charge, maybe realizing even Everett might play out on easy answers soon. "And it was a little off, as we obviously had no intent to mine. It's been our in-joke, our solidarity for two years now. Our secret weapon. It wasn't the sort of information you volunteer."

As if to say, so Jules, we were in it together. He still bargained on divisiveness kicking in some day soon, now that the original four were down to two. It was a little like *Ten Little Indians,* and he wondered if it made them nervous, too.

The phone was ringing off the hook and Jules stretched in his chair. Hugh and Everett popped up with palpable relief, but he wasn't done with them.

"Why such obvious names?"

"No one out here knows anything anymore," said Hugh. "I told you we meant it as a joke. It's a tedious process, putting through a claim. And then there was the symbolism."

Jules shook his head at Grace, who waved her arm toward his phone. "What symbolism? The outlaw angle? Theoretically saving the trees while you cram the meadow with buildings?"

"In a way," said Hugh stiffly. "Though that's not quite how we thought about it."

"Sylvia thought that was funny, too?"

"Yes, she did," said Hugh defiantly. "Why should any of us be on the Forest Service's side? What good ranching girl wouldn't love the joke of controlling land without paying more than a few dollars for it, no taxes, nothing. Cheaper even than grazing rights."

Jules suddenly and absolutely believed that Hugh had loved and known Sylvia in the way you know and love someone you giggle in the dark with. He could hear Sylvia laughing over the irony of free land, and he could imagine her picking her name, Hazel instead of Haze, the worst man in the Plummer lot.

"I have a couple of stray questions," he said. "The only claim that's been patented is one of yours, Everett. It went through at the end of last week."

Everett had been staring blankly out the window, and turned slowly, as if he hadn't really heard.

"It was a test," said Hugh impatiently. "To see how easily it would go through. And it means something to Ev. He'll own it, and he'll have his cabin there. We couldn't get away with that on a claim."

"Which one of you broke into Otto's house?"

Silence and much inspection of the linoleum.

"Did you take anything besides this map?" He held it up.

They shook their heads.

"Why didn't you just tell your employee to give it to you before he left?" he asked Hugh acidly.

"That gets back to my not wanting to address the problems between Otto and Everett," said Hugh, with an effort.

"Why did Sylvia slap you after the parade?"

He looked hunted and weepy. "Small town," said Jules for the second time.

"I asked her why Otto left her a note." Hugh spoke softly, and Everett averted his gaze. "I thought they were seeing each other again."

"And what did Sylvia say?"

Hugh smiled. "She seemed to think I was trying to kill her. It was a hard time at the end. I wish it had been better."

By one that Friday it was ninety degrees, and two fires started in the valley, one of which moved through a full chicken coop and incinerated eighty tons of hay. In town, people had headed for the water, which temporarily gave the illusion of quiet. At three, Grace answered a call for a possible drowning in the old mining dredge behind the valley hot springs. Forty more miles at top speed, chasing an ambulance, and when Jules and Al and Bean, the paramedics, finally ran down the steep gravel slope the man was the color of an enameled bathtub. Twenty-five years old, a good-looking waiter at Blue Deer's very bad, very pretentious nouvelle restaurant. He'd moved that spring from Savannah, Georgia, where people surely knew how to swim, and he'd been showing his friends how long he could hold his breath underwater. Bean was of the opinion "his heart just popped." Jules surveyed the man's friends and thought they were a little extra edgy, but this determination could be left to Horace, who got to start his twenty-first year of marriage with a double autopsy that night.

Jules spent the rest of the afternoon cooling down a particularly onerous dispute, one in which the even division of property was taken literally. After he'd carted the sawdust-covered attacker to jail, he decided dinner would be a bad idea, and was only ten minutes late for the autopsies.

"Did you have a good time last night?"

Horace nodded. "I recommend marriage. Have you ever considered it?"

"I came close once."

"Easy to say if you didn't do it."

"She died," said Jules. "A car accident."

Horace was struggling with his rubber gloves and sighed. "On that cheerful note, we can flip for who to start with."

Blue Deer used an old restaurant walk-in for a morgue. It didn't make the state boys happy, but it worked. Jules and Horace stood in the doorway looking at a fresh set of toes.

"Is that the waiter?" asked Jules.

Horace pulled back the sheet abruptly. "Yep."

"Stop it," said Jules. "Goddamn water sports. Did you find anything in his blood?"

"Not yet, but I scraped plenty of goo out of his nose when they brought him in, water or no," said Horace. "And I don't think he had a talcum powder fetish. There's not much point to slicing him up." He reached for Sylvia's cart. "You don't have to see this."

"Somebody's supposed to be here, and Harvey and Ed can't,

and I don't want Jonathan to start with Sylvia."

Horace nodded, and started to pull back the sheet.

"I have a quick question," said Jules.

Horace snorted.

"Why did Otto come to see you, right before he left?"

"Don't you think the dead are entitled to their privacy?" asked Horace.

Jules, flanked by naked bodies, wondered at the ironies. "Not when they came to be dead in this fashion."

"Christ," said Horace. "Let me think." He drummed his fingers on the steel examining table, and flinched when he touched Sylvia's wrist. "Colitis," he said finally. "Stress. The man was a classic internalizer, blood pressure inching up every year despite a fair amount of exercise. I wanted to put him on a gentler diet, but he was having work done on his teeth, and a healthy amount of roughage was difficult for him."

Jules doodled on his notepad, and Horace misread his silence. "Fruit was the answer, I said, fruit and prune juice and a vacation. He said he was going to take a break, but he was having his car worked on after it broke down somewhere in Wyoming, which I guess scared the living shit out of him and didn't exactly help his blood pressure."

"A lot of bad luck in a small population."

Horace looked at their two companions. "You could put it that way."

"I don't just mean the horse, or the car. I heard that Sylvia was nearly electrocuted by a juicer a couple of weeks ago." Jules pointed to her half-healed elbow. It was unmistakable, though the colors were wrong; a burn didn't look like a burn anymore, once someone was dead.

"I wondered what that was," said Horace, bending to look. "Shorted, huh?"

"I guess."

Horace stared at Jules, obviously disliking the tangent. "So go check out the goddamn juicer."

"I gather Hugh threw it away."

The doctor threw up his arms in exasperation. "Who the hell wouldn't, if it nearly killed someone? Do you mind if we get started here?"

They found nothing to indicate why she might have died on life support. Her heart showed some damage, but that was only natural as it had stopped several times a few days before it stopped for good. The needle marks on her arms added up to the numbers and types on the chart with two exceptions, and Horace put those down to false starts on a vein pending the blood tests.

Jules woke Saturday morning with a great ball of pain in his head. It stuck with him through four speeders, a possibly rabid skunk, a fencing dispute, and the mercy killing of a hit-and-run German shepherd. At one he walked home for some ibuprofen, silence, and a can of chicken soup, but Moe was out of shape about something, and Fred had vomited yet again, splattering some books. Jules took refuge on the front porch with his bowl and indulged in a series of classic, alcoholic, postbinge thoughts: He missed someone, but couldn't think of who it might be. It wasn't a friend, or the woman who'd written the postcard, or his dead father. It certainly wasn't his mother or his sister, and only in the vaguest way did the feeling apply to the girlfriend he'd told Horace about. What he really missed was feeling vital enough to want someone, immediately and in perpetuity. He felt sorry for himself, and he was sick of feeling sorry for himself.

Only two years into a theoretically meaningful job and already he had a sense of repetition. You got the bad guy or you didn't, you saved someone or you didn't, you found someone or you didn't, your judgment was good or it wasn't. The truly memorable incidents were often so grisly that others shied away from the topic, leaving you no one to talk to; they faded in everyone else's memory, and if you brought them up you sounded like a broken record, a man with no life. Jules spent much of his existence shying away from a multiplying list of people and problems he'd rather not deal with. Edie, Donald Parsons, survivors of people who'd died in car wrecks, encountered in grocery stores while he tried to decide between whole and two-percent milk. He didn't mind staring back at the brother of a man he'd put in jail, but why endure the moment if he didn't have to?

It wasn't until he was washing up, gazing blankly out his back window as he scrubbed, that Jules focused on Alice and Edie, who were picking flowers in his neglected garden while Everett reclined in the hammock, accepting bouquets as a pasha might accept a peeled grape. He'd wondered at the odd giggles he'd heard when he was mooning out in front, and now the laughter seemed like theme music for his depression. He knew Alice was trying to cheer Everett up, and he knew Edie was probably trying to do the same thing, and he loved them for it, but they didn't need to do it in his yard when he was convinced no one within two thousand miles loved him.

It was a little like finding his wife in bed with another man, and since Everett didn't hear him coming Jules kicked him in the ass through the hammock mesh. "The tough life of a lobbyist."

"Stop," shrieked Everett. "These are for Sylvia."

Alice and Eddie straightened in the garden patch, and Alice saw the look on Jules's face. "For the funeral, Jules. I need to save some of mine for the fair."

At the Lutheran church Hugh flexed his hands as if he were preparing to play a piano. "I wanted to say a few words about the woman I had come to love more than any other human in my life, but she knew how I felt, and I will bury those feelings with her. So all I can tell you is that though I have no peace, I believe she has won it, and that I will always feel her death is as unfair and as unbelievable as the death of a child.".

No one moved. Jules looked at the dark wood casket and thought about the sewn-together body he'd seen the night before. He wondered why they hadn't had the kindness to cremate her, as if doing so might exorcise the pain and damage, truly send her to heaven.

"I would like to read a short passage for Sylvia Charlotte Coburg, who believed in God, but who also believed in a heaven on earth."

Oh boy, thought Jules. He tried to make his body relax. Two rows ahead Everett was white as a sheet, but Diane was smiling next to Sylvia's sons, who looked confused.

Hugh cleared his throat.

Hear my prayer, O Lord, and let my cry come unto thee.
Hide not thy face from me in the day when I am in trouble;
*   incline thine ear unto me: in the day when I call answer me*
*   speedily.*
For my days are consumed like smoke, and my bones are
*   burned as a hearth.*
My heart is smitten, and withered like grass; so that I forget
*   to eat my bread.*
By reason of the voice of my groaning my bones cleave to my
*   skin.*
I am like a pelican of the wilderness; I am like an owl of the
*   desert.*

Jules, despite newfound respect for the orator, nearly stood and screamed enough. Hugh wasn't a cheap romantic after all.

I watch, and am as a sparrow alone upon the house top.
Mine enemies reproach me all the day; and they that are mad
*   against me are sworn against me.*

*For I have eaten ashes like bread, and mingled my drink with
weeping,*
*Because of thine indignation and thy wrath: for thou hast
lifted me up, and cast me down.*
*My days are like the shadow that declineth; and I am
withered like grass . . .*
*I said, O my God, take me not away in the midst of my days:
thy years are throughout all generations.*

He finished and stepped back to his pew, and the congrega-
tion sighed. The minister was purple with indignation and immediately recited "The Lord is my shepherd," an infinitely more
comforting psalm. He spoke of "our sister Sylvia, safe in God's
caring hands," her weeping sons and sad maiden aunts, and
frail, heartbroken grandmother; mentioned her love for animals
(without delving into the irony of this love having killed her); her
love for the landscape she'd been born into; her good works; and
her humor. He did a fine job, all in all, and after he led the con-
gregation in singing a hymn he stepped down.

Sylvia's ninety-year-old grandmother nodded to him, and
Jules walked up to the casket. She'd asked him to say the final
verse because he had a good voice, she said, and because he was
young, and it was good to end death with youth. Jules had stayed
up until three wondering what to read. He didn't feel young, but
he spoke clearly.

*Consider the lilies of the field, how they grow: they neither toil
nor spin. And yet I tell you that not even Solomon in all his
glory was robed like one of these.*

FAUNA

BLUE DEER BULLETIN

SHERIFF'S REPORT, WEEK OF JULY 5–11

July 5—A report was received of horrible smelling smoke coming from the exit at mile marker 377. An officer was advised and reported an incinerator was burning.

July 6—A driver reported prairie dogs all over the highway and cars hitting them. She thought someone should take care of the prairie dogs or they should be put in a zoo.

July 7—An individual complained about children wielding water balloons. An officer suggested he tell the children to go away.

An officer was requested to help with a situation involving a juvenile.

July 8—An individual reported a dog locked in a vehicle with closed windows. An officer responded and found the owner had returned. The owner was warned.

July 9—An individual reported a prowler. No prowler was discovered.

An individual reported that a neighbor was on a roof with a chain saw. An officer responded and discovered a domestic disturbance. The man was taken into custody.

July 10—An individual reported finding an unconscious man in her flower bed. An officer responded and took the man to the hospital.

July 11—An individual reported a male walking along a highway with nothing on but a thin pair of pants. An officer responded and discovered the man was intoxicated, and had been kicked out of his car by his wife.

A report was received of a moose chasing a dog. The individual was advised to control his dog.

It was a pisser being a grownup. On July 12, Jules's fourth week back at work began with the much-delayed inquest into the deaths of Otto Scobey and Bonnie Siskowitz. Jules still didn't see the point in the formality—what, after all, did anyone have to add to the mess?—but as usual, no one had asked for his opinion, and he'd begun to husband his fights.

He put on his much-used funeral suit instead of a uniform and walked into the courtroom without bothering to bring notes, or check into who was on the jury, or touch base again with Scotti. He scanned the onlookers from the doorway. No one for Otto but Hugh, now that Sylvia was dead; no one for Sylvia. Then again, it wasn't her inquest, and there was no real reason to suppose she deserved one.

The irony was that almost everyone in the courtroom who felt true sorrow was there for Bonnie, the forgotten woman, the woman who'd slept with one last wrong man. Her mother, father, brothers, cousins, aunts and uncles, friends and coworkers. Twenty-three people, all told, for someone he had barely thought of in the last week.

Three hours later, when it was evident to the world at large that the Absaroka County Sheriff's Department didn't have a clue as to who had crushed the tent, he tried to be one of the first out of the door and collided with Mary Peach, the owner of the

Martinsdale Inn. They joked quietly out in the hall about how one day he might actually have the time and the appetite to eat on a visit to Martinsdale, and she told him Everett's last visit had really perked things up for the first time since the parade. Which made her think of poor Sylvia Coburg, and how awful that was, and how much she wished she'd had a chance to really speak with her the day after.

"The day after what?" said Jules.

"The day after the parade," said Mary Peach. "A month or so ago, on a Sunday."

Jules stared at her, wondering if she could possibly mean the last Sunday of Otto and Bonnie's life.

"She came in to eat dinner with her new boyfriend," said Mary, oblivious. "He ate a lot, and she was just as pretty and sweet as ever."

Lies, lies, lies. People died lying, but at least it would give him and Hugh yet another topic to discuss. By the time he'd marched down the hall to the station life seemed so bleak and Scandinavian that he decided, out of sheer stubbornness, to clear up a few odds and ends before he ran the asshole to earth.

He and Otto had shared a mechanic, Erb Arnslatter. Erb was deaf from too many pneumatic tools, and talked at a scream even over the phone. Jules found himself screaming back as he explained his reason for calling, which gave him a bit of a cheering section in the station room. So it was something of a shock when Erb fell silent.

"What?" yelled Jules, deafened by the lull.

"Somebody killed him?"

"Sure enough. Crushed him in a tent. Don't you read the papers?"

"No."

More silence. Jules did a Morse code tap with his pencils. "All I need to know is whether he showed for an appointment or not. Was it an oil change? Brake job?"

Erb snorted. "I'll say it was a brake job. Someone had cut his goddamn line. Nearly killed him."

Jules fumbled for a pencil. "You know that?"

"No doubt."

"Did he say where? In Boulder?"

"Nah, outside of Cody. He made it halfway up a mountain and found out he couldn't stop when he braked for a switchback. Quite a job towing that sucker all that way back."

"Did it just let go there? Could it have broken on its own or been cut earlier?"

"No, it was just about clean. Probably a puddle of fluid wherever he'd had it parked, but he didn't look 'cause he didn't know what the problem was till I told him. And then I can tell you he was pretty goddamn upset."

Otto, not bothering with pablum like "that goddamn bad luck," feeling hunted. "How so?"

"All quiet. And he wanted the car fixed, right away. Said he had to go somewhere."

Jules hung up and stared into space. He would have been thrilled if he could have figured out a way either Hugh or Everett could have been in Cody to cut a brake line.

Loose ends, little shit, everywhere. He'd have saved time by stockpiling thorny questions, but a roomful of Bonnie's relatives had made him jumpy, and he tracked Hugh down to earth at the Blue Bat, still in his inquest tie. Everett, also in a tie on the next stool, was fresh from the county commissioners and nursing a soda. Hugh, the man who claimed to stick to beer to avoid violence, had a big fat whiskey.

Three men in suits. Jules hauled Hugh into the back hall, while Everett watched with minimal interest. No, he hadn't known the nature of Otto's car problem; yes, they were in the *general* area, looking at horses on a ranch a hundred miles from Otto's vehicle, with other people all afternoon; no, Everett hadn't known about his and Sylvia's trip to Martinsdale that last

Sunday, and Hugh would appreciate it if Jules didn't tell him now.

"We didn't mention it because we knew you'd make a big deal about it. We were worried about Everett's mental state."

"I'm glad someone was. Did Otto suspect Everett of something?"

"Of course not."

"Then why the second thoughts about having him in charge?"

"Well," said Hugh, pulling out a hankie and dabbing his brow, "I'm sure he just didn't think the man was solid."

Jules tried to be patient. Hugh had to be on his third drink already; possibly Everett wasn't alone in guilty misery. "This was a month ago, more. What was he doing that so alarmed you?"

Hugh looked confused. "It's hard to put into words."

Jules gritted his teeth. "What did Sylvia think?"

"She didn't want to go up there."

"What did Otto say?"

"We never saw them. They weren't in their tent, and the car was gone."

Jules looked toward the bar, to where Everett sat slumped next to his ginger ale. All the fight seemed to have gone out of him. It might have been his new prescription, but it was just as likely exhaustion.

"What's the occasion this afternoon?"

Hugh looked longingly at his stool. "We just received final approval on Dragonfly."

It didn't seem to make him that happy, but Everett turned and slowly raised his glass in their direction.

Jules left by the back door and blinked in the sunlight and the cool, clean breeze. He looked toward the Baird and thought for a moment of trying to make peace with Edie, then decided to drop everything for the afternoon—slit brake lines, dead rodeo queens, lost loves—and be a civilian. He walked into the bookstore and bought three novels that he'd someday have time to read, ambled into the music store and picked up two CDs. He bought a newspaper, some socks on sale, and a pair of pretty candlesticks for Alice's birthday, still months away. He was on his way to buy a water gun for his nephew Artie when a glance through the window of the photo supply store gave him Diane's unmistakable backside, a compelling sight for a variety of reasons.

The bell on the door rang when he entered, but she continued to pore over her prints, not, as usual, bothering to acknowledge the rest of the world. Even after she flicked through another five photos—three Dragonfly landscapes and two of the rodeo steer pens—and he cleared his throat, she only turned enough to note his shoes and went back to her stack. The broncs, the empty chutes, a profile of Hugh yelling at someone.

Jules heard a whistle approaching from the back of the store and brought his hand along her butt ever so softly. Diane wheeled, her face rigid; it was one of the rare times when he really had surprised her.

"Can I look through them?" he asked sweetly.

She still wasn't quite back to her version of normal. "What's with the white shirt?"

"Inquest." He seized the stack she'd already inspected and felt her twitch.

She definitely had an eye for the strange. It was like seeing a series of extras for a Fellini movie, and in the landscape shots the black and white mountains looked about to shatter. She'd caught one black bull's silvery ribbon of snot making a perfect lariat around its own head, and the bull's eyes looked like a shark's. Close-ups of a whole series of riders, and more shots of Hugh, Everett, Peter, but not a single picture of Sylvia that bothered to focus on her face. He thought of some old Alice advice—never trust a woman who doesn't like other women—but it had never occurred to him to trust Diane anyway. Then he reached Sylvia's final ride, and found a sole clear shot, so clear that he could see a smudge on her cheek as she smiled and put her foot in the stirrup. It gave him goosebumps. His eyes moved to the background and there was Richie Berko, a little fuzzy but obviously distraught, bashing at something that proved to be a man's hand, connected to the even blurrier profile of Genie Jordan.

Diane's proof sheet and an eyeglass lay on the counter, and his hand snaked out for them. The good print of Sylvia was followed by four more as she mounted, adjusted her stirrups and ropes, talked to another rider. In the background, Richie Berko retreated, his back to the camera, and Genie followed. They faced each other, both now specks even with the glass, and in the third frame Genie open-handed Berko's curly head. In the fourth they'd disappeared.

Diane watched him, unreadable. The owner had emerged and retreated again to his darkroom. "Who is that man?"

"Someone named Genie Jordan."

She pointed again. "Is that the clown who blew up?"

"Yes."

"Do you want my film?"

"Yes."

"How about, 'Yes, thank you, Diane. You've made my life better, once again.' "

Jules smiled, tucked Genie and the clown to one side, and reached for the rest of the prints. "Just as you say, ma'am."

A gorgeous shot of the river; clusters of cowboys taking shelter downtown during the Saturday afternoon rainstorm; some dark interiors, out of sequence, from the wake. Then there he was, a true native son in the next print, smiling at the photographer on Saturday evening, immediately after their set-to in the sheep barn.

"You think I don't like anything, but I like that picture of you." She took the prints from him and dropped them into an envelope.

"It's flesh and blood that's the problem, huh?"

Diane gave her trademark smile. "Have I acted like I had a problem with it? Walk back to the Baird with me?"

"No," said Jules. "I need to deal with these now. But I'd love to take you to dinner later."

He sent the Gardiner deputy in search of Genie without luck; sent Jonathan in search of Richie Berko, without luck; and had the other images in the sequence enlarged. He and Diane had a very domesticated night, a date, though without the usual datey compulsion to fill silences.

Genie and his girlfriend didn't turn up the next day, or the one after that, and Richie Berko's partner said Berko had left via Greyhound to visit his mother, somewhere in Wyoming, and would be back Thursday or Friday. Construction began in earnest at Dragonfly, and when Hugh wasn't there he worked on his screenplay, alone, in his room. Everett took his pills, put on his suit and tie, and simmered down into a worker-bee catatonia. Everyone went through the motions of citizenship. Jules used the lull to catch up on all the job's other messes, the DUIs and domestic abuses and bad checks and petty thefts.

He spent the next two nights with Diane in an odd drifting mood, relaxed but watchful, fascinated by her tenderness to Everett, who was asleep by ten every night, and her low opinion of everyone else on earth. She didn't struggle with civilities. Her sense of humor was marginal, and never emerged at her own expense. She'd read a lot, though without empathy. When she slept she looked young, potentially surprisable, and free of ulterior motives. In bed, she'd retreated a bit from her early tendency toward kinkiness, but not too far; she'd simply stopped showing off.

She didn't exactly blend in, and it still fascinated him sometimes that she had any soft parts, that she was human, and maybe that was one of the reasons he kept at it. He wasn't going to learn a thing by sitting on his porch alone, and he might learn quite a bit from her about the logistics between Everett and Hugh and Otto and Sylvia. He wasn't blind to the idea that she might want to learn something from him. She seemed fascinated by the idea that someone she knew may have murdered someone she'd known, without acknowledging or bothering to deny that the first someone could conceivably have been her, and theorized without encouragement. Genie had the brains of a beagle, and would have taken an Uzi to the tent. Hugh—well, Hugh didn't have enough money of his own. Maybe he didn't want to split it with Otto, maybe Otto had cottoned to some plot and Hugh, or Hugh and Sylvia, had shut him up. Everett didn't have enough money of his own either, but then he never would be satisfied. Though he might have wanted to kill Otto, Diane had once witnessed him vomit when he accidentally stepped on a large roach. According to Diane, Everett redefined not having the stomach for murder. She thought Sylvia had killed Otto. Maybe she'd intended to cheat Hugh and Otto found out, or maybe Otto was blackmailing her over something else. Sylvia had been the smartest of the bunch, and when people who had a lot wanted more, they tended to be decisive about getting it. Maybe the accident had been cosmic vengeance.

This theory didn't exactly put Jules in the mood. "And how about you?" he asked, wrestling naked with the window fan in her room at the Baird.

"Woo hoo hoo," she laughed. "I'd have poisoned them."

The Absaroka County Future Farmers of America
Proudly Present

SUPER AGRICULTURAL COUPLES CONTEST

It's a Family A-Fair

BALE TOSS The husband picks up a square straw bale and tosses it over a six-foot-high crossbar. The bar will be raised in one-foot increments.

WHEELBARROW RACE The husband will load the wife into a wheelbarrow and transport her across the first marker and then remove her from the wheelbarrow and carry her across the finish line.

TRACTOR BACKING The wife will be required to back a tractor up through a set of pylons while she is facing forward and using only the husband's directions. Once through the pylons the husband will hook up a trailer which the wife will drive back through the pylons. Each pylon hit will be a five-second penalty.

EGG SEARCH Wife is assigned a nest of eggs and the object of the contest is to gather an egg which she believes to be hard-boiled and check it on her husband's head. She must check each egg until the hard-boiled one is found.

Alice had been reading out loud, but now it seemed likely that she'd choke from laughter and roll off her own front porch.

"I think you'd better sign up," said Jules. "Alice is doubtless the fastest egg cracker in the west."

"Only if you try it with Diane," said Peter. "I'd give a lot to see you push her in a wheelbarrow."

"Ho ho ho," said Jules.

In a way, the fair weekend was the rodeo's counterpoint, a revisiting of the range wars, the fancy plow versus the free cow. These days it all fit together, and in fact the FFA/4-H rodeo was more amusing than the self-important adult event, what with highlights like a potato race, goat tying, and the immortal pig wrestling contest, a thirty-second mudbath. (Rule #3: "Pig has to be put butt first into 55 gal. barrel. Barrel stays in the center of the pen. Barrel is tipped upright when pig is in.")

The crowd was definitely easier to get along with, and Jules didn't anticipate problems. When he left dinner at Peter and Alice's Thursday evening he planned to look up Richie Berko, see what he had to say about the old bruises on his forehead, maybe look in on Diane after the shift change at the Baird. He was touring the town, looking for a shabby orange Happy Cab, when the station radio announced a minor rollover with loose livestock on the freeway just outside of town. It proved to be the two dozen wrestling pigs, all colors, shapes, and sizes, heading all different directions. He gave up at one A.M. after retrieving eighteen, and decided the search for Berko's cab could wait.

He saw it soon enough. Once again, at noon on Friday, he stood in a dark Blue Bat on a beautiful, sunny day. This time he was in uniform, grilling Richie Berko on the topic of death threats, inquiring, as gently as possible, why his car was flaming in the alley behind the Blue Bat. Berko had had two shots of bourbon in the ten minutes since the car had made a popping sound and he'd run from it, abandoning the passengers, but the liquor hadn't settled him down. His whole body shook and tears cascaded down his cheeks; sometimes he waved his bandaged hand weakly over his eyes, as if to clear them, but this had only smeared the ink signatures on the cast and rubbed them into his forehead.

Jules gave up and fell silent. He patted Richie on his back and peered toward the dark corner booth where the passengers cowered. He asked Delly to go slow pouring the shots, and trudged out the back door to check on the fire department's progress.

David Eaton and his men stood in a semicircle on the wet pavement around the smoldering Delta 88. Jules walked toward the car, waving away the stink of burned vinyl. "Let's pop the hood," he said.

"You do it," said David, with a cherubic smile.

Jules made a face. David tossed him some gloves, shooed back the small crowd, and called for a hose as Jules edged toward the Olds and gingerly felt for the hood latch.

Everyone jumped back when it creaked skyward. Jules peered into a black, twisted, steaming landscape.

"Bang," yelled David into his ear.

"Die, gravysucking pig," muttered Jules. He pulled a knife

from his pocket and scraped a bit of tin fireworks confetti from the side of the oozing battery. Eaton pointed to the ghostly outline of a parachute and tube, pasted to the inside of the hood.

"A Sunrise Siren," he said.

Jules used the knife to pry up some charcoaled hoses. "Here's a Twitter Glitter and a Ground Bloom," he said. He walked around to look through the driver's door, and there on the passenger seat was an unlit Chicken Laying Eggs, affectionately known as a pooping chicken. Someone had a sense of humor.

"Some kid felt like using up his collection," said David. "That had to be an M-80 in the tailpipe."

"I don't think so," said Jules, extricating an Autumn Drizzle and a simple timer from next to a wiper fluid container. "Richie and fireworks have a real affinity for each other."

David stared at him. "He's the clown?"

"Same guy."

"Talk about bad luck. They'd all be dead if anything had been put in the gas tank. Can you take prints?"

Jules snorted and headed for the back door of the Blue Bat. He told Richie to keep his skinny little butt planted and walked over to the unmarked but glaze-eyed couple from Toledo. They'd been in the cab for three minutes when it blew; they'd been taking a cab to begin with because they'd taken out a cow and a rental car on the East River Road forty-eight hours earlier. No, Jules said soothingly, this wasn't a typical Montana vacation. He spoke to them gently and deliberately, and he had to repeat almost every question. They'd been walking, grown tired, seen the cab parked at a diner and gone in to find the driver. End of story.

When it became clear they didn't know a thing and couldn't walk back to their bed and breakfast, didn't in fact know where they were on the planet, he brought them the two go-cup martinis they agreed were a fine idea and returned them to their quarters.

When he got back, Richie Berko was sedated enough to give the illusion of calm, but he didn't remember any man hitting him at the rodeo, and no one had threatened him or told him to keep his mouth shut. He was stoic in his no's until they reached his tiny shed of a house and found his front door open. Jules told Richie to wait, took a brief look, and called the Bat to tell Harvey to make a second stop with the fingerprint powder. He took Richie back to the bar, for lack of a better baby-sitter.

Someone had cleaned out every cupboard and dumped every drawer in the place onto the floor, which probably hadn't been clean to start with. The mayhem was complicated by the fact that Berko had once intended to be a taxidermist, and many of his early projects had been ripped from the walls and shed when they hit the floor.

Harvey thought it had been a search; Jules thought it was simple destruction. Their one discovery came when Harvey shook a conch shell and two finger bones, threaded together with a wire, rattled out. Harvey screamed.

"He kept his goddamn finger?"

"Looks like it," said Jules. He picked up the shell, peered inside, and pulled out a small plastic bag filled with a gray, grainy substance.

"Toot?"

"I don't think so."

Ed got to look for Genie, but Jules and Harvey worked on Berko's latest disaster all day long, except for a break to retrieve two more errant pigs. They had Berko's logbook, and Jules was heard to wonder how many cab rides such an asshole could pick up on a Friday morning. Quite a few, as it turned out. Several infirm elderly, who'd visited the supermarket, hair dresser, and doctor. It was the kind of minute work that made Jules want to brain himself against a wall. From the commissioners' and council's point of view they were spending hours that could have gone into the profitable collaring of wealthy speeders, but when the mayor visited to make sighing noises Jules pointed out that most tourists don't expect to be blown up in a cab west of New York, on the far side of the world from Tel Aviv. By the end of the day the couple from Toledo had talked to the *Bulletin,* the Bozeman paper, the chamber of commerce, and their lawyer. Doom, doom, doom, said Jules to the mayor. Get off my ass and find my money, and I'll find your gunpowder fiend.

They had five sets and two partials left from the car after clearing all of Richie Berko's known fares, and no prints at all on the bag from the conch shell, the contents of which the hospital lab was trying to identify. Harvey started running the prints they had through state records on the computer, and Jules took over phone complaints for Grace, who was scheduled to judge rabbits, of all things, at the fairgrounds. A half hour later a child on a bicycle was hit by a car, and Jules rang the ambulance and left.

It wasn't so bad after all; the kid had zigzagged, needed a few stitches and lost some teeth, and the man who hadn't killed him was only mildly hysterical. Jules charged back, ready for bad news. Harvey met him in the hallway, beaming, chewing his gum with extra vigor.

"What do you want first?"

"Don't tease me," said Jules.

"A half-wiped partial on the edge of the hood belongs to Eugene Jordan."

"No shit?" said Jules. "There's more?"

Harvey smiled and slapped him on the back affectionately. "A thumb print on that conch shell belongs to him, too. And the hospital thinks the stuff in the bag is cyanide."

Jules could only stare. Nobody was this stupid, not even Genie, but how could he complain? All this in the time it had taken to locate one uprooted incisor. "I think I'm happy, but I'm not sure yet."

Harvey blew a bubble. "Mark just called in from Gardiner to say he'd found Genie's girlfriend in a bar, showing off $900 in cash. Also, you're supposed to call the state vets; they've got something on that horse."

On Saturday afternoon Peter was at his *Bulletin* desk, picking and choosing headlines and striving to not cackle out loud. What to cut? The cow-car incident? The porcupine-septuagenarian incident? The skunk–dog–trail bike incident? Perhaps the campers from San Diego who'd gone into a wasp nest for honey, or the unfortunate standard poodle that had inadvertently saved his master from a mountain lion.

The best story came first:

BULL ON THE RAMPAGE

On the eve of the Absaroka County Fair, Hamburgh, a 2,300-lb Angus-Brahma cross, has escaped and seems displeased with his surroundings. Hamburgh exited his enclosure at the fairgrounds at about four A.M., and was last sighted at noon near the lagoon. In between he dented a pickup, splintered two decks, attempted to gore one fair official, trampled a dog . . .

A very obese husky named Fur, owned by an insurance agent who doubled as a fowl judge. One of the decks had belonged to a very annoyed Donald Parsons, Jules's favorite human. Soren was in the darkroom, working on the film.

. . . and generally tore up the playground. Hamburgh was initially angered when stock company officials circled him, tried to lasso him, and then shot him several times with a small-caliber pistol. The sheriff's department responded after a call from a concerned citizen, and impounded the gun and warned the men to call the department of F,W & P for a tranquilizer gun, or to leave the matter up to the department. According to Sheriff Jules Clement, "the bull was the least dangerous mammal out there."

Peter cackled. What Jules had actually said was "I'd like to neuter those stupid motherfuckers." He'd been so enraged that when Peter had pressed him for a cleaner quote he'd screamed, "Print it. I'm sick of this shit," before spitting out the appropriately laconic sound-bite ten minutes later. The men had literally stood in a circle and fired away, making painful, maddening red holes in Hamburgh, which encouraged him to play Red Rover and head for the weak link of the circle—the realtor and Fur. All this on the children's playground, between the monkey bars and the tallest slide, on a sunny day in the midst of an exceptionally busy tourist season.

Hamburgh, the third lead bull of last year's Rocky Mountain Cattle Drive, had lead billing at this year's fair, with a purse of $2,000 offered to a six-second rider, and proceeds from event tickets going toward the Absaroka High junior class's planned trip to Japan. At press time, Hamburgh had been seen in a garden on West Cottonwood, slowly making his way north toward Cottonwood Street and downtown. Fair officials were unsure of when an F,W & P representative might arrive, but held out hope that Hamburgh would be safe in his pen by nightfall.

Someone dropped an extra large soda on his desk, and Peter jumped. It was the man of the hour himself, and he peered over Peter's shoulder at the screen and shook his head.

"Hamburgh's history, sweetheart."

"There's a headline," said Peter. "Give me the ugly details. I only have half an hour."

"He crossed Main and the same crew of assholes tried to hem him in with cars. Main Street, one in the afternoon, the biggest day of the fair, with a muscle car show going on across from the Fry and Chew only three blocks down. This time one of them had a thirty-eight, and someone else had a goddamn rifle, and they still didn't quite do the job even on each other and the bull ran through the train yard and into a westbound engine, which was only going ten miles an hour but still took its back leg off."

"He's dead?" asked Peter, stunned by the ratatatat of the story and already wondering how to translate it.

Jules raised his eyebrows in a kind of silent "duh." He wanted information and wasn't in the mood to dole any more out. He didn't, for instance, tell Peter that he'd gotten back a set of autopsy results that morning, and would have another when he met Horace later that afternoon. He didn't mention the fact that Jonathan had left his Beretta on the patrol car hood when he sped toward the railroad tracks in hot pursuit of the dumb, terrified, wounded beast and his great white hunters. Somewhere in town, a common tourist might pick up a pistol and become a psychopath due to simple happenstance and a hiring error. And Jules didn't tell Peter that when he caught up with the posse, after the train had struck the bull, broken its spine and severed one leg, the men had been standing around the still live animal, chitchatting about it all while the bull moaned and watched them with a blood-flecked white eye. Jules shot the bull behind the ear and ended it finally, but then one of the men laughed and joked, something to the effect of "Hey, give it a sporting chance." White light: He put the jokester and two of his gun-happy friends into the back of the squad car, laid their fancy rifles on a cement slab, borrowed the train engineer's sledgehammer, and sent the guns to the great scrapyard in the sky. Peter would hear about it all eventually, when the men filed complaints. There was no point in getting into it now.

"Why are you smiling?" asked Peter.

"Good question." He was smiling because when he'd learned that Jonathan had joined in the shooting spree with his shotgun, Jules had told Jonathan to pick up each and every shell with his teeth after he picked up the body parts and scrubbed the engine. "If you send Soren up there he might still find a photo opportunity."

"He's got to leave for the 4-H judging." Peter looked around the room for other candidates, then shrugged. "We've got a picture of Hamburgh live. That's what Teddy will want. Unless the engine is damaged."

"Not a dent. A few smears. They wouldn't play in black and white."

Peter started typing while Jules looked around the room, sipped his soda, and enjoyed the padded chair. Peter worked on titles, muttering each for the proper ring. The occasion called for a *New York Post*–style phrase, something like HEADLESS WOMAN IN TOPLESS BAR. The old rule of thumb was that you had to be able to sing it to the melody of "Camptown Races."

"Hamburgh Eats It on a Track, *doo dah, doo dah . . .*"

Jules opened one eye.

"Bull and Train Meet at Noon, *oh de doo dah day.*"

"Can you tell me what Hugh's screenplay is about?"

"I haven't paid attention. Go ask Alice. I think she'll know." Peter cracked his knuckles and went back to typing.

Jules drained half of his soda and gave Peter a foul look. "She's not home."

"She's probably in Bozeman. The shrubbery sales are on." He finished with a crescendo on the keyboard and turned to stare at Jules. "Why are you here? Have you found Genie? Need someone to pull his nails out?"

"Nah. I'm hiding. The commissioners and council were almost done with a special session in the basement, and I couldn't bear the sounds of plotting through the jail wall."

Peter nodded, reread his lead, and stood. "Caption time."

Jules rubbed his shoulder and sank farther back in the chair. "Will you see if Soren still has his rodeo shots out and about?"

"Sure." Peter started off and then turned around. "Why?"

"Just curious."

"My ass. You haven't spent so much time in one chair since May."

Soren Rue was literally black and white, as if he truly lived in the darkroom. It was always a little shocking when you saw him in daylight, despite the fact that Soren's job constantly called for him to encounter wildlife, stand in rushing rivers, and endure subzero sporting events. Peter found him agonizing over three shots of a large, angry bull, but knew enough to stand back and let the process continue. Soren would miss half the 4-H judging, but Soren was perpetually late, and the only person this surprised was their new publisher. Peter found the Wrangle outtakes gathering dust on a shelf, and sifted through until he hit the bull riding.

"Hamburgh sure was bigger than most of the bulls at the rodeo."

"He looked like an elephant to me," said Soren, earnestly.

"You got some good shots," said Peter politely. "I especially like the one on the left, where he's charging you."

"It's a little out of focus."

"That's understandable."

It took another five minutes for Soren to pick the blandest shot. Peter brought it back to his desk with the rodeo pictures. Jules was looking through the day's pages, and held up a large personal from page two. "Did you see this?"

Thanks

To all the kind people who helped Eric after his bike accident on Fifth and Pyrite yesterday. Special thanks to the ambulance drivers and police officer who found the teeth and to Dr. Bolan for reattaching them.

The Eschelman Family

"Horace is a very talented man," said Jules. "And by the way, I only found an eyetooth."

Peter shuddered and showed him the two bulls. "Check out

the size difference. What will they do with the carcass?"

"I have no idea," said Jules, snatching away the stack.

"Those fireworks were tampered with somewhere else," said Peter, watching him scan every inch.

"I know," said Jules.

"The mare looks normal in every shot. I checked through right after the fact."

"It would have happened in the barn," said Jules.

"You're a paranoid bastard," said Peter. "You don't believe in natural causes anymore."

"It was the horseshit that bothered me," said Jules, flipping another black and white. "If a heart blows up you don't keep going like that, you drop. With a stroke it's even faster. And the horse had diarrhea."

"Everyone shits when they die. Maybe it was an epileptic seizure."

Jules took a sip from his soda and looked at one photo with a pretty cowgirl in the foreground and Genie and Everett Parsons apparently having a sign language conversation in the right corner. He put it next to another that showed Hugh watching Richie Berko. "It was foamy, and it was happening by the time she came out of the gate."

"Is that so." Peter made another attempt at a caption. The photo showed Hamburgh splintering redwood, while Donald Parsons screamed in the background. Sometimes heaven beamed down in strange ways.

"I found a funny-looking smear on the corral post. And as it happens, the mare's death was caused by a cyanide suppository."

Peter stopped scribbling. *"What?"*

"A suppository, just a big old fillable capsule, probably. It would have taken about ten minutes to dissolve."

Peter threw his pen so violently that it broke on his desk. "Ten minutes to deadline, and you're telling me you've got evidence of another fucking *murder?"*

"Time to go," said Jules. "If you stop screaming, you'll still have the story first, but you'll have to wait a couple of days."

"It turns out," said Horace, "that Sylvia had quite a bit of potassium in her blood. Now, some of that could be naturally occurring, and some could have resulted from an honest mistake—"

"What would potassium have done?"

"Stopped her heart."

Jules flipped through the lab report. All sorts of people were working that weekend. He thought of Lot's wife, seeing something she should have left unseen. Why bother killing a woman who'll never talk again? Then he remembered the overly optimistic minister and his pamphlets on miraculous recovery. "Have you figured out who at the hospital made this honest mistake?"

Horace drummed his fingers on his desk.

"No. It may have been a confusion with the I.V.s."

"Have you tried to?"

"Yes. Before I even called you."

"If it was so honest, wouldn't it be easy to document? Wouldn't somebody have written down an injection and an amount?"

"Usually," said Horace, miserable.

"How quickly would it have happened?"

"Almost immediately."

"Who was on shift?"

"Renee was doing rounds. Arlanna was keeping an eye on a birth."

Jules remembered the birth. "Neither of them seems sloppy."

"No one at this hospital is sloppy."

Jules nodded.

Moe had a cough, and this time Fred had thrown up on Jules's bed, with little dribbles leading from the sheets to the stairs and across the living room, where he sat staring at the hacking bird. Jules had a sore throat. All of them were falling apart.

Jules bit the bullet and called San Francisco. Olive wanted to gossip, and he tried to satisfy her.

"You're missing all kinds of funerals," he said.

"Carlotta told me you picked a strange passage for Sylvia but read it well. What else is happening?"

Jules made a childish face into the receiver and Fred started to retch again, on cue. "That's about it. The weather's been hot, and we've had a few fires. The usual drunks."

"Let's get back to the cat," said Olive. "Fred never throws up. You need to take him to the vet."

"I arrested the new vet just the other day, in that riot. I don't like him. Who did we used to go to?"

"We?" said his mother sarcastically. "The last time you took an animal to the vet yourself you were six and it was a dying frog. I even had to take Marv in that last time."

Marv, an airedale, had been put to sleep at age sixteen the year before, and Jules had gotten thoroughly and absolutely drunk for the event. "Okay," said Jules. "Who did you selflessly haul my animals to?"

"Donald Parsons, but he lost his license right after he started practicing. I can't remember the name of the next guy, but he died in 1980 or so. Then someone who moved, and now we're stuck with that man you arrested, unless you'd like to drive to Bozeman with a parrot and a cat in the same car."

Jules didn't say anything. "Hello," said Olive, annoyed. "Jules?"

He drew a breath. "Parsons?"

"That's what I said. Lost his license for shooting a horse-dose of bute into a nice setter by mistake. One from Joseph's line, actually. Plus a lot of other problems. I think he neutured someone's prize stallion. By mistake. Try that, someday."

"Donald Parsons? The county commissioner?"

"Jules, did we or did we not live in the same town for your first seventeen years?"

"We did," he muttered. "But some things didn't seem worth remembering at the time."

"I'm glad you can pick and choose." In the background, he could hear Artie, three, yammering his name. "Hang on," said Olive. "He wants to talk to you."

"Steaming hot weiner," shrieked Artie. "Eat a bug."

A wrestling match ensued between Olive and her grandson while Jules found a chair and thought about how much he'd prefer to talk to Artie than most of his suspects. Olive won possession of the phone. "Isn't he a sweetheart? He can't wait to visit. So what are you going to do?"

"About what?" He wanted to get off the line, try to pin down, order his thoughts.

"What are you going to do about my sick cat?"

"Well," said Jules, "I might ask Everett if his dad taught him much."

★ 13 ★

TERRA AURA

BLUE DEER BULLETIN

SHERIFF'S REPORT, WEEK OF JULY 12–18

July 12—An individual reported that a man had been hurt in a fight, and had wandered off. An officer responded with negative contact.

July 13—A valley resident reported that someone had shot out her front window with a BB gun.

A report was received of someone doing "brodies" on the Absaroka Heights golf course. A deputy discovered tracks.

July 14—A traveler reported a mattress on the interstate between the Blue Deer and White Sulphur exchanges.

A report was received of customers refusing to pay for a room at a local motel. An officer was advised and the situation was resolved.

July 15—A traveler reported that someone had placed a rotten whitefish on his car seat. An officer removed the fish.

July 16—An individual reported sighting a mountain lion. The caller was advised to keep her child inside.

A motorist reported seeing a man in a wheelchair on the interstate, but could not recall the location. An officer investigated and found no one.

July 17—Several early-morning callers reported sighting a moose. The animal proved to be a bull.

July 18—An individual reported that his neighbor appeared to be plucking chickens in his garage. An officer advised him that this activity was not illegal.

Numerous hood ornaments were reported missing. An officer is investigating.

Jules tried to avoid blatant hints and questions, but his timing was bad, and Everett made subtlety impossible. He'd been in the midst of an argument with Diane, and for the first time Jules was aware of a well of resentment in Everett. Feigned surprise when Jules said Diane wasn't the object of his visit; a backlog of anger when he got the point.

"Are you accusing me of killing a horse just because you've decided I might know how to use a needle?"

Jules shrugged. That wasn't actually what he was saying; maybe Everett was smart enough to misread the question, as an honest man might. But he wasn't going to confide that his curiosity about needles had to do with Sylvia. Veterinary knowledge would provide an added plus in terms of equine suppositories, but he supposed you could read about those, and he was fairly sure someone had hired out that bit of dirty work. Needles you had to know.

They were standing in the lobby of the Baird on Monday, and Everett was wearing a suit, on his way to yet another meeting. It was six o'clock and the temperature on the bank clock was still ninety-one. Jules hoped Everett was as hot as he was. Served him right for throwing a scene in a public place.

"I watched my dad work twenty years ago and you're saying I'm responsible for the death of someone I *loved*?"

Jules raised an eyebrow and held his ground. The public, after all, consisted of Edie, trying to make herself one with the computer monitor, and Diane, legs crossed on the couch, flipping angrily through *Architectural Digest*.

"All I said, other than I'd forgotten that your father was a vet, was that Sylvia's horse did not die naturally."

"When's the last time you saw me even go near a goddamn horse?"

Jules squeezed out a tight-lipped smile. "Did I say I saw you go near a horse?"

"What about that psychotic you pulled in a couple of weeks ago?"

"I was going to ask you how well you knew Eugene Jordan."

"I don't, but I've heard he has a morphine problem. Ask *him* about needles."

"I will when I find him," said Jules. "I have a photo of you talking, but maybe you were just asking for bathroom directions."

He caught Edie's startled look and made to leave, but he'd started a chain reaction, and Everett lunged for his arm.

"Hugh ever mention to you how he began his film career?"

Jules waited patiently for the man to bite the hand that fed him.

"Did he?"

"Stunts. I've seen his knees. Then he was a techie."

"Don't be such a smug prick. You think you've done your research. He started staging stunts himself."

Jules shook off Everett's hand. "Keep talking."

"He was an FX guy. The only guy in England who really specialized in explosions. Not a big call for it in costume dramas, and he always said he was glad he got out of that line before he killed someone. But he was looking forward to the mining movie because he'd get to use it again."

"Well, Everett, thanks for letting me know." Jules was annoyed, despite himself. "As it happens, the fireworks in question here weren't particularly clever."

"You should ask him something else, too." Everett was white and stiff, on a roll. Diane was the same color, and Jules had the sense she wanted to kill him. "Ask him how well he and Sylvia were really getting along."

"Since you're so in love with the sound of your own voice, why don't you just tell me?" said Jules.

"All those accidents," said Everett.

"Everett," said Diane.

"What?" he snapped.

"You're late for your meeting."

Everett shut his eyes and rocked on his heels, then walked calmly out the door and climbed into the BMW.

Jules turned to Diane. "You can't keep protecting him."

"Why not?" She looked at him evenly, then stared at his crotch.

Jules left, feeling used.

Only twelve thousand people in the county, and still they couldn't turn up a white-trash psychopath named Genie Jordan, despite reports that he was floating around Blue Deer with plenty of cash and attitude. He'd told friends his girlfriend had made a bundle, but this was news to the lady who owned the cafe where she worked. Jules ached to ask Genie if he enjoyed inserting cyanide balloons in equine assholes, got an extra thrill blowing up and beating up clowns, trusted whoever had paid him to handle both these tasks and the second assault on poor Richie Berko, who'd embarked on a bender and was beyond answering questions. The planting of the cyanide in Berko's apartment had been such a clumsy maneuver that Jules thought it was the only thing Genie had done on his own, for free.

At the end of the day on Monday, with Genie still invisible,

Jules and Scotti met at a polite, mayor-approved bar and wrangled over whether to tell anyone about Sylvia and her horse. Jules wanted to do so, and up the ante on his cast of suspects; he pointed out that Horace could only be asked to keep such a secret for so long. Scotti was worried about how the hospital might look. Jules pointed out that Hugh, theoretically innocent of murder, deserved to know. Scotti wanted him to be guilty, and his bad temper increased when Jules was noncommittal and refused to give an opinion. Jules pointed out that Peter planned to drop the bomb about the horse poisoning by Wednesday, and even if Peter could be talked out of it, Henckle, the mare's owner, would know by then; once this came out, no one would blame a nurse for Sylvia. They settled on a Wednesday morning compromise, and Scotti said he'd handle Peter; he planned to offer him a job, get him off his ass and onto his side, and might as well make the offer an out-and-out bribe.

Alice lay on a sandy bank of the Yellowstone, letting the breeze and the hot sun dry her, putting off reading more horror stories about nineteenth-century white men's greed. Jules and Peter and Edie bobbed in inner tubes twenty feet out in the current. The inner tubes were a wonderful idea, but a person could only freeze her ass in a cold river for so long. They'd planned on floating and fishing, but a thunderstorm in Yellowstone Park had muddied the river, and Edie had volunteered the tubes. Her children were in Missoula with their father, and it seemed when the children returned he'd be staying behind. It was a relief to Alice, who'd always thought of the situation as a Mexican standoff, a no-win war of attrition. Alice had liked Edie's husband just fine, as had Edie, until he admitted he'd been having an affair, and Alice had never been good at forgiving anyone but Peter and the occasional charming asshole, like Jules. This wasn't why Edie and Jules were in the water together, now; that was simply due to the fact that it was more trouble to keep them apart.

Alice dozed.

"Don't move," said Jules.

Her eyes flapped open. He was crouched down, dripping wet and grinning.

"I came in very slowly, so that you could see all the black snakes enjoying the sun, too. They must have thought you were a log."

He pointed and she swiveled her eyes to the side without moving her head. Ten feet away, a black coil on a black rock moved ever so slightly, and suddenly Alice was airborne, screaming obscenities as she plunged into the water. All the rocks moved at once and even Jules scooted back toward the water, where Alice punched him.

"You lousy son of a bitch."

Much laughter from the inner tubes. Jules led her back to shore, where she demanded and received wine. It took half a glass before she showed any semblance of humor.

Jules pointed to her untouched bag of history books. "Why do you bother lugging it around?"

"Hugh's in a hurry now. He's got time on his hands, and says he'd rather write than think."

At least he had an option. "What's the screenplay about again, a mining disaster? He wrote it a long time ago, right?"

"Not a disaster, but something that happened during a strike, when he was a kid in Wales. And yeah, it's been going on forever. It's his baby. This is how he got to know Everett—Otto suggested he'd be a good reader for the mining details. Hugh got to know Sylvia because of the script, too, because Otto told him about her grandfather's old mine, and Sylvia took him on a tour. My whole job is to find a way to move the central scam here and give it a lot of local color."

"My whole job" was a hell of a way to describe ten hours of

weekly reading in nice weather. He smiled and stretched out in the sand, wondering if his memory served him right. "What's the scam?"

"A bunch of striking miners bombed the road to a mine closed to keep the scabs out."

Jules stared up into the dark blue sky. "That's a direct approach."

"Yeah, it was. But unfortunately, Ralph, the guy the studio wants in the lead, says he likes the story line but not the period. Hugh wanted to get into Butte in the teens, Frank Little and the Wobblies—"

"Which would make a great movie," said Jules. He'd go, and lately he only saw one a year.

"Which would make a great movie, but Ralph wants to ride a horse, and he wants a prettier landscape and older guns and bloodthirsty and not very accurate Native Americans. So now it's about prospecting in the 1860s or 1870s. Which is why I was bothering to read about Plummer and the rest."

Jules lay back down on the grass. "Tough to get all the prospectors in Montana to want to close a road together."

"Aren't you a riot," said Alice sarcastically. "I admit he's going to lose the noble brotherhood aspect. Now a bunch of poor, honest, and extraordinarily well-washed explorers will find gold in a wash, and follow it up a canyon, and dynamite the wash behind them as the bad guys close in."

"Wouldn't the bad guys go around?"

"There's only one way in, and everyone assumes the good guys are dead."

"How do they get out?"

"There's another way. Only our heroes know about it."

Jules swatted an ant on his stomach. "Seems geographically difficult to pull that off."

Alice pointed to a cliff and a rivulet across the river. "They should do the panning scene right here."

He lifted his head and let it drop again. "Wrong formations."

"Easy for you to say."

"You forget I spent my youth studying rocks." He peered at Alice, who was waving her arms in the air as if exercising. "Why are you doing that?"

"Keeping the snakes away."

They unpacked the food, roast pork sandwiches and potato salad and fruit, and Edie and Peter waded in. Edie deigned to share a blanket with Jules, and Jules deigned to eye her goosebumps, and the white strips between her tan line and her suit. When she wrapped herself in a towel he thought about the story Hugh had told Everett, the miners in Wales who were the reason for their first meeting, and ate another sandwich while he sorted out the chicken versus egg order of it all.

Peter talked about all the scripts he'd been reading, borrowed from Hugh; Jules sensed that he hoped for an end run against having to go back to work for Scotti: fortune, fame, and no grim child abuse prosecutions. Fittingly enough, Peter had been reading legal thrillers, and thought most of them were bad, just like most mysteries were bad. "You ask yourself, what's the con? What's the screw? Who's good, who's bad, who doesn't know *what* they are anymore? It's only the last question that seems to make them any good, because you can pick out the rest in the first twenty pages."

"Can you," said Jules. "I agree with you, about the last question."

"Sure you can," said Peter. "Then it's just finding the grave, digging it, and filling it again with a guilty body." He looked at Jules and almost blushed. "I'll shut up now."

A silence settled on the beach, a kind of mutual embarrassment, as if everyone had to avert their eyes from Jules, who would indeed have to find the grave, dig it, and fill it with the correct bad guy. He smiled and pulled a shirt over his scarred shoulder on cue, feeling utterly apart.

Alice patted him on the back and stopped avoiding the subject. She wanted to talk about poisoned horses, how long it might have taken the cyanide to leak through its container and kill the horse. Five or ten minutes, said Jules, and no, the poisoner or the person who hired him couldn't have known for sure that it would result in Sylvia's death. And yes, people and animals seemed to fly with balloons of cocaine all the time, but those were made of rubber, and this had been a glycerine capsule, meant to dissolve. And yes, quite likely the same person had blown up the clown twice, and yes, he thought more than one person was involved. Jules wondered how many questions Alice had asked when she was his nephew Artie's age. He'd met her parents several times, and they didn't seem exceptionally exhausted.

Now Alice brought up a bull rider who'd just died in Texas, ten thousand people at his funeral. "What do they do with the killer bull? What would they have done with Sylvia's horse? I know it's moot, but I'm curious."

"It's up to the owner," said Jules. "In this case Henckle would never have put the horse down, because she was worth too much. But when a bull kills a golden boy, it's probably curtains."

"Kill the messenger," said Peter. "Or maybe it's like the mafia rubbing out someone who flubs a hit, makes it too public."

"Sink the bagman in cement," muttered Jules, wondering when he'd find Genie. "Then get a manicure or go golfing."

A canoe laden with two men and two women rounded the bend. They were in their early twenties, sunburned and blasted, howling instead of talking, using the paddles like they were modern dance props. The girls were wearing string bikinis, and one waved. The frat boys were cultivating the very beginnings of beer guts and ignored their existence.

Edie was tracking the canoe the way you'd follow a plummeting airliner. "Doesn't look too safe."

"No, it doesn't," said Jules, amused by the dour way they were all watching.

"No life preservers," said Alice, who was terrified of everything but bathwater and luxury pools. "You should yell at them."

"What?" asked Jules. "Tell them to pick some up at the next bridge?"

"Don't worry," said Peter. "They'll make it around the bend. It's your first day off in weeks."

The girl who'd waved to them bent over the edge of the canoe, staring into the water and pushing the structural engineering of her bikini top to the limits.

"Would that be for your benefit, Peter, or for Jules's?" asked Alice, a B-cup.

"Hard to tell," said Jules. Edie, still fixed on the canoe, had stood in front of him, and her inner thighs were approximately two feet from his face. A few hours off, and he was ready for life and hope.

"She'll tip them over the line," said Peter.

They all watched as the other girl ripped at a willow branch, discovered it wouldn't uproot, and let go a second too late, shooting her buxom friend over the opposite side. The canoe started to spin, one of the boys reached to the sputtering girl, and they all disappeared.

"There he goes," said Alice, watching Jules head downriver at a dead run. "So much for the break."

"Someone called three times and asked for you," said Grace. "But I said it was your day off."

Jules was still pretty soggy, and wished he heard some irony, or maybe even a little sympathy, in her voice.

"It sounded like Genie."

He was sorting through the day's incident reports. "And how does Genie sound, these days?"

"Panicky."

"Speed," said Jules, signing off at the bottom of three, an assault and two petty robberies. "The asshole's heart will probably give out before he comes to trial on anything."

"He said someone was trying to kill him."

Jules still didn't look up, but his crooked jaw twitched.

"Did you check up on it?"

"He wouldn't give me his name, wouldn't say where he was. But Ed called Gardiner, and Mark found a box left in the girlfriend's driveway with some M-80s in it and a lot of fake wire to make it look official. He's going to drive it up tomorrow morning, but he gave a pretty good description."

"No one in sight at the trailer?"

"No. Ed called the girlfriend at work, and she didn't know a thing. Mark knocked, the whole nine yards, and he poked around a little in the garage."

Jules eyed her.

Grace looked defensive. "He said the door was open. He just *looked.* And he found a bucket of stuff he said smelled like gunpowder, with some feathers in it."

Jules stared at her, mouth ajar, remembering his own misspent youth. Feathers, to cut down on the friction when you mixed in extra phosphorus. He'd burned the bejesus out of himself once, and incurred the last paddling before his father died. He handed her the cites and incident reports. "And how was the package described?"

"An opened shoebox, five M-80s, but none of them were connected to the fuse on the outside. It had been wrapped in white freezer paper, and someone had taped a picture of three monkeys to the top—"

"Run that by me again," said Jules.

"The deputy said it looked like it had been cut out of a kid's book, proverbs or some such."

"No words?"

"Guess," said Grace, rubbing her eyes.

He drove home very slowly in his patrol car after the thunderstorm had finally broken and vanished. Clean, wet, crisp streets, rushing gutters and no one in sight. Hear no evil, see no evil, speak no evil.

Ten o'clock. He pulled out a container of frozen stew Alice had given him when he'd first come home from the hospital. A lamb shank daube; he found some leftover rice and nuked it all, but ate only half. He was fidgety, unsettled, and tried calling Alice and Peter for the sake of discussing something meaningless, then remembered they'd been planning on a movie. He fed Moe some old grapes, one by one, and opened a can of tuna for Fred.

He climbed the stairs, turned the fan on, mixed himself a huge drink, and sat on the porch reading a book called *How to Lie with Maps* by the window light behind him. At 11:30 he tried Edie at home, but she'd already left for work. He flicked on the television and stared at the black and white image of fingers wriggling through a sewer grate, wondering if it was a waking nightmare or an hallucination. No, it was *The Third Man,* and he turned the set off, unwilling to linger over the ironies.

An hour later, on his fourth short story, he tried the Baird. He was nonchalant. She was wary. "Get to the point."

"There isn't much of one. Is Everett in tonight?"

"I think so. A call just went through."

"Hugh?"

"The call came from his room."

She waited patiently. "It just seems like a strange night," Jules said lamely.

"Aren't you going to ask about Diane?"

He sighed. "Is she in?"

"I don't know. Want me to ring?"

"No. Call me if it really is strange, okay?"

"Okay," said Edie, bemused. "Has something happened since the river?"

"Not really," said Jules.

When the phone rang at three-thirty he was on his bed, but still wearing jeans and a T-shirt. It was Edie, whispering, and he ran for the car.

He didn't use lights or the siren, and he cut the headlights when he coasted to a stop in the alley parking lot. Edie was standing in a corner of the half-darkened lobby, facing the stairwell and the elevator.

"It's the breaker for the southern wing," she told him.

Uh huh, thought Jules. This wasn't a normal cause for alarm in a woman who'd wired her own house.

"No one's complained; I guess everyone up there's asleep. The box is in the basement, but that breaker handles the basement as well. I was cleaning the bathroom, and when I came out it was dark and I thought I heard a noise, so I went into the restaurant to find a flashlight, and when I came out the elevator was moving."

The elevator had been manufactured in 1908, and the shaft was dark. "It has its own breaker, except for the lights," explained Edie.

"What kind of noise?" asked Jules.

"Breathing."

"Can you tell what floor the elevator's on?"

She shook her head.

"Let's go to the basement."

The fuse was missing and the spares were missing. Jules thought of swapping one of the others, but he faced three different generations of electrical equipment, and the thought of waking two dozen guests to an iffy situation was unattractive. His guests, the Dragonfly trio, apparently hadn't minded the darkness on their portion of the fourth floor at all, and he'd hate to throw off their visitor's sense of direction.

Edie, who held the shaking flashlight, wore an impassive look he recognized as her version of mental paralysis, and they bargained about where she'd wait. They settled on her car, locked, with the remote phone. She wanted to call the station, and he didn't have the heart to admit no one was actually on call. Harvey deserved more than four hours' sleep. They found another flashlight, very small, so he started up the stairs in the dark.

The elevator was parked on the fourth floor. Jules edged toward it and almost pitched forward at the open doorway, because the person who'd run it had misjudged the floor by a foot. Jules crouched and caught his breath, and when he looked up he saw a pattern of phosphorus fingerprints on the wall and the gate handle and the lever.

Shit, shit, shit, thought Jules, crawling back into the hall and around the stair railing.

"I hear you," said Genie. He sounded whistly and terrified, also terrifying. His meeting with his employer didn't seem to be going according to plan.

"I'm not the person you're looking for," said Jules.

"The fuck you aren't. You tried to kill me a few times. You just tried to kill me."

"Listen to my voice, Genie."

"No," he hissed. "Don't move."

Jules was crouched two steps down the open stairwell and he thought Genie was five yards or so away, in the darkest corridor leading to the north side of the hotel and Hugh's apartment. The alley side, the south side where Everett and Diane presumably still slept, had more windows, and a little more light, despite the cloudy moon; when Jules peered down that hallway he saw movement, low to the floor.

But something seemed to be moving at the other end, past Genie and near Hugh's place, and Genie heard it, too, without knowing the direction. Jules, dead center in a four-story opening, was a noise machine.

"Fuck you. I said don't move."

Jules listened instead of answering, and heard another step. He knew what Genie would do, and braced himself. One more step, and the flick of the third person's lighter, and Genie ran right at Jules. But Jules had a new set of concerns, and came out of the stairwell like a linebacker, smacking Genie in the stomach with his shoulder at the top of the stairs and knocking him backward down the south hall, screaming "Run!" to Genie and "Stay in your rooms!" to anyone else who might be listening, and scrabbling on like an awkward crab. Then light and noise burst out of the stairwell, and Genie's face in front of him looked like an overexposed print. Jules kept scrabbling for the window and the fire escape at the end of the hall, while Genie retreated in front of him. When he saw Genie fumbling with his own lighter, he didn't bother turning around to see what it was that Genie saw, but threw himself against a door on the left, the last door before the open window, and counted on antique wood.

He'd come to a rest inside, facing the hall again, when another explosion came from the direction of the stairwell. He saw Genie loop one leg over the windowsill before something landed near his other foot, and Jules once again willed himself into movement, jumping over the familiar bed to the far wall, where Diane had already retreated.

As it happened, the last of Genie's homemade explosives never blew. It had been so poorly made that the fuse had detached, and some of the tube's contents spilled out onto the Baird carpeting. Jules moved quickly one last time to throw Diane's bedtime glass of water on the spark while she sat glittery-eyed on the edge of the bed. She never said a word, and still didn't when he swung open Everett's bedroom door and found it empty. By then Jules had already looked out the fire-escape window where he'd last seen Genie. There was really no point in hurrying in that direction, as long as he could use the stairwell to evacuate.

Not that anyone had asked what route they should take. If there'd been any embers on the stairs from the first explosion, they'd have been long since trampled out. The fourth-floor guests, twenty or more people, were so many ants charging out of a flooded hill. Jules, without much humor, yelled at them to slow the hell down. He stopped to help one elderly couple, grinding his teeth with impatience and wondering where Everett was, and where Hugh was.

Harvey and Ed and the fire trucks arrived a few seconds after Jules hit the street and spied Everett and Hugh in the crowd. Everett was wrapping Diane's robe tighter around her and Hugh was patting her on the shoulder, a community of people with hair pointed in the wrong direction. Jules pulled Ed around the corner to the alley, and pointed up to the dim outline of the fire escape.

Genie dangled ten feet from the ground, his neck clamped in the accordioned ladder. His arm was caught, too, which had kept him from being decapitated, but blood still dripped onto the oily dirt of the alley. "Who is it?" asked Ed, squinting.

"Eugene Jordan."

Ed turned and stared at Jules. "What happened?"

"He was trying to get out of the way."

"No point in checking on him, huh?"

"No," said Jules. "I saw his neck. And look at the angle of his back."

They were quiet for a minute, watching the dark shape move ever so slightly in a breeze. When bad things happened to bad people . . . what? Jules knew the answer, already: You shift gears and feel sorry for them, see them as the happy child on a mother's knee, who didn't deserve his eventual place in the world. How many people died with any grace?

"Now what?" asked Ed.

It was a quarter after four, and growing lighter. Another beautiful, hot day in tourist country was on its way. "Let's try to keep people around the corner, and we'll try to get him down fast. I don't suppose Harvey brought the camera."

"He's probably wearing pajamas, with the rest of the crowd. I doubt he was thinking of the public record when he jumped out of bed."

Jules rubbed the back of his neck and discovered it was singed. Ed watched him. "Your back is a little tie-dyed. Does it hurt?"

"No."

Harvey peered down from the fourth-story window. "How do we handle this?"

"I don't think it's going to work from above, but you might as well see how close you can get," said Jules.

Harvey, the lightest of all of them, took a tentative step on the metal platform. Two stories down, the ladder lurched and Genie swayed. It was light enough now to see the shower of droplets on the dirt below him.

David Eaton rounded the corner and Jules waved him over. "Everything okay inside?"

"Everyone's out, and nothing's burning anymore. No heart attacks or burns. Did you know that your face was black?" He squinted at Jules. "You might tell me what happened."

Jules pointed up. "We could use your truck ladder."

"Oh echh," said David. "What a fucking summer."

It didn't seem that Jules and Axel Scotti were going to have a meeting of the minds that month. This time around they wrangled at the hospital, where Jules and a dozen of the Baird guests were getting patched up. Even Genie was on hand, though in the basement cooler; it was a regular party.

It was six A.M., and Scotti wasn't an early-rising sort of man. "Thousands of dollars of damage, in the middle of the summer season. You had one gun, which you didn't use, no handcuffs, no badge, no radio. A dead felon, just *hanging* there, for everyone to see."

"I want their hands tested." Jules was hunkered forward on an examination table, and Horace's stitchwork on his back was making him more stubborn than usual.

"You said it was a goddamn accident. Who the hell would we charge? The guests say you were the idiot who yelled run."

"Hush," said Horace, trying to concentrate. Scotti was screaming, reverting to a Sicily he'd never seen.

"I am not the idiot who threw explosives around the hallway," hissed Jules, breaking into another sweat as Horace tugged. "Everett wasn't in his room. I didn't see either him or Hugh go down the stairs with the rest."

"Maybe the goddamn smoke was in your eyes," snarled Scotti. "If you heard someone in the hallway, why the hell didn't you shoot them?"

Jules looked at him in disgust.

"If you were worried about Genie going there, why the hell didn't you have your stuff with you?"

"I wasn't necessarily worried."

"Edie Linders says you were, told her to watch out and call you. Or was that another cocksucking social call?"

"Axel," said Horace. "Women and children use this facility, and you have high blood pressure at the best of times."

"Start working on your lines for another inquest," said Scotti, giving Jules a vicious pat on the knee.

Horace sponged some antiseptic on Jules's back and smiled as he writhed. "More than a scratch, less than a war wound. Are you starting to feel at home here?"

Eugene F. Jordan

Eugene Franklin Jordan, 31, of Gardiner died early Wednesday morning in Blue Deer of injuries sustained in a fall. Arrangements will be announced by the Babaski Funeral Home.

He was born August 12, 1962, in Gardiner, the son of Frank and Barbara Jordan, and spent most of his life in the Blue Deer area. Genie was loved by his family and his friends. He is survived by his brothers Dale, Wayne, and Gregory.

Alice looked up from the paper. "Peter, didn't you have to deal with Eugene Jordan's brothers a few years ago? What are they like?"

He was trussing a chicken in the kitchen. "Awful."

"How awful?"

"Awful enough to kill Jules if they bother coming back to town for the funeral."

"Eugene Jordan was throwing around his own fireworks?"

"Yeah. With someone else."

"When are you going to print that he poisoned the horse?"

"After Jules talks to the owner, and a few other things."

Alice folded the paper and stood up. "What sort of other things?"

"After Jules knows who wanted Sylvia dead."

She tossed the *Bulletin* in the trash. "Just make sure he really takes the day off tomorrow."

"He will. Ankeny's going along."

Jules had called Ankeny early that morning for the name and particulars of Everett's Forest Service contact. Larry Nellikov was the man who'd speeded up the one patent Everett had bothered to pursue out of fifteen Dragonfly claims, his prospective home site.

Ankeny had meant to call Jules anyway, about the fact they'd be fishing together the next day and because he wanted Jules to know that a stray Forest Service truck had just been retrieved from long-term parking at the Billings airport, and that the Gallatin station, near Bozeman, was one truck short. Lo and behold, they were the same truck, and Jules called the Billings station to ask for a copy of the tread.

Larry Nellikov, Bozeman regional supervisor, actually answered his own phone, a heartening public-service detail that Jules was fairly sure was a complete anomaly. They struggled through the first five minutes before the conversation grew truly testy.

"Are you accusing me of something?"

"I wouldn't see the point," said Jules. "I'm just asking you how well you know Everett, and if your friendship has anything to do with him being granted the fastest patent since Anaconda."

"Everett knows a lot of people here," said Nellikov. He had an oddly pleasant, singsong voice. "Everybody wants favors, and he's one of the one percent who don't throw money around. He just gets things done."

"Is this your way of telling me the patent is on the up-and-up and won't be challenged?"

Yes, said the pause. "He did the work, filed everything, gave us samples, paid his money. I went over there with him, knowing it was all to prevent logging, but the fact was he had his ducks in a row. Challenging the patent would be expensive and take years, and there's really no point if he never mines."

"What about improvements he needed to make for a patent? Five hundred worth, right?"

"The road."

"He didn't pay for that."

"Moot. He works for the corporation, and the road runs over his claim. It cost at least five thousand dollars, and we were of course happy that it opened the glacier trail back up for the public."

Jules looked down at the map, squinting at the black line of the road on the north side of Dragonfly Creek and the yellow dot of Everett's patent on the south side. "The road work was last year, right?"

"I think so."

"It occurred to me the other day that all your maps are at least five years old."

"More like ten."

Jules rubbed his forehead. Once upon a time he'd enjoyed being right. "What did Everett find for the patent anyway?"

"Industrial grade sapphires. There's quite a few of them, right at the canyon mouth. Just enough to prove marketability." Jules could hear the happiness in the man's voice. "I really like Everett. We all do. Don't you?"

"Sometimes," said Jules.

Jules spent another few hours on the phone and drove up to Martinsdale in the late afternoon, passing ditches filled with miles and miles of sunflowers, opportunistic and beautiful. The fields were brown from the summer heat, and the air was hazy from a cluster of fires in Washington. He stood on the edge of the reservoir, looking down toward the dam. Now it was a puddle, and the tent would have been marooned in the center. At least they'd found it sooner rather than later.

It's the little shit you gotta keep an eye on, Ed had said two years earlier, when Jules signed up to be a deputy. It's the little shit that'll get you down, or clear things up.

He found Clarence at the gas station, telling the owner how to run his business. He'd probably been doing so for forty years. It took a long time to disengage him from the argument and park him on a sidewalk bench, and longer to bring him back to their last conversation, about who it was Clarence may have seen the day Otto and Bonnie had been killed.

"So this guy came in," said Jules. "What time was it?"

"Late."

"Eight? Nine?"

"Yeah."

"And you don't remember anything about him, the color of his hair, how old, anything."

"I told you. Not young, not old."

Jules gave a little prayer and took a stab in the dark.

"But he was familiar."

"Yeah, a little, but I didn't know him. Couldn't place him."

"Someone from around here you didn't know?"

"Maybe."

Familiar could be a newspaper photo; familiar could be a family resemblance. It could also, of course, be someone you'd seen on a street one or two years earlier, the guy in front of you in the bank line who took so long, the jerk you'd watched give the waitress a hard time in a restaurant. Jules tried not to think about all the arguments he'd had with Scotti about leading witnesses.

"Do you think he knew you?"

Clarence looked suspicious, as if Jules was asking him a trick question. "He didn't know me."

"You get our paper?"

Clarence looked like he didn't want to admit it, but he nodded. Jules pulled the Hamburgh issue from his pocket.

"Did the guy look a little like this man?"

"Well, you know, I thought maybe so for a sec there, but now that I really look I know it wasn't him."

"Did he have anyone with him?"

Clarence thought, this time in earnest. "I think I remember so, but she stayed in the car."

"Couldn't really see her?"

"Nah."

"Short? Tall?"

"Like I said, she was in the goddamn truck. She looked pretty tiny to my bad eyes."

"Did you notice what kind of truck it was? Before you told me you hadn't seen one that day."

"Did I say truck?" Clarence scowled. "I don't think so. Anyway, I was trying to look at the lady. Could have been a semi."

Jules grinned. "Thanks, Clarence. You've been a help."

"Huh," said Clarence. He watched from the bench while Jules drove away.

At Dragonfly, thirty-six miles and fifty-two minutes away, Sylvia's new house was almost done. This was another part of her estate Hugh wouldn't have to share with the sons; they got the cash, and some of the profits, but the corporation land remained intact. The house looked huge to Jules, and whether or not Hugh had a clean conscience it probably looked too large to him now.

He walked all the way to the glacier and made out four bugs through the ice, far fewer than he'd seen as a child in the same amount of time. More proof that people forgot how to notice what was right in front of them. He walked back slowly, wishing he could camp with someone he liked, disappear for a week or so. He'd brought Otto's map along and looked up the meadow toward some of the claims, most of them heavily wooded on rounded slopes. Then he backtracked all the way to the narrow canyon, the main gateway, and stood in the expensive new roadbed running on the south side of the pinched, swollen creek. Across from him the old roadbed was a narrow pile of avalanched rock. Jules looked up at the fresh rock of the shorn cliff. If he went in for climbing, he was sure he could find some evidence of where the dynamite had been placed, but he'd never been able to bear the idea of falling.

He stood smack in the middle of Everett's patented claim and looked down at Otto's map, still the Forest Service version of the way the world lay, at the hasty, faint pencil marks showing the new course of the road, there all along. He wondered if Otto had figured it out before his brake line was sliced, or if he and Bonnie had made a quick trip here on that last weekend. The road was the only way in, unless you walked ten miles up and around.

DAYS LIKE THIS

HUGH WAS PACKING UP SOME OF SYLVIA'S THINGS IN THE BAIRD apartment. Not all of them; he didn't intend to give her away to sons who hardly knew her. Music, for instance, he would keep. If she'd liked it, he could still listen to it, and pretend she heard. But the presence of certain photographs, posters, vases and blankets was unbearable. Hugh couldn't work with them about, and he had to work or he'd shoot around the bend like that asshole Everett and half the town.

Jules stared out the window, thinking of how innocuous a loaded subject could seem. Maps, for instance. "Didn't Everett help you research the script?"

"Four or five years ago, when I first started," Hugh said. "He checked it for realism." He looked flushed and puffy, and his face was covered with spidery lines. He stared morosely at a shelf of cookbooks. "Do you suppose Alice could use any of them?"

Jules squinted at the shelf. "I think she has everything. Edie might like them. Do you mind if I look around?"

Hugh went back to sorting through a pile of papers and photos. "Go ahead. Most of the small stuff is on her bedside table."

Jules took a few minutes to poke through Sylvia's jewelry box, the carefully folded love letters and school snapshots of her sons. He didn't expect to find Otto's last note, and even if it had been there he was sure Otto had warned her against both men, leaving her no one to confide in.

He flipped the box shut and walked back out to the living room. Hugh looked up from a pile of photographs.

"I have something I need to tell you," said Jules. "We ran some last tests on Sylvia's blood, and I wanted to wait to talk to you about the results until I was sure of what they meant."

Hugh gave him a long look and climbed to his feet.

Jules walked down the hall and knocked softly on Diane's door. A minute later she was pushing bottles around in the mini fridge, looking for wine, while he sat on her bed.

Everett was playing the radio on the other side of the hall, yodeling along from time to time. Jules watched Diane pour two glasses of wine, kick off her high-heeled sandals and start on her blouse. Honest-to-God pearl buttons. Once again he didn't know whether to laugh or cry, strip and lie down or jump out the window fully clothed. Usually, with Diane, he simply watched until she made the final approach.

"Have you ever been married?" he asked.

It was a testimony to the nature of their relationship that he hadn't asked before, and that she would never think he was asking her for the usual reason.

"Yes," she said. "I don't necessarily recommend it. Have you?"

"Almost."

"Almost doesn't count," she said, finding this funny. "You do or you don't, and it's always on your record."

There was an echo in the room, Everett singing along to the next song. It was still hot outside but there was enough of a breeze to wave the curtains. Jules kicked off his shoes and lay down on the bed.

"Slow night in a slow town." Diane smiled. "It's been a while. Did you forget your vitamins? I have an apple, also a wonderful cheese from your friend Alice, who's decided to give in and be nice."

She bit into the chunk of hard, crumbly cheese, pulled on his hand until he was upright again, and sat on his lap. Jules looked down at the cheese, then up at her teeth, six inches away.

"Do you and Everett still sleep together?" asked Jules.

"Ah," said Diane. "You care."

He grinned in a moment of horrible honesty. "I care professionally."

Diane raised her eyebrows and stretched her legs around him, letting her blue miniskirt accordion to her hips.

"I don't think our arrangement has helped his already unstable mental health," added Jules.

"Fuck him if he can't take a joke," said Diane.

Jules watched her and she chortled, true glee burbling out from a childhood cranny. "Tell me the truth," said Diane. "You're usually more energetic."

"I'm scared of your teeth," said Jules.

"Richie," said Jules, "we need to talk about life here. You've got to pay attention."

Scotti watched. Jules knew he didn't expect much.

"Why did Genie Jordan hit you?"

"No one hit me."

Jules picked up a photo. "This man was Genie Jordan. He's dead now. Did this man hit you?"

Berko, who'd been drunk for a week, according to his partner, nodded slowly. The white of his right eye was deep red, and the left a soft yellow. The bandages on his hand were stained, and Jules didn't have much faith in the healing process.

"Why?" asked Jules.

Berko shrugged and looked away.

"Because he didn't want you to talk about something you'd seen?"

"I guess," said Berko. "But I wouldn't have anyway."

"I guess he didn't believe you," said Jules. "But it doesn't matter now, does it?"

"No," said Berko.

"What did you see that had him so upset?"

"I don't *know,*" said Berko, querulous and flailing his paddle hand. "I never saw a thing that seemed strange. I saw him at the chute and outside the barn smoking and that was it. He just wouldn't believe me." He looked back and forth at Jules and Scotti. "I never saw a thing worth forgetting."

Scotti looked bleakly out the window. Jules doodled another moon shape onto his pad. He wanted to get something out of the way. "Richie, why did you save your finger bones?"

Richie Berko stared at him. "Why would I throw them away?"

Scotti left immediately, deep in a funk and muttering about futility, cruelty, stupidity. Jules checked Richie into the hospital, had a huge lunch with Harvey, and returned to the station for the long haul, taking a phone from the communal room into the kitchen.

Three hours later his ears were ringing and hot from the phone receiver. He'd started with the car rental companies at the Bozeman airport, the closest airport to Blue Deer: Had they levied any extra charges for picking up a rental at a different site on June 11 or 12? One, rented to a Nat Langford on the evening of June 12, to be picked up on the fourteenth near Big Sky, half a mile from the Gallatin ranger station where a truck with tires that matched the Martinsdale tread had gone missing. Langford had paid in cash, and the company had kept no record of the ID he must have shown. Jules checked the likely afternoon flights from Denver and came up with Nat Langford on the 6:10. The same man had left Billings Monday morning on a 7:25 flight for Denver.

Jules had given Jonathan the task of tracking down all the taxi fares from Stapleton to Boulder that Monday morning while Everett's sedate and handsome BMW had decorated the sidewalk in front of his house. Harvey, hunkered down at his desk, had come up with an admission from Everett's landlord: He'd heard music, and seen the nice car, without actually having seen Everett between midday Saturday and midday Monday, when the moving truck arrived. But out of all the fares to Boulder, most were to hotels and not one was to the address they were looking for.

Nathaniel Langford had been one of the most enthusiastic of the vigilantes who'd hung Plummer and Co., as well as their historian. Jules thought of Hugh claiming no one remembered any history anymore, but Langford had hung Stinson, Everett's other alias, and now Jules knew it meant that Everett had hung himself. Why use one of those trucks at all? Why not? Scam the state and pile on the ironies; use something so big you won't be able to tell when the tires crush bone and dog and breast.

He'd asked Scotti to call Donald Parsons, saddling him with some troublesome family questions that Jules knew Donald would never answer if he had asked them. But by the time Scotti called back with a tentative answer, Jules had already gotten a confirmation from the IRS that Everett had claimed a dependent on his last return.

Thursday morning he called Everett, and watched Fred flick his tail on the porch while the phone rang. Another day when they wouldn't be going to the vet. He wished it was over already.

Everett was happy to meet, later, over a drink.

"Later is better for me," said Jules. "Any time after four or so. I'm going fishing. It's my day off."

"Now that's funny," said Everett, whose voice was thin and reedy.

"I've been meaning to tell you," said Alice, "that I had lunch with Renee yesterday, and she said some strange stuff was going on at the hospital around the time Sylvia died."

Jules kept rocking, trying to keep the illusion that he could actually watch the garden grow. He didn't want to talk.

"Doors that should have been locked, missing hypodermics, somebody's locker open . . ."

"Hospitals are filled with strange stuff," said Jules wearily. "By definition. This spring I remember some old lady looking through my window, and Renee's the one who pointed out to me there're always creeps around. And if there aren't, the nurses are tired and seeing ghosts. Look at that IV drip long enough and you'll see things, too. I did."

Alice smiled. "If Renee pointed all this out to you, why did she bother telling this story to me?"

He kept rocking, watching a woodpecker beat his brains against her new garden fence. "They've been taken through that night a dozen times, and now they've had enough time to think it over, come up with a collective memory." He smiled. "Renee's not used to me just asking questions. When I was there earlier she always had to tone me down, keep my twitchy fingers on *Reader's Digest*. The medication and all."

"I bet."

Jules gave her a sweet smile. Alice tsk tsked and clipped some more beans. "Anyway, they finished inventory, and some stuff is missing, including an attendant's uniform, and the nurse on duty that night found a trolley in the bathroom."

"With a discarded uniform, size eighteen, a permed wig, and an empty syringe dripping undetectable blowfish poison. The custodian is about to wash the prints off, as we speak, and here I sit on my skinny ass, wishing Renee was still around to scrub my legs in the shower."

Alice slapped him with an overgrown romano bean. "Shut your mouth. No one will help you if you don't learn to say thank you."

Jules rocked for another minute. "Thank you."

"You're welcome. Do I get bonus points if I finally tell you Otto and Sylvia still slept together sometimes?"

"Who told you that?"

Alice smiled. "Doesn't matter anymore, does it?"

"For some reason," said Jules, "that makes me very happy."

"I'm ready," said Peter, who'd come around the side of the house with Ankeny. "We finally fixed the hitch."

Jules thanked Alice for an iced tea and they walked to the truck.

They'd floated for five miles and two hours by the time Jules volunteered some of the story. Peter was annoyed by knowing so little and rowed with unnecessary vigor.

"You're saying Everett's going to mine? To spite Hugh, fuck over the project, he's going to open an ugly pit in the earth? Why spend a fortune digging dirt?"

"Everett doesn't want to dig." Jules cast a fly toward a riffle. "He doesn't have to spend a fortune to ruin everything for Hugh. He *owns* the road, and he can get whatever he wants out of Hugh if he threatens to close it. He might have to let the feds through to the glacier, but that's it. No construction crews, no tourists, just eight thousand pretty acres. They could get in eventually, legally, but it might take years, and even a few months would ruin the project financially."

Peter rowed. Ankeny chugged a beer and watched the rocks slide by under the boat.

"He's a partner now," said Jules. "Hugh doesn't have a clue, yet, but Everett's name might as well be on the deed."

"Otto must have gotten an easement from the Forest Service," said Peter. "If the patent just went through, Dragonfly's right-of-way would take precedence. No court would turn away Hugh's trucks."

"That's what I asked Patrick about," said Jules. "The problem is that no easement was ever requested or granted."

Peter gaped. "Otto never requested one?"

"I think that might have been a job he delegated," said Jules, "and he found out too late it hadn't been done. He probably planned to file an injunction on the patent when he got back from his trip with Bonnie. He just wanted to think it over first."

Ankeny made a bad cast and swore.

Peter dug into the water hard and they scooted past. "What the hell are you doing here then?"

"Killing time," said Jules. "There's a little problem of proof."

Jules had already asked to be let off in town rather than continuing east to Sheep Mountain, where they'd parked his truck to haul the boat back. He could tell Peter and Ankeny wanted out, too; it was hard being stuck in a boat with a murder on your mind. They'd probably set a new speed record, row their little hearts out and skip fishing.

He'd gone home early to do mindless things like his laundry before he talked to Everett, but everything had to be complicated that day; he was out of laundry detergent, and the idea of needing to buy something so mundane maddened him. He walked to the grocery, a trip somewhat redeemed by the fact that a new, freckled cashier, thinking he was a normal human, commented on his sunburn and his T-shirt, which plugged a band called the Bad Livers. The front showed a red combine, and the back read "Corn Fed, Inbred, and Brain Dead." "Don't tell me they made that shirt for you," she said. Actual flirting in a small town;

someone would whisper a warning in her ear before he was through the automatic doors.

Jules circled back to the river on his way home and counted fishing tourists. Six of them in a one-mile stretch, and a dozen craft floated by; the memorable sight, though, was a man in bathing trunks and flippers, who did not treat Jules as an authority figure when he was advised that scuba diving, especially with flippers, was a dangerous sport in a rushing river. Maybe it was Jules's T-shirt or ratty shorts and stained sneakers; maybe it was the fact that the man was surly from a first try, which had given him an abraded belly on the bottom gravel. Jules took another minute of abuse and walked away, leaving the man to his sure drowning.

When he heard a car accelerate behind him he thought for one instant that some former victim of justice was taking revenge, but it was Alice, wild-eyed in her Subaru, and she lurched to a stop.

"Get in. Now."

He didn't want the delay of going home for his gun, and bargained on Edie having called the station once she got off the phone to Alice. But Alice and Edie's talk had just been a lucky coincidence, and Everett hadn't let Edie dial again. Everything seemed normal enough when they reached the Baird lobby except for the way Everett and Diane were facing each other in chairs, and the fact that Edie, who was stiff as a board on the couch, had told Alice that Everett had a gun. He and Diane had come downstairs together, but Diane had refused to go any farther.

"Diane's being difficult," said Everett calmly to Jules. He held the gun flat on his lap, all but the barrel covered by his jacket. "We were just on our way out the door."

"Shoot him," said Diane.

"No," said Jules. He held up his empty hands to Everett. "I'm just a little early for our drink here. I don't know what the problem is—"

"Don't fucking lie," said Everett. "Yes, you do. Diane, get in the car."

"No. You're on your own."

Jules looked her over. She was very white in a ruby-colored sundress, looking more out of her element than usual. The key, of course, was that she had no element. She didn't belong anywhere.

Everett didn't move his eyes from her. "I'm going to blow your vicious little head right off your shoulders. Get in the goddamn car."

Diane managed to cry and look mean at the same time, which probably meant she was terrified. "Screw you."

"Don't do this to me," hissed Everett. He was flushed and shaking.

"Everett, I don't have a gun. I can go with you," said Jules.

"You're not my idea of good company," said Everett. "And the ice queen here probably wants you to stick around, for when I'm gone."

A couple walked down the stairs and smiled at Edie. "Hello," they said. "Do you think it will rain tonight?"

Edie opened her mouth and nothing came out. She did better on a second try. "Not a chance."

They walked out the door, only bothering to look askance at Jules's T-shirt.

"You know what she's like, don't you?" Everett was looking at Jules.

"Yes."

He turned back to Diane. "Come on, honey."

She shook her head. "Go away, Everett," she said softly.

Everett stared at her and blinked, then stood.

"Don't get in that car, Everett," said Jules. "Stick around."

"You're flat out of fucking luck," said Everett, walking toward him. "Don't chase me. I need more time."

He smashed Jules on the side of the head with the pistol, and walked out the door.

When Jules sat up Diane was gone and Edie was on the portable phone to Grace while she dribbled a mixture of cold water and ice onto his face, with much of it going into his eyes and up his nose. Alice was there, too, saying "Of course she didn't want to die with him," and giving instructions, this after she'd followed Everett far enough to guess that he was heading north. A few minutes later Jules was on his feet at the door, clutching his liquid ear, when Ed showed up.

They saw nothing for twenty miles and Ed kept on for Martinsdale when they saw no telltale plume of dust settling on the long dirt road to Dragonfly. Ed's theory was that Everett wanted to jump into the reservoir. Jules wondered how fast the BMW was going. Grace let them know that the car had made it through Wilsall, so blurred with speed that three people had called to complain. She'd warned them that the patrol car would be almost as fast.

They paused at the road to Martinsdale, and Jules got out of the car to listen and think, even though a minute's pause probably gave Everett another two miles. His left ear buzzed with pain and his right with the buffeting wind from the open car window. He only heard the whine of grasshoppers and a faraway tractor.

"I think he's heading north," he said to Ed. "I don't think he gives a shit about the reservoir."

"We've passed the county line."

"I don't care. Keep it under a hundred and no one will bother us."

They had to go slower anyway, now that the road ran between the Castle and Big Belt ranges. There'd been road construction and orange cones were sprayed for twenty yards on either side of the road. Everett, having a little fun. They'd crossed Sixteen-mile Creek and the south fork of the Smith, heading straight for a massive, black thundercloud, when Jules suddenly realized that the last patch of cones had still been in place, and asked Ed to turn around.

The skid marks were just a little darker than the shiny new pavement, but the grass was gone all the way to the narrow gul-ley. The green BMW had crumpled on its nose and Everett had been thrown forty feet. He lay face up and open-eyed in the small stream, staring at nothing and looking very young.

Ed, uncharacteristically, began to cry. "Turn that shit off."

Jules walked back to the BMW, where the radio was still play-ing.

☆ 15 ☆

DOING THE
WIDOW WALK

"WHY YOU ANYWAY?" ASKED PETER, PULLING COTTONWOOD fluff from a dove gray suit. "It's a stretch to say you two were close."

They were moving away from the grave, and Jules pulled out his pallbearer's carnation and jammed it in his pocket. "Donald Parsons told Scotti that Everett had called him and said I'd given him time for a graceful out. I hadn't, really, but it's not the sort of thing you argue about."

"How could he ask Hugh?"

"Nerve."

They reached a rise and waited for Alice and Edie. Twenty yards away, Hugh had his arm around Diane's shoulder, his head turned toward hers, listening with a patient, exhausted, loving expression.

"The last ones left," said Peter, starting to walk again. "Maybe now they can settle down together."

Maybe, thought Jules, watching carefully and not finding it likely they'd have much contact beyond wired deposits in her direction. Hugh didn't find it likely either, suddenly, because his expression changed and his pink skin turned white, as if someone had just kicked him in the balls, told him he had cancer. He still stared at Diane, and she was still explaining life patiently to him. Jules took only one step in their direction before he thought better of it and waited near an immense marble tombstone that commemorated the death of a cigar manufacturer.

A few moments later Diane turned away to join the Parsons clan. Hugh looked up and saw Jules walking toward him.

"How's it feel to have a new partner?" asked Jules.

Hugh was hardly breathing. "Do something," he said.

"I can't," said Jules.

EVERETT O. PARSONS

Everett Owen Parsons, 35, of Blue Deer and Boulder, Colorado, passed away in a car accident on Thursday, July 22, 1993. Services were held at Trinity Methodist Church with the Reverend Ralph Haird officiating. Music was provided by soloist Kay Rosch and organist Millie Babaski. Casket bearers were Ronald Tuttle, Lawrence Nellikov, Jules Clement, Edward Salz, Mark Fredling, and Hugh Lesy. Interment was in Cottonwood Cemetery, in Blue Deer.

He was born February 1, 1958, in Billings, Montana, the son of Donald and Alceste Brigg Parsons. After attending Blue Deer High he received a full scholarship to Dartmouth, and later received a graduate degree from George Washington University. Mr. Parsons began his career as the press officer for Senator Mapes Dillon of Indiana, and served on several corporate boards. He also served on the advisory committees of the Colorado office of the Nature Conservancy.

Survivors include his parents; his wife, Opal D. Meek; three sisters, Miranda Salz of Redondo Beach, California, Constance Parsons of Denver, and Camilla Fredling of St. Albans, Vermont; and five nieces and nephews. He was preceded in death by a brother, Calvin.

The family asks that memorials be made in Mr. Parsons' name to the Blue Deer High business and vocational education departments.

"Criminy," said Alice. "Only in a small town."

"What?"

"That your casket bearer was sleeping with your wife and might have killed you if you hadn't killed yourself."

"Probably happens all the time," said Peter. "And Everett was young. Think of how complicated it could have gotten. Also, I think it's likelier that his wife would have killed Everett, than Jules. Jules has been there."

Jules checked one last time with the airlines in Billings for the weekend Otto and Bonnie had died. Early morning flights to the hubs in Minneapolis, Salt Lake, and Spokane, as well as back to Bozeman, Missoula, Great Falls, Helena and Rapid City; Jules found a likely seeming reservation to Minneapolis and on to New York for one Ruby Owen, who'd paid cash for a flight leaving Billings at eight A.M. on Monday, arriving at LaGuardia at two P.M. A nice grandmotherly, bland sound to it, with Everett's middle name and Ruby instead of Opal. Her studio assistant said she'd seen her that Sunday morning; a magazine said they'd received photos Monday afternoon that could only have been taken that weekend in the city. The cops in New York started to look into the matter, but only turned up a lover, who said he'd spent Sunday night with her. They didn't necessarily believe him, and they'd dig a little deeper, but it didn't look promising. Her alibis were looser for the weekend Otto Scobey's brake line had been cut, but this was a double-edged sword: no one had seen her, anywhere.

Jules didn't have faith in progress. Diane had never tended toward loose ends. She was also multitalented: helping her dad with car repair as a child, helping her grandfather with horses in the Dakotas as a teen, helping RNs as a student nurse, helping Everett through all the other difficult tasks Jules would never be able to tie her to, from paying Genie for services rendered to crushing an old friend. Diane wasn't the sort to believe in miraculous recoveries, but Everett had been, and Jules thought she'd returned a favor only once. She'd probably looked fine in a nurse's uniform; the only time she'd really risked her own neck. Maybe she'd made him watch. Probably she hadn't felt the need for company.

There was no way to prove a thing. He said as much to Scotti, and Scotti found this unbearable. Jules promised to quiz ticket agents and stewardesses across America, should the budget bear such abuse. They'd found one of Everett's prints in the Forest Service truck, but Clarence had pulled another blank when presented with a photo of Diane.

"You're saying that's it?" asked Scotti.

Jules had a half-eaten granny smith in his freezer, but when he'd asked the dentist about a match, the man had laughed in his face.

"I think that's it," said Jules.

Ten days after Everett died, on another Monday morning, he was parked at an exit on the freeway, scanning speeds without bothering to pull anyone over. When he finally accelerated it was for a white rental car, headed for the airport and only going seventy-three. He put on his lights and had the satisfaction of seeing her do a double-take in the rearview before she signaled.

"Officer," she said softly. "Are you here because I forgot to say good-bye? I left some photos behind at the Baird. I thought your mom might like that one of you at the rodeo."

"Would you mind taking your sunglasses off while we talk?"

She pulled them off and looked at him evenly. "Why are you here? I'm not going to make any speeches, and I get the feeling you're not up for a quickie in the ditch."

He drummed his fingers on the window. "Why'd you bother

breaking Everett's heart in the end? Couldn't you have found any way around that?"

"Short of dying with him, no." She bit her lip and looked down, then up again, coldly. "It was time for Everett to grow up."

Jules straightened. "Are you going back to New York?"

"Shall I send you my address when I find a new place?"

"I'm sure Hugh will have it." Jules smiled, one corner of his mouth traveling upward, the other stayed where it was. "Enjoy that apple on the plane."

It took her a moment but then she laughed and laughed, slapping her skinny legs, great burbling little girl giggles; he'd never heard her laugh quite like that.

As she drove away he walked backward to his car and watched her go, then made the briefest, simplest of little boy gun gestures with his right hand, blowing smoke from his index finger as she shrank against the landscape. He couldn't resist. He drove home with the image of her eating an apple on a windy late spring night, in a truck next to poor Everett, telling him he had to do it, that he could own it all, that she'd always be there to hold his hand when he could no longer remember what he'd wanted or why he wanted it so badly, killing time together before they accelerated toward a frail sapphire tent.

Buy These Books and We'll Kill You Sweepstakes
No purchase necessary
OFFICIAL RULES

1. **To Enter:** Complete the Official Entry Form. Or you may enter by hand printing on a 3" × 5" postcard your name, address (including zip code), daytime and evening phone numbers and the words, "BUY THESE BOOKS AND WE'LL KILL YOU." Mail entries to BUY THESE BOOKS AND WE'LL KILL YOU Sweepstakes, c/o St. Martin's Paperbacks, 175 Fifth Avenue, Suite 1615, New York, NY 10010-7848. Entries must be received by April 1, 1998. Limit one entry per person. No mechanically reproduced or illegible entries accepted. Not responsible for lost, misdirected, mutilated or late entries. For a copy of the rules send a stamped, self-addressed envelope to Rules—"Buy These Books and We'll Kill You," c/o St. Martin's Paperbacks, 175 Fifth Avenue, Suite 1615, New York, NY 10010-7848. attn: CF.

2. **Random Drawing.** Winner will be determined in a random drawing to be held on or about April 10, 1998 from all eligible entries received. Odds of winning depend on the number of eligible entries received. Potential winner will be notified by mail on or about April 30, 1998, and will be asked to execute and return an Affidavit of Eligibility/Release/Prize Acceptance Form within fourteen (14) days of attempted notification. Non-compliance within this time may result in disqualification and the selection of an alternate winner. Return of any prize/prize notification as undeliverable will result in disqualification and an alternate winner will be selected. If you choose to have "someone you love" receive the prize, they will be required to execute a release.

3. **Prize and Approximate Retail Value:** Winner will be written into the author's next book as a character who is killed off, or winner may choose to submit the name of a "loved one" to be the character instead. (No retail value).

4. **Eligibility.** Open to U.S. and Canadian residents (excluding residents of the province of Quebec) who are 18 at the time of entry. Employees of St. Martin's, its parent, affiliate and subsidiaries, its and their directors, officers and agents, and their immediate families or those living in the same household, are ineligible to enter. Potential Canadian winners will be required to correctly answer a time-limited arithmetic skill question by mail. Void in Puerto Rico and wherever else prohibited by law.

5. **General Conditions:** No substitution or cash redemption of prize permitted by winner. Prize is not transferable. Acceptance of prize constitutes permission to use winner's (and "loved one's," if a "loved one" is the chosen victim) name, photograph and likeness, for purpose of advertising and promotion without additional compensation or permission, unless prohibited by law. "Loved one" must be over the age of 18 on date prize is awarded.

6. All entries become the property of sponsor, and will not be returned. Winner agrees that the author, St. Martin's, its parent, subsidiaries and affiliates, and its and their officers, directors, employees, agents, and promotion agencies shall not be liable for the use of winner or "loved one's" name as character in the author's next book and works based on that book. By participating in this sweepstakes, entrants agree to be bound by these official rules and the decision of the judges, which are final in all respects.

7. For the name of the winner, available after April 30, 1998, send by May 31, 1998 a stamped, self-addressed envelope to Winner's List, BUY THESE BOOKS AND WE'LL KILL YOU Sweepstakes, St. Martin's Paperbacks, 175 Fifth Avenue, Suite 1615, New York, NY 10010-7848.

BUY THIS BOOK AND WE'LL KILL YOU (OR SOMEONE YOU LOVE)!

We won't *really* kill you, but we will use YOUR name—or one of your choosing—as the name of a corpse in Jamie Harrison's next book! Aren't you a lucky stiff—Jamie will write you into her book, and you'll get a little piece of immortality!

OFFICIAL ENTRY FORM

Mail to:

St. Martin's Paperbacks
Attn: JP/GL
Suite 1615
175 Fifth Avenue
New York, NY 10010

Name: _____

Address:_____

City/State/Zip:_____

Phone (day):_____ Phone (night):_____

See next page for Official Rules. No purchase necessary. Void in the province of Quebec, Puerto Rico and wherever else prohibited by law. Ends April 1, 1998. No photo copies accepted.

Perched at the foot of Montana's Crazy Mountains, Blue Deer is a small town boasting an uneasy mix of longtime residents and hotshots from both coasts looking to possess their own piece of the Big Sky. Local sheriff Jules Clement manages the town's tensions fairly well...until someone blasts a hole in screenwriter George Blackwater's office window— and in George himself.

As more of the town's prominent citizens start turning up dead, the pressure on Jules keeps rising. It starts to look like this rookie sheriff may not survive the next election...if he lives to see it.

THE EDGE OF THE CRAZIES

JAMIE HARRISON

THE EDGE OF THE CRAZIES
Jamie Harrison